Praise for #1 *New York Times* bestselling author

NORA ROBERTS

"You can't bottle wish fulfillment, but Nora Roberts certainly knows how to put it on the page."

—*New York Times*

"When Roberts puts her expert fingers on the pulse of romance, legions of fans feel the heartbeat."

—*Publishers Weekly*

"Roberts…is at the top of her game."

—*People* magazine

"Roberts has a warm feel for her characters and an eye for the evocative detail."

—*Chicago Tribune*

"Nora Roberts is among the best."

—*Washington Post*

"America's favorite writer."

—*New Yorker*

Dear Reader,

Bold men, daring women and sweeping passions—nobody does it better than the phenomenal Nora Roberts! At Silhouette, we're delighted to offer two stories that deliver on that promise—one contemporary and one historical.

Confirmed bachelor Nathan Powell had his life mapped out—until he discovered author Jackie "Jack" MacNamara living in his house. This mismatched couple are like oil and water, but there's absolutely no doubt who will be *Loving Jack*.

A rare historical novel from Nora Roberts, *Lawless* tells the story of Sarah Conway, a refined Eastern lady who travels west to meet the father she hasn't seen since childhood. When she finds herself alone in the rough town of Lone Bluff, she gains a protector in handsome gunslinger Jake Redman. According to Jake, the frontier is the last place she should be—but Sarah is nothing if not determined. Be prepared for an unstoppable force meeting an immovable object!

Though the journey is different for each of our couples, their final destination is the same!

We hope you enjoy this classic collection.

The Editors
Silhouette Books

NORA ROBERTS

WRITTEN IN THE STARS

Includes *Loving Jack* & *Lawless*

 *Silhouette Books*

SILHOUETTE™

Recycling programs for this product may not exist in your area.

Written in the Stars

ISBN-13: 978-1-335-42602-4

Copyright © 2022 by Harlequin Enterprises ULC

Loving Jack
First published in 1988. This edition published in 2022.
Copyright © 1988 by Nora Roberts

Lawless
First published in 1989. This edition published in 2022.
Copyright © 1989 by Nora Roberts

For questions and comments about the quality of this book, please contact us at CustomerService@Harlequin.com.

Silhouette
22 Adelaide St. West, 41st Floor
Toronto, Ontario M5H 4E3, Canada
www.Harlequin.com

Printed in Lithuania

MIX
Paper from responsible sources
FSC® C021394

CONTENTS

LOVING JACK

To Kasey Michaels,
because Jackie is a heroine she'll understand.

Chapter 1

The minute Jackie saw the house, she was in love. Of course, she acknowledged, she did fall in love easily. It wasn't that she was easily impressed, she was just open, wide-open, to emotions—her own and everyone else's.

The house had a lot of emotion in it, she felt, and not all of it serene. That was good. Total serenity would have been all right for a day or two, but boredom would have closed in. She preferred the contrasts here, the strong angles and arrogant juts of the corners, softened occasionally by curving windows and unexpectedly charming archways.

The white-painted walls glittered in the sunlight, set off by stark ebony trim. Though she didn't believe the world was black-and-white, the house made the statement that the two opposing forces could live together in harmony.

The windows were wide, welcoming the view from both east and west, while skylights let in generous slices of sun. Flowers grew in profusion in the side garden and in terracotta pots along the terraces. She enjoyed the bold color they added, the touch of the exotic and lush. They'd have to be tended, of course—and religiously, if the heat continued and the rain didn't come. She didn't mind getting dirty, though, especially if there was a reward at the end.

Through wide glass doors she looked out at the crystalline waters of a kidney-shaped tiled pool. That, too, would require tending, but that, too, offered rewards. She could already picture herself sitting beside it, watching the sun set with the scent of flowers everywhere. Alone. That was a small hitch, but one she was willing to accept.

Beyond the pool and the sloping slice of lawn was the Intracoastal Waterway. Its waters were dark, mysterious, but even as she watched, a motorboat putted by. She discovered she liked the sound of it. It meant there were people close enough to make contact but not so close as to interfere.

The water roads reminded her of Venice and a particularly pleasant month she had spent there during her teens. She'd ridden in gondolas and flirted with dark-eyed men. Florida in the spring wasn't as romantic as Italy, but it suited her just fine.

"I love it." She turned back to the wide, sun-washed room. There were twin sofas the color of oatmeal on a steel-blue carpet. The rest of the furniture was an elegant ebony and leaned toward the masculine. Jackie approved of its strength and style. She rarely wasted her time looking for flaws and was willing to accept them when they jumped out at her. But in this house and everything about it she saw perfection.

She beamed at the man standing casually in front of the white marble fireplace. The hearth had been cleaned and swept and was a home for a potted fern. The man's tropical-looking white pants and shirt might have been chosen for precisely that pose. Knowing Frederick Q. MacNamara as she did, Jackie was sure it had been.

"When can I move in?"

Fred's smile lit up his round, boyish face. No one looking at it would have been reminded of a shark. "That's our Jack, always going on impulse." His body was rounded, too—not quite fat, but not really firm, either. Fred's favorite exercise was hailing—cabs or waiters. He moved toward her with a languid grace that had once been feigned but was now second nature. "You haven't even seen the second floor."

"I'll see it when I unpack."

"Jack, I want you to be sure." He patted her cheek—older, more experienced cousin to young scatterbrain. She didn't take offense. "I'd hate for you to regret this in a day or two. After all, you're proposing to live in this house by yourself for three months."

"I've got to live somewhere." She gestured, palm out, with a hand as slim and delicate as the rest of her. Gold and colored stones glittered on four fingers, a sign of her love of the pretty. "If I'm going to be serious about writing, I should be alone. Since I don't think I'd care for a garret, why shouldn't it be here?"

She paused a moment. It never paid to be too casual with Fred, cousin or not. Not that she didn't like him. Jackie had always had a soft spot for Fred, though she knew he had a habit of skimming off the top and dealing from the bottom.

"You're sure it's all right for you to sublet it to me?"

"Perfectly." His voice was as smooth as his face. Whatever wrinkles Fred had were carefully camouflaged. "The owner only uses it as a winter home, and then only sporadically. He prefers having someone in residence rather than leaving it empty. I told Nathan I'd take care of things until November, but then this business in San Diego came up, and it can't be put off. You know how it is, darling."

Jackie knew exactly how it was. With Fred, "sudden business" usually meant he was avoiding either a jealous husband or the law. Despite his unprepossessing looks, he had constant problems with the former, and not even a prepossessing family name could always protect him from the latter.

She should have been warier, but Jackie wasn't always wise, and the house—the look, the feel, of it—had already blinded her.

"If the owner wants it occupied, I'm happy to accommodate him. Let me sign on the dotted line, Fred. I want to unpack and spend a couple of hours in the pool."

"If you're sure." He was already drawing a paper from his pocket. "I don't want a scene later—like the time you bought my Porsche."

"You failed to tell me the transmission was held together with Krazy Glue."

"Let the buyer beware," Fred said mildly, and handed her a monogrammed silver pen.

She had a quick flash of trepidation. This was cousin Fred, after all. Fred of the easy deal and the can't-miss investment. Then a bird flew into the garden and began to sing cheerily, and Jackie took it as an omen. She signed the lease in a bold, flowing hand before drawing out her checkbook.

"A thousand a month for three months?"

"Plus five hundred damage deposit," Fred added.

"Right." She supposed she was lucky dear cousin Fred wasn't charging her a commission. "Are you leaving me a number, an address or something so I can get in touch with the owner if necessary?"

Fred looked blank for a moment, then beamed at her. It was that MacNamara smile, charming and guileless. "I've already told him about the turnover. Don't worry about a thing, sweetie. He'll be in touch with you."

"Fine." She wasn't going to worry about details. It was spring, and she had a new house, a new project. New beginnings were the best thing in the world. "I'll take care of everything." She touched a large Chinese urn. She'd begin by putting fresh flowers in it. "Will you be staying tonight, Fred?"

The check was already stashed in the inside pocket of his jacket. He resisted the urge to add a loving pat. "I'd love to hang around, indulge in some family gossip, but since we've got everything squared away, I should catch a flight to the Coast. You'll need to get to the market pretty soon, Jack. There're some essentials in the kitchen, but not much else." As he spoke, he started across the room toward a pile of baggage. It never occurred to him to offer to take his cousin's bags upstairs for her, or for her to ask him to. "Keys are there on the table. Enjoy yourself."

"I will." When he hefted his cases, she walked over to open the door for him. She'd meant her invitation to spend the night sincerely, and she was just as sincerely glad he'd refused. "Thanks, Fred. I really appreciate this."

"My pleasure, darling." He leaned down to exchange a kiss with her. Jackie got a whiff of his expensive cologne. "Give my love to the family when you talk to them."

"I will. Safe trip, Fred." She watched him walk out to a long, lean convertible. It was white, like his suit. After stowing his cases, Fred scooted behind the wheel and sent her a lazy salute. Then she was alone.

Jackie turned back to the room and hugged herself. She was alone, and on her own. She'd been there before, of course. She was twenty-five, after all, and had taken solo trips and vacations, had her own apartment and her own life. But each time she started out with something new it was a fresh adventure.

As of this day…was it March 25, 26? She shook her head. It didn't matter. As of this day, she was beginning a new career. Jacqueline R. MacNamara, novelist.

It had a nice ring, she thought. The first thing she was going to do was unpack her new typewriter and begin chapter one. With a laugh, she grabbed the typewriter case and her heaviest suitcase and started upstairs.

It didn't take long to acclimate herself, to the South, to the house, to her new routine. She rose early, enjoying the morning quiet with juice and a piece of toast—or flat cola and cold pizza, if that was handier. Her typing improved with practice, and by the end of the third day her machine was humming nicely. She would break in the afternoon to have a dip in the pool, lie in the sun and think about the next scene, or plot twist.

She tanned easily and quickly. It was a gift Jackie attributed to the Italian great-grandmother who had breached the MacNamara's obsessively Irish ranks. The color pleased her, and most of the time she remembered the face creams and moisturizers that her mother had always touted. "Good skin and bone structure make a beauty, Jacqueline. Not style or fashion or clever makeup," she'd often declared.

Well, Jackie had the skin and bone structure, though even her mother had to admit she would never be a true beauty. She was pretty enough, in a piquant, healthy sort of way. But her face was triangular rather than oval, her mouth wide rather than bowed. Her eyes were just a shade too big, and they were brown. The Italian again. She hadn't inherited the sea green or sky blue that dominated the rest of her family. Her hair was brown, as well. During her teens she'd experimented with rinses and streaks, often to her mother's embarrassment, but had finally settled for what God had given her. She'd even come to like it, and the fact that it curled on its own meant she didn't have to spend precious time in salons. She kept it short, and its natural fullness and curl made a halo around her face.

She was glad of its length now, because of her afternoon dips. It only took a few shakes and a little finger-combing to make it spring back to its casual style.

She took each morning as it came, diving headfirst into writing after she woke, then into the pool each afternoon. After a quick forage for lunch, she went back to her machine and worked until evening. She might play in the garden then, or sit and watch the boats or read on the terrace. If the day had been particularly productive, she would treat herself to the whirlpool, letting the bubbling water and the sultry heat of the glass enclosure make her pleasantly tired.

She locked the house for the owner's benefit rather than for her own safety. Each night Jackie slipped into bed in the room she'd chosen with perfect peace of mind and the tingling excitement of what the next morning would bring.

Whenever her thoughts turned to Fred, she smiled. Maybe the family was wrong about Fred after all. It was true that more than once he'd taken some gullible relative for a ride down a one-way street and left him—or her—at a dead end. But he'd certainly done her a good turn when he'd suggested the house in Florida. On the evening of the third day, Jackie lowered herself into the churning waters of the spa and thought about sending cousin Fred some flowers.

She owed him one.

He was dead tired, and happy as hell to be home at last. The final leg of the journey had seemed interminable. Being on American soil again after six months hadn't been enough. When Nathan had landed in New York, the first real flood of impatience had struck. He was home, yet not home. For the first time in months he had allowed himself to think of his own house, his own bed. His own private sacrosanct space.

Then there had been an hour's delay that had left him roaming the airport and almost grinding his teeth. Even once he'd been airborne he hadn't been able to stop checking and rechecking his watch to see how much longer he had to hang in the sky.

The airport in Fort Lauderdale still wasn't home. He'd spent a cold, hard winter in Germany and he'd had enough of the charm of snow and icicles. The warm, moist air and

the sight of palms only served to annoy him, because he
wasn't quite there yet.

He'd arranged to have his car delivered to the airport,
and when he'd finally eased himself into the familiar interior he'd felt like himself again. The hours of flying from
Frankfurt to New York no longer mattered. The delays and
impatience were forgotten. He was behind the wheel, and
twenty minutes from pulling into his own driveway. When
he went to bed that night it would be between his own
sheets. Freshly laundered and turned back by Mrs. Grange,
who Fred MacNamara had assured him would have the
house ready for his arrival.

Nathan felt a little twist of guilt about Fred. He knew he'd
hustled the man along to get him up and out of the house
before his arrival, but after six months of intense work in
Germany he wasn't in the mood for a houseguest. He'd have
to be sure to get in touch with Fred and thank him for keeping an eye on things. It was an arrangement that had solved
a multitude of problems with little fuss. As far as Nathan
was concerned, the less fuss the better. He definitely owed
Frank MacNamara a very large thank-you.

In a few days, Nathan thought as he slipped his key into
the lock. After he'd slept for twenty hours and indulged in
some good, old-fashioned sloth.

Nathan pushed open the door, hit the lights and just
looked. Home. It was so incredibly good to be home, in the
house he'd designed and built, among things chosen for his
own taste and comfort.

Home. It was exactly as he—no, it wasn't exactly as he'd
left it, he realized quickly. Because his eyes were gritty with
fatigue, he rubbed them as he studied the room. His room.

Who had moved the Ming over to the window and stuck
irises in it? And why was the Meissen bowl on the table in-

stead of the shelf? He frowned. He was a meticulous man, and he could see a dozen small things out of place.

He'd have to speak to Mrs. Grange about it, but he wasn't going to let a few annoyances spoil his pleasure at being home.

It was tempting to go straight to the kitchen and pour himself something long and cold, but he believed in doing first things first. Hefting his cases, he walked upstairs, relishing each moment of quiet and solitude.

He flipped on the lights in his bedroom and stopped short. Very slowly, he lowered the suitcases and walked to the bed. It wasn't turned down, but made up haphazardly. His dresser, the Chippendale he'd picked up at Sotheby's five years before, was crowded with pots and bottles. There was a definite scent here, not only from the baby roses that had been stuck in the Waterford—which belonged in the dining room cabinet—but a scent of woman. Powder, lotion and oil. Neither strong nor rich, but light and intrusive. His eyes narrowed when he saw the swatch of color on the spread. Nathan picked up the thin, almost microscopic bikini panties.

Mrs. Grange? The very idea was laughable. The sturdy Mrs. Grange wouldn't be able to fit one leg inside that little number. If Fred had had a guest... Nathan turned the panties over under the light. He supposed he could tolerate Fred having had a companion, but not in his room. And why in hell weren't her things packed and gone?

He got an image. It might have been the architect in him that enabled him to take a blank page or an empty lot and fill it completely in his mind. He saw a tall, slim woman, sexy, a little loud and bold. Ready to party. A redhead, probably, with lots of teeth and a rowdy turn of mind. That was fine for Fred, but the agreement had been that the house was to be empty and back in order on Nathan's return.

He gave the bottles on his dresser one last glance. He'd have Mrs. Grange dispose of them. Without thinking, he stuffed the thin piece of nylon in his pocket and strode out to see what else wasn't as it should be.

Jackie, her eyes shut and her head resting on the crimson edge of the spa, sang to herself. It had been a particularly good day. The tale was spinning out of her head and onto the page so quickly it was almost scary. She was glad she'd picked the West for her setting, old Arizona, desolate, tough, dusty and full of grit. That was just the right backdrop for her hard-bitten hero and her primly naive heroine.

They were already bumping along the rocky road to romance, though she didn't think even they knew it yet. She loved being able to put herself back in the 1800s, feeling the heat, smelling the sweat. And of course there was danger and adventure at every step. Her convent-raised heroine was having a devil of a time, but she was coping. Strong. Jackie couldn't have written about a weak-minded woman if she'd had to.

And her hero. Just thinking about him made her smile. She could see him perfectly, just as if he'd popped out of her imagination into the tub with her. That dark black hair, thick, glinting red in the sun when he removed his hat. Long enough that a woman could get a handful of it. The body lean and hard from riding, brown from the sun, scarred from the trouble he never walked away from.

You could see that in his face, a lean, bony face that was often shadowed by the beard he didn't bother to shave. He had a mouth that could smile and make a woman's heart pump fast. Or it could tighten and send shivers of fear up a man's spine. And his eyes. Oh, his eyes were a wonder. Slate gray and fringed by long, dark lashes, crinkled at the corners from squinting into the Arizona sun. Flat and hard when he pulled the trigger, hot and passionate when he took a woman.

Every woman in Arizona was in love with Jake Redman. And Jackie was pleased to be a little in love with him herself. Didn't that make him real? she thought as the bubbles swirled around her. If she could see him so clearly, and feel for him this intensely, didn't it mean she was doing the job right? He wasn't a good man, not through and through. It would be up to the heroine to mine the gold from him, and accept the rough stones along with it. And boy, was he going to give Miss Sarah Conway a run for her money. Jackie could hardly wait to sit down with them so that they could show her what happened next. If she concentrated hard enough, she could almost hear him speak to her.

"What in the hell are you doing?"

Still dreaming, Jackie opened her eyes and looked into the face of her imagination. Jake? she thought, wondering if the hot water had soaked into her brain. Jake didn't wear suits and ties, but she recognized the look that meant he was about to draw and fire. Her mouth fell open and she stared.

His hair was shorter, but not by much, and the shadow of beard was there. She pressed her fingers to her eyes and got chlorine in them, then blinked them open. He was still there, a little closer now. The sound of the spa's motor seemed louder as it filled her head.

"Am I dreaming?"

Nathan's eyes narrowed. She wasn't the rowdy redhead he'd pictured, but a cute, doe-eyed brunette. Either way, she didn't belong in his house. "What you're doing is trespassing. Now who the hell are you?"

The voice. Good grief, even the voice was right. Jackie shook her head and struggled to get a grip on herself. This was the twentieth century, and no matter how real her characters seemed on paper, they didn't come to life in five-hundred-dollar suits. The simple fact was that she was alone with a stranger and in a very vulnerable position.

She wondered how much she remembered from her karate course, then took another look at the man's broad shoulders and decided it just wasn't going to be enough.

"Who are you?" The edge of fear gave her voice haughty, rounded tones her mother would have been proud of.

"You're the one who has questions to answer," he countered. "But I'm Nathan Powell."

"The architect? Oh, I've admired your work. I saw the Ridgeway Center in Chicago, and…" She started to scoot up, no longer afraid, but then she remembered she hadn't bothered to put on a suit and slumped back again. "You have a marvelous flair for combining aesthetics with practicality."

"Thanks. Now—"

"But what are you doing here?"

His eyes narrowed again, and for the second time Jackie saw something of her gunslinger in them. "That's my question. This is my house."

"Yours?" She rubbed the back of her wrist over her eyes as she tried to think. "You're Nathan? Fred's Nathan?" Relieved, she smiled again. "Well, that explains things."

A dimple appeared at the corner of her mouth when she smiled. Nathan noticed it, then ignored it. He was a fastidious man, and fastidious men didn't come home to find strange women in their tubs. "Not to me. I'm going to repeat myself. Who the hell are you?"

"Oh. Sorry. I'm Jack." When his brow rose, she smiled again and extended a wet hand. "Jackie—Jacqueline MacNamara. Fred's cousin."

He glanced at her hand, and at the glitter of jewels on it, but didn't take it in his. He was afraid that if he did he might just haul her out onto the tiled floor. "And why, Miss Mac-Namara, are you sitting in my spa, and sleeping in my bed?"

"Is that your room? Sorry, Fred didn't say which I was to take, so I took the one I liked best. He's in San Diego, you know."

"I don't give a damn where he is." He'd always been a patient man. At least that was what he'd always believed. Right now, though, he was finding he had no patience at all. "What I want to know is why you're in my house."

"Oh, I sublet it from Fred. Didn't he get ahold of you?"

"You what?"

"You know, it's hard to talk with this motor running. Wait." She held up a hand before he could hit the off button. "I'm, ah…well, I wasn't expecting anyone, so I'm not exactly dressed for company. Would you mind?"

He glanced down automatically to where the water churned hot and fast at the subtle curve of her breast. Nathan set his teeth. "I'll be in the kitchen. Make it fast."

Jackie let out a long breath when she was alone. "I think Fred did it again," she muttered as she hauled herself out of the tub and dried off.

Nathan made himself a long gin and tonic, using a liberal hand with the gin. As far as homecomings went, this one left a lot to be desired. There might have been men who'd be pleasantly surprised to come home after an exhausting project and find naked women waiting in their sunrooms. Unfortunately, he just wasn't one of them. He took a deep drink as he leaned back against the counter. It was, he supposed, just a question of taking one step at a time—and the first would be disposing of Jacqueline MacNamara.

"Mr. Powell?"

He glanced over to see her step into the kitchen. She was still dripping a bit. Her legs were lightly tanned and long—very long, he noticed—skimmed at the thighs by a

terry-cloth robe that was as boldly striped as Joseph's coat
of many colors. Her hair curled damply around her face in
a soggy halo, with a fringe of bangs that accented dark,
wide eyes. She was smiling, and the dimple was back. He
wasn't sure he liked that. When she smiled she looked as
though she could sell you ten acres of Florida swampland.

"It appears we're going to have to discuss your cousin."

"Fred." Jackie nodded, still smiling, and slipped onto
a rattan stool at the breakfast bar. She'd already decided
she'd do best by being totally at ease and in control. If he
thought she was nervous and unsure of her position... Well,
she wasn't positive, but she had a very good idea she'd find
herself standing outside the house, bag in hand. "He's quite
a character, isn't he? How did you meet him?"

"Through a mutual friend." He grimaced a little, thinking he was going to have to talk with Justine, as well. "I had
a project in Germany that was going to keep me out of the
country for a few months. I needed someone to house-sit.
He was recommended. As I knew his aunt—"

"Patricia—Patricia MacNamara's my mother."

"Adele Lindstrom."

"Oh, Aunt Adele. She's my mother's sister." It was more
than a smile this time. Something wickedly amused flashed
in Jackie's eyes. "She's a lovely woman."

There was something droll, a bit too droll, in the comment. Nathan chose to ignore it. "I worked with Adele
briefly on a revitalization project in Chicago. Because of
the connection, and the recommendation, I decided to have
Fred look out for the house while I was away."

Jackie bit her bottom lip. It was her first sign of nerves,
and though she didn't realize it, that small gesture cleared a
great deal of ground for her. "He wasn't renting it from you?"

"Renting it? Of course not." She was twisting her rings,
one at a time, around her fingers. Don't get involved, he

warned himself. Tell her to pack up and move out. No explanations, no apologies. You can be in bed in ten minutes. Nathan felt rather than heard his own sigh. Not many people knew that Nathan Powell was a sucker. "Is that what he told you?"

"I suppose I'd better tell you the whole story. Could I have one of those?"

When she indicated his glass, he nearly snapped at her. Manners had been bred carefully into him, and he was irritated at his oversight, even though she was hardly a guest. Without speaking, he poured and mixed another drink, then sat it in front of her. "I'd appreciate it if you could condense the whole story and just give me the highlights."

"Okay." She took a sip, bracing herself. "Fred called me last week. He'd heard through the family grapevine that I was looking for a place to stay for a few months. A nice quiet place where I could work. I'm a writer," she said with the audacious pride of one who believed it. When this brought no response, she drank again and continued. "Anyway, Fred said he had a place that might suit me. He told me he'd been renting this house… He described it," Jackie explained, "and I just couldn't wait to see it. It's a beautiful place, so thoughtfully designed. Now that I know who you are, I can see why—the strength and charm of the structure, the openness of the space. If I hadn't been so intent on what I was doing, I'd have recognized your style right away. I studied architecture for a couple of semesters at Columbia."

"That's fascinating, I'm sure… LaFont?"

"Yes, he's a wonderful old duck, isn't he? So pompous and sure of his own worth."

Nathan raised a brow. He'd studied with LaFont himself—a lifetime ago, it seemed—and was well aware that the old duck, as Jackie had termed him, only took on the most promising students. He opened his mouth again, then shut it. He wouldn't be drawn out. "Let's get back to your cousin, Miss MacNamara."

"Jackie," she said, flashing that smile again. "Well, if I hadn't been really anxious to get settled, I probably would have said thanks but no thanks. Fred's always got an angle. But I came down. I took one look at the place, and that was that. He said he had to leave for San Diego right away on business and that the owner—you—didn't want the house empty while you were away. I suppose you don't really just use it as a winter home sporadically, do you?"

"No." He drew a cigarette out of his pocket. He'd successfully cut down to ten a day, but these were extenuating circumstances. "I live here year-round, except when a project takes me away. The arrangement was for Fred to live here during my absence. I called two weeks ago to let him know when I'd be arriving. He was to contact Mrs. Grange and leave his forwarding address with her."

"Mrs. Grange?"

"The housekeeper."

"He didn't mention a housekeeper."

"Why doesn't that surprise me?" Nathan murmured, and finished off his drink. "That takes us to the point of your occupation."

Jackie drew a long breath. "I signed a lease. Three months. I wrote Fred a check for the rent, in advance, plus a damage deposit."

"That's unfortunate." He wouldn't feel sorry for her. He'd be damned if he would. "You didn't sign a lease with the owner."

"With your proxy. With whom I thought was your proxy," she amended. "Cousin Fred can be very smooth." He wasn't smiling, Jackie noted. Not even a glimmer. It was a pity he couldn't see the humor in the situation. "Look, Mr. Powell—Nathan—it's obvious Fred's pulled something on both of us, but there must be a way we can work it out. As far as the thirty-five hundred dollars goes—"

"Thirty-five hundred?" Nathan said. "You paid him thirty-five hundred dollars?"

"It seemed reasonable." She was tempted to pout because of his tone, but she didn't think it would help. "You do have a beautiful home, and there was the pool, and the sunroom. Anyway, with a bit of family pressure, I may be able to get some of it back. Sooner or later." She thought about the money a moment longer, then dismissed it. "But the real problem is how to handle this situation."

"Which is?"

"My being here, and your being here."

"That's easy." Nathan tapped out his cigarette. There was no reason, absolutely no reason, why he should feel guilty that she'd lost money. "I can recommend a couple of excellent hotels."

She smiled again. She was sure he could, but she had no intention of going to one. The dimple was still in place, but if Nathan had looked closely he would have seen that the soft brown eyes had hardened with determination.

"That would solve your part of the problem, but not mine. I do have a lease."

"You have a worthless piece of paper."

"Very possibly." She tapped her ringed fingers on the counter as she considered. "Did you ever study law? When I was at Harvard—"

"Harvard?"

"Very briefly." She brushed away the hallowed halls with the back of her hand. "I didn't really take to it, but I do think it might be difficult and, worse, annoying to toss me out on my ear." She swirled her drink and considered. "Of course, if you wanted to get a warrant and take it to court, dragging cousin Fred into it, you'd win eventually.

I'm sure of that. In the meantime," she continued before
he could find the right words, "I'm sure we can come up
with a much more suitable solution for everyone. You must
be exhausted." She changed her tone so smoothly he could
only stare. "Why don't you go on up and get a good night's
sleep? Everything's clearer on a good night's sleep, don't
you think? We can hash through all this tomorrow."

"It's not a matter of hashing through anything, Miss Mac-
Namara. It's a matter of your packing up your things." He
shoved a hand into his pocket, and his fingers brushed the
swatch of nylon. Gritting his teeth, he pulled it out. "These
are yours?"

"Yes, thanks." Without a blush, Jackie accepted her underwear. "It's a little late to be calling the cops and explaining all of this to them. I imagine you could throw me out
bodily, but you'd hate yourself for it."

She had him there. Nathan began to think she had a lot
more in common with her cousin than a family name. He
glanced at his watch and swore. It was already after midnight, and he didn't—quite—have the heart to dump her in
the street. The worst of it was that he was nearly tired enough
to see double and couldn't seem to come up with the right,
or the most promising, arguments. So he'd let it ride—for
the moment.

"I'll give you twenty-four hours, Miss MacNamara. That
seems more than reasonable to me."

"I knew you were a reasonable man." She smiled at him
again. "Why don't you go get some sleep? I'll lock up."

"You're in my bed."

"I beg your pardon?"

"Your things are in my room."

"Oh." Jackie scratched at her temple. "Well, I suppose
if it was really important to you, I could haul everything
out tonight."

"Never mind." Maybe it was all a nightmare. A hallucination. He'd wake up in the morning and discover everything was as it should be. "I'll take one of the guest rooms."

"That's a much better idea. You really do look tired. Sleep well."

He stared at her for nearly a full minute. When he was gone, Jackie laid her head down on the counter and began to giggle. Oh, she'd get Fred for this, make no mistake. But now, just now, it was the funniest thing that had happened to her in months.

Chapter 2

When Nathan woke, it was after ten East Coast time, but the nightmare wasn't over. He realized that as soon as he saw the muted striped paper on the wall of the guest room. He was in his own house, but he'd somehow found himself relegated to the position of guest.

His suitcases, open but still packed, sat on the mahogany chest under the garden window. He'd left his drapes undrawn, and sunlight poured in over the neatly folded shirts. Deliberately he turned away from them. He'd be damned if he'd unpack until he could do so in the privacy of his own room.

A man had a right to his own closet.

Jacqueline MacNamara had been correct about one thing. He felt better after a full night's sleep. His mind was clearer. Though it wasn't something he cared to dwell on, he went over everything that had happened from the time he'd unlocked his door until he'd fallen, facefirst, into the guest bed.

He realized he'd been a fool not to toss her out on her pert little ear the night before, but that could be rectified. And the sooner the better.

He showered, taking his shaving gear into the bathroom with him, but meticulously replacing everything in the kit when he was finished. Nothing was coming out until it could be placed in his own cabinets and drawers. After he'd dressed, in light cotton pants and shirt, he felt in charge again. If he couldn't deal with a dippy little number like the brunette snuggled in his bed, he was definitely slipping. Still, it wouldn't hurt to have a cup of coffee first.

He was halfway down the stairs when he smelled it. Coffee. Strong, fresh coffee. The aroma was so welcome he nearly smiled, but then he remembered who must have brewed it. Strengthening his resolve, he continued. Another scent wafted toward him. Bacon? Surely that was bacon. Obviously she was making herself right at home. He heard the music, as well—rock, something cheerful and bouncy and loud enough to be heard a room away.

No, the nightmare wasn't over, but it was going to end, and end quickly.

Nathan strode into the kitchen prepared to shoot straight from the hip.

"Good morning." Jackie greeted him with a smile that competed with the sunshine. As a concession to him, she turned the radio down, but not off. "I wasn't sure how long you'd sleep, but I didn't think you were the type to stay in bed through the morning, so I started breakfast. I hope you like blueberry pancakes. I slipped out early and bought the berries. They're fresh." Before he could speak, she popped one into his mouth. "Have a seat. I'll get your coffee."

"Miss MacNamara—"

"Jackie, please. Cream?"

"Black. We left things a bit up in the air last night, but we've got to settle this business now."

"Absolutely. I hope you like your bacon crisp." She set a platter on the counter, where a place was already set with his good china and a damask napkin. She noticed that he'd shaved. With the shadow of beard gone, he didn't look quite as much like her Jake—except around the eyes. It wouldn't be wise, she decided, to underestimate him.

"I've given it a lot of thought, Nathan, and I think I've

come up with the ideal solution." She poured batter onto the griddle and adjusted the flame. "Did you sleep well?"

"Fine." At least he'd felt fine when he'd awakened. Now he reached for the coffee almost defensively. She was like a sunbeam that had intruded when all he'd really wanted to do was draw the shades and take a nap.

"My mother's fond of saying you always sleep best at home, but it's never mattered to me. I can sleep anywhere. Would you like the paper?"

"No." He sipped the coffee, stared at it, then sipped again. Maybe it was his imagination, but it was the best cup of coffee he'd ever tasted.

"I buy the beans from a little shop in town," she said, answering his unspoken question as she flipped the pancakes with an expert hand. "I don't drink it often myself. That's why I think it's important to have a really good cup. Ready for these?" Before he could answer, she took his plate and stacked pancakes on it. "You've a wonderful view from right here." Jackie poured a second cup of coffee and sat beside him. "It makes eating an event."

Nathan found himself reaching for the syrup. It wouldn't hurt to eat first. He could still toss her out later. "How long have you been here?"

"Just a few days. Fred's always had an excellent sense of timing. How are your pancakes?"

It seemed only fair to give her her due. "They're wonderful. Aren't you eating?"

"I sort of sampled as I went along." But that didn't stop her from plucking another slice of bacon. She nibbled, approved, then smiled at him. "Do you cook?"

"Only if the package comes with instructions."

Jackie felt the first thrill of victory. "I'm really a very good cook."

"Studied at the Cordon Bleu, I imagine."

"Only for six months," she said, grinning at him. "But I did learn most of the basics. From there I decided to go my own way, experiment, you know? Cooking should be as much of an adventure as anything else."

To Nathan, cooking was drudgery that usually ended in failure. He only grunted.

"Your Mrs. Grange," Jackie began conversationally. "Is she supposed to come in every day, do the cleaning and the cooking?"

"Once a week." The pancakes were absolutely fabulous. He'd grown accustomed to hotel food, and as excellent as it had been, it couldn't compete with this. He began to relax as he studied the view. She was right, it was great, and he couldn't remember ever having enjoyed breakfast more. "She cleans, does the weekly marketing, and usually fixes a casserole or something." Nathan took another forkful, then stopped himself before he could again be seduced by the flavor. "Why?"

"It all has to do with our little dilemma."

"Your dilemma."

"Whatever. I wonder, are you a fair man, Nathan? Your buildings certainly show a sense of style and order, but I can't really tell if you have a sense of fair play." She lifted the coffeepot. "Let me top that off for you."

He was losing his appetite rapidly. "What are you getting at?"

"I'm out thirty-five hundred." Jackie munched on the bacon. "Now, I'm not going to try to make you think that the loss is going to have me on the street corner selling pencils, but it's not really the amount. It's the principle. You believe in principles, don't you?"

Cautious, he gave a noncommittal shrug.

"I paid, in good faith, for a place to live and to work for three months."

"I'm sure your family retains excellent lawyers. Why don't you sue your cousin?"

"The MacNamaras don't solve family problems that way. Oh, I'll settle up with him—when he least expects it."

There was a look in her eyes that made Nathan think she would do just that, and beautifully. He had to fight back a surge of admiration. "I'll wish you the best of luck here, but your family problems don't involve me."

"They do when it's your house in the middle of it. Do you want some more?"

"No. Thanks," he added belatedly. "Miss—Jackie—I'm going to be perfectly frank with you." He settled back, prepared to be both reasonable and firm. If he'd known her better, Nathan would have felt his first qualms when she turned her big brown eyes on him with a look of complete cooperation. "My work in Germany was difficult and tiring. I have a couple of months of free time coming, which I intend to spend here, alone, doing as little as possible."

"What were you building?"

"What?"

"In Germany. What were you building?"

"An entertainment complex, but that isn't really relevant. I'm sorry if it seems insensitive, but I don't feel responsible for your situation."

"It doesn't seem insensitive at all." Jackie patted his hand, then poured him more coffee. "Why should you, after all? An entertainment complex. It sounds fascinating, and I'd really love to hear all about it later, but the thing is, Nathan—" she paused as she topped off her own cup "—is that I kind of see us as two people in the same boat. We both expected to spend the next couple of months alone, pursuing our own projects, and Fred screwed up the works. Do you like Oriental food?"

He was losing ground. Nathan didn't know why, or

when, the sand had started to shift beneath his feet, but there it was. Resting his elbows on the counter, he held his head in his hands. "What the hell does that have to do with anything?"

"It has to do with my idea, and I wanted to know what kind of food you liked, or particularly didn't like. Me, I'll eat anything, but most people have definite preferences." Jackie cupped her mug in both hands as she tucked her legs, lotus-style, under her on the stool. She was wearing shorts today, vivid blue ones with a flamingo emblem on one leg. Nathan studied the odd pink bird for a long time before he lifted his gaze to hers.

"Why don't you just tell me your idea while I still have a small part of my sanity?"

"The object is for both of us to have what we want—or as nearly as possible. It's a big house."

She lifted both brows as his eyes narrowed. That look, she thought again. That Jake look was hard to resist. Nathan's coming back when he did might have been the sort of odd bonus fate sometimes tossed out. Jackie was always ready to make the grab for it.

"I'm an excellent roommate. I could give you references from several people. I went to a variety of colleges, you see, so I lived with a variety of people. I can be neat if that's important, and I can be quiet and unobtrusive."

"I find that difficult to believe."

"No, really, especially when I'm immersed in my own project, like I am now. I write almost all day. This story's really the most important thing in my life right now. I'll have to tell you about it, but we'll save that."

"I'd appreciate it."

"You have a wonderfully subtle sense of humor, Nathan. Don't ever lose it. Anyhow, I'm a strong believer in atmosphere. You must be, too, being an architect."

"You're losing me again." He shoved the coffee aside. Too much stimulation, that must be it. Another cup and he might just start understanding her.

"The house," Jackie said patiently. Her eyes were the problem, Nathan decided. There was something about them that compelled you to look and listen when all you really wanted to do was hold your hands over your ears and run.

"What about the house?"

"There's something about it. The minute I set up here, everything just started flowing. With the story. If I moved, well, don't you think things might stop flowing just as quickly? I don't want to chance that. So I'm willing to make some compromises."

"You're willing to make some compromises," Nathan repeated slowly. "That's fascinating. You're living in my house, without my consent, but you're willing to make some compromises."

"It's only fair." There was that smile again, quick and brilliant. "You don't cook. I do." Jackie gestured with both hands as if to show the simplicity of it. "I'll prepare all of your meals, at my expense, for as long as I'm here."

It sounded reasonable. Why in the hell did it sound so reasonable when she said it? "That's very generous of you, but I don't want a cook, or a roommate."

"How do you know? You haven't had either yet."

"What I want," he began, careful to space his words and keep his tone even, "is privacy."

"Of course you do." She didn't touch him, but her tone was like a pat on the head. He nearly growled. "We'll make a pact right now. I'll respect your privacy and you'll respect mine. Nathan…" She leaned toward him, again covering his hand with hers in a move that was natural rather than calculated. "I know you've got absolutely no reason to do me any favors, but I'm really committed to this book. For reasons of my own, I've a great need to finish it, and I'm sure I can. Here."

"If you're trying to make me feel guilty because I'd be sabotaging the great American novel—"

"No, I'm not. I would have if I'd thought of it, but I didn't. I'm just asking you to give me a chance. A couple of weeks. If I drive you crazy, I'll leave."

"Jacqueline, I've known you about twelve hours, and you've already driven me crazy."

She was winning. There was just the slightest hint of it in his tone, but she caught it and pounced. "You ate all your pancakes."

Almost guiltily, Nathan looked down at his empty plate. "I've had nothing but airplane food for twenty-four hours."

"Wait until you taste my crepes. And my Belgian waffles." She caught her lower lip between her teeth. "Nathan, think of it. You won't have to open a single can as long as I'm around."

Involuntarily he thought of all the haphazard meals he'd prepared, and about the barely edible ones he brought into the house in foam containers. "I'll eat out."

"A fat lot of privacy you'd have sitting in crowded restaurants and competing for a waiter's attention. With my solution, you won't have to do anything but relax."

He hated restaurants. And God knew he'd had enough of them over the past year. The arrangement made perfect sense, at least while he was comfortably full of her blueberry pancakes.

"I want my room back."

"That goes without saying."

"And I don't like small talk in the morning."

"Completely uncivilized. I do want pool privileges."

"If I stumble over you or any of your things even once, you're out."

"Agreed." She held out a hand, sensing he was a man who would stand by a handshake. She was even more certain of it when she saw him hesitate. Jackie brought out what she hoped would be the coup de grâce. "You really would hate yourself if you threw me out, you know."

Nathan scowled at her but found his palm resting against hers. A small hand, and a soft one, he thought, but the grip was firm. If he lived to regret this temporary arrangement, he'd have one more score to settle with Fred. "I'm going to take a spa."

"Good idea. Loosen up all those tense muscles. By the way, what would you like for lunch?"

He didn't look back. "Surprise me."

Jackie picked up his plate and did a quick dance around the kitchen.

Temporary insanity. Nathan debated the wisdom of pleading that cause to his associates, his family or the higher courts. He had a boarder. A nonpaying one at that. Nathan Powell, a conservative, upstanding member of society, a member of the Fortune 500, the thirty-two-year-old wunderkind of architecture, had a strange woman in his house.

He didn't necessarily mean strange as in unknown. Jackie MacNamara *was* strange. He'd come to that conclusion when he'd seen her meditating by the pool after lunch. He'd glanced out and spotted her, sitting cross-legged on the stone apron, head tilted back, eyes closed, hands resting lightly on her knees, palms up. He'd been mortally afraid she was reciting a mantra. Did people still do that sort of thing?

He must have been insane to agree to her arrangement because of blueberry pancakes and a smile. Jet lag, he decided as he poured another glass of iced tea Jackie had made to go with a truly exceptional spinach salad. Even a competent, intelligent man could fall victim to the weakness of the body after a transatlantic flight.

Two weeks, he reminded himself. Technically, he'd only agreed to two weeks. After that time had passed, he could gently but firmly ease her on her way. In the meantime, he would do what he should have done hours ago—make certain he didn't have a maniac on his hands.

There was a neat leather-bound address book by the kitchen phone, as there was by every phone in the house. Nathan flipped through it to the *L*'s. Jackie was upstairs working on her book—if indeed there was a book at all. He would make the call, glean a few pertinent facts, then decide how to move from there.

"Lindstrom residence."

"Adele Lindstrom, please, Nathan Powell calling."

"One moment, Mr. Powell."

Nathan sipped tea as he waited. A man could become addicted to having it made fresh instead of digging crystallized chemicals out of a jar. Absently he drew a cigarette out of his pocket and tapped the filter on the counter.

"Nathan, dear, how are you?"

"Adele. I'm very well, and you?"

"Couldn't be better, though March insists on going out like a lion here. What can I do for you, dear? Are you in Chicago?"

"No, actually I've just arrived home. Your nephew Fred was, ah…house-sitting for me."

"Of course, I remember." There was a long, and to Nathan pregnant, pause. "Fred hasn't done something naughty, has he?"

Naughty? Nathan passed a hand over his face. After a moment, he decided not to blast Adele with the sad facts of the situation, but to tone it down. "We do have a bit of a mix-up. Your niece is here."

"Niece? Well, I have several of those. Jacqueline? Of course it's Jacqueline. I remember now that Honoria—that's Fred's mother—told me that little Jack was going south. Poor Nathan, you've a houseful of MacNamaras."

"Actually, Fred's in San Diego."

"San Diego? What are you all doing in San Diego?"

Nathan tried to remember if Adele Lindstrom had been quite this scattered in Chicago. "Fred's in San Diego—at least I think he is. I'm in Florida, with your niece."

"Oh… Oh!" The second *oh* had enough delight in it to put Nathan on guard. "Well, isn't that lovely? I've always said that all our Jacqueline needed was a nice, stable man. She's a bit of a butterfly, of course, but very bright and wonderfully good-hearted."

"I'm sure she is." Nathan found it necessary to put the record straight, and to put it straight quickly. "She's only here because of a misunderstanding. It seems Fred…didn't understand that I was coming back, and he…offered the house to Jackie."

"I see." And she did, perfectly. Fortunately for Nathan, he couldn't see her eyes light with amusement. "How awkward for you. I hope you and Jacqueline have worked things out."

"More or less. You're her mother's sister?"

"That's right. Jackie favors Patricia physically. Such a piquant look. I was always jealous as a child. Otherwise, none of us have ever been quite sure who little Jackie takes after."

Nathan blew out a stream of smoke. "That doesn't surprise me."

"What is it now…painting? No, it's writing. Jackie's a novelist these days."

"So she says."

"I'm sure she'll tell a delightful story. She's always been full of them."

"I'll just bet."

"Well, dear, I know the two of you will get along fine. Our little Jack manages to get along with just about anyone. A talent of hers. Not to say that Patricia and I hadn't hoped she'd be settled down and married by now—put some of that energy into raising a nice family. She's a sweet girl—a bit flighty, but sweet. You're still single, aren't you, Nathan?"

With his eyes cast up to the ceiling, he shook his head. "Yes, I am. It's been nice talking to you, Adele. I'll suggest to your niece that she get in touch when she relocates."

"That would be nice. It's always a pleasure to hear from Jack. And you, too, Nathan. Be sure to let me know if you get to Chicago again."

"I will. Take care of yourself, Adele."

He hung up, still frowning at the phone. There was little doubt that his unwanted tenant was exactly who she said she was. But that didn't really accomplish anything. He could talk to her again, but when he'd tried to do that over lunch, he'd gotten a small, and very nagging, headache. It might be the coward's way, but for the rest of the day he was going to pretend that Jacqueline MacNamara, with her long legs and her brilliant smile, didn't exist.

Upstairs, in front of her typewriter, Jackie wasn't giving Nathan a thought. Or if she was she'd twined him so completely with the hard-bitten and heroic Jake that she wasn't able to see the difference.

It was working. Sometimes, when her fingers slowed just a bit and her mind whipped back to the present, she was struck by the wonderful and delightful thought that she was really writing. Not playing at it, as she had played at so many other things.

She knew her family tut-tutted about her. All those brains and all that breeding, and Jackie could never seem to make up her mind what to do with them. She was happy to announce that this time she had found something, and that it had found her.

Sitting back, her tongue caught between her teeth, she read the last scene over. It was good, she was sure of that. She knew that back in Newport there were those who would shake their heads and smile indulgently. So what if the scene was good, or even if several chapters were good? Dear little Jack never finished anything.

In her stint at remodeling, she'd bought a huge rattrap of a house and scraped, planed, painted and papered. She'd learned about plumbing and rewiring, haunted lumberyards and hardware stores. The first floor—she'd always believed in starting from the bottom up—had been fabulous. She was creative and competent. The problem had been, as it always had been, that once the first rush of excitement was over something else had caught her interest. The house had lost its charm for her. True, she'd sold it at a nice profit, but she'd never touched the two upper stories.

This was different.

Jackie cradled her chin in her hand. How many times had she said that before? The photography studio, the dance classes, the potter's wheel. But this *was* different. She'd been fascinated by each field she'd tampered in, and in each had shown a nice ability to apply what she'd learned, but she was beginning to see, or hope, that all those experiments, all those false starts, had been leading up to this.

She had to be right about the story. This time she had to carry it through from start to finish. Nothing else she'd tried had been so important or seemed so right. It didn't matter that her family and friends saw her as eccentric and fickle. She *was* eccentric and fickle. But there had to be something, something strong and meaningful, in her life. She couldn't go on playing at being an adult forever.

The great American novel. That made her smile. No, it wouldn't be that. In fact, Jackie couldn't think of many things more tedious than attempting to write the great American novel. But it could be a good book, a book people might care about and enjoy, one they might curl up with on a quiet evening. That would be enough. She hadn't realized that before, but once she'd really begun to care about it herself she'd known that would be more than enough.

It was coming so fast, almost faster than she could handle. The room was stacked with reference books and manuals, writers' how-tos and guides. She'd pored over them all. Researching her subject was the one discipline Jackie had always followed strictly. She'd been grateful for the road maps, the explanations of pitfalls and the suggestions. Oddly, now that she was hip deep in the story, none of that seemed to matter. She was writing on instinct and by the seat of her pants. As far as she could remember—and her memory was keen—she'd never had more fun in her life.

She closed her eyes to think about Jake. Instantly her mind took a leap to Nathan. Wasn't it strange how much he looked like her own conception of the hero of her story? It really did make it all seem fated. Jackie had a healthy respect for fate, particularly after her study of astrology.

Not that Nathan was a reckless gunslinger. No, he was rather sweetly conservative. A man, she was sure, who thought of himself as organized and practical. She doubted seriously that he considered himself an artist, though he was undoubtedly a talented one. He'd also be a list-maker and a plan-follower. She respected that, though she'd never been able to stick with a list in her life. What she admired even more was that he was a man who knew what he wanted and had accomplished it.

He was also a pleasure to look at—particularly when he smiled. The smile was usually reluctant, which made it all the sweeter. Already she'd decided it was her duty to nudge that smile from him as often as possible.

It shouldn't be difficult. Obviously he had a good heart; otherwise he would have given her the heave-ho the first night. That he hadn't, though he'd certainly wanted to, made Jackie think rather kindly of him. Because she did, she was determined to make their cohabitation as painless for him as possible.

She didn't doubt that they could deal very nicely with each other for a few months. In truth, she preferred company, even his reluctant sort, to solitude.

She liked his subtlety, and his well-bred sarcasm. Even someone much less sensitive than she would have recognized the fact that nothing would have made him happier than to dispose of her. It was a pity she couldn't oblige him, but she really was determined to finish her book, and to finish it where she had started it.

While she was at it, she'd stay out of his way as much as was humanly possible, and fix him some of the best meals of his life.

That thought made her glance at her watch. She swore a little, but turned off her machine. It really was a pain to have to think about dinner when Jake was tethered by a leather thong to the wrist of an Apache brave. The knife fight was just heating up; but a bargain was a bargain.

Humming to herself, she started down to the kitchen.

Once again it was the scents that lured him. Nathan had been perfectly happy catching up on his back issues of *Architectural Digest*. He burrowed in his office, content simply to be there with the warm paneled walls and the faded Persian carpet. Terrace doors opened onto the patio and out to the garden. It was his refuge, with the faint scent of leather from books and the sharp light of sun through etched glass. If a man couldn't be alone in his office, he couldn't be alone anywhere.

Late in the afternoon he'd nearly been able to erase Jackie MacNamara and her conniving cousin from his mind. He'd heard her humming, and had ignored it. That had pleased him. A servant. He would think of her as a servant and nothing more.

Then the aromas had started teasing him. Hot, spicy aromas. She was playing the radio again. Loud. He really was going to have to speak to her about that. Nathan shifted in his office chair and tried to concentrate.

Was that chicken? he wondered, and lost his place in an article on earth homes. He thought about closing the door, flipped a page and found the Top 40 number Jackie was playing at top volume juggling around in his head. Telling himself she needed a lecture on music appreciation, he set the magazine aside—after marking his place—then headed toward the kitchen.

He had to speak to her twice before she heard him. Jackie kept a hand on the handle of the frying pan, shaking it gently as she pitched her voice to a shout.

"It'll be ready in a few minutes. Would you like some wine?"

"No. What I'd like is for you to turn that thing off."

"To what?"

"To turn that thing—" Almost growling in disgust, Nathan walked over to the kitchen speaker and hit the switch. "Haven't you ever heard about inner-ear damage?"

Jackie gave the pan another shake before turning off the flame. "I always play the music loud when I'm cooking. It inspires me."

"Invest in headphones," he suggested.

With a shrug, Jackie took the lid off the rice and gave it a quick swipe with a fork. "Sorry. I figured since you had speakers in every room you liked music. How was your day? Did you get plenty of rest?"

Something in her tone made him feel like a cranky grandfather. "I'm fine," he said between his teeth.

"Good. I hope you like Chinese. I have a friend who owns a really wonderful little Oriental restaurant in San Francisco. I persuaded his chef to share some recipes." Jackie poured Nathan a glass of wine. She was using his Waterford this time. In the smooth and economical way she had in the kitchen, she scooped the sweet-and-sour chicken onto a bed of rice. "I didn't have time for fortune cookies, but there's an upside-down cake in the oven." She licked sauce from her thumb before she began to serve herself. "You don't want to let that get cold."

Wary of her, he sat. A man had to eat, after all. As he forked a cube of chicken, he watched her. Nothing seemed to break her rhythm, or her breezy sense of self-confidence. He'd see about that, Nathan thought, and waited until she'd joined him at the bar.

"I spoke with your aunt today."

"Really? Aunt Adele?" Jackie hooked one bare foot around the leg of the stool. "Did she give me a good reference?"

"More or less."

"You brought it on yourself," she said, then began to eat with the steady enthusiasm of one who liked food for food's sake.

"I beg your pardon?"

Jackie sampled a bamboo shoot. "Word's going to spread like wildfire, through the Lindstrom branch and over to the MacNamaras. I imagine it'll detour through the O'Brians too. That's my father's sister's married name." She took a forkful of saffron rice. "I can't take the responsibility."

Now it was he who'd lost his rhythm. Again. "I don't know what you're talking about."

"The wedding."

"What wedding?"

"Ours." She picked up her glass and sipped, smiling at him over the rim. "What do you think of the wine?"

"Back up. What do you mean, our wedding?"

"Well, I don't mean it, and you don't mean it. But Aunt Adele will mean it. Twenty minutes after you spoke with her she'd have been chirping happily about our romance to anyone who'd listen. People do listen to Aunt Adele. I've never understood why. You're letting that chicken get cold, Nathan."

He set his fork down, keeping his voice even and his eyes steady. "I never gave her any reason to think we were involved."

"Of course you didn't." Obviously on his side, Jackie squeezed his arm. "All you did was tell Aunt Adele I was living here." The timer buzzed, so Jackie scooted up to pull the cake out of the oven. Wanting a moment to think, Nathan waited until she'd set it out to cool and joined him again.

"I explained there'd been a misunderstanding."

"She has a very selective memory." Jackie took another generous bite. "Don't worry, I won't hold you to it. Do you think there's enough ginger in this?"

"There's nothing to hold me to."

"Not between us." She sent him a sympathetic glance. "Don't let it ruin your appetite. I can handle the family. Can I ask you a personal question?"

Nathan picked up his fork again. Somehow he'd opened the door to his own house and fallen down the rabbit hole. "Why not?"

"Are you involved with anyone? It doesn't have to be particularly serious."

She liked the way his eyes narrowed. There was something about gray eyes, really gray eyes, that could cut right through you.

He debated half a dozen answers before settling on the truth. "No."

"That's too bad." Her forehead wrinkled briefly before smoothing out again. "It would have helped if you were, but I'll just make something up. Would you mind very much if I threw you over, maybe for a marine biologist?"

He was laughing. He didn't know why, but when he reached for his wine, his lips were still curved. "Not at all."

She hadn't counted on that—that his laugh would be so appealing. The little flutter came. Jackie acknowledged it, savored it briefly, then banked it down. It wouldn't do. No, it wouldn't do at all. "You're a good sport, Nathan. Not everyone would think so, but they don't know you like I do. Let me get you some more chicken."

"No, I'll get it."

It was a small mistake, the kind people make every day when they step into a doorway at the same time or bump elbows in a crowded elevator. The kind of small mistake that is rarely recognized and soon forgotten.

They rose simultaneously, both reaching for his plate. Their hands closed over it, and each other's. Their bodies bumped. He took her arm to steady her. The usual quick smile and the automatic apology didn't come from either of them.

Jackie felt her breath snag and her heart stumble. The feeling didn't surprise her. She was too much in tune with her emotions, too comfortable with them, to be surprised. It was the depth of them that caught at her. The contact was casual, more funny than romantic, but she felt as though she'd been waiting all her life for it.

She'd remember the feel of his hand, and the china, and the heat of his body as it barely brushed hers. She'd remember the look of surprised suspicion in his eyes, and the scent of spices and wine. She'd remember the quiet, the absolute and sudden quiet. As if the world had held its breath for a moment. For just a moment.

What the hell was this? That was his first and only coherent thought. He was gripping her harder than he should have, as if he were holding on—but that was absurd. However absurd it was, he couldn't quite make himself let go. Her eyes were so big, so soft. Was it foolish to believe he saw absolute honesty in them? That scent, her scent, was there, the one he'd first come across in his own bedroom. The one, Nathan thought now, that still lingered, ridiculously, after she'd moved into a guest room. He heard her breath suck in, then shudder out. Or maybe it was his own.

And he wanted her, as clearly and as logically as he'd ever wanted anything. It lasted only a moment, but the desire was strong.

They moved away together, with the quick, almost jerky motion one uses when one steps back from an unexpected flame. Jackie cleared her throat. Nathan let out a long, quiet breath.

"It's no trouble," she said.

"Thanks."

She moved to the stove before she thought she could breathe easily. As she scooped up chicken and vegetables, she wondered if this was one adventure she should have passed on.

Chapter 3

When he looked at her something happened, something frantic, something she'd never experienced before. Her heart beat just a little too fast, and dampness sprang out on the palms of her hands. A look was all that was necessary. His eyes were so dark, so penetrating. When he looked at her it was as if he could see everything she was, or could be, or wanted to be.

It was absurd. He was a man who lived by the gun, who took what he wanted without regret or compassion. All of her life she'd been taught that the line between right and wrong was clear and wide, and couldn't be crossed.

To kill was the greatest sin, the most unforgivable. Yet he had killed, and would surely kill again. Knowing it, she couldn't care for him. But care she did. And want she did. And need.

Sitting back, Jackie reviewed Sarah's confused and contrasting feelings for Jake. How would a sheltered young woman, barely eighteen, respond to a man who had lived all his life by rules she couldn't possibly understand or approve of? And how would a man who had seen and done all that Jake Redman had seen and done react to an innocent, convent-bred woman?

There was no way their dealings with each other could run smoothly. Their coming together and its resolution couldn't be impossible, it just had to be difficult. Two different worlds, she thought. Two sets of values, two opposing ambitions. Those would be difficult conflicts to overcome. Then you added gunfights, betrayal, kidnapping and revenge. Just to keep things interesting. Still, for all the action and adventure, Jackie had come to think that the love story was really the heart of her book. How these two people were going to change and complement each other, how they would compromise, adjust and stand firm.

She didn't think Sarah or Jake would understand about emotional commitment or mutually supportive relationships. Those were twentieth-century terms. Her psychology course on modern marriage had given Jackie a basketful of catchphrases. The words might change, but love was love. As far as she was concerned, Sarah and Jake had a good chance. That was more than a great many people could say.

It occurred to her that that was all she wanted for herself. A good chance. Someone to love who would love her back, someone to make adjustments for, to make long-range plans with. Wasn't it strange that in making a relationship on paper she had begun to fantasize about making one for herself?

She wouldn't ask for perfection, not only because it would be boring but because she would never be able to achieve perfection herself. It wouldn't be necessary, or even appealing, to settle down with a man who agreed with you on every point.

Would she like dashing? Probably. It might be fun to have someone flash in and out of your life, dropping off dew-kissed roses and magnums of champagne. It would be a nice interlude, but she was dead certain she couldn't live with dashing. Dashing would never take out the trash or unclog a drain.

Sensitive. Jackie rolled the word around in her mind, coming up with a picture of a sweet, caring man who wrote bad poetry. Horn-rimmed glasses and a voice like cream. Sensitive would always understand a woman's needs and a woman's moods. She could be very fond of sensitive. Until sensitive began to drive her crazy.

Passionate would be nice, as well. Someone who would toss her over his shoulder and make mad love in sun-drenched fields. But it might get a bit tough to do that sort of thing once they hit eighty.

Funny, intelligent, reckless and dependable.

That was the trouble, she supposed. She could think of a dozen different qualities she would enjoy in a man, but not of a combination that would pull her in for the long haul. With a sigh, she cupped her chin in her hand and stared over the typewriter through the window. Maybe she just wasn't ready to think about wedding rings and picket fences. Maybe she'd never be ready.

It wasn't easy to accept, but if it was true she could see herself living in some quaint little house near the water and writing about other people's love affairs. She could spend her days dreaming up characters and places, put-tering around in a garden and playing aunt to all the little MacNamaras. It wouldn't be so bad.

She wouldn't be a hermit, of course. And it wasn't as though she didn't appreciate men. Any man she'd ever been close to had possessed at least one of the qualities she ad-mired. She'd cared for and about them, even loved them a little. But then, love was easy for her, falling in and falling out of it without bruises or scars. That wasn't real romance, she thought as she looked at the words she'd written. Real romance scraped off a little skin. It had to if love was going to bloom out of it and heal.

Lord, she was getting philosophical since she'd started putting words on paper. Maybe that explained her reac-tion to Nathan.

The problem was, though she was clever with words and always had been, she couldn't quite come up with the right ones to describe that one brief moment of contact.

Intense, confusing, illuminating, scary. It had been all of those, yet she wasn't sure what the sum of the parts equaled.

Attraction, certainly. But then, she'd found him attractive even when she'd thought she was hallucinating. Most women found dark, brooding types with aloof qualities attractive. God knew why. Yet that one moment, that quick link, had been more than simple attraction. The fact was, it hadn't been simple anything. She'd wanted him in the strong, vital way that usually came only with understanding and time.

I know you, something had seemed to say inside her. *And I've been waiting.*

He'd felt something too. She was certain of that. Maybe it had been that same kind of instant knowledge and instant desire. Whatever he'd felt hadn't pleased him, because he'd been very careful to avoid her for the better part of two days. Not an easy trick, since they were living in the same house, but he'd managed.

She still thought it had been rather rude of him to go out on his boat for an entire day and not ask her along.

Maybe he had to think things through. Jackie gauged him as the type of man who would have to compute and analyze and reason out every area of his life, including the emotional. That was too bad, but she'd have been the first to say that everyone was entitled to their own quirks.

He didn't have to worry about her, she decided as she dipped into a bowl of cheese curls. She wasn't interested in flirting with a relationship, and certainly not one with a man as buttoned-down as Nathan Powell. If she were, then he'd have reason to worry. Jackie chuckled to herself as she nibbled. She could be very tenacious and very persuasive when her mind was set. Fortunately for him, and perhaps for both of them, she was much too involved with writing to give him more than a passing thought.

Still, she checked her watch and noticed that it was nearly dinnertime and he wasn't back. His problem, she thought as she took another handful of cheese curls. She'd agreed to cook, but not to cater. When he came home he could make himself a sandwich. It certainly didn't matter to her.

She peered out her window at the sound of a boat, then settled back with the smallest of sighs when it passed by.

She wasn't really thinking of him, she told herself. She was just...passing the time. She didn't really wish he'd asked her to join him today so that they could have spent some time alone together, getting to know each other better. She wasn't really wondering what kind of man he was— except in the most intellectual terms.

What did it matter that she liked the way he laughed when he briefly let his guard down? It certainly wasn't important that his eyes were dark and dangerous one minute and quietly sensitive another. He was just a man, bound up in his work and his self-image in the same way she was bound up in her work and her future. It wasn't any of her business that he seemed more tense than he should be, and more solitary. It wasn't her goal in life to draw him out and urge him to relax and enjoy.

Her goal in life, Jackie reminded herself, was to finish the story, sell it and reap the benefits of being a published novelist. Whatever they might be. Straightening in her seat, she pushed Nathan Powell aside and went back to work.

This was what he'd come home for, Nathan told himself as he cruised down one of the narrow, deserted channels. Peace and quiet. There were no deadlines, no contract dates to worry about, no supply shortages to work around or inspectors to answer to. Sun and water. He didn't want to think beyond them.

He was beginning to feel almost like himself again. It was odd that he hadn't thought of this before—taking the boat out and disappearing for the day. He might have agreed to have a boarder for a couple of weeks, but that didn't mean he had to chain himself to the house. Or to her.

He couldn't say that it was entirely unpleasant having her there. She was keeping her end of the bargain. Most days passed without him seeing her at all except in the kitchen. Somehow he'd even gotten used to hearing her pounding away at the keys of her typewriter for hours on end. She might have been writing nursery rhymes for all he knew, but he couldn't say she wasn't keeping at it.

Actually, there were a lot of things he couldn't say about her. The problem started with the things he could say.

She talked too fast. It might have seemed an odd complaint, but not for a man who preferred quiet and structured conversations. If they talked about the weather she'd mention her brief career as a meteorologist and end by saying she liked rain because it smelled nice. Who could keep up with that sort of thought pattern?

She anticipated him. He might just begin to think he could use a cold drink and he'd find her in the kitchen making iced tea or pouring him a beer. Though she hadn't yet indicated that she'd trained as a psychic, he found it disconcerting.

She always looked at ease. It was a difficult thing to fault her for, but he found himself growing tenser the more casual she became. Invariably she was dressed in shorts and some breezy top with no makeup and her hair curling as it chose. She stopped just short of being sloppy, and he shouldn't have found it alluring. He preferred well-groomed, polished women—women with a little gloss and style. So why couldn't he keep his mind off one coltish, unpainted throwback who didn't do anything more to attract him than scrub her face and grin?

Because she was different? Nathan could easily reject that notion. He was a man who preferred the comfortable, and the comfortable usually meant the familiar. There was certainly nothing remotely familiar about Jackie. Some might accuse him of being in a rut, but he thought himself entitled. When your career took you to different cities and different countries and involved different people and problems on a regular basis, you deserved a nice comfortable rut in your personal life.

Solitude, quiet, a good book, an occasional congenial companion over drinks or dinner. It didn't seem like too much to ask. Jacqueline MacNamara had thrown a wrench in the works.

He didn't like to admit it, but he was getting used to her. After only a few days, he was used to her company. That in itself, for a loner, was a shattering discovery.

Nathan opened the throttle to let his boat race. He might have been more comfortable if she'd been dull or drab. For social purposes he preferred refined and composed, but for a housemate—boarder, he reminded himself firmly—for a boarder he'd have been happy with dull.

The trouble was, no matter how quiet or unobtrusive she was for most of the day, she was impossible to ignore with her rapid-fire conversations, her dazzling smiles and her bright clothes. Especially since she never seemed to dress in anything that covered more than ten percent of her.

Maybe he could admit it now, alone, with the wind breezing through his hair and over his face, that as annoying and inconvenient as it was to have his sanctuary invaded, she was, well…fun.

He hadn't allowed himself a great deal of fun in the past few years. Work had been and still was his first priority. Building, the creative process and the actual nuts and bolts, absorbed his time. He'd never resented the responsibility. If anyone had asked him if he enjoyed his work, he would have given them a peculiar look and answered, "Of course." Why else would he do it?

He would have accepted the term *dedicated* but would have knit his brows at the word *obsessed*, though obsessed was exactly what he was. He could picture a building in his mind, complete, down to the smallest detail, but he didn't consider himself an artist when he drew up the blueprints. He was a professional, educated and trained, nothing more or less.

He loved his work and considered himself lucky to have found a profession for which he had both skill and affection. There were moments of sweaty, gritty work, head-throbbing concentration and absolute pride. Nothing, absolutely nothing, had ever given him the same thrill of accomplishment as seeing one of his buildings completed.

If he absorbed himself in his work, it wasn't that his life was lacking in other areas. It was simply that no other area had the same appeal or excitement for him. He enjoyed the company of women, but had never met one who could keep him awake at night the way an engineering problem with a building could.

Unless, of course, he counted Jackie. He didn't care to.

He squinted into the sun, then steered away from it until it spread its warmth across his back. Still his frown remained.

Her conversations were like puzzles he had to sort out. No one had made him think that intricately in years. Her constant cheerfulness was contagious. It would be foolish to deny he hadn't eaten better since his childhood—and probably not even then.

She did have an affecting smile, he thought as he wound his way down an alley of the waterway. And her eyes were so big and dark. Dark, yes, but they had this trick, this illusion of lighting up when she smiled. And her mouth was so wide and so generous, always ready to curve.

Nathan pulled himself up short. Her physical attributes weren't of any consequence. Shouldn't be.

That one moment of connection had been a fluke. And he was undoubtedly exaggerating the depth of it. There might have been a passing attraction. That was natural enough. But there certainly hadn't been the affinity he'd imagined. He didn't believe in such things. Love at first sight was a convenience used by novelists—usually bad ones. And instant desire was only lust given a prettier name.

Whatever he had felt, if he'd felt anything at all, had been a vague and temporary tug, purely physical and easily subdued.

Nathan could almost hear her laughing at him, though he was alone on the water and the banks of the waterway were almost deserted. Grimly he headed home.

It was dusk when she heard his boat. Jackie was certain it was Nathan. For the past two hours her ears had been fine-tuned for his return. The wave of relief came first. He hadn't met with any of the hideous boating accidents her mind had conjured up for him. Nor had he been kidnapped and held for ransom. He was back, safe and sound. She wanted to punch him right in the mouth.

Twelve hours, she thought as she dived cleanly into the pool. He'd been gone for nearly twelve hours. The man obviously had no sense of consideration.

Naturally, she hadn't been worried. She'd been much too busy with her own projects to give him more than a passing thought—every five minutes for the last two hours.

Jackie began to do laps in a steady freestyle to release her pent-up energy. She wasn't angry. Why, she wasn't even mildly annoyed. His life was most certainly his own, to do with exactly as he chose. She wouldn't say a word about it. Not a word.

She did twenty laps, then tossed her wet hair back before resting her elbows on the edge of the pool.

"Training for the Olympics?" Nathan asked her. He stood

only a few feet away, a glass of clear, fizzing liquid in his hand. Jackie blinked water out of her eyes and frowned at him.

He was wearing shorts, pleated and pressed, and a short-sleeved polo shirt that was so neat and tidy it might have come straight from the box. Nathan Powell's casual wear, she thought nastily.

"I didn't realize you were back." She glanced at his feet as she lied. Despite all her accomplishments, Jackie had never been able to manage an eyeball-to-eyeball lie.

"I haven't been for long." She was annoyed, Nathan realized. He found it enormously satisfying. Abandoning his rule against small talk, he smiled down at her. "So, how was your day?"

"Busy." Jackie pushed away from the side and began lazily treading water. In the east, the sky was nearly dark, but the last light from the sun touched the pool and garden. She didn't trust the way he was smiling right now, but she found she liked it. There was probably nothing more tedious than a man a woman could trust unconditionally. "And yours?"

"Relaxing." He had an urge, odd and unexpected, to slide into the pool with her. The water would be cool and soft; so would her skin. Maybe he was punchy, Nathan thought, after a hot day on the water.

As she continued to float, Jackie studied him. He did look relaxed—for him. She'd already discovered he was one of those people who carried around tension like a responsibility. She smiled, forgiving him as abruptly as she'd become angry.

"Want an omelet?"

"What?" Distracted, he pulled himself back. She was wearing two thin strips as an excuse for a bathing suit. The water, and perhaps a trick of the light, made them glimmer against her skin. A great deal of skin.

"Are you hungry? I could fix you an omelet."

"No. No, thanks." He took a sip of his drink to ease a suddenly dry throat, then sat the glass down to stuff his hands in his pockets. "It's cooling off." If that was the best he could do, he thought with a scowl, he'd best put the lid on small talk again.

"You're telling me." After sleeking her hair back, Jackie pulled herself out of the pool. She was skinny, Nathan told himself. There was no reason such a skinny, even lanky woman should move so athletically. In the fading sunlight, drops of water scattered over her skin like some primitive decoration.

"I forgot a towel." She shrugged, then shook herself. Nathan swallowed and looked elsewhere. It wasn't wise to look when he'd begun to imagine how easy it would be to slip those two tiny swatches of material off her and slide back into the water with her.

"I should go in," he managed after a moment. "I've got reading to catch up on."

"Me too. I'm reading tons of Westerns. Ever try Zane Grey or Louis L'Amour?" She was walking toward him as she spoke, and he found himself fascinated by the way the water clung to and darkened her hair and lashes. "Great stuff. I'll take this in for you."

"That's all right."

For the second time they reached at the same instant. For the second time their fingers touched and tangled. Nathan felt hers tense on the glass. So she felt it, too. That jolt… that connection, as he'd come to think of it. It wasn't his imagination. Wanting to avoid it, Nathan loosened his grip and stepped back. For the same reason, Jackie mirrored his move. The glass tipped, teetering on the edge of the table. They made the grab simultaneously, caught it, then stood holding the glass between them.

It should have been funny, she thought, but she managed

only a quick, nervous laugh. In his eyes she saw exactly what she felt. Desire, hot and dangerous and edgy.

"Looks like we need a choreographer."

"I've got it." His voice was stiff as they waged a brief tug-of-war.

After relinquishing the glass to him, Jackie let out a slow, careful breath. She made the decision quickly, as she believed all the best decisions were made. "It might be better if we just got it over with."

"Got what over with?"

"The kiss. It's simple, really. I wonder what it would be like, you wonder what it would be like." Though her voice was casual, she moistened her lips. "Don't you think we'd be more comfortable if we stopped wondering?"

He set the glass down again as he studied her. It wasn't a romantic proposal, it was a logical one. That appealed to him. "That's a very pragmatic way of looking at it."

"I can be, occasionally." She shivered a little in the cooling air. "Look, odds are it won't be nearly as important after. Imagination magnifies things. At least mine does." The smile came again, quick and stunning, with the flash of a dimple at the corner of her mouth. "You're not my type. No offense. And I doubt I'm yours."

"No, you're not," he answered, stung a bit.

She took this statement with an agreeable nod. "So, we get the kiss out of the way and get back to normal. Deal?"

He didn't know if she'd done it on purpose—in fact, he was all but certain she hadn't—but she'd managed a direct hit to his male pride. She was so casual, so damn friendly about it. So sure that kissing him would leave her unaffected. Kissing him would be like brushing a pesky fly aside. Get it over with and get back to normal. He'd see about that.

She should have been warned by the look in his eyes— what she still thought of as his Jake look. Perhaps she had been, but it was knowledge gained too late.

With one hand he cupped her neck so that his fingers tangled in her dripping hair. The touch itself was a surprise—quietly intimate. There was a quick and sudden instinct to back away, but she ignored it. Jackie was used to approaching things head-on. So she stepped forward, tilting her head up. She expected something pleasant, warm, even ordinary. It wasn't the first time in her life she'd gotten more than she'd bargained for.

Rockets. They were her first image as his lips closed over hers. Rockets, with that flash of color and that fast, deadly boom. It had always been the boom she'd liked the best. Her little murmur wasn't of protest but of surprise and of pleasure. Accepting the pleasure, she leaned into him and absorbed it.

She could smell the water on him, not the clear, chlorinated water of the pool, but the darker, more exciting water that ran out to sea. The air was cooling rapidly as night fell, but the chill was gone. Her skin warmed as she moved against him and felt the soft brush of his shirt, and then of his hands.

And she *had* been waiting. The knowledge clicked quietly into place. She had been waiting years and years for this. Just this.

Unlike Jackie, Nathan had stopped thinking almost instantly—or thought he had. She tasted…exotic. There had been no warning of that in her pretty, piquant looks and wiry body, no indication of milk and honey heated with spice. She tasted of the desert, of something a dying man might drink greedily in the oasis of his mind.

He hadn't meant to hold her, not closely. He hadn't meant to let his hands roam over her, not freely. Somehow he'd lost control over them. With each touch and stroke over her damp skin, he lost a bit more.

Her back was long and lean and slick. He trailed his fingers over it and felt her tremble. The need jolted again until his mouth was hard on hers, more demanding than he'd ever intended. He pillaged. She accepted. When her sigh whispered against his tongue, his heartbeat doubled.

She pressed against him, her mouth open and willing, her body soft but not submissive. Her generosity was all-consuming. As was his temptation.

She'd never forget this, Jackie thought, not one detail. The heavy, heated scent of flowers, the soft hum of insects, the lapping of water close by. She'd never forget this first kiss, begun at dusk and carried into the night.

Her hands were in his hair, a smile just forming on her lips, as they drew apart. Unashamed of her reaction to him, she let out a long, contented sigh.

"I love surprises," she murmured.

He didn't. Nathan reminded himself of that and pulled back before he could stroke a hand through her hair. It amazed him and infuriated him to see that it wasn't steady. He wanted, unbearably, what he had no intention of taking.

"Now that we've satisfied our curiosity, we shouldn't have any more problems."

He expected anger. Indeed, that came first, a flash in her eyes. They were exceptionally expressive, he thought, and felt a pang when he read hurt in them. Then that, like the anger, disappeared, to be replaced by amusement.

"Don't bet the farm on it, Nathan." She patted his cheek—though she would have preferred to use her fist—and strolled into the house.

She was going to give him problems, all right, she thought as the screen door shut behind her. And it would be her pleasure.

Chapter 4

She would poison his poached eggs. Jackie could see the justice in that. He would come down for breakfast, cool-eyed and smug. She could even imagine what he'd be wearing—beige cotton slacks and a navy-blue shirt. Without a wrinkle in either.

She, giving him no reason to suspect, would serve him a lovely plate of Canadian bacon, lightly grilled, and poached eggs on toast. With a touch of cyanide.

He would sip his coffee. Nathan always went for the coffee first. Then he'd slice the meat. Jackie would fix herself a plate so everything would seem perfectly normal. They'd discuss the weather. A bit humid today, isn't it? Perhaps we're in for some rain.

As he took the first forkful of eggs, the sweat would break out cold on her brow as she waited…and waited.

In moments he would be writhing on the floor, gasping for air, clutching his throat. His eyes would be wide and shocked, then all too aware, as she stood over him, triumphant and smiling. With his last breath, he would beg for forgiveness.

But that wasn't subtle enough.

She was a great believer in revenge. People who forgave and forgot with a pious smile deserved to be stepped on. Not that she couldn't forgive small slights or unconscious hurts, but the big ones, the deliberate ones, required—no, demanded—payback.

She was going to give Nathan Powell the payback he deserved.

She told herself he was a cold fish, an unfeeling slug, a cardboard cutout. But she didn't believe it. Unfortunately for her, she'd seen the kindness and sense of fair play in him. Perhaps he was rigid, but he wasn't cold.

Maybe, just maybe, she had read too much into the kiss. Perhaps her emotions were closer to the surface than most people's, and there was a possibility that he hadn't heard the boom. But he'd felt something. A man didn't hold a woman as if he were falling off a cliff if he'd only slipped off a curb.

He'd felt something, all right, and she was going to see to it that he felt that and more. And suffered miserably.

She could take rejection, Jackie told herself as she ground fresh beans for coffee. Smashing something into dust gave her enormous satisfaction. Rejection was that part of life that toughened you enough to make you try harder. True, she hadn't had to deal with it very often, but she thought of herself as gracious enough to accept it when it was warranted.

Frowning, she watched the kettle begin to steam. It wasn't as though she expected men to fall at her feet— though she had enough ego to want one to trip a little now and again. She certainly didn't expect pledges of undying love and fidelity after one embrace, no matter how torrid.

But damn it, there had been something special between them, something rare and close to wonderful. He'd had no business turning it off with a shrug.

And he'd pay, she thought viciously as she poured boiling water over the ground coffee. He'd pay for the shrug, for the pretending disinterest, and more, he'd pay for the night she'd spent tossing in bed remembering every second she'd been in his arms.

It was a pity she wasn't stunning, Jackie mused as she

heated a skillet. Really stunning, with razor-edged cheek-bones and a statuesque build—or petite and fragile-looking, with melting blue eyes and porcelain skin. Frowning a bit, she tried to get a good look at her reflection in the stainless-steel range hood. What she saw was distorted and vague. Experimenting, she sucked in her cheeks, then let them out again with a puff of air.

Since her appearance was something she couldn't change, she would make the very best of what she had. Nathan Powell, man of stone and steel, would be eating out of her hand in no time.

She heard him come in but took her time before turning. The skimpy halter made the most of her tanned back. For the first time in days she'd raided her supply of makeup. Nothing jarring, she'd told herself. Just a bit of blush and gloss, with most of the accent on the eyes.

Jackie tossed one of her best smiles over her shoulders and had to stifle a shout of laughter. He looked dreadful. Wasn't that a shame?

He felt worse. While Jackie had been fuming and toss-ing in her bed, Nathan had been cursing and turning in his own. Her cheerful smile made him want to bare his teeth and snarl.

One kiss and they'd get back to normal? He'd have liked to strangle her. Things hadn't been normal since she'd forced herself into his life. As far as he could recall, his body hadn't ached like this since he'd been a teenager, when, fortunately, his imagination had outdistanced his experience. Now he knew exactly what it could be like and had spent most of the night thinking about it.

"Morning, Nate. Coffee?"

Nate? *Nate?* Because he was sure it would hurt too much to argue, he merely nodded.

"Hot and fresh, just the way you like it." If her voice had

been any sweeter, she'd have grown wings. "We have Canadian bacon and eggs on the menu this morning. Ready in five minutes."

He downed the first cup. He set it back on the counter, and she filled it again. She'd used a freer hand with her scent. Her fragrance still wasn't rich or overpowering, but this morning it seemed just a bit more pungent than usual. *Remember?* it seemed to say. Cautious, he glanced up at her.

Did she look prettier, or was it just his imagination? How did she manage to make her skin always look so glowing, so soft? It wasn't right, it wasn't even fair, that her hair could be constantly disheveled and appealing whether she was tossing a salad or napping on his couch.

He'd have sworn he'd never seen anyone look so alive, so vivid, in the morning. It was infuriating that she should be so fresh when he felt as though he'd spent the night being pummeled by rubber-tipped sledgehammers.

Despite his best intentions, his gaze was drawn to her mouth. She'd put something on it, something that left it looking as moist and as warm as he remembered it tasted. Dirty pool, he thought, and scowled at her.

"Mrs. Grange is coming in today."

"Oh?" Jackie smiled at him again as she turned the sizzling bacon. "Isn't that nice? Things really are getting back to normal, aren't they?" Jackie broke an egg, one-handed, and dropped it in the poacher. "Do you plan to be here for lunch?"

The yolk didn't break, and the shell was neatly dispatched. A nice trick, Nathan thought. He was sure she had a million of them. "I'll be in all day. I've got a lot of calls to make."

"Good. I'll be sure to fix something special." She turned to him again to give him a long, interested study. "You know, Nathan, you look a little haggard this morning. Trouble sleeping?"

No matter how much it cost him, he wouldn't snarl. "I had some paperwork I wanted to clear up."

Jackie clucked her tongue sympathetically as she arranged his breakfast on a plate. "You work too hard. It makes you tense. You should try yoga. There's nothing like a little meditation and proper exercise to relax the body and mind."

"Work relaxes me."

"A common misconception." Jackie set the plate neatly in front of him, then scooted around the counter. "The fact is that work occupies your mind and can take your mind off other problems, but it doesn't cleanse. Take a good massage."

Jackie began to knead his neck and shoulders while she spoke, pleased that at the first touch he jerked like a spring. "A really good massage," she continued as her fingers pressed and stroked, "relieves both mind and body of tension. A little oil, some soothing music, and you'll sleep like a baby. Oh, you've got yourself a real knot here at the base of your neck."

"I'm fine," he managed. In another minute the fork he was holding was going to snap in two. She had magic in her hands. Black magic. "I'm never tense."

Jackie frowned a moment, losing track of the purpose of the exercise. Did he believe that? she wondered. Probably. When a man was always tense, he obviously thought of it as normal. When her heart started to warm toward him, she lectured herself.

"Let's just say there's relaxed and there's relaxed." She concentrated on the teres minor. "After a really good rub, my muscles are like butter. I slide right off the table. I've got some wonderful oil. Hans swears by it."

"Hans?" Why was he asking? Nathan thought as, despite himself, he stretched under her hands.

"My masseur. He's from Norway and has the hands of an artist. He taught me his technique."

"I'll just bet," Nathan muttered, and had Jackie grinning behind his back.

God, who would have suspected he had muscles like this? The man drew up blueprints and argued with engineers. Jackie hadn't suspected that his conservative shirts hid all those wonderful ridges. Last night, when he'd held her, she'd been too dazed to notice how well he was built. She ran her hands over his shoulders.

"You've got a terrific build," she told him. "I've got lousy deltoids myself. When I was into bodybuilding, I never managed to do much more than sweat."

Enough was enough, Nathan thought. One more squeeze of those long, limber fingers and he'd do something embarrassing. Like whimpering. Instead, he spun around on the stool and caught her hands in his.

"What the hell are you trying to do?"

She didn't mind her heart skipping a beat. In fact, it was a delightful feeling. Still, she remembered that revenge was her first order of business.

"Just trying to loosen you up, Nate. Tension's bad for the digestion."

"I'm not tense. And don't call me Nate."

"Sorry. It suits you when you get that look in your eyes. That look," she explained, and she would have gestured if her hands hadn't been clamped in his. "The one that says shoot first and ask questions later."

He would be patient. Nathan told himself to count to ten, but only made it to four. "Careful, Jack. You're here on probation. You'd be wise to back off from whatever game you're playing."

"Game?" She smiled, but her eyes held the first hint of frost he'd ever seen in them. For some reason, even that attracted him. "I don't know what you're talking about."

"What about that stuff you put on your mouth?"

"This?" Deliberately she ran her tongue over her upper, then her lower lip. "A woman's entitled to a little lipstick now and then. Don't you like it?"

He wouldn't dignify the question with an answer. "You put stuff on your eyes, too."

"Are cosmetics against the law in this state? Really, Nate—sorry, Nathan—you're being silly. Surely you don't think I'm trying to…seduce you?" She smiled again, daring him to comment. "I'd think a big strong man like you could take care of himself." She liked the way his eyes could darken from slate to smoke. "But if it stirs you up, I'll be certain to keep my mouth absolutely naked from now on. Will that be better?"

His voice was so soft, so very controlled, that she was fooled into thinking she was still at the wheel. "People who fight dirty end up in the mud themselves."

"So I've heard." She tossed back her head and looked at him from beneath her lashes. "But you see, I can take care of myself, too."

She saw then that she had misjudged him. Perhaps by no more than a few degrees, but such miscalculations could often be fatal. The look that came into his eyes was so utterly reckless, so coolly dangerous, that her heart thudded to a halt.

Jake was back, and his guns were smoking.

It would be more than a kiss now, whether she wanted it or not. It would be exactly as he chose, when he chose and how he chose. No amount of glib chatter or charming smiles was going to help.

When the doorbell rang, neither of them moved. With a

hard, painful thump, Jackie's heart started again. Saved by the bell. She would have giggled if she hadn't been ready to collapse.

"That must be Mrs. Grange," she said brightly, just a shade too brightly. "If you'd let go of my hands now, Nathan, I'd be glad to answer the door while you finish your breakfast."

He did release her, but only after making her suffer through the longest five seconds of her life, during which she believed he would ignore the door and finish what his eyes had told her he intended to do. Saying nothing, Nathan let her go, then swiveled back around to the counter. The pity of it was that he no longer wanted coffee, but a nice stiff drink.

Jackie slipped out of the kitchen. She hoped his eggs were stone-cold.

She loved Mrs. Grange. When Jackie opened the door, she wasn't sure what to make of the large woman in the flowered housedress and high-top sneakers. Mrs. Grange gave Jackie a long, narrowed look with watery blue eyes, pursed her lips and said, "Well, well."

Understanding the implications of that, Jackie smiled and offered a hand. "Good morning. You must be Mrs. Grange. I'm Jack MacNamara, and Nathan's stuck with me for a few weeks because he can't bring himself to toss me out. Have you had breakfast?"

"An hour ago." After she stepped inside, Mrs. Grange set a huge canvas bag on the floor. "MacNamara. You must be related to that no-account."

Jackie didn't need a name. "Guilty. We're cousins. He's gone."

"And good riddance." With a sniff, Mrs. Grange cast a look around the living area. Though she approved of the fresh flowers, she was determined to withhold final judgment. "I'll tell you like I told him. I don't clean up after pigs."

"And who could blame you?" Jackie's grin was fast and brilliant. If dear cousin Fred had tried to charm Mrs. Grange, he'd fallen flat on his baby face. "I'm using the guest room, the blue-and-white one? I'm working in there, too, so if you'll just let me know where that room fits into your schedule I'll make sure I'm out of your way. I'm planning on fixing lunch about twelve-thirty," she continued, mentally adjusting her menu with the idea of carving a few pounds from Mrs. Grange's prodigious bulk.

Mrs. Grange's lips pursed again. It was a rare thing for an employer to offer her a meal. For the most part she was treated with polite, and bland, disregard. "I brought some sandwiches."

"Of course, if you'd rather, but I was hoping you'd join us. I'll be upstairs if you need anything. Nathan's in the kitchen and the coffee's fresh." She smiled again, then left Mrs. Grange to begin while she went upstairs.

Throughout the morning, Jackie heard the sounds of vacuuming and the heavy thud of Mrs. Grange's sneakers moving up and down the hallway. It pleased her that the noise and activity didn't intrude on her concentration. A real writer, in her opinion, should have imagination enough to overcome any outside interference. By noon, she was well on her way to sending Jake and Sarah on another adventure.

Jackie decided on a cracked-wheat-and-parsley salad for the lunch break. With the radio on, she set about dicing and cubing and humming to herself while she tried to imagine what it would be like to outrun desperadoes. When Nathan came in, she turned the music down, then set a huge bowl on the counter.

"Iced coffee all right?"

"Fine." His answer was casual, but he was watching her.

One wrong move, he thought, and he was going to pounce. He wasn't certain what would constitute a wrong move, or what he'd do once he'd pounced, but he was ready for her.

"I'd like to use the phone later, if you don't mind. Anything long-distance I'll charge to my credit card."

"All right."

"Thanks. I think it's about time to start planting the seeds of Fred's downfall."

With his fork halfway to his mouth, Nathan stopped. "What kind of seeds?"

"You're better off not knowing. Oh, hello, Mrs. Grange."

Annoyed with the interruption, Nathan turned to look at his housekeeper. "Mrs. Grange?"

"Sit down right here," Jackie said before Nathan could continue. "I hope you like this. It's called *tabouleh*. Very popular in Syria."

Mrs. Grange settled her bulk on a stool and eyed the bowl doubtfully. "It doesn't have any of that funny stuff in it, does it?"

"Absolutely not." Jackie set a glass of iced coffee next to the bowl. "If you like it, I'll give you the recipe for your family. Do you have a family, Mrs. Grange?"

"Boys are grown." Cautiously Mrs. Grange took the first forkful. Her hands, Jackie noticed, were work-reddened and ringless.

"You have sons?"

With a nod, Mrs. Grange dipped into the salad again. "Had four of them. Two of them are married now. Got three grandkids."

"Three grandchildren. That's marvelous, isn't it, Nathan? Do you have pictures?"

Mrs. Grange took another forkful. She'd never tasted anything quite like this. It wasn't cold meat loaf on rye, but it was nice. Real nice. "Got some in my bag."

"I'd love to see them." Jackie took a seat that set Mrs. Grange squarely between her and Nathan. He was eating in silence, like a man who found himself placed next to strangers at a diner. "Four sons. You must be very proud."

"They're good boys." Her wide, stern face relaxed a bit. "The youngest is in college. Going to be a teacher. He's smart, that one, never gave me a minute's trouble. The others…" She paused, then shook her head. "Well, that's what having kids is all about. This is a real nice salad, Miss Mac-Namara. Real pretty."

"Jack. And I'm glad you like it. Would you like some more coffee?"

"No, I'd best get back to work. You want me to take those shirts to the cleaners, Mr. Powell?"

"I'd appreciate it."

"If you don't need to use it now, I'll do your office."

"That's fine."

She turned to Jackie, and her eyes were friendly. "Don't worry about keeping out of the way upstairs. I can work around you."

"Thanks. Don't bother, I'll get these." She started to gather up bowls as Mrs. Grange plodded out. Nathan frowned at her over the rim of his iced coffee.

"What was all that about?"

"Hmm?" Jackie glanced at him as she transferred the leftover salad into a smaller dish.

"That business with Mrs. Grange. What were you doing?"

"Eating lunch. Would you mind if I gave her the rest of this to take home?"

"No, go ahead." He drew out a cigarette. "Do you usually have lunch with the help?"

She looked at him again, one brow lifting. "Why not?"

Every answer he thought of seemed stilted and snobbish,

so he merely shrugged and lit his cigarette. Because she could see he was embarrassed, Jackie let it pass.

"Is Mrs. Grange divorced or widowed?"

"What?" Nathan blew out a stream of smoke and shook his head. "How would I know? How do you know she's either?"

"Because she talked about her sons and her grandchildren, but she didn't mention her husband. Therefore it's elementary, my dear Nathan, that she hasn't got one." As an afterthought, she popped one last crouton into her mouth. "I opt for divorce because widows usually continue to wear a wedding ring. Hasn't it ever come up?"

"No." He brooded, staring into his coffee. For some reason he didn't want to confess that Mrs. Grange had worked for him for five—no, it was nearly six years now—and he hadn't known she had four sons and three grandchildren until five minutes ago. "It wasn't part of her job description, and I didn't want to pry."

"That's nonsense. Everyone likes to talk about their families. I wonder how long she's been single." She moved around the kitchen rinsing bowls, tidying counters. The rings on her fingers flashed with wealth, while her hands spoke of confidence. "I can't think of anything tougher than raising kids on your own. Do you ever think about that?"

"Think about what?"

"About having a family." She poured herself another glass with the idea of taking the coffee upstairs. "Thinking about kids always makes me feel very traditional. White picket fence, two-car garage, wood-paneled station wagon and all of that. I'm surprised you're not married, Nathan. Being a traditional man."

Her tone had him scowling. "I know when I've been insulted."

"Of course you do." She touched his cheek lightly with

her fingertips. "Being traditional's nothing to be ashamed of. I admire you, Nathan, really I do. There's something endearing about a man who always knows where his socks are. When the right woman comes along, she's going to get a real prize."

His hand clamped over her wrist before she could draw away. "Have you ever had your nose broken?"

Absolutely delighted, she grinned at him. "Not so far. Want to fight?"

"Let's try this."

Jackie found herself sprawled over him as he sat on the stool. He'd caught her off balance, and she had to grab his shoulders to keep from falling on her face. She hadn't expected him to move that quickly, or precisely in that way. Before she could decide how to counter it—or whether she should counter it—his mouth was on hers. And it was searing.

He didn't know why he'd done it. What he'd really wanted to do, ached to do, was slug her. Of course, a man didn't slug a woman, so he'd really been left with no choice.

Why he'd thought a kiss would be revenge was beyond him now that it was begun. She didn't struggle, though he knew from the way her breath caught and her fingers tightened that he had at least surprised her.

But she couldn't have been more surprised than he.

Damn it, he wasn't the kind of man who yanked women around. Yet it seemed right when it was Jackie. It seemed… fated. He could rationalize for hours, he could reason and deliberate until everything was crystal-clear. Then he could touch her and blow logic to smithereens.

He didn't want her. He was eaten up with wanting her. He didn't even like her. He was fascinated by her. He thought she was crazy. And he was beginning to be sure he was.

Always he'd known there was a pattern to everything, a structure. Until Jackie.

He nipped his teeth into her bottom lip and heard her low, quiet moan. Apparently life wasn't always geometrical.

She'd asked for it, Jackie thought to herself. And, thank God, she'd gotten it. Thoughts of revenge, of making him suffer and sweat, flew out of her mind as she dived into the kiss. It was wonderful, sweet, sharp, hot, trembling, the way she'd imagined and hoped a kiss might be.

Her heart went into it, completely, trustingly. This was a man who could love her, accept her. She wasn't a fool, and she wasn't naive. She felt it from him as clearly as if he'd spoken the words. This was special, unique, the kind of loving poems were written about and wars were fought for. Some people waited a lifetime for only this. And not everyone found it. She knew it, and she wrapped her arms around him, ready to give him everything she was. No questions, no doubts.

Something was happening. Over the desire, over the passion, he could sense it. There was a change inside him, an opening, a recklessness. When her mouth was on his, her body melting in his arms, he couldn't think beyond the moment. That was crazy. He never thought of today without taking tomorrow into account. But now, just now, he could think only of holding her like this. Of tasting more of her, bit by slow bit. Of exploring her, discovering her. He couldn't think of anything but her.

It was insanity. He knew it, feared it, even as he pressed her closer. Sinking. He was sinking into her. It was an odd and erotic sensation to feel himself lose his grip. He had to stop this, and stop it cold, before whatever was growing inside him grew too big to be controlled.

He drew her away, struggling to be firm, planning to be cruel. If she smiled at him instead of striking back, he knew, he'd be on his knees. He knew he should tell her all bets were off, to pack her things and leave. But he couldn't. No matter how much he told himself he wanted her out of his life, he couldn't ask her to go.

"Nathan." Aroused, pliant, already in love, she cupped her hand over his cheek. "Let's give Mrs. Grange the rest of the day off. I want to be with you."

Words caught in his throat, trapped in a fresh surge of desire. He'd never known a woman who was more open with her feelings, more honest with her needs. She scared him to death. He gave himself an extra moment. He couldn't afford to have his voice sound unsteady or to have her see how flexible his resolve was.

"You're getting ahead of yourself." As if the kiss had been only a kiss, he set her back on the floor. He hadn't realized how much warmth she'd brought to him until he'd no longer been touching her. "I don't think having an affair is in your best interests, or mine, considering our current arrangement. But thanks."

She went pale, and he knew that he'd gone too far in his rush for self-protection.

"Jackie, I didn't mean that the way it sounded."

"Didn't you? Well, whatever." She was amazed, absolutely amazed, at how much it hurt. She'd always dreamed of falling in love, deeply, blindly, beautifully in love. So this was how it felt, she thought as she pressed a hand to her stomach. The poets could keep it.

"Jack, listen—"

"No, I'd really rather not." When she smiled at him now, he realized just how special her genuine smile was. "No explanations required, Nathan. It was only a suggestion. I should apologize for coming on too strong."

"Damn it, I don't want an apology."

"No? Well, that's good, because I think I'd choke on

it. I really should get back to work, but before I go there's just one thing." Deadly calm, Jackie picked up her glass of iced coffee and emptied it in his lap. "See you at dinner."

She worked like a maniac, barely noticing when Mrs. Grange came in to change the bed linen and dust the furniture. She was both amazed and infuriated at how close, how dangerously close, she'd been to tears. It wasn't that she minded shedding tears. There were times when she enjoyed nothing more than a wailing crying jag. But she knew that if she gave in to this one she wouldn't enjoy it a bit.

How could he have been so insensitive, so unfeeling, as to think she'd been offering him nothing more than sex, a quick afternoon romp? And how could she have been so stupid as to think she'd fallen in love?

Love took two people. She knew that. Wasn't she even now pouring her heart out in a story that involved two people's feelings and needs? And those feelings hadn't sprung out of a kiss but out of time and struggle.

Same old Jack, she accused herself. Still believing that everything in life came as easily as slipping off a log. She'd deserved a swift kick and gotten one. But deserving or not, it didn't make it any less humiliating that Nathan had been the one to plant it.

Mrs. Grange cleared her throat for the third time as she fluffed Jackie's pillows. The minute the typewriter stilled, she stepped in.

"You sure do type fast," she began. "You do secretarial work?"

There was no reason to take out her foul mood on the housekeeper, Jackie reminded herself as she forced a smile. "No, actually I'm writing a book."

"Is that so?" Interested, Mrs. Grange walked to the foot of the bed to tug on the spread. "I like a good story myself."

Mrs. Grange was the first person Jackie had told about her writing who hadn't raised a brow or rolled her eyes. Encouraged, she swiveled around in her chair. The devil with Nathan, she thought. Jacqueline R. MacNamara had come to write a book, and that was just what she was going to do.

"Do you get much of a chance to read?"

"Nothing I like better after a day on my feet than to sit down with a nice story for an hour or two." Mrs. Grange edged a little closer, passing a dustrag over the lamp. "What kind of book are you writing?"

"A romance, a historical romance."

"No fooling? I'm partial to love stories. You been writing long?"

"Actually, this is my first try. I spent about a month doing research and compiling information and dates and things, then I just dived in."

Mrs. Grange shifted her gaze to the typewriter, then looked back at the lamp. "I guess it's like painting. You don't want anybody looking till it's all done."

"Are you kidding?" Laughing, Jackie tucked her feet under her. "I've been dying for somebody to want to read some of it." But not her family, Jackie thought, nibbling on her lower lip. They had already seen too much of what she'd begun, then left undone. "Want to see the first page?" Jackie was already whipping it from the pile and offering it.

"Well, now." Mrs. Grange took the typed sheet and held it out at arm's length until she focused on it. She read with her lips pursed and her eyes narrowed. After a moment she let out three wheezes that Jackie recognized as a laugh. Nothing, absolutely nothing, could have pleased her more.

"You sure did start out with a bang, didn't you?" There was both admiration and approval in Mrs. Grange's eyes as she looked over the end of the sheet. "Nothing like a gunfight to pique the interest."

"That's what I was hoping. Of course, it's just a first draft, but it's going fast." She accepted the page back and studied it. "I'm hoping to have enough to send off in a couple of weeks."

"I'll be mighty pleased to read the whole thing when you've finished."

"Me too." Jackie laughed again as she placed the first page on top of the pile. "Every day when I see how many pages I've done I can't believe it." A bit hesitantly, she laid her hand on top of the manuscript pages. "I haven't figured out what I'm going to do when it's all finished."

"Well, I guess you'll just have to write another one, won't you?" Bending, Mrs. Grange hefted her box of cleaning tools and clumped out.

Why, she was right, Jackie thought. Win or lose, life didn't begin or end on the first try. There couldn't be anyone who knew that better than herself. If something worked, you kept at it. And if something didn't work, and you wanted it, you kept right at that, too.

Turning around, she smiled at the half-typed page in her machine. She could apply that philosophy nicely to her writing. And while she was at it she might just apply it to Nathan.

Chapter 5

He was furious with himself. Still, it was easier, and a lot more comfortable, to turn his fury on her. He hadn't wanted to kiss her. She'd goaded him into it. He certainly hadn't wanted to hurt her. She'd forced him to do so. In a matter of days she'd turned him into a short-tempered villain with an overactive libido.

He was really a very nice man. Nathan was certain of it. Sure, he could be tough-minded, and he was often an impatient perfectionist on the job. He could hire and fire with impersonal speed. But that was business. In his personal life he'd never given anyone reason to dislike him.

When he saw a woman socially, he was always careful to see that the rules were posted up front. If the relationship deepened, both would be fully aware of its possibilities and its limitations. No one would ever have called him a womanizer.

Not that he didn't have a certain number of female… friends. It would be impossible for a grown man, a healthy man, to go through life without some companionship and affection. But, damn it, he made the moves, the overtures—and there was a certain flow to how these things worked. When a man and a woman decided to go beyond being friends, they did so responsibly, with as much caution as affection. By the time they did, if they did, they'd developed a certain rapport and understanding.

Groping in the kitchen after a parsley salad wasn't his idea of a sensible adult relationship.

If that was old-fashioned, then he was old-fashioned.

The problem was, that kiss over the kitchen counter had meant more, had shaken him more, than any of the carefully programmed, considerate and mature relationships he'd ever experienced. And it wasn't the way he wanted his life to run.

He hadn't learned much from his father, other than how to knot a tie correctly, but he had learned that a woman was to be treated with respect, admiration and care. He was—always had been—a gentleman. Roses for the proper occasion, a light touch and a certain amount of courtship.

He knew how to treat a woman, how to steer a relationship along the right course and how to end one without scenes and recriminations. If he was overly careful not to allow anyone to get too close, he had good reason. Another thing he'd learned from his father, in reverse, was never to make promises he wouldn't keep or establish bonds he would certainly break. It had always been a matter of pride to him that whenever it had become necessary to end a relationship he and the woman involved had parted as friends.

How could he and Jackie part as friends when they hadn't yet become friends? In any case, Nathan considered himself sharp enough to know that if a relationship was begun, then ended, with a woman like Jackie, it wouldn't end without scenes or recriminations. The end, he was sure, would be just as explosive and illogical as the beginning.

He didn't like mercurial personalities or flash-fire tempers. They interfered with his concentration.

What he needed to do was to get back in gear—start the preliminaries on his next project, resume his social life. He'd spent too much time on the troubles and triumphs with the complex in Germany. Now that he'd gotten home, he hadn't had a peaceful moment.

His own fault. Nathan was willing to accept responsibility. His uninvited guest had another week—after all, she had his word on that. Then she was out. Out and forgotten. Well, out, in any case.

He started upstairs with the intention of changing and drowning himself in the pool. Then he heard her laugh. It was just his bad luck, he supposed, that she had such an appealing laugh. He heard her speak in that quicksilver way she had, and he stopped. Her bedroom door was open, and her voice raced out. It wasn't eavesdropping, he told himself. It was, after all, his house.

"Aunt Honoria, what in the world gave you that idea?" Kicked back in a chair, Jackie held the phone between her shoulder and chin as she painted her toenails. "Of course I'm not annoyed with Fred. Why should I be? He did me a wonderful favor." Jackie dipped her brush in the bottle of Sizzling Cerise polish and played her cards close to her chest. "The house is absolutely perfect, exactly what I'd been looking for, and Nathan—Nathan's the owner, darling—yes, he's just adorable."

She held her foot out to admire her handiwork. Between writing and cooking, she hadn't had time for a pedicure in weeks. No matter how busy, her mother would have said, a woman should always look her best from head to toe.

"No, dear, we've worked things out beautifully. He's a bit of a hermit, so we keep to ourselves. I'm fixing his meals for him. The darling's developing a bit of a paunch."

Outside the door, Nathan automatically reached a hand to his stomach.

"No, he couldn't be sweeter. We're rubbing along just fine. He might be one of my uncles. As a matter of fact, his hairline's receding just like Uncle Bob's."

This time both of Nathan's hands went to his hair.

"I'm just glad I could put your mind at ease. No, be sure to let Fred know everything couldn't be better. I'd have gotten in touch with him myself, but I wasn't sure just where he'd popped off to."

There was a pause. For some reason, Nathan felt it was a particularly cold one.

"Of course, dear, I know exactly how our Fred is."

In the hallway, Nathan heard little murmurs of agreement and a few light laughs. He was just about to continue when Jackie spoke again.

"Oh, Aunt Honoria, I nearly forgot. What was the name of that wonderful Realtor you used on the Hawkins property?"

Jackie switched feet and moved in for the kill.

"Well, dear, it's rather confidential still, but I know I can trust you. It seems there's this block of land, about twenty-five acres. South of here, a place called Shutter's Creek. Yes, it is rather precious, isn't it? In any case...you will keep this to yourself, won't you?"

Jackie smiled and continued to paint as she received her aunt's assurances. Aunt Honoria's promises were as easily smeared as wet nail polish. "Yes, I knew you would. Anyway, it's being sold at rock bottom, and naturally I wouldn't have been interested. Who would? It's hardly more than a swamp at this point. But the beauty is, dear, that Allegheny Enterprises—you know, the contractors who put up all those marvelous resorts? Yes, that's the one. They're scouting out the location. They're thinking about pumping it and filling it in and putting up one of those chichi places like they did in Arizona. Yes, it was marvelous what they did with a few acres of desert, wasn't it?"

She listened a few more moments, knowing how to play a line until the bait was well taken.

"Just a little tip from a friend of mine. I want to snap it up quickly, then resell it to Allegheny. Word from my friend is that they'll pay triple the asking price. Yes, I know, sounds too good to be true. Do keep this under your hat, Auntie. I want to see if I can have the Realtor rush this through settlement before the lid's off."

Jackie listened for a moment as she debated putting on a third coat.

"Yes, it could be exciting, and very hush-hush. That's why I don't want to tip my hand to the Realtor here in Florida. No, I haven't said a thing to Mother and Daddy yet. You know how I love surprises. Oh, darling, there's the door. Must run. Do give my best to everyone. I'll be in touch. *Ciao.*"

Delighted with herself, Jackie stretched in the chair and sent it spinning in a circle.

"Well, hello, Nathan."

"I don't know where you get your information," he began, "but unless you want to lose even more money, I'd look for someplace other than Shutter's Creek. It's twenty-five acres of sludge and mosquitoes."

"Yes, I know." With the ease of the limber, Jackie brought her leg around so that she could blow on her painted toenails. Nathan wouldn't have been surprised if she'd tucked her heel behind her ear and grinned at him. "And unless I miss my guess, dear old Fred will own all those lovely mosquitoes within forty-eight hours." Smiling at Nathan, she pillowed her head on her folded arms. "I always figure when you pay back you should pay back where it'll hurt the most. For Fred, that's his wallet."

Impressed, Nathan stepped farther into the room. "You planted the seeds of his downfall?"

"Exactly, and like Jack's beanstalk, it should sprout overnight."

Nathan mulled it over. It was a nasty trick, a very nasty trick. He only wished he'd thought of it. "How do you know he'll go for it?"

Jackie merely continued to smile. "Want to make a wager on it?"

"No," he said after a moment. "No, I don't think I do. How much are they asking an acre?"

"Oh, only two thousand. Fred should be able to beg, borrow or steal fifty without too much trouble." Deciding against a third coat, she capped the bottle. "I always pay my debts, Nathan. Without exception."

He was aware he'd been warned and decided he deserved it. "If it's any consolation, I doubt I'll be able to drink iced coffee again."

She crossed her legs lazily. "I suppose that's something."

"And I'm not losing my hair."

She flicked her gaze over it. It was thick and full and dark. She could remember with absolute clarity how it had felt between her fingers. "Probably not."

"Nor do I have a paunch."

With her tongue caught between her teeth, she let her glance slide down to his taut and very flat stomach. "Well, not yet."

"And I am not adorable."

"Well…" Her eyes were laughing when they came back to his. "Cute, then—in a staid and very masculine sort of way."

He opened his mouth to argue, then decided it was safer to give up. "I'm sorry," he said instead before he knew he'd meant to tell her.

Jackie's eyes softened along with her smile. Revenge always took a back seat to an apology. "Yes, I think you are. Do you like fresh starts, Nathan?"

So it was that easy. He should have known it would be that easy with her. "Yes, actually, I do."

"All right, then." She unwound herself from the chair. If he found himself looking at her legs again, he was only human. When she stood, she offered a hand. "Friends?"

He knew he could have given her a list of reasons they couldn't be, certainly a lengthy one of reasons why they shouldn't be. But he put his hand in hers. "Friends. Do you want to take a swim?"

"Yeah." She could have kissed him. God, she wanted to. Lecturing herself, Jackie smiled instead. "Give me five minutes to change."

She took less than that. When she arrived, Nathan was just surfacing. Before he had the chance to shake the water out of his eyes and spot her, she dived in beside him. She came up cleanly, head tilted back so that her hair was slick against her head.

"Hi."

"You move fast."

"Mostly." She moved into a smooth sidestroke and did a length and a half. "I love your pool. That helped sell me on the place, you know. I grew up with a pool, so I'd have hated to spend three months without one."

"Glad I could oblige," he told her, but it didn't come out nearly as sarcastic as he'd expected. She smiled and switched to a breaststroke that barely rippled the water. "I take it you do a lot of swimming."

"Not as much as I used to." With what looked like no effort at all, she rolled onto her back to float. "I was on a swim team for a couple of years in my teens. Gave some serious thought to the Olympics."

"I'm not surprised."

"Then I fell in love with my swim coach. His name was Hank." She sighed and closed her eyes on the memory. "I couldn't seem to concentrate on my form after that. I was fifteen and Hank was twenty-five. I imagined us married and raising a relay team. He was only interested in my backstroke. I've always been able to go backward well."

"You don't say."

"No, really. I was all-state with my backstroke. Anyway, Hank was about five-eight, with shoulders like I beams. I've always been a sucker for shoulders." She opened her eyes briefly to study him. Without a shirt, his body seemed tougher and more disciplined than she had expected. "Yours are very nice."

"Thanks." He discovered it was both relaxing and invigorating to float beside her.

"Also, Hank had the greatest blue eyes. Like lanterns. I wove some wonderful fantasies around those eyes."

Irrationally he began to detest Hank. "But he was only interested in your backstroke."

"Exactly. To get him to notice me, I pretended I was drowning. I imagined him pulling me out and doing mouth-to-mouth until he realized he was madly in love and couldn't live without me. How was I supposed to know that my father had picked that day to come in and watch practice?"

"No one could have."

"I knew you'd understand. So there's my father jumping into the pool in his three-piece wool suit and Swiss watch. Neither were ever quite the same again, by the way. By the time he dragged me to the side he was hysterical. Some of my teammates thought it was a reaction from shock, but my father knew me too well. Before I could blink, I was off the swim team and on the tennis courts. With a female pro."

"Your father sounds like a very wise man."

"Oh, he's as sharp as they come, J. D. MacNamara. No one's ever been able to put anything over on him for long. God knows I've tried." She sighed and let the water lap around her. "He'll get a tremendous charge out of it when I tell him about the sting I pulled on Fred."

"You're close to your family?"

Jackie thought, but couldn't be sure, that his voice sounded wistful. "Very. Sometimes almost too much, which may be why I'm always pulling myself off somewhere to try something new. If Daddy had his way, I'd be safely housed in Newport with the man of his choice, raising his grandchildren and keeping out of trouble. Do you have any family here in Florida?"

"No."

She didn't have any doubts about it this time. The subject was definitely on posted ground. Not wanting to irritate him again so soon, Jackie let it pass. "Want to race?"

"Where?" He nearly yawned as he said it. He couldn't remember the last time he'd been so completely relaxed.

"To one end and back to the other. I'll give you a three-stroke lead."

He opened his eyes at that. Jackie was treading water now, her face only inches from his. As he looked at her, Nathan realized he could yank her to him and have his mouth on hers in a heartbeat. Racing, he decided, was a much better idea.

"Fine." He took three easy strokes, then saw the bullet pass him. Amused, and challenged, he kicked in.

It might have been a few years since she'd been on a swim team, but after five yards Nathan saw that she'd retained her competitive spirit. With some women, with most women, he'd have been inclined to lose, knowing that the woman involved would know he'd done so purposely.

He didn't feel inclined to lose to Jackie.

When they touched the wall and rolled into a turn, they were head-to-head. He couldn't, as he'd expected, sprint ahead of her. Her long legs propelled her forward, and her slim arms cut through the water in quick, smooth strokes. Gradually he inched ahead, one stroke, then two, with the advantage of his longer reach. When they came to the side he touched only half a body length ahead.

"I must be slipping." A little breathless, Jackie leaned

her forearms on the edge, pillowed her cheek on them and studied him. His skin was shiny with water now, drops running off of and clinging to muscular forearms and shoulders. The kind of arms and shoulders, Jackie thought, that a woman could depend on. "You're in good shape, Nathan."

"You too." He was out of breath himself.

"No handicap next time."

He grinned. "I'll still beat you."

"Maybe." Jackie dragged a hand through her hair so that it curled, wet and charming, around her face. "How's your tennis?"

"Not bad."

"Well, that's a possibility." She pulled herself up and out, then sat on the edge, legs dangling. "How about Latin?"

"What about Latin?"

"We could have a Latin tournament."

With a shake of his head, he pulled himself up to sit beside her. "I don't know any Latin."

"Everyone knows some Latin. Corpus delicti or magna cum laude." She leaned back on her elbows. "I can never understand why they call it a dead language when it's used every day."

"That's certainly something to think about."

She laughed. She couldn't help it. He had such a droll way of telling her he thought she was crazy. When his eyes were light and friendly and the smile was beginning to play around his mouth, he seemed like someone she'd known all her life. Or wished she had.

"I like you, Nathan. I really do."

"I like you, too. I think." It wasn't possible not to smile back at her, just as it wasn't possible not to look at her if she was anywhere nearby. She drew you in. Being with her was like plunging into a cold lake on a sultry day. It was a shock to the system, but a welcome one.

Before he realized what he was doing, Nathan reached over to tuck a dripping curl behind her ear. It wasn't like him; he didn't touch casually. The moment his fingers brushed her cheek he knew it was just one more mistake. How could you want more when you weren't even certain what it was you were taking?

As he started to draw away, she leaned up just a little and took his hand in hers. She brought his fingers to her lips in a gesture that stunned him with the naturalness of it.

"Nathan, is there some woman I should be concerned about?"

He didn't pull away, though he knew he should. Somehow his fingers had curled with hers and were holding on. "What do you mean?"

"I mean, you said you weren't involved, but I wondered if there was someone. I don't mind competing, I just like to know."

There was no one. Even if there had been, her memory would have vanished like a puff of smoke. That was what worried him. "Jack, you're taking two steps to my one."

"Am I?" She shifted. It only took a small movement to have her lips whisper against his. She didn't press, content for now with only a taste. "How long do you think it'll take you to catch up?"

He didn't remember moving, but somehow his hands were framing her face. He could feel the water turning to steam on his skin. It should have been easy, uncomplicated. She was willing, he was desirous. They were adults who understood the rules and the risks. There were no promises between them, and no demands for any.

But even as her lips parted beneath his, even as he took what she offered and ached for more, he knew there would be nothing simple about it.

"I don't think I'm ready for you," he murmured, but lowered her onto the concrete apron of the pool.

"Then don't think." Her arms went around him. She'd been waiting. There was no way she could explain to him that she'd been waiting for him, just for him, all her life. It was so easy, so natural, to want him and to give in to that wanting.

Somehow, even as a girl, she'd known there would only be one man for her. She hadn't known how or when she'd find him, or even if she would. Without him, she would have been content to live on her own, satisfying herself with the love of family and friends. Jackie had never believed in settling for second best.

But now he was here, his mouth on her mouth, his body warming hers. She didn't have to think about tomorrow or the day after that when she was holding a lifelong dream in her arms.

What she wanted was here and now. Turning into him, Jackie murmured his name and cherished the sensation of being wanted in turn.

She wasn't like other women. But why? He'd wanted before, been charmed and baffled and achy before. But not like this. He couldn't think when he was close to her. He could only feel. Tenderness, passion, frustration, desire. It was as if when he held her intellect clicked off and emotion, pure emotion, took over.

Was it that she was every man's fantasy? A generous, willing woman with needs and demands to match a man's— a woman without inhibitions or pretenses. He wished he could believe it was that. He wanted to believe it was only that. But he knew it was more. Somehow it was much more.

And he was losing himself, degree by degree, layer by layer. All his life he'd known where he was going and why.

It wasn't possible, it wasn't right, to allow this—to allow her—to change it.

He had to stop it now, while he still had a choice, or at least while he could still pretend he had one.

Slowly, and with much more difficulty than he'd imagined, he pulled away from her. The sun was hanging in the west, still bright, vivid enough to bring out the highlights in her hair. It wasn't just brown as he'd thought, it had dozens and dozens of variations of the shade. Soft, warm, rich. Like her eyes. Like her skin.

He forced himself not to lift a hand to her cheek to touch just once more.

"We'd better go in."

She'd melted inside. Completely. He could have asked anything of her in that moment and she'd have given it without a second thought. Such was the power of loving. She blinked, struggling against coming back to earth. If the choice had been hers, and hers alone, she would have stayed where she was, in his arms, forever.

But she wasn't a fool. He wasn't talking about going in to continue what they'd begun, but to end it. She closed her eyes, accepting the hurt.

"Go ahead. I think I'll get a little more sun."

"Jack."

She opened her eyes. He was surprised to see such patience in them. He shifted away, knowing that if he remained too close he'd touch her again and start the merry-go-round spinning. "I don't like to start anything until I know how it's going to finish."

She let out a long sigh because she understood. "That's too bad. You miss an awful lot that way, Nathan."

"And make less mistakes. I don't like to make mistakes."

"Is that what I am?" There was just enough amusement in her voice for him to be relieved.

"Yes. You've been a mistake right from the beginning." He turned to her again, noting that she was looking at him the way he sometimes saw her look when she was putting together a complicated dish. "You know it would be better if you didn't stay here."

She lifted a brow. It was the only change in the quietly intense look. "Are you kicking me out?"

"No." He said it too quickly and cursed himself for it. "I should, but I don't seem to be able to."

She laid a hand on his shoulder lightly. He was tense again. "You want me, Nathan. Is that so terrible?"

"I don't take everything I want."

She frowned a moment, thinking. "No, you wouldn't. You're too sensible. It's one of the things I like best about you. But you will take me eventually, Nathan. Because there's something right about us. And we both know it."

"I don't sleep with every woman who attracts me."

"I'm glad to hear it." Jackie sat up completely, tucked up her knees and wrapped her arms around them. "Indulging like that is dangerous in more ways than one." Turning her head, she studied him. "Do you think I sleep with every man who raises my blood pressure?"

Restless and not entirely comfortable, he moved his shoulders. "I don't know you or your lifestyle."

"Well, that's fair." She preferred things to be fair. "Let's get the sex out of the way, then. It dims the romance a bit, but it's sensible. I'm twenty-five, and I've fallen in and out of love countless times. I like falling in better, but I've never been able to stick. Nathan, this might be difficult for you to accept, but I'm not a virgin."

When he shook his head and dropped his chin on his chest, she patted his shoulder.

"I know, shocking, isn't it? I confess, I've been with a

man. Actually, I've been with two. The first time was on my twenty-first birthday."

"Jack—"

"I know," she interrupted with a wave of her hand. "That's a little late in this day and age, but I hate to follow trends. I was crazy about him. He could quote Yeats."

"That explains it," Nathan muttered.

"I knew you'd understand. Then a couple of years ago I was into photography. Moody black-and-whites. Very esoteric. I met this man. Black leather jacket. Very sullen good looks." There was more amusement in her eyes now than sentiment.

"He moved in with me and sat around being attractive and despondent. It only took me a couple of weeks to discover I wasn't meant to be depressed. But I got some wonderful pictures. Since then, there hasn't been anyone who's made my toes curl. Until you."

He sat still, wondering why he should be glad there had only been two important men in her life. And why he was now jealous of both of them. After a moment he looked at her again. The light had changed subtly. It warmed her skin now.

"I can't decide whether you have no guile whatsoever or if you have more than anyone I've ever met."

"Isn't it nice to have something to wonder about? I guess that's why I want to write. You can 'I wonder' yourself from beginning to end." She was silent only a moment. Jackie's debates with herself never lasted long. "Nathan, there's another thing you might want to wonder about. I'm in love with you."

She rose after she told him, feeling it would be best for both of them.

"I don't want you to worry about it," she said as he sat in stunned silence. "It's just that I hate it when people try to pretend things away. Good things, I mean. I think I'll go in after all and change before I start dinner."

She left him alone. He wondered if anyone else could drop a bombshell so casually, then wander off without checking the damage. Jackie could.

He frowned, watching the way the sun danced in diamonds on the water. There was a boat running north. He could just hear the purr of the motor. The air smelled richly of spring, flowers sun-warmed and burgeoning, grass freshly cut. The days were lengthening, and the heat remained well into evening.

That was life. It went on. It had a pattern.

She was in love with him.

That was absurd…so why wasn't he surprised? It all had to do with who she was, he decided. While he wasn't one to use words like *love* casually, she would be much freer with words, and with feelings.

He didn't even know what love meant to her. An attraction, an affection, a spark. That would be more than enough for many people. She was impetuous. Hadn't she just told him she'd fallen in and out of love countless times? This was just one more adventure for her.

Wasn't that what he wanted to believe? If it was, why did the thought leave him cold and angry?

Because he didn't want to be another adventure. Not for her. He didn't want her to be in love with him…but if she was, he wanted it to be real.

Rising, Nathan walked over to where his land gave way to the wall and the wall to the water. Once his life had moved that smoothly—like a calm channel flowing effortlessly out to sea. That was what he wanted, and that was what he had. He didn't have time to deal with impulsive women who talked about love and romance.

Sometime in the future there would be time for such

things—with the proper woman. Someone sensible and polished, Nathan thought. Then he wondered why that suddenly
sounded like a nice piece of furniture instead of a wife.

She was doing this to him, he realized, and he resented
it. She had no business telling him she was in love with
him, making him think that maybe, just maybe, what he
was feeling was—

No. He brought himself up short as he turned to scowl
back at his house. It was beyond ridiculous to imagine,
even for an instant, that he could be in love with her. He
barely knew the woman, and for the most part she was an
annoyance. If he was attracted it was simply because she
was attractive. And he'd kept himself so tied up with work
in Germany that he hadn't had time for the softer things a
man needed.

And, damn it, that was a lie. Disgusted, he turned back
to the water again. He did feel something for her. He wasn't
sure what or why, but he felt it. He wanted more than to
tumble into bed with her and satisfy an itch. He wanted to
be with her, hold her, let that low, fascinating voice drain
away his tensions.

But that wasn't love, he assured himself. It might have
been a little like caring. That was almost acceptable. A
man could come to care for a woman without sinking in
over his head.

But not a woman like Jackie.

Dragging a hand through his hair, he started back to
the house. They weren't going to talk about this, not now,
and not later. Whatever it took, he was going to get back
to normal.

He told himself it was expedient, not cowardly, to go in
through the side door and avoid her.

Chapter 6

Jackie wasn't ashamed of having told Nathan what she felt. Nor did she wish the words back. One of her firmest beliefs was that it was useless to second-guess a decision once it had been made.

In any case, taking the words back or regretting them wouldn't change the fact that they were true. She hadn't meant to fall in love with him, which made it all the sweeter and more important. At other times in her life she had seen a man, thought that he might be the one and set about falling in love.

With Nathan, love had come unexpectedly, without plan or consideration. It had simply happened, as she had always secretly hoped it would. In her heart she'd known that love couldn't be planned, so she'd begun to believe that it would never be there for her.

He was not the perfect match for her, at least not in the way she'd once imagined. Even now she couldn't be sure he had all the qualities she had sometimes listed as desirable in a man.

None of that mattered, because she loved him.

She was willing to give him time—a few days, even a week—to respond in whatever way suited him. As far as she was concerned, there were no doubts as to how things would resolve themselves. She loved him. Fate had taken a hand, in the person of cousin Fred, and tossed them together. Perhaps Nathan didn't know it yet. As she whipped eggs for a soufflé, Jackie smiled. In fact, she was sure Nathan didn't know it yet, but she was exactly what he needed.

When a man was logical, conservative and—well, yes, even just a tad stuffy—he needed the love and understanding of a woman who wasn't any of those things. And that same woman—herself, in this case—would love the man, Nathan, because he was all the things he was. She would find his traits endearing and at the same time not allow him to become so starched he cracked down the middle.

She could see exactly the way it would be for them over the years. They would grow closer with an understanding so keen that each would be able to know what the other was thinking. Agreement wouldn't always be possible, but understanding would. He would work at his drawing board and attend his meetings, while she wrote and took occasional trips to New York to lunch with her publisher.

When his work took him away, she'd go with him, supporting his career just as he would support hers. While he supervised the construction of one of his buildings, she would fill reams of notebooks with research.

Until the children came. Then, for a few years, they would both stay closer to home while they raised their family. Jackie didn't want to imagine boys or girls or hair color, because something that precious should be a surprise. But she was sure that Nathan would be a marshmallow when it came to his children.

And she would be there for him, always, to knead the tension from his shoulders, to laugh him out of his sullen moods, to watch his genius grow and expand. With her, he would smile more. With him, she would become more stable. She would be proud of him, and he of her. When she won the Pulitzer they would drink a magnum of champagne and make love through the night.

It was really very simple. Now all she had to do was wait for him to realize how simple.

Then the phone rang.

With her mixing bowl held in the crook of her elbow, Jackie picked up the receiver from the wall unit. "Hello."

After a brief hesitation came a beautifully modulated voice. "Yes, is this the Powell residence?"

"Yes, it is. May I help you?"

"I'd like to speak to Nathan, please. This is Justine Chesterfield calling."

The name rang a bell. In fact, it rang several. Justine Chesterfield, the recently divorced darling of the society pages. The name opened doors in Bridgeport, Monte Carlo and St. Moritz. All in the proper season, naturally. Jackie believed in premonitions, and she didn't care for the one she was having at the moment.

She was tempted to hang up, but she didn't think that would solve anything.

"Of course." Her mother would have been delighted with the richly rounded tones. "I'll see if he's available, Mrs. Chesterfield."

It was ridiculous to be jealous of a voice over the phone. Besides, she didn't have a jealous bone in her body. Regardless, Jackie gained enormous satisfaction from sticking her tongue out at the receiver before she went to find Nathan.

Since he was just coming down the stairs, she didn't have to look far. "You have a phone call. Justine Chesterfield."

"Oh." He had a flash of guilt that baffled him. Why should receiving a call from an old friend make him feel guilty? "Thanks. I'll take it in my office."

She didn't linger in the hall. Not on purpose, anyway. Could she help it if she had a sudden and unavoidable itch on the back of her knee? So she stood, scratching, while Nathan stepped into his office and picked up the phone.

"Justine, hello. A few days ago. A new housekeeper? No, that was…" How did he, or anyone, explain Jackie?

"Actually, I've been meaning to call you. Yes, about Fred MacNamara."

When she decided that if she scratched much longer she'd draw blood, Jackie wandered back into the kitchen. Once there, she stared at the phone. It would be easy to pick up the receiver, very slowly, very quietly—just to see if he was still on the line, of course. She began to, and very nearly did. Then, with a muttered oath, she set it back on the hook. Audibly.

She wasn't interested in anything he had to say to *that woman*. Already Justine had taken on an italicized quality in her mind. Let him explain to *her* why he had a woman living with him. Because the idea amused her, Jackie turned up the radio a little louder and began to sing along with it.

With the care of a woman who loved to cook, she continued to mix the soufflé. She wouldn't slam pots and pans around the kitchen. Jackie knew how to control herself. She didn't make a habit of it, but she knew how. It was only a phone call, after all. As far as Jackie knew, *that woman* had phoned Nathan to make a plug for her favorite charity. Or maybe she wanted to remodel her den. There were a dozen very innocent and perfectly logical reasons for Justine Chesterfield to call Nathan.

Because she wants to get her hooks into him, Jackie thought, and made herself pour the soufflé mixture into the pan without spilling a drop.

"Jackie?"

She turned, as careful with her smile as she'd been with the batter. "All done? Did you have a nice chat with Justine?"

"I wanted to let you know I'll be going out so you wouldn't worry about dinner."

"Mmm-hmm." Without missing a beat, Jackie set a cucumber on the chopping block and began to slice it. "I wonder, did Justine's second—or is it third—divorce ever come through?"

"As far as I know." He paused a moment, leaning against the doorjamb as he watched Jackie bring the knife down with deadly accuracy. Jealousy, he thought, recognizing it when it slammed into his face. He had a jealous woman on his hands, through no fault of his own. Nathan opened his mouth, then shut it again. He'd be damned if he'd explain himself. Perhaps it was absurd, but if she thought he and Justine were romantically involved it might be the best thing for everyone. "I'll see you later."

"Have a good time," she said, and brought the knife down with a satisfying *thwack*.

Jackie didn't turn, nor did she stop her steady slicing until she heard the front door shut. Blowing the hair out of her eyes, she poured the soufflé mixture down the drain. She'd eat a hot dog.

It helped to get back to work, to hear the comforting hum of her typewriter. What helped even more was the development of a new character. Justine—make that Carlotta—was the frowsy, scheming, overendowed madam of the local brothel. Her heart was brass, like her hair. She was a woman who used men like poker chips.

Jake, being only a man, was taken in by her. But Sarah, with the clear eyes of a woman, saw Justine—Carlotta— for exactly what she was.

Afraid of his growing feelings for Sarah, Jake turned to Carlotta. The cad. Eventually Carlotta would betray him, and her betrayal would nearly cost Sarah her life, but for now Sarah had to deal with the fact that the man she'd come to love would turn to another woman to release his passion.

Jackie would have preferred to make Carlotta frumpy and faded. She'd even toyed with a wart. Just a small one.

But a hard-faced woman wouldn't do justice to Jake or her book. Dutifully tearing up the first page, Jackie got down to business.

Carlotta was stunning. In a cold, calculated sort of way. Jackie had seen Justine's picture often enough to describe her. Pale and willowy, with eyes the clear blue of a mountain lake and a thin, almost childish mouth. A slender neck and wheat-blond hair. There were ice-edged cheekbones and balletic limbs. Taking literary license, Jackie allowed herself to toughen the looks, add a few dissipated lines and a drinking problem.

As she wrote, she began to see the character more clearly, even began to understand Carlotta's drive to use and discard men, to make a living off their baser drives and weaknesses. She discovered that Carlotta had had a miserable childhood and an abusive first marriage. Unfortunately, this softened her mood toward Justine even as she had Carlotta plotting dreadful problems for Jake and Sarah.

When Jackie ran out of steam, it was still shy of midnight. Telling herself it had nothing to do with waiting up for Nathan, she dawdled, applying a facial she remembered once or twice a month at best, filing her nails and leafing through magazines.

At one she deliberately turned the bedside light off, then lay staring at the ceiling.

Maybe everyone was right after all. Maybe she *was* crazy. A woman who fell in love with a man who had virtually no interest in her had to be asking for trouble. And heartache. This was her first experience with real heartache, and she couldn't say she cared for it.

But she did love him, with all the energy and devotion she was capable of. It wasn't anything like the way it had been with the Yeats buff or the leather jacket. They had brought on a sense of excitement—the way a runner might feel, she thought, when she was about to race the fifty-yard dash full-out. It was different, very different, from preparing for a marathon. The excitement was still there, but with it was a steady determination that came from the knowledge of being ready to start and finish, of being prepared for the long haul.

Like her writing, Jackie thought, and sat up in bed. The parallel was so clear. With all her other projects there had been that quick, almost frantic flash of energy and power. It had been as if she'd known going in that there would be a short, perhaps memorable thrill, then disenchantment.

With the writing, there had been the certainty that this was it for her. It hadn't been her last chance so much as her only one. What she was beginning now was the one thing she'd been looking for through all the years of experimenting.

Falling for Nathan was precisely the same. Other men she'd cared for had been like stepping-stones or springboards that had boosted her up for that one and only man she would want for the rest of her life.

If someone had gotten in the way of her and her writing, would she have tolerated it? Not for a minute. Mentally pushing up her sleeves, she settled back. No one was going to step in the way of her and her man, either. Justine Chesterfield was going to have a fight on her hands.

He'd been home for nearly an hour, but Nathan sat in his parked car and let the smoke from his cigarette trail out the window. It was an odd thing for a man to be wary about going into his own house, but there it was. She was in there. In the bedroom. Her bedroom now. It would never be just a guest room again.

He'd seen her light burning, and he'd seen her light shut

off. She might be sleeping. He wasn't sure he'd ever get a decent night's sleep again.

My God, he wanted to go in, walk up the stairs into her room and lose himself in the promise of her. Or the threat.

There was nothing in his feelings for her that made sense, nothing he could put his finger on and analyze. Over and over again his mind played back the way she'd looked at him as they'd sat by the pool, the way her skin had felt with water drying on it, the way her voice had sounded.

I'm in love with you.

Could it be, could it possibly be that easy for her? Yes, he thought it was. Now that he was beginning to know and understand her, he was sure that falling in love and declaring that love would be as natural for Jackie as breathing. But this time she was in love with him.

He could take advantage of it. She wouldn't even blame him for it. He could, without conscience or guilt, do exactly what he was dreaming of doing—walk into her room and finish what had been started that evening.

But he couldn't. He'd never be able to forget the way her eyes had looked. Trusting, honest and incredibly vulnerable. She thought she was tough, resilient. And he believed that she was, to a point. If she really loved him and he hurt her by casually taking what love urged her to give, she wouldn't bounce back.

So how did he handle her?

He'd thought he'd known earlier that evening. Going to see Justine had been a calculated move to distance himself from Jackie and to show both her and himself how ridiculously implausible any relationship between them would be.

Then he'd found himself in Justine's elegant condo with its gold-and-white rooms and its tasteful French antiques and he'd been unable to think of anything but Jackie. There'd been an excellent poached salmon, prepared to a turn by

Justine's housekeeper. Nathan had found himself with a yen for the spicy chicken Jackie had prepared that first night.

He'd smiled as Justine, dressed in sleek white lounging pajamas, her wheat-colored hair twisted back in a sleek knot, had served him brandy. And he'd thought of the way Jackie looked in shorts.

With Justine he'd discussed mutual friends and compared viewpoints on Frankfurt and Paris. Her voice was low and soothing, her observations were concise and mildly amusing. He'd remembered the fits and starts and wild paths Jackie's conversations could take.

Justine was an old friend, a valued one. She was a woman he had always been completely at ease with. He knew her family, and she knew his. Their opinions might not always agree precisely, but they were invariably compatible. Over the ten years they'd known each other, they'd never become lovers. Justine's marriages and Nathan's travels had prevented that, though there had always been a light and companionable attraction between them.

That could change now, and they were both aware of it. She was single, and he was home. There would very likely never be a woman he knew better, a woman better suited to his tastes, than Justine Chesterfield.

He'd wanted, as he'd sat comfortably, to be back in his kitchen watching Jackie concoct a meal, even if the damn radio was playing.

He thought it entirely possible that he was losing his mind.

The evening had ended with a chaste, almost brotherly kiss. He hadn't wanted to make love with Justine, though God knew he was stirred up enough to need a woman. It infuriated him to realize that if he'd slept with Justine he would have thought of Jackie and felt like an adulterer.

There was no doubt about it. He was going crazy.

Giving up on trying to reason, even with himself, Nathan got out of the car. As he let himself in to the house he thought a long soak in the whirlpool might tire him out enough to let him sleep.

Jackie heard the movement downstairs and sat up in bed again. Nathan? She hadn't heard a car drive up and stop. She'd been listening for his return for over a half hour, and even in a half doze she would have heard. Crawling down to the foot of the bed, she strained to hear.

Silence.

If it was Nathan, why wasn't he coming upstairs? Annoyed because her heart was beginning to race, she crept to the door and peeked out.

If it was Nathan, why was he walking around in the dark?

Because it wasn't Nathan, she decided. It was a burglar who'd probably been watching the house for weeks, learning the routine and waiting for his chance. He'd know that she was alone in the house and asleep, so he'd broken in to rob Nathan blind.

With a hand to her heart, she glanced back toward her bed. She could call the police, then crawl under the covers. It sounded like a wonderful idea. Even as she took the first tiptoeing step back, she stopped.

But what if she hadn't really heard anything other than the house settling? If Nathan wasn't already fed up, he certainly would be if he got home from *that woman*'s and found the house full of police because she'd jumped the gun.

Taking a deep breath, Jackie decided to creep down and make sure there was a good reason to panic.

She descended the stairs slowly, keeping her back to the wall. Still no sound. The house was absolutely dark and absolutely silent. A burglar had to make some noise when he stole the family silver.

Probably just your imagination, she told herself as she reached the lower landing. In the dark she strained her ears but still heard nothing. As her heartbeat slowed to normal she decided to take one quick check around the house, knowing her imagination would play havoc if she went back to bed without satisfying her curiosity.

She began to whistle, just under her breath, as she moved from room to room. There was no one there, of course, but if there was, Jackie preferred to have them know she was on her way. Jackie's imagination, according to her mother, had always been bizarre.

By the time she'd wound through the living room, passed by Nathan's office and the powder room and gone into the dining area, she'd imagined not just your everyday intruder but a gang of psychotic thugs who'd recently escaped from a maximum-security prison in Kentucky. Determined to beat her own wayward fantasies, she stepped into the kitchen. Every light in the house blazed behind her. Now, as she reached for the switch in the kitchen, she heard a shuffle of footsteps.

Her fingers froze, but her mind didn't. They were in the sunroom—at least six of them by now. One of them had a scar running from his temple to his jawline and had been serving time for bludgeoning senior citizens in their sleep. She took a step back, thinking of the phone in her room behind a locked door when the footsteps came closer.

Too late, her mind flashed. Going with impulse and desperation, she grabbed the closest weapon—the soufflé pan. Swinging it above her head, she prepared to defend herself.

When Nathan stepped into the room, dressed only in his briefs, it was a toss-up as to who was the more surprised. He jerked back, finding himself ridiculously embarrassed as Jackie let out a scream and dropped the pan. It landed with a resounding clatter just before she doubled over with hysterical giggles.

"What the hell are you doing, sneaking around the

house?" If it wouldn't have made him feel that much more foolish, Nathan would have grabbed a dishcloth for cover.

Jackie slammed both hands over her mouth as she gasped and choked. "I thought you were six men with homicidal intentions. One of you had a scar, and the little one had a face like a weasel."

"So naturally you came down to beat us all off with a soufflé pan."

"Not exactly." Still giggling, she propped herself against the counter. "I'm sorry, I always laugh when I'm terrified."

"Who doesn't?"

"It was just that I thought there was a burglar, then I convinced myself there wasn't, and then..." She began to hiccup. "Then I thought you were this gang from Kentucky led by a man named Bubba. I need some water." Grabbing a glass, Jackie filled it to the rim while Nathan tried to follow.

"You've obviously picked the right field at last, Jack. With an imagination like that, you'll make a million."

"Thanks." Picking up the glass, she drank while running her finger in circles over the bottom.

"What the hell are you doing now?"

"Getting rid of the hiccups. Surefire." She set the glass down and waited. "See? All clear. Now it's your turn. What were you doing sneaking around the house in the dark in your underwear?"

"It's my house."

"Right you are. And it's very nice underwear, too. Sorry I scared you."

"You didn't scare me." Finding his temper once more on a short fuse, he bent down and scooped up the pan. "I was about to take a spa and decided I wanted a drink."

"Oh. Well, that explains that." Jackie pressed her lips together. It wouldn't do to start giggling again. "Did you have a nice time?"

"What? Yes, fine." This was a hell of a time, Nathan decided, to notice that she was wearing nothing but an oversize T-shirt with a faded picture of Mozart on the front. With care and effort, he kept his eyes on her face, but it didn't help very much. "I don't want to keep you up."

"Oh, that's okay. I'll fix you a drink."

"I can do it." He had his hand on her wrist before she could open the cupboard.

"No need to be cranky. I said I was sorry."

"I'm not cranky. Go to bed, Jack."

"I'm bothering you, aren't I?" she murmured as she turned to face him. With her free hand, she reached up to touch his cheek. "That's nice."

"Yes, you're bothering me, and it's not particularly nice." Her face was scrubbed free of cosmetics, but her scent still lingered. "Now go to bed."

"Want to come with me?"

His eyes narrowed at the smile in hers. "You're going to push too far."

"It was only a suggestion." She felt a wave of tenderness as she thought of how he would view his position and what was happening between them. An honorable man who thought his intentions were dishonorable. "Nathan, is it so hard for you to understand that I love you and want to make love with you?"

He didn't want it to make sense, couldn't allow it to make sense. "What's hard for me to understand and impossible for me to believe is that anyone could consider themselves in love after a matter of days. Things don't work that easily, Jack."

"Sometimes they do. Look at Romeo and Juliet. No, that's a bad example when you think of how things worked out." Fascinated by his mouth, warmed by the memory of how it felt on hers, she traced it with her fingertip. "Sorry,

I guess I can't think of a good example right now because I'm thinking about you."

His stomach wound itself into a tight knot. "If you're trying to make this difficult, you're succeeding."

"Impossible was the idea, but I'll settle for difficult." She shifted closer. Their thighs brushed. Her eyelids lowered. "Kiss me, Nathan. Even my imagination falls short of what it's like when you do."

He swore at her, or tried to, but his mouth was already against hers. Each time it was a little sweeter, a little sharper, a little more difficult to forget. He was losing, and he knew it. Once he gave in to his own needs, he wasn't sure he'd be able to pull back. Nor did he know precisely what he would find himself trapped in.

She was a drug to a man who had always been obsessively clear-minded, a slide down a cliff to one who had always been firmly surefooted.

And she was naked beneath that loose shirt. Soft and naked and already warm for him. He found himself reaching, testing, taking, even as warning bells rang inside his head. DANGER. PROCEED AT YOUR OWN RISK.

His own risk. He'd always carefully calculated the risk, the odds, the degrees and angles, before he took the first step. Her body seemed to have been molded for his hands, for his pleasure, for his needs. There was no way to calculate this, or her, or what happened every time they touched each other.

It was so easy, so mindlessly easy, to take the next step. Blindly, recklessly. She was murmuring his name as her hands glided up his back, then down to his hips. He could feel every curve and angle of her body as his hands moved over and under the thin cotton. How could it be so familiar yet so fresh, so comforting yet so unnerving?

He wanted to scoop her up, to wallow in her, to lose himself. It would have been so easy. Her body was poised against his, ready, waiting, eager. And the heat, the heat he'd begun to recognize and expect, was weighing down on his brain. There was nothing and no one he'd ever wanted more.

Somewhere in the back of his mind he heard a door slam and a key turn in a lock. In a last attempt at self-defense, he pulled her away.

"Hold it."

Sighing, half dreaming, she opened her eyes. "Hmm?"

If she kept looking at him like that he was going to fall apart. Or rip that excuse for nightgear off her back. "Look, I don't know why this is happening, but it has to stop. I'm not hypocrite enough to say I don't want you, but I'm not crazy enough to start something that's going to make us both miserable."

"Why should making love make either of us miserable?"

"Because it could never go beyond that." Because she swayed toward him, he put his hands on her shoulders. Damn it, she was trembling. Or he was. "I don't have room for you, for anyone, in my life, Jack. I don't want to make room. I don't think you understand that."

"No, I don't." She leaned forward to brush her lips over his chin. "If I believed it, I'd think it was very sad."

"Believe it." But he was no longer certain he did. "My work comes first. It takes all my time, my energy and my concentration. That's the way I want it. A blistering affair with you has its appeal, but…for some reason I care about you, and I don't think that's all you want or need."

"It doesn't have to be all."

"But it does, and that's something for you to think about." He had to stay calm now, calm enough to make her listen. "In six weeks I go to Denver. When I've finished there, it's Sydney. After that I don't know where I'll be or for how long. I travel light, and that doesn't include a lover, or the worry about someone waiting for me back home."

She shook her head as she took a small step back. "I wonder what happened to make you so unwilling to share yourself, so determined to keep to some straight-and-narrow path. No curves, no detours, Nathan?" She tilted her head to study him. There was no anger in her eyes, just a sympathy he didn't want. "It's more than sad, it's sinful, really, to turn away someone who loves you because you don't want to spoil your routine."

He opened his mouth so that the words nearly tumbled out. Reasons, explanations, an anger he barely remembered or thought he'd forgotten. Years of control snapped into place.

"Maybe it is, but that's the way I live. The way I've chosen to live." He'd hurt her again, badly this time. The shiver of pain sliced back at him, and he knew he was hurting himself, as well. "I can tell you that if you were another woman it would be a lot easier to turn away. I don't want to feel what I'm feeling for you. Do you understand?"

"Yes. I wish I didn't." She looked down at the floor. When her eyes lifted again, the hurt was still there, but it had been joined by a flash of something stronger. "What you don't understand is that I don't give up. Blame it on the Irish. A stubborn breed. I want you, Nathan, and no matter how far you run or how fast, I'll catch up. When I do, all your neat little plans are going to tumble like a stack of dominoes." Taking his face in her hands, she kissed him hard. "And you'll thank me for it, because no one's ever going to love you the way I do."

She kissed him again, more gently this time, then turned away. "I made some fresh lemonade, if you still want a drink. Night."

He watched her go with the sinking feeling that he could already hear the clatter of dominoes.

Chapter 7

She should have hated him. Sarah wanted to, wished the strong, destructive emotions would come, filling all the cracks in her feelings, blocking out everything else. With hate, a coolheaded, sharply honed hate, she would have felt in control again. She needed badly to feel in control again. But she didn't hate him. Couldn't.

Even knowing Jake had spent the night with another woman, kissing another woman's lips, touching another woman's skin, she couldn't hate him. But she could grieve for the loss, for the death of a beauty that had never had the chance to bloom fully.

She had come to understand what they might have had together. She had nearly come to accept that they belonged together, whatever their differences, whatever the risks. He would always live by his gun and by his own set of rules, but with her, briefly, perhaps reluctantly, he had shown such kindness, such tenderness.

There was a place for her in his heart. Sarah knew it. Beneath the rough-hewn exterior was a man who believed in justice, who was capable of small, endearing kindnesses. He'd allowed her to see that part of him, a part she knew he'd shared with few others.

Then why, the moment she had begun to soften toward him, to accept him for what and who he was, had he turned to another woman, a woman of easy virtue?

* * *

A woman of easy virtue? Jackie said to herself, and rolled her eyes. If that was the best she could come up with, she'd better hang it up right now.

It hadn't been one of her better days. Nathan had been up and gone before she'd started breakfast. He'd left her a note—she couldn't even say a scribbled note, because his handwriting was as disciplined as the rest of him—telling her he'd be out most of the day.

She'd munched on a candy bar and the last of the ginger ale as she'd mulled over the current situation. As far as she could see, it stank.

She was in love with a man who was determined to hold her, and his own feelings, at arm's length. A man who insisted on rationalizing those feelings away—not because he was committed to another woman, not because he was suffering from a fatal disease, not because he was hiding a criminal past, but because they were inconvenient.

He was too honorable to take advantage of the situation, and too stubborn to admit that he and she belonged together.

No room in his life for her? Jackie thought as she pushed away from the typewriter and began to pace. Did he really believe she would take a ridiculous statement like that and back off? Of course she wouldn't, but what bothered her more was that he would make a statement like that in the first place.

What made him so determined not to accept love when it was given, so determined not to acknowledge his own emotions? Her own family could sometimes be annoyingly proper, but there had always been a wealth of love generously given. She'd grown up unafraid of feelings. If you didn't feel, you weren't alive, so what was the purpose? She knew Nathan felt, and felt deeply, but whenever his emotions took control he stepped back and put up those walls.

He did love her, Jackie thought as she flopped down on the bed. She couldn't be mistaken about that. But he was going to fight her every inch of the way. So she'd handle it. It wasn't that she objected to a good fight, it was just that this one hurt. Every time he drew back, every time he denied what they had together, it hurt a little more.

She'd been honest with him, and that hadn't worked. She'd been deliberately provocative, and that hadn't done so well, either. She'd been annoying, and she'd been cooperative. She wasn't sure what step to take next.

Rolling onto her stomach, she debated the idea of taking a nap. It was midafternoon, she'd worked nonstop since breakfast, and she couldn't drum up any enthusiasm for the pool. Perhaps if she went to sleep with Nathan on her mind she would wake up with a solution. Deciding to trust the Fates—after all, they'd gotten her this far—she closed her eyes. She'd nearly dozed off when the doorbell rang.

Someone selling encyclopedias, she thought groggily, with the idea of ignoring them. Or it was three men in white suits passing out pamphlets for a tent revival—which actually might be fairly interesting. With a yawn, she snuggled into the pillow. She'd nearly shut off her mind when a last thought intruded. It was a telegram from home, and someone had been in a horrible accident.

Springing up, she sprinted downstairs.

"Yes, I'm coming!" As she pushed the hair out of her eyes, she yanked the door open.

It wasn't a telegram or a door-to-door salesman. It was Justine Chesterfield. Jackie decided it really wasn't one of her better days. She leaned on the door and offered a chilly smile.

"Hello."

"Hello. I wonder if Nathan might be around."

"Sorry, he's out." Her fingers on the knob itched to close

the door quietly and completely. That would be rude. Jackie could almost hear her mother upbraiding her. She took a long breath before moderating her tone. "He didn't say where he was going or when he'd be back, but you're welcome to wait if you'd like."

"Thanks." They exchanged appraising glances before Justine stepped over the threshold.

The woman's dressed as if she's just stepped off a yacht, Jackie thought nastily. In Hyannis Port. At the beginning of the season. Justine's tall, softly curved body was set off nicely by white slacks and a boat-necked silk T-shirt in crimson. She'd added a quietly elegant necklace of twisted gold links and discreetly stylish matching earrings. Her hair had been left down to wave gently on her shoulders, scooped back at the temples by two mother-of-pearl combs.

She was perfect. Perfectly lovely, perfectly groomed, perfectly mannerly. Jackie was glad she could hate her.

"I hope I'm not disturbing you…" Justine began.

"Not at all." Jackie gestured toward the living room. "Make yourself at home."

"Thanks." Justine wandered in, then set her envelope bag on a small table. The bag matched her open-toed white snakeskin pumps. "You must be Jacqueline, Fred's cousin."

"I must be."

"I'm Justine Chesterfield. An old friend of Nathan's."

"I recognized your voice." Ingrained manners had Jackie offering a hand. As their fingers touched briefly, a smile hovered around Justine's mouth. Unfortunately for Jackie, the smile was friendly and entirely too appealing.

"And I yours. According to Nathan, Fred's as devious as he is charming."

"More so, believe me." So this was the kind of woman Nathan preferred. Quietly polished, quietly stylish, quietly stunning. Trying not to sigh, Jackie played hostess. "Can I get you something? A cold drink, some coffee?"

"I'd love something cold, if you wouldn't mind."

"All right, have a seat. I'll just be a minute."

Jackie muttered to herself the entire time she fixed lemonade and arranged shortbread cookies on Nathan's Depression glass platter. It rarely occurred to her to think how she looked when she planned on staying in. But she would have picked today to wear her most comfortable and most ragged pair of cutoffs, with a baggy athletic-style T-shirt in garish green-and-yellow stripes. There was a small fortune in gold and gems on her fingers, and her feet were bare. The Sizzling Cerise on her toes had begun to chip.

The hell with that, she thought, and made one vague and futile attempt to finger-comb her hair. She'd let Ms. Sleek-and-Stylish have her say.

She was sure that Sarah would have been just as gracious to Carlotta, but she had a feeling that Sarah was a much nicer person than Jacqueline R. MacNamara. Determined to give Nathan nothing to snarl about, she lifted the tray and started back to her guest. Nathan's guest.

The sunlight and the strong masculine colors of the room were certainly flattering to Justine. It didn't help to admit it, but Jackie was nothing if not honest.

"This is awfully nice of you," Justine began as she took a seat. "Actually, I was hoping we'd have a chance to talk. Are you very busy? Nathan told me you were working on a book."

"He did?" It was surprise more than a desire to chat that had Jackie sitting. She hadn't thought Nathan even remembered she was writing, much less that he would tell someone else about it. And Justine was the second person, after Mrs. Grange, who hadn't smirked when she'd spoken of her writing.

"Yes, he said you were writing a novel and that you were very dedicated and disciplined about your work. Nathan's a big believer in discipline."

"So I've noticed." Jackie discovered she didn't mind sipping a glass of lemonade after all. Justine had just handed her the perfect route to make her excuses and disappear back upstairs. After a second sip, Jackie decided to detour around it. "As it turns out, I was just taking a break when you rang the bell."

"That's lucky." Justine chose a cookie and nibbled. Her scent was very sophisticated, not opulent but rich and feminine. Jackie noticed that her nails were long, rounded and painted a pale rose. She wore only one ring, a stunning opal surrounded by diamonds. "I suppose I should apologize first."

Jackie left off her study long enough to lift a brow. "Apologize?"

"For the mix-up here between you and Nathan." Justine noticed with a little stab of envy that Jackie's skin was free of cosmetics and as clear as springwater. "It was I who talked Nathan into letting Fred move in while he was away in Europe. It seemed like such a perfect solution at the time, as Nathan was concerned about leaving his house empty for that length of time and Fred seemed to be at loose ends."

"Fred's always at loose ends," Jackie said over the rim of her glass. She looked at Justine with a trace of sympathy. Fred's charm might not have swayed Mrs. Grange, but the housekeeper was the exception to the rule. "He also has a way of making you believe he can spin straw into gold. As long as you're paying for the straw."

"So I understand." Appreciation for the analogy showed in Justine's eyes. "I feel, well…a little guilty that Fred absconded with your money under false pretenses."

"No need." Jackie took a healthy bite out of a cookie.

"I've known Fred all my life. If anyone should have seen through him, I should have. In any case," she added with what she thought was a wonderfully cool smile, "Nathan and I have come to a satisfactory arrangement."

"So he said." Justine took another sip of lemonade, watching Jackie over the rim. "Apparently you're a first-class cook."

"Yes." She didn't believe in denying the truth, but she wondered what else Nathan had felt obligated to tell Justine. If they were going to fight, she thought restlessly, why didn't they just get on with it?

"I've never been able to put two ingredients together and have either one come out recognizable. Did you really study in Paris?"

"Which time?" Despite herself, Jackie smiled. She hadn't wanted to like Justine. True, the woman was very cool and very polished, but there was something kind in her eyes. Kindness, no matter what the package, always drew her in.

Justine smiled in return, and the restraint between them lowered by another few degrees. "Miss MacNamara— Jacqueline—may I be frank?"

"Things usually get done faster that way."

"You're not at all what I expected."

Jackie sat back, tucking up her legs beneath her. "What did you expect?"

"I always thought when Nathan became besotted about someone she'd be very sleek and self-contained. Possibly boring."

The lemonade that was halfway down Jackie's throat had to be swallowed in a hard gulp. "Back up. Did you say Nathan was besotted?"

"A wreck. Didn't you know?"

"He hides it well," Jackie murmured.

"Well, it was perfectly obvious to me last night." The heat in Jackie's eyes came instantly and automatically. "We've never been anything but friends, by the way." Justine gave a small shrug. "If I were in your position, I'd appreciate someone making that clear to me."

The heat simmered a moment longer, then snuffed itself out. She didn't often feel like a fool, but she was willing to accept it when she did. "I do appreciate it—your telling me, and the fact that you've never been anything but friends. Would you mind if I asked you why?"

"I've wondered myself." With the ease of a woman who never gained an ounce, Justine took another cookie. "The timing's never been quite right. I'm not independent." This was said with another shrug. "I enjoy being married, being part of a couple, so I end up doing it quite a bit. I was married when I met Nathan. Then, after my first divorce, we were in different parts of the country. It's continued to work out about the same way for close to a decade. In any case, it's enough to say that I was always involved with someone else and Nathan was always involved with his work. For his own reasons, he prefers things that way."

Jackie wanted to ask why, suspected that Justine might have some of the answers. But she couldn't go that far. If what she had with Nathan was going to work, the explanations would have to come from him. "I appreciate you telling me. I suppose I should tell you that you're not what I expected, either."

"And what did you expect?"

"A calculating adventuress with icicles on her heart and designs on my man. I spent most of last night detesting you." When Justine's lips curved at the description, Jackie was very glad she'd refrained from giving Carlotta that wart.

"Then I wasn't wrong in thinking you care about Nathan?"

"I'm in love with him."

Justine smiled again. There was a trace of wistfulness in it that told Jackie more than words could have. "He needs someone. He doesn't think so, but he does."

"I know. And it's going to be me."

"Then I'll wish you luck. I didn't intend to when I came."

"What changed your mind?"

"You invited me in and offered me a drink when you wished me to hell."

Jackie grinned. "And I thought I was so discreet."

"No, you weren't. Jack...that's what Nathan calls you, isn't it?"

"Most of the time."

"Jack, my track record with relationships isn't what you would call impressive—in fact, let's continue to be frank and admit it's lousy—but I'd like to offer you a little advice."

"I'll take anything I can get."

"Some men need more of a push than others. Use both hands with Nathan."

"I intend to." With her head tilted to one side, Jackie considered. "You know, Justine, I have this cousin. Second cousin on my father's side. Not Fred," she said quickly. "This one's a college professor at the University of Michigan. Do you like the intellectual type?"

With a laugh, Justine set down her glass. "Ask me again in six months. I'm on sabbatical."

When Nathan arrived home a few hours later, he knew nothing of Justine's visit or of the conclusions that had been reached in his living room. Perhaps that was for the best.

It was bad enough that he was glad to be home. It was a different sort of glad from the feeling he'd had when he'd arrived from Germany. Then he'd been looking forward to the familiar, to solitude, to the routine he had set for himself over the years. He didn't—wouldn't have—considered it stuffy, just convenient.

Now a part of him, a part he still wasn't ready to acknowledge, was glad to come home to Jackie. There was an anticipation, a surge of excitement at knowing she was there to talk with, to relax with, even to spar with. The unfamiliar, and the companionship, added a new dimension to an evening at home. The challenge of outmaneuvering her had become a habit he hadn't been aware of forming. Somewhere along the line he'd stopped resenting the fact that she'd invaded his privacy.

He heard the music the moment he opened the door. It wasn't the rock he'd grown accustomed to hearing from the kitchen but one of Strauss's lovely and sensual waltzes. Though he wasn't sure if her change in radio stations was something to worry about, he was cautious as he slipped into his office to put away his briefcase and the reinforced tubes that held the blueprints from his project in Denver.

Loosening his tie, he started into the kitchen. As usual, something smelled wonderful.

She wasn't wearing her habitual shorts. Instead, she wore a jumpsuit in some soft, silky material the color of melted butter. It didn't cling to her body so much as shift around it, offering hints. Her feet were bare, and she wore one long wooden earring. She was busy slicing a round loaf of crusty bread. He had a sudden feeling, strong and lucid, that he should turn and run, as fast and as far as he could. Because it annoyed him, Nathan stepped through the archway.

"Hello, Jack."

She'd known he was there, but she managed to look mildly and credibly surprised when she turned. "Hi." He looked so attractive in a suit, with the knot of his tie pulled loose. Because her heart turned to mush, she walked over and kissed his cheek. "How was your day?"

He didn't know what to make of her. So what else was new? But he did know that her casual greeting kiss was exactly what he'd needed, and it worried him. "Busy," he told her.

"Well, you'll have to tell me all about it, but you should have some wine first." She was already pouring two glasses. The sun hit the liquid as it rushed into the crystal and shot it through with gold. "I hope you're hungry. It'll be ready in just a couple minutes."

He accepted the wine and didn't ask why her timing always seemed so perfect. It made him wonder if she'd managed to slip a homing device on him. "Did you get much done today?"

"Quite a bit." Jackie began to arrange the bread she'd sliced in a basket. "I had a little lull this afternoon, but things really picked up afterward." Her lips curved as she lifted her wine, and once again he had the feeling that there was something he should know, but he didn't want to ask. "I've decided to concentrate on the first hundred pages for the next week or so, until it's ready to send off to an agent I know in New York."

"That's good," he managed, wondering why the idea sent him into a panic. He wanted her to progress, didn't he? The more she did, the less guilty he'd feel about telling her that her time was up. No amount of logic could erase the niggling fear that she would tell him she no longer needed the house to work in and was moving on. "It must be going well."

"Better than I expected, and I always expect quite a lot." The timer buzzed, and she turned to the oven. Fortunately, the move hid her smile. "I thought we'd eat on the patio. It's such a nice evening."

The warning bells sounded again, but they were dimmer and less urgent. "It's going to rain."

"Not for a couple of hours yet." With her hands buried in oven mitts, she drew out a casserole. "I hope you like this. It's called *schinkenfleckerln*." Jackie whipped out the foreign name like a native.

There was something very homey and nonthreatening about the pot of browned noodles and ham in bubbling sauce. "It looks terrific."

"A very simple Austrian recipe," she told him. That explained the Viennese waltz, he thought. "Grab the bread, will you? I've already set up outside."

Again, she timed it perfectly. The sun was dropping in the sky. The clouds that were gathering to bring rain during the night were tipped with pink and orange. The air was cool, with a catchy breeze from the east that brought just a hint of the sea.

The round patio table was set for two. Informally. Nathan would have to have stretched a point to call it deliberately romantic. Colorful mats she must have bought herself were under his white everyday dishes. She'd added flowers, but they were only a few sprigs of daisies in a colored bottle. The bottle wasn't his, either, so he could only suppose that she'd been foraging in some of the local shops.

He settled back as Jackie began the business of serving. "I haven't thanked you for all the meals."

She only smiled as she sat across from him. "That was the deal."

"I know, but you've gone to more trouble than you had to. I appreciate it."

"That's nice. I really like to cook when there's someone to share it with. Nothing more depressing than cooking for one."

He hadn't thought so. Once. "Jack…" She looked up at

him, her eyes big and round and soft, and he lost track of what he'd planned to say. Groping, he picked up his wine. "I, ah… I feel like we got off on the wrong foot. Since we're both victims, so to speak, I'd like to call a truce."

"I thought we had."

"An official one."

"All right." She lifted her glass and tapped it against his. "Live long and prosper."

"I beg your pardon?"

Jackie chuckled into her wine. "I should have known you wouldn't be a fan of *Star Trek*. That's the Vulcan greeting, Nathan, but to keep it simple, I'll just wish you the best."

"Thanks." Unconsciously he loosened his tie a little more. "Why don't you tell me about your book?"

It was a first, Nathan decided, to see Jackie speechless. Her lips parted, not to smile or to toss a quip, but in utter surprise. "Really?" she managed after a moment.

"Yes, I'd like to hear what it's about." He picked up a hunk of bread and began to butter it. "Don't you want to talk about it?"

"Well, yes, it's just that I didn't think you were interested. You never asked, or even commented, and I know that I usually beat people over the head with whatever I'm doing at the time because I get too involved and lose perspective. So I thought it would be better if I just kept the book to myself since I was already driving you crazy. I figured under the circumstances, counting Fred and six months in Frankfurt, you'd probably hate it anyway."

Nathan scooped up some of the casserole, chewed and considered. "I understand that," he said. "I can't tell you how much that terrifies me, but I understand. Now, why don't you tell me about your book?"

"Okay." She moistened her lips. "I've set it in what is now Arizona, in the 1870s—a decade or so after the Mex-

ican War, when it was ceded to the U.S. as part of New
Mexico. I'd toyed around with doing a generational thing
and starting in the eighteenth century, when it was still a
European settlement, but I found that I wanted to get into
the meat right away."

"No meat in the eighteenth century?"

"Oh, pounds of it." She took a piece of bread herself and
shredded it before she realized she was nervous. "But Jake
and Sarah weren't alive then. My protagonists," Jackie explained. "It's really their story, and I was too impatient to
start the book a hundred years before they came along. He's
a gunfighter and she's convent-bred. I liked the idea of putting them in Arizona because it really epitomizes America's
Old West. The Earps, the Claytons, Tombstone, Tucson,
Apaches." Nerves disappeared as she began to imagine.
"It gives it that nice bloody frontier tradition."

"Shoot-outs, bounty hunters and Indian raids?"

"That's the idea. The setup has Sarah coming West after
her father dies. He, Sarah's father, had led her to believe
that he's a prosperous miner. She's grown up in the East,
learning all the things that well-bred young ladies of good
families are supposed to learn. Then, after his sudden death,
she comes out to the Arizona Territory and discovers that
for all the years she was living in moderate luxury back
East, her father had barely been scraping by on this dilapi-
dated gold mine, spending every penny he could spare on
her education."

"Now she's penniless, orphaned and out of her element."

"Exactly." Pleased with him, Jackie poured more wine.
"I figure that makes her instantly vulnerable and sympathetic, as well as plunging her into immediate jeopardy.
Anyway, it doesn't take her long to discover that her father
didn't die in an accidental cave-in, but was murdered. By
this time, she's already had a few run-ins with Jake Red-

man, the hard-bitten gun-for-hire renegade who stands for everything she's been taught to detest. He saved her life during an Apache raid."

"So he's not all bad."

"A diamond in the rough," Jackie explained over a bite of bread. "See, there were a lot of miners and adventurers in the territory during this period, but the War between the States and troop withdrawal were delaying settlement, so the Apaches were still dominant. That made it a very wild and dangerous place for a gently bred young woman to be."

"But she stays."

"If she'd turned to run, she'd have been pitiful rather than sympathetic. Big difference. She's compelled to discover who killed her father and why. Then there's the fact that she's desperately, though unwillingly, attracted to Jake Redman."

"And he to her?"

"You've got it." She smiled at him as she toyed with her wine. "You see, Jake, like a lot of men—and women, for that matter—doesn't believe he needs anyone, certainly not someone who would interfere with his lifestyle and convince him to settle down. He's a loner, has always been a loner, and intends to keep it that way."

His brow lifted as he sipped. "Very clever," he said mildly.

Pleased that he saw the correlation, she smiled. "Yes, I thought so. But Sarah's quite determined. Once she discovers that she loves him, that her life would never be complete without him, she wears him down. Of course, Carlotta does her best to botch things up."

"Carlotta?"

"The town's leading woman of ill repute. It's not so much that she wants Jake, though of course she does. They all do. But she hates Sarah and everything Sarah stands for. Then there's the fact that she knows Sarah's father had been mur-

Loving Jack

dered because, after five years, he'd finally hit the mother lode. The mine Sarah now holds the claim for is worth a fortune. That's as far as I've gotten."

"But how does it end?"

"I don't know."

"What do you mean, you don't know? You're writing it, you have to know."

"No, I don't. In fact, I'm almost certain if I knew, exactly, it wouldn't be half as much fun to sit down every day." She offered him more of the casserole, but he shook his head. "It's a story for me, too, and I am getting closer, but it's not like a blueprint, Nathan."

Because she could see he didn't understand, she leaned closer, elbows propped on the table. "I'll tell you why I think I'd never have made a good architect, though I found the whole process fascinating and the idea of taking an empty lot and bringing it alive with a building incredible."

He glanced over again at that. What she'd said, and how she'd phrased it, encompassed his own feelings so perfectly that he could almost believe she'd stepped into his mind.

"You have to know every detail, beginning to end. You have to be certain before you take out the first shovel of dirt how it's going to end up. When you build, you're not just responsible for creating an attractive, functional piece of work. You're also responsible for the lives of the people who will work or live in or pass through the building, climb the stairs, ride the elevators. Nothing can be left to chance, and imagination has to conform to safety and practicality."

"I think you're wrong," he said after a moment. "I think you'd have made an excellent architect."

She smiled at him. "No, just because I understand doesn't mean I can do. Believe me, I've been there." She touched his hand easily, friend to friend. "You're an excellent architect because not only do you understand, but you're able to combine art with practicality, creativity with reality."

He studied her, both moved and pleased by her insight. "Is that what you're doing with your writing?"

"I hope so." She sat back to watch the clouds roll in. It would rain soon after nightfall. "All my life I've been scrambling around, looking for one creative outlet after another. Music, painting, dancing. I composed my first sonata when I was ten." Her lips tilted in a self-deprecating grin. "I was precocious."

"No, really?"

She chuckled as she slipped her hand under the bowl of her glass. "It wasn't a particularly good sonata, but I always knew there was something I had to do. My parents have been very patient, even indulgent, and I didn't always deserve it. This time… I guess this sounds silly at my age, but this time I want them to be proud of me."

"It doesn't sound silly," he murmured. "We never grow out of wanting our parents' approval."

"Do you have yours, Nathan?"

"Yes." The word was clipped. Because he heard it himself, he added a smile. "They're both very pleased with the route my career's taken."

She decided to press just a little farther. "Your father isn't an architect, is he?"

"No. Finance."

"Ah. That's funny, when you think of it. I imagine our parents have had cocktails together more than once. J.D.'s biggest interests are in finance."

"You call your father J.D.?"

"Only when I'm thinking of him as a businessman. He'd always get such a kick out of it when I'd march into his office, plop on his desk and say, 'All right, J.D., is it buy or sell?'"

"You're very fond of him."

"I'm crazy about him. Mother, too, even when she nags. She's always wanting me to fly to Paris and be redone." With only the faintest of frowns, she touched the tips of her hair. "She's certain the French could find a way to make me elegant and demure."

"I like you the way you are."

Again he saw that quick look of astonishment on her face. "That's the nicest thing you've ever said to me."

He thought, as he stared into her eyes, that he heard the first rumble of thunder. "We'd better get this stuff inside. Rain's coming."

"All right." She rose easily enough and helped clear the table. It was foolish to be moved by such a simple statement. He hadn't told her she was beautiful or brilliant. He hadn't said he loved her madly. He'd simply told her that he liked her the way she was. Nothing he could have said would have meant more to a woman like Jackie.

Inside the kitchen, they worked together for a few moments in companionable silence.

"I suppose," she began, "since you're dressed like that, you didn't spend the day at the beach."

"No, I had meetings. My clients from Denver."

Jackie looked at what was left in the wine bottle, decided it wasn't enough to cork and poured the remainder into their glasses. "You never mentioned what you were going to build."

"S and S Industries is putting a branch in Denver. They need an office building."

"You designed another one of them in Dallas a few years ago."

Surprised, he glanced over. "Yes, I did."

"Is this one going to be along the same lines?"

"No. I went for slick and futuristic in Dallas. Lots of

glass and steel, with an uncluttered look. I want something more classic for this. Softer, more distinguished lines."

"Can I see the drawings?"

"I suppose, if you'd like."

"I really would." She dried her hands on a cloth, then handed him his half-filled glass. "Can I see them now?"

"All right." He didn't question the fact that he wanted her to see them, that her opinion mattered to him. Both were new concepts for him, and something to think about later. They walked through the house as the light grew dim from the gathering clouds.

His desk was clear. Nathan would never have gone to a meeting without dealing with any leftover paperwork or correspondence. Drawing the blueprints from the tube, he spread them out. Genuinely interested, Jackie leaned over his shoulder with her lips pursed.

"The exterior is brown brick," he began, trying to ignore the brush of her hair against his cheek as she leaned closer. "I'm using curves rather than straight lines."

"It has a deco look."

"Exactly." Why hadn't he noticed her scent earlier? Was he just growing accustomed to it, or was it because she was standing so close, close enough to touch or to taste with the slightest effort? "I've arched the windows, and…"

When he let his words trail off, she glanced up and smiled. Understanding and patience shouldn't make a man uncomfortable, but he looked back deliberately at the papers on his desk.

"And every individual office will have at least one. I've always felt that it's more conducive to productivity if you don't feel caged in."

"Yes." She was still smiling, and neither of them were looking at the blueprints. "It's a beautiful building, very strong without being oppressive. Classic without being staid. The trim and accents are in rose, I imagine."

"To blend with the bricks." Her mouth was rose, a very soft, very subtle rose. He found himself turning his head just enough to taste it.

This time he knew he heard thunder, and it was much closer.

He drew away, shaken. Without speaking, he began to roll up the blueprints.

"I'd like to see the sketches of the interior."

"Jack—"

"It's not really fair to leave things half done."

Nodding, Nathan unrolled the next set. She was right. He supposed he'd known that all along. A thing begun required a finish.

Chapter 8

Jackie drew a long, steadying breath. She felt like a diver who'd just taken the last bounce on the board. There could be no turning back now.

She hadn't known when she'd started the evening that he would allow her to get this close. The defenses he had were lowering, and the distance he insisted on was narrowing. It was difficult, very difficult, to accept that the reason for that might only be his own desire. But if that was all he could feel for her now, that was all she would ask for. Desire, at least, was honest.

She couldn't love him any more than she already did. That was what she had thought, but now she knew it wasn't true. With every step closer, with every hour spent with him, her heart expanded.

Patient, even sympathetic to his dilemma, she listened while he explained the floor plans.

It was an excellent piece of work. Her eye and her knowledge were sharp enough to recognize that. But so was he. An excellent piece of work. His hands were wide palmed and long fingered, tanned from the hours he spent outdoors watching over his projects, artistic in their own competent, no-nonsense way. His voice was strong, masculine without being gruff, cultured without being affected. There was a trace of lime scent on his skin from his soap.

She murmured in agreement and put a hand on his arm as he pointed out a facet of the building. There were muscles beneath the creaseless material of his tailored, conservative suit. She heard his voice hesitate at her touch. And she, too, heard the thunder.

"There'll be an atrium here, in the executive offices. We're going to use tile rather than carpet for a cooler, cleaner look. And here…" His mouth was drying up on the words, his muscles tightening at her casual touch. He found it necessary to sit.

"The boardroom?" Jackie prompted, and sat on the arm of his chair.

"What? Yes." His tie was strangling him. Nathan tugged at it and struggled to concentrate. "We'll continue with the arches, but on a larger scale. The paneling will—" He wondered why in the hell the paneling had ever mattered. Her hand was on his shoulder now, kneading away the tension he hadn't even been aware had lodged there.

"What about the paneling?"

What about it? he thought as she leaned forward to trail one of her slender, ringed fingers over the prints. "We're going with mahogany. Honduras."

"It'll be beautiful. Now, and a hundred years from now. Indirect lighting?"

"Yes." He looked at her again. She was smiling, her head tilted just inches above his, her body curved just slightly toward him. The ink on the blueprint of his life seemed to fade. "Jack, this can't go on."

"I agree completely." In one lithe move, she was in his lap.

"What are you doing?" It shouldn't have amused him. His stomach had just contracted into a fist, one with claws, but he found himself smiling at her.

"You're right, this can't go on. I'm sure you're going as crazy as I am, and we can't have that, can we?" A trio of rings glittered on her hand as she tucked her hair back.

"I suppose not."

"No. So I'm going to put a stop to it."

"To what?" He put a hand on her wrist as she slipped off his tie.

"To the uncertainty, to the what-ifs." Ignoring his hand, she began to unbutton his shirt. "This is very nice material," she commented. "I'm taking full responsibility, Nathan. You really have no say in the matter."

"What are you talking about, Jack?" He took her by the shoulders when she started to peel off his jacket. "What the hell do you think you're doing?"

"I'm having my way with you, Nathan." She pressed her mouth to his, and the laugh he'd thought he was ready to form became a moan. "It's no use trying to fight it, you know," she murmured against his lips as she pulled off his jacket. "I'm a very determined woman."

"So I see." He felt her tug at his shirt from the waistband of his slacks and tried again. "Jack—damn it, Jackie, we'd better talk about this."

"No more talk." She nipped lightly at his collarbone, then slid her tongue to his ear. "I'm going to have you, Nathan, willing or not." She closed her teeth over his earlobe. "Don't make me hurt you."

This time he did laugh, though not steadily. "Jack, I outweigh you by seventy pounds."

"The bigger they are…" she told him, and unhooked his slacks. In an automatic defensive gesture, his hands covered hers.

"You're serious."

She drew back far enough to look at him just as the first slice of lightning lit the sky. The flash leaped into her eyes as if it had always been there, waiting. "Deadly." With her eyes on his, she caught the zipper of her jumpsuit between her thumb and fingers and drew it down. "You're not getting out of this room until I'm finished with you, Nathan. Cooperate, and I'll be gentle. Otherwise…" She shrugged, and the jumpsuit slithered tantalizingly down her shoulders.

It was too late, much too late, to pretend he didn't want to be with her, didn't have to be with her. The game she was playing was taking the responsibility and the repercussions away from him and onto her. Though it touched him, he couldn't allow it.

"I want you." He brushed her cheeks with his hands and combed his fingers through her hair as he said it. "Come upstairs."

She turned her face so that her lips pressed into his palm. It was a gesture of great tenderness, a gesture that bordered on submission. But when she looked back at him, she shook her head. "Right here. Right now." Jackie pressed her open mouth to his, leaving him no choice.

She tantalized, tormented, teased. Her body curled itself around his, and her lips were quick and urgent. They lingered on his, drawing in, drawing out, then sped away to trace the planes and angles of his face. His blood was hammering. He could feel it, in his head, in his loins, in his fingertips. Her hands were unmerciful…wonderful…as they roamed over him.

No hesitation. She didn't know the meaning of the word. Like the storm that whipped at the windows, she was all flash and fire. A man could get burned by her, he thought, and always bear the scars. Yet his arms banded around her, holding her hard and close as he fought to maintain some control. She was driving him beyond the limits he'd always set for himself, away from reason, away from the civilized.

That was his own breath he heard, fast and uneven. That was his skin springing moist and hot from a need that had grown titanic in mere moments. He was pulling the material from her shoulders with a gnawing demand to feel her flesh against his. And it was with an insatiable greed that he took it.

"Jack." His mouth was against her throat as he tasted, devoured. More…he could only think of having more. He'd have absorbed her into him if he'd known how. "Jack," he repeated. "Give me a minute, will you?"

But her mouth was just as greedy when it came to his. She only laughed.

He swore, but even the oath caught in his throat. He was tearing the jumpsuit from her as they slid to the floor.

She couldn't make her fingers work fast enough. Jackie pulled and yanked to strip the last barriers of his clothing away. She wanted to feel him, all of him. As they rolled over on the carpet, her skin was on fire from the friction of flesh against flesh.

She'd thought she would guide him, coerce, cajole, seduce. She'd been wrong. Like a pebble in a slingshot, she'd been flung high and fast, no longer in control. But with some trace of reason, she knew he was as lost as she.

Desire held control, steered by a love only one of them could admit. But in the lamplight, with the storm reaching its peak, desire was enough.

Wrapped together, they rolled mindlessly, each searching and finding more. The capacity for intense concentration was inherent in them both, but neither had used it so fully in the act of love until tonight. The clothes they'd discarded tangled with their naked legs and were kicked heedlessly away. Rain, tossed by a restless wind, hit the windows like bullets but was ignored. Something teetered on a table as it was jolted, then thudded to the carpet. Neither of them heard.

There were no murmured promises, no whispered endearments. Only sighs and shudders. Neither were there tender caresses or gentle kisses. Only demands and hunger.

Breath heaving, Nathan moved above her. Lightning still flashed sporadically, highlighting her face and hair. Her head was thrown back, her eyes clear and open, when he took her.

Perfect. Naked, damp and dazed, Jackie curled into him while that one word ran around in her head. Nothing had ever been so perfect. His heart was still pounding against hers, his breath still warming her cheek. The rain had slowed, and the thunder was only a murmur in the distance. Storms passed. Some storms.

She hadn't needed the physical act of love to confirm her feelings for Nathan. Lovemaking was only an extension of being in love. But even with her vivid and often far-reaching imagination, she'd never known anything could be like this.

He'd emptied her, and he'd filled her.

No matter how many times they came together, no matter how many years they shared, there would never be another first time. Her eyes closed, her arms wrapped around him, she savored it.

He didn't know what to say to her, or if he was capable of speech at all. He'd thought he knew himself, the man he was and the man he'd chosen to be. The Nathan Powell he'd lived with most of his life wasn't the same man who had plunged so recklessly into passion, giving and taking with greedy disregard.

He'd lost all sense of time, of place, even of self, as he'd driven himself restlessly, even abandonedly, into her. The way he had never done before. The way, he already understood, he would never do again. Unless it was with Jackie.

He should have taken her with more care, and certainly with more consideration. But once begun he had lost whatever foothold he'd still had on reason and had cartwheeled off the cliff with her.

It had been what she'd wanted—what he'd wanted—but did that make it right? There had been no words, no questions. He hadn't even given a thought to his responsibility or her protection. That had made him wince a bit even as he stroked a hand through her hair.

They'd have to talk about that, and soon, because he was going to have to admit that what had happened between them was going to happen again. That didn't make it permanent, he assured himself as his hand fitted possessively over the curve of her shoulder.

"Jack?"

When she tilted her head to look up at him, he was struck by such an unexpected wave of tenderness that he couldn't speak at all. Lips curved, she leaned closer and pressed them to his. It took no more than that to have the embers of desire glowing again. The fingers that had been stroking her hair tightened and dragged her closer. Limber and sleek, she shifted onto him.

"I love you, Nathan. No, don't say anything." Her lips nibbled and rubbed against his as she sought to soothe more than to arouse. "You don't have to say anything. I just need to tell you. And I want to make love with you again and again."

Her hands had already told him as much, and now her mouth was moving lower, nipping and gliding along his neck. His response was so immediate it stunned him.

"Jack, wait a minute."

"No more complaints," she murmured. "I ravished you once, and I can do it again."

"Thank God for that, but wait." Firmly now, thinking only of her, he drew her away by the shoulders. "We have to talk a minute."

"We can talk when we're old—though I did want to mention that I'm crazy about your carpet."

"I've grown fond of it myself. Now, hold on," he said again when she tried to squirm away from his restraining hands. "Jack, I'm serious."

She let out a huge and exaggerated sigh. "Do you have to be?"

"Yes."

"All right, then." She composed her features and settled herself comfortably. "Shoot."

"I'm already doing it backward," he began, furious with himself. "But I don't intend to make the same mistake again. Things happened so quickly before that I never asked, never even thought to ask, if it was all right."

"Of course it was all right," she began with a laugh. "Oh." Her brows rose as realization struck. "You really are a very good man, aren't you?" Despite his grip on her shoulders, she managed to kiss him. "Yes, it's all right. I realize I look like a scatterbrain, but I'm not. Well, at least I'm a responsible one."

The tenderness crept back unexpectedly, and he cupped her face in his hands. "You don't look like a scatterbrain. You may act like one, but you look beautiful."

"Now I know I'm getting to you." She tried to say it lightly, but her eyes glistened. "I'd like you to think I'm beautiful. I always wanted to be."

Her hair fell over her brow, tempting him to brush at it, to tangle his fingers in it. "The first time I saw you, when I was tired and annoyed and you were sitting in my whirlpool, I thought you were beautiful."

"And I thought you were Jake."

"What?"

"I'd been sitting there, thinking about my story, and about Jake—the way he looked, you know." Her fingers roamed over his face as she remembered. "Build, color-

ing, features. I opened my eyes and saw you and thought…
there he is." She rested her cheek on his chest. "My hero."

Troubled, he curled an arm around her. "I'm no hero,
Jack."

"You are to me." She shimmied up his body a bit, then
rested her forehead against his. "Nathan, I forgot the strudel."

"Did you? What strudel?"

"The apple strudel I made for dessert. Why don't I dish
some out and we can eat it in bed?"

Later, he thought, later he'd think about Jackie's idea of
love and heroes. "Sounds very sensible."

"Okay." She kissed the tip of his nose, then smiled.
"Your bed or mine?"

"Mine," he murmured, as though the word had been
waiting to be said. "I want you in mine."

Laziness was its own reward. Jackie embraced the idea
as she stretched in bed. Nothing seemed more glorious at
the moment than to sleep in after so many days of rising
early and going straight to the typewriter.

She snuggled, half dozing, pretending she was twelve
and it was Saturday. There had been nothing she'd liked
better at twelve than Saturdays. But as she shifted her leg
brushed against Nathan's. It took no more than that for her
to be very, very glad she was no longer twelve.

"Are you awake?" she asked without opening her eyes.

"No." His arm came around her possessively and remained.

Still drowsy, a smile just forming on her lips, she nibbled
on him. "Would you like to be?"

"Depends." He shifted closer to her, enjoying the quiet,
cozy feel of warm body against warm body. "Did we get
all the strudel out of the bed?"

"Can't say for sure. Shall I look?" With that, Jackie tossed the sheets over their heads and attacked him.

She had more energy than she was entitled to, Nathan thought later as she lay sprawled over him. The sheets were now balled and twisted somewhere below their feet. Still trying to catch his breath, he kept his eyes half-shut as he looked at her.

She was long and lean and curved very subtly. Her skin was gold in the late-morning light, except for a remarkably thin line over her hips where it remained white, unexposed to the sun. Tousled from the pillow and from his hands, her hair sprang in a distracted halo.

He'd always thought he preferred long hair on a woman, but with Jackie's short, free-swinging style he could stroke the curve at the back of her neck. He did so now, and she began to purr like a satisfied cat.

What was he going to do with her?

The idea of nudging her gently along was no longer even a remote possibility. He wanted her with him. Needed her. *Need.* That was a word he'd always been careful to avoid. Now that it had slammed into him, he hadn't any idea how to handle it.

He tried to think of what he would do tomorrow, a week, even a month from now, without her. His mind remained stubbornly blank. This wasn't like him. He hadn't been like himself since she'd spun her way into his life.

What did she want from him? Nathan detested himself because he knew he wouldn't ask her. He already knew what she wanted, as if it had been discussed and debated and deliberated. She loved him, at least for today. And he…he cared for her. *Love* was one four-letter word he wouldn't allow himself. Love meant promises. He never made promises unless he was sure he could keep them. A promise given casually and broken was worse than a lie.

With the morning sun shining through the windows and the birds singing the praises of spring, he wished it could be as simple as Jackie would like it. Love, marriage, family. He knew all too well that love didn't guarantee the success of a marriage and that marriage didn't equal family.

His parents had a marriage in which love no longer was an issue. No one would ever have accused the three of them of being a family.

He wasn't his father, Nathan thought as he held Jackie and studied the ceiling. He'd made certain that he would never be his father. But he understood the pride in success and the drive for accomplishment that had been his father's. That were still his father's. And were his.

He shook his head. He hadn't thought of his father or his lack of family life as much in a decade as he had since he'd met Jackie. She did that to him, as well. She made him consider possibilities that he'd rejected long ago with perfect logic and sense. She made him wish and regret what he'd never had reason to wish or regret before.

He couldn't let himself love her, because then he would make promises. And when the promises were broken he'd hate himself. She deserved better than what he could give her or, more accurately, what he couldn't give her.

"Nathan?"

"Hmm."

"What are you thinking about?"

"You."

When she lifted her head, her eyes were unexpectedly solemn. "I hope not."

Puzzled, he combed his fingers through the tangle of her hair. "Why?"

"Because you're tensing up again." Something came and went in her face—the first shadow of sorrow he'd ever seen in it. "Don't regret. I don't think I could bear it."

"No." He drew her up to cradle her in his arms. "No, I don't. How could I?"

She turned her face into his throat. He didn't know she was forcing back tears, and she couldn't have explained them to him. "I love you, Nathan, and I don't want you to regret that, either, or worry about it. I want you to just let things happen as they're meant to happen."

He tilted her head back with a finger under her chin. Her eyes were dry now. His were intense. "And that's enough for you?"

"Enough for today." The smile was back. Even he couldn't detect the effort it cost her. "I never know what's going to be enough for tomorrow. How do you feel about brunch? You haven't had my crepes yet. I make really wonderful crepes, but I don't remember if there's any whipping cream. There's always omelets, of course—if the mushrooms haven't dried up. Or we could make do with leftover strudel. Maybe we should have a swim first, and then—"

"Jack?"

"Uh-huh?"

"Shut up."

"Right now?" she asked as his hand slid down to her hip.

"Yes."

"Okay."

She started to laugh, but his lips met hers with such quiet, such fragile tenderness that the laughter became a helpless moan. Her eyes, once alight with amusement, shuttered closed at the sound. She was a strong woman, often valiant in her way, but she had no defense against tenderness.

It had been just as unexpected for him. There had been no flash of fire, no rumble of thunder. Just warmth, a drugging, languorous warmth that crept under his skin, into his brain, into his heart. With one kiss, one easy merging of lips, she filled him.

He hadn't thought of her as delicate. But she was delicate now, as her bones seemed to dissolve under his hands, leaving her smaller somehow, softer. Woman at her most vulnerable. As the kiss spun out, he lifted a hand to her cheek, as if to hold her there, captive.

Patience. She'd known there was a steady, rock-solid patience in him. But until now he'd never shown it to her. Compassion. That, too, she'd sensed in him. But to feel it now, to have him give her the gift of it, was more precious than diamonds. She was lost in him again, not in the frantic race she'd become used to, but in a slow, lengthy search she already knew would lead her where she had always wanted to go.

He caressed where he'd once taken greedily. Her skin was like satin and shivered under his touch. There was a fluidity to her now rather than a frenzy, a quiescence that had taken the place of energy.

His fingertips skimmed over her, and he delighted in making discoveries in territory already conquered. The same woman, yet a different one; her generosity was still there, but merged now with a vulnerability that humbled him. He found her flavor somehow sweeter. When he pressed his lips to her breast, he felt her heartbeat. It hammered fast, not with the heady, energetic rhythm of their past loving, but quick and light.

Experimentally he ran a finger over the inside of her wrist, feeling her pulse beating there, as well. For him. Curling his fingers through hers, he brought them to his lips to kiss and caress them one by one.

The bottom seemed to drop out of her world. With each touch she had fallen deeper, still deeper, into his. Into him. Now, as he did nothing more than brush his mouth over her fingertips, she tumbled headfirst into the dark, trusting him implicitly to catch her.

He could have asked her anything, demanded anything. In that moment her love was so overwhelming that she would have granted any wish without a thought to self or survival. It wasn't possible for her to gather him close and take their loving to another plane. He had a prisoner. Though he might not know it, she would stay enslaved as long as he'd have her.

He only knew that something had changed yet again. He was protector now as well as lover, giver as well as taker. The excitement that knowledge brought was tinged with a trace of fear he struggled to ignore. He couldn't think about tomorrow and tomorrow's consequences when he wanted her, possibly more, impossibly more, than he had only moments ago. She wouldn't object if he took her quickly, if he dragged them both to the top without preamble or delicacy. Perhaps it was because of that, because he understood that she would accept him on any terms, that he found himself needing to give her everything he could.

Slow loving. Almost tortuous. Tender stroking. Lazy tastes. There were quiet sighs that rippled the air until even the sunlight seemed to dim. If it had been possible, he would have had flowers for her, a bouquet of them. Soft petals, shimmering fragrances; he would have poured them over her skin. But he only had himself.

It was enough. He was more than enough for her. She showed him that in the way her lips parted, in the way her arms encircled him. No dream she'd ever indulged in, no wish she'd ever given herself, could compare with the reality of him cherishing her.

His hands were so cool, so calm, on her skin. With each touch she felt herself glow. The heat came from within her now, so that it was possible to bank it, to prevent it from becoming overpowering. Just flickers of flame, burning softly.

As gentle as he, she reached for him, offering the pleasure and temptation of unconditional love. When she trembled, he murmured. In reassurance. And she, who had never believed she would need a man to watch over her, understood that she would wither to dust without him.

Generosity, given without restrictions. That she offered, openhanded, was no longer a surprise to him. But to discover that he could give equally, to find that he was compelled to match her, was something new.

He slipped into her, and the tenderness remained.

Slow, harmonious movements. A breath caught, then sighed away like the wind. With his mouth on hers, they continued. Like a Viennese waltz, their dance was light and elegant. When the tempo increased, they surged with the music, spinning, whirling, their eyes open and locked together.

The dance ended as gently as it had begun.

The sun was higher now. Contentedly, her body curved into his, Jackie watched the curtains move with the faint breeze. If she concentrated hard enough she could catch the light fragrance of flowers from the garden below. Nothing identifiable, but a mixture of scents that spoke of spring and new life.

Every moment of the hours they'd had together was lodged firmly in her mind. She knew she would take them out often and enjoy them over and over.

"You know what I'd like?" she asked him.

"Hmm?" If he hadn't been so dazed, it would have amazed him that he could be dozing in bed this close to noon.

"To stay here, right here in this bed, all day."

"We've got a pretty good start."

Her grin wicked, she turned to face him. Nose to nose, she leered. "Why don't we—" She swore when the phone rang. "It's the wrong number," she told him, climbing over his shoulder as he reached for it. "It's just a woman with a squeaky voice who's going to tell you your name's been selected in a sweepstakes and you've won ten free magazine subscriptions as long as you pay $7.75 a month for handling."

He hesitated a moment because when she said it it was too easy to believe. "What if it isn't?"

"Ah, but what if it is? Do you have enough willpower to resist ten free magazines a month? Be sure, Nathan. Be very sure."

He put a hand over her face and shoved her back against the pillows. "Hello."

"You were warned," Jackie said in a voice that spoke of doom. This time he put the pillow over her face.

"Carla?"

"Carla?" Her voice was muffled by the pillows. Jackie tossed it aside and sank her teeth into his shoulder.

"Ouch! Damn it! No, Carla, I— What is it?" To protect himself, Nathan rolled and trapped Jackie under him. "Yes, I was expecting that." Ignoring the flailing arms and muttered curses beneath him, Nathan listened. "All right, we'll push up the schedule if necessary. No, I've already taken care of that from here. Set this up for tomorrow. Nine. Ten, then," he said. "Contact Cody. I'll want him there. Fine, Carla." Jackie wriggled beneath him and made loud gasping noises. He ignored that, as well. "Yes, I've enjoyed having a few days of relaxation. See you tomorrow."

When he leaned over to hang up the receiver, Jackie managed to squirm out from under him. Face flushed, pulling in exaggerated gulps of air, she thudded a pillow over his head.

"So," she began. "You decided to smother me so that you could run off with the Italian countess and make mad, illicit passion in the Holiday Inn. Don't try to deny it," she warned. "The signs are all too clear."

"Okay. Which Italian countess was that?"

"Carla." She slammed the pillow at him again, aiming lower, then had to bite back a laugh when he grabbed her around the waist. "No, don't try to make up, Nathan. It's too late. I've already decided to murder both you and the countess. I'll electrocute you while you're sharing your bubble bath. No jury would convict me."

"Not if they did a psychiatric profile first."

She made another grab, this time for a very vulnerable area. He avoided her by throwing her onto her back and once again using his body to shield and protect himself. Arms locked, they rolled. Nathan was just beginning to enjoy it when her momentum sent them tumbling to the floor.

Out of breath and rubbing his shoulder, he narrowed his eyes. "You are crazy."

Jackie straddled him and planted her arms on either side of his head. "Okay, Powell, if you value your life, come clean. Who's Carla?"

He considered her. Her eyes were bright, her cheeks flushed with amusement. Her wide, incredible mouth was curved. Casually he cupped her hips in his hands. "You want the truth?"

"And nothing but."

"The Countess Carla Mandolini and I have been having a blazing adulterous affair for years. She fools her husband, the elderly and impotent count, by doubling as my secretary. The fool actually believes that the twins are his."

He really was adorable, Jackie decided as she leaned closer. "A likely story," she told him just before her mouth covered his.

Chapter 9

"All right, Nathan, consider yourself kidnapped. You might as well go peacefully."

As he wrapped a towel around his waist, Nathan glanced up. Without bothering to knock, Jackie pushed open the door to the bathroom and strode in. He should be used to it by now, he thought as he secured the towel. She could pop up anytime and anywhere.

"Mind if I put my shoes on?"

"You've got ten minutes."

Before she could turn to go, he had her by the arm. "Where have you been?"

He was becoming too attached to her, Nathan told himself even as the words came out. When he'd woken up alone that morning it had taken all of his control not to dash around the house looking for her. They'd been lovers three days, and already he felt bereft if she wasn't beside him when he opened his eyes in the morning.

"Some of us have work to do, even on Saturdays." She let her gaze roam down, then up. He was damp, tanned and mostly naked. She thought it a pity she'd made plans. "Downstairs in ten minutes, or I'll make you suffer."

"What's going on, Jack?"

"You're not in a position to ask questions." With a last smile, she left him. He heard her run lightly downstairs.

What did she have in store for him now? Nathan wondered as he reached for his razor. With Jackie there were never any guarantees, and there was rarely any rhyme or reason. It should have annoyed him, he thought as he lathered his face. It was supposed to annoy him. He'd already planned his day.

A few hours in his office dealing with the preliminaries on the Sydney project and snipping any loose ends from Denver would take care of the morning. After that he'd thought it might be nice to treat Jackie, and himself, to lunch and tennis at the country club. Being kidnapped hadn't been in his plans.

But he wasn't annoyed. Nathan brought the razor over lather and beard in short, smooth strokes. Because he'd left the window open, the mirror was only lightly steamed at the edges. He could see himself clearly. What had changed?

He was still Nathan Powell, a man with certain responsibilities and priorities. It wasn't a stranger looking back at him in the mirror, but a man he knew very well. The eyes were the same, as was the shape of the face, the hairline. If he looked the same, why didn't he feel the same? More, why couldn't he, a man who knew himself so well, put his finger on exactly what his feelings were?

Shaking the thought aside, he rinsed off the traces of lather. It was absurd. He was exactly who he had always been. The only change in his life was Jackie.

And what the hell was he going to do about her?

It wasn't a question he could avoid much longer. The more involved he became with her, the more certain he was that he was going to hurt her. That was something he would regret the rest of his life. In a matter of weeks he would have to leave her to go to Denver. He couldn't leave her with promises and vows, nor could he expect her to stay when he couldn't tell her what she needed to hear.

He wanted to believe she was nothing more than a few colorful pages in the very straightforward book of his life.

But he knew, he already knew, that as his life went on he would keep turning back to look over those few pages again and again.

They should talk. He slapped on aftershave that left his skin cool and stinging. It was up to him to see that they did, quietly, seriously and as soon as possible. The world, as much as he might now wish it could be, was not composed of two people. And neither of them had begun to live the moment they'd met.

"You're running out of time, Nathan."

Jackie's voice came rushing up the stairs and caught him daydreaming. Daydreams were also something new in his life. Swearing at himself, Nathan whipped off the towel and began to dress.

He found her in the kitchen, securing the lid on a cooler, while on the radio some group from the fifties harmonized about love and devotion.

"You're lucky I decided to be generous and give you another five minutes." She turned to study him. He wore black shorts with a white shirt, and his hair was still slightly damp. "I guess it was worth it."

He was almost but not quite used to her frank and unabashed appraisals. "What's going on, Jack?"

"I told you. You're kidnapped." She stepped forward to slip her arms around his waist. "If you try to escape, it'll go hard on you." Pressing her face in his throat, she began to sniff. "I love your aftershave."

"What's in the cooler?"

"Surprises. Sit down, you can have some cereal."

"Cereal?"

"Man doesn't live by hotcakes alone, Nathan." She kissed him quick. "And some bananas." She moved away to get one, changed her mind and took two. As she peeled her own, she began to explain. "You might as well consider yourself my hostage for the day and make this simple."

"Make what simple?"

"We've both been working hard the last few days—well, except for one very memorable day." She smiled as she took the first bite. "And that was exhausting in its own way. So…" She slapped a palm on the cooler. "I'm taking you for a ride."

"I see." Nathan sliced the banana over a bowl of corn-flakes. "Anywhere in particular?"

"No. Anywhere at all. You eat, I'll put this in the boat."

"Boat?" He paused, the banana peel in his hand. "My boat?"

"Of course." Hefting the cooler, she turned back with an easy smile. "As much as I love you, Nathan, I know even you can't walk on water. Coffee's hot, by the way, but make it quick, will you?"

He did, because he was more interested in what she had up her sleeve than in a bowl of cold cereal. She'd left the radio on, he supposed for his benefit. After he'd rinsed his bowl, Nathan switched it off. As a matter of course he went to check the front door. Jackie had left it open. He shut it, locked it, then went to join her.

Outside, he found her competently storing supplies in the hatch. She wore a visor in a blazing orange that matched her shorts and the frames of a pair of mirrored wraparound sunglasses.

"All set?" she asked him. "Cast off, will you?"

"You're driving?"

"Sure. I was practically born on a boat." She slipped be-hind the wheel and tossed a look over her shoulder as Nathan hesitated, his hands on the line. "Trust me. I looked at a map."

"Well, then." Wondering if he was taking his life in his hands, he cast off and came aboard.

"Sun block," she said, handing him a tube. With that she pulled smoothly away from the dock. "How do you feel about St. Thomas?"

"Jack…"

"Only kidding. I've thought what a kick it would be to travel the whole Intracoastal. Take a whole summer and just cruise."

He'd thought of it, too, as something he might find time for—someday. After retirement, perhaps. When Jackie said it, it seemed possible it could happen tomorrow. And it made him wish it would happen tomorrow. He only murmured as he watched her handle the boat.

He should have known she'd be fine. Maybe she couldn't remember to close doors behind her, but it seemed to him that whatever she did she did with careless skill. Her hand was light on the wheel as she negotiated the channel. Even when she picked up speed, he relaxed.

"You picked a good day for a kidnapping."

"I thought so." She threw him a grin, then settled more comfortably in her seat.

The boat handled like a dream. Of course, she'd known that Nathan would keep it in tip-top shape. That was one of the things she admired about him. He didn't take his possessions for granted. If it belonged to him, it deserved his attention. Too many people she knew, herself included, could develop a casual disregard for what was theirs. She'd learned something from him about pride of possession and the responsibility that went along with it.

She belonged to him now. Jackie hoped he'd begin to care for her with the same kind of devotion.

You're moving too fast, as usual, she cautioned herself. Caution was something else she'd learned from Nathan. It had to be enough, for now, that he no longer looked alarmed whenever she told him she loved him. The fact that he was beginning to accept that she did was a giant step. And soon—eventually, she thought, correcting herself— eventually he would accept the fact that he loved her back.

She knew he did. It wasn't a matter of wish fulfillment or hopeful dreams. She saw it when he looked at her, felt it when he touched her. Because she did, it made it that much more difficult to wait.

She'd always looked for instant gratification. Even as a child she'd been able to learn quickly and apply what she'd learned so that the rewards came quickly. Writing had shown her more than a love for storytelling. It had also shown her that some rewards were best waited for. Having Nathan, really having him, would be worth waiting a lifetime.

She turned down an alley of water where the bush was thick and green. It was hardly wide enough for two boats to pass. Near the verges, limbs of deadwood poked through the surface like twisted arms. Behind them the wake churned white, while ahead the water was darker, more mysterious. Above, the sun was a white flash, hinting, perhaps threatening, of the sultry summer still weeks away. Spray flew, glinting in the light. The motor purred, sending a flurry of birds rocketing above the trees.

"Ever been on the Amazon?"

"No." Nathan turned to her. "Have you?"

"Not yet," she told him, as if it were only a small oversight. "It might be something like this. Brown water, thick vegetation hiding all sorts of dangerous jungle life. Is it crocodiles or alligators down there?"

"I couldn't say."

"I'll have to look it up." A dragonfly dashed blue and gleaming across the bow, catching her attention. It skimmed over the water without making a ripple, then flashed into the bush. "It's wonderful here." Abruptly she cut the engine.

"What are you doing?"

"Listening."

Within moments the birds began to call, rustling through the leaves and growing bold in the silence. Insects sent up a soprano chorus. There was a watery plop, then two, as a frog swallowed an insect for an early lunch. Even the water itself had sound, a low, murmurous voice that invited laziness. From far off, too far off to be important, came the hum of another boat.

"I used to love to go camping," Jackie remembered. "I'd drag one of my brothers, and—"

"I didn't know you had any brothers."

"Two. Fortunately for me, they've both taken an avid interest in my father's many empires, leaving me free to do as I please." He couldn't see her eyes as she spoke, but from the tone of her voice he knew they were smiling.

"Never any interest in being a corporate climber?"

"Oh, God, no. Well, actually, I did think of being chairman of the board when I was six. Then I decided I'd rather be a brain surgeon. So I was more than happy when Ryan and Brandon took me off the hook." Lazily she slipped out of her deck shoes to stretch her toes. "I've always thought it would be difficult to be a son of a demanding father and not want to follow in his footsteps."

She'd said it casually, but Nathan was so completely silent that she realized she'd hit part of the mark. She opened her mouth to question, then shut it again. In his own time, she reminded herself. "Anyway, even though it often took blackmail to get one of my brothers to go with me, I really loved sitting by the fire and listening. You could be anywhere you wanted to be."

"Where did you go?"

"Oh, here and there. Arizona was the best. There's something indescribable about the desert when you're sitting beside a tent." She grinned again. "Of course, there's also something special about the presidential suite and room service. Depends on the mood. You want to drive?"

"No, you're doing fine."

With a laugh, Jackie kicked the motor on. "I hate to say it, but you ain't seen nothin' yet."

She spun the boat through the waterway, taking any out-of-the-way canal or inlet that caught her fancy. She was delighted to chug along behind the *Jungle Queen*, Lauderdale's triple-decker party boat, and wave to the tourists. For a time she was content to follow its wake and direction as it toured the Intracoastal's estates.

The houses pleased her, with their sweeping grounds and sturdy pillars. She enjoyed the flood of the spring flowers and the wink and shimmer of the pools. When another boat passed, she'd make up stories about the occupants that had Nathan laughing or just rolling his eyes.

It pleased her just as much to turn off the more traveled routes and pretend she was lost in the quiet, serpentine waters where the brush grew heavy and close at the edges. Shutting down again under the shade of bending palms and cypress, she took out Jackie's idea of a picnic.

There was Pouilly-Fuissé in paper cups, and cracked crab to be dug out with plastic forks, and tiny Swiss meringues, white and glossy. After she'd badgered Nathan into taking off his shirt, she rubbed sunblock over him, rambling all the while about the idea of setting a book in the Everglades.

But what she noticed most as she stroked the cream over his skin was that he was relaxed. There was no band of tension over his shoulders, no knot of nerves at the base of his neck. When he reciprocated by applying the cream to wherever her skinny blue tank top exposed her skin, there was none in her, either.

When the cooler was packed away again, she jumped

back behind the wheel. The morning laziness was over, she told him. Turning the boat around, she headed out.

She burst into Port Everglades to join the pleasure and cruise ships, the freighters and sailboats. Here the water was wide and open, the spray cool and the air full of sound.

"Do you ever come here?" she shouted.

"No." Nathan clamped a hand on the orange visor she'd transferred from her head to his. "Not often."

"I love it! Think of all the places these ships have been before they come here. And where they're going when they leave. Hundreds of people, thousands, come here on their way to—I don't know… Mexico, Cuba."

"The Amazon?"

"Yes." Laughing, she turned the boat in a circle that had spray spurting up the sides. "There are so many places to go and see. You don't live long enough, you just can't live long enough to do everything you should." Her hair danced madly away from her face as she rode into the wind. "That's why I'm coming back."

"To Florida?"

"No. To life."

He watched her laugh again and raise her arm to another boat. If anyone could, Nathan thought, it would be Jackie.

He let her have her head. Indeed, he didn't know if he could have stopped her if he'd been inclined to. Besides, he'd long since acknowledged that he enjoyed the race.

At midafternoon, she pulled up to a dock and advised Nathan to secure the lines. While he obliged, she dug her purse out of the hatch.

"Where are we going now?"

"Shopping."

He held out a hand to help her onto the pier. "For what?"

"For anything. Maybe nothing." With her hand in his, she began to walk. "You know, spring break's nearly here.

In a couple of weeks the college crowd will flock to this, the mecca of the East."

"Don't remind me."

"Oh, don't be a stick-in-the-mud, Nathan. Kids have to blow off steam, too. But I was thinking the shops would be a madhouse then, and as much as I might appreciate that, you wouldn't, so we should do this now."

"Do what now?"

"Shop," she explained patiently. "Play tourist, buy tacky souvenirs and T-shirts with vulgar sayings, haggle over a shell ashtray."

"I can't tell you how much I appreciate you thinking of me."

"My pleasure, darling." She planted a quick kiss on his cheek. "Listen, unless I miss my guess, this is something you never do."

He was surprised when she paused, waiting for his answer. "No, it's not."

"It's time you did." She adjusted the visor to a cockier angle. "You very sensibly moved south and chose Fort Lauderdale because of its growth, but you don't take too many walks on the beach."

"I thought we were going shopping."

"It's the same thing." She slipped her arm around his waist. "You know, Nathan, as far as I can see, you don't have one T-shirt with a beer slogan, a rock concert or an obscene saying."

"I've been deprived."

"I know. That's why I'd like to help you out."

"Jack." He stopped, turning around to gently take her shoulders. "Please don't."

"You'll thank me later."

"We'll compromise. I'll buy a tie."

"Only if it has a naked mermaid on it."

Jackie found exactly what she wanted bordering Las Olas Boulevard. There was a labyrinth of small cross streets bulging with shops selling everything from snorkels to sapphires. Telling him it was for his own good, Jackie dragged him into a small, crowded store with a doorway flanked by two garish red flamingos.

"They're becoming entirely too trendy," she said to Nathan with a flick of her hand toward the slim-legged birds. "It's a shame I'm so fond of them. Oh, look, just what I've always wanted. A music box with shells stuck all over it. What do you suppose it plays?"

Jackie wound up what Nathan considered one of the most hideous-looking things he'd ever seen. It played "Moon River."

"No." Jackie shook her head over the melody. "I can do without that."

"Thank God."

Chuckling, she replaced it and began to poke through rows of equally moronic whatnots. "I understand, Nathan, that you have an eye for the aesthetic and harmonious, but there really is something to be said for the ugly and useless."

"Yes, but I can't say it here. There are children present."

"Now take this."

"No," he said as she held up a pelican made entirely of clamshells. "Please, I can't thank you enough for the thought, but I couldn't."

"Only for demonstration purposes. This has a certain charm." She laughed as his brow rose. "No, really. Think of this. Say a couple comes here on their honeymoon and they want something silly and very personal to remember the day by. They need something they can look at in ten years and bring back that very heady, very intimate time before insurance payments and wet diapers." She flourished the bird. *"Voilà."*

"*Voilà?* One doesn't *voilà* a pelican, especially a shell one."

"More imagination," she said with a sigh. "All you need is a little more imagination." With what seemed like genuine regret, she set the pelican down. Just when he thought it was safe, Jackie dragged him over to a maze of T-shirts. She seemed very taken with one in teal with an alligator lounging in a hammock drinking a wine cooler. Passing it by, she dragged out one of a grinning shark in dark glasses.

"This," she told him grandly, "is you."

"It is?"

"Absolutely. Not to say you're a predator, but sharks are notorious for being loners, and the sunglasses are a symbol of a need for privacy."

He studied it, frowning and intrigued. "You know, I've never known anyone to be philosophical about T-shirts."

"Clothes make the man, Nathan." Draping it over her arm, she continued to browse. When she loitered by a rack of ties screen-printed with fish, he put his foot down.

"No, Jack, not even for you."

Sighing at his lack of vision, she settled for the shirt.

She hauled him through a dozen shops until pictures of neon palms, plastic mugs and garish straw hats blurred in his head. She bought with a blatant disregard for style or use. Then, suddenly inspired, she shipped off a huge papier-mâché parrot to her father.

"My mother will make him take it off to one of his offices, but he'll love it. Daddy has a wonderful sense of the ridiculous."

"Is that where you get it?"

"I suppose." Hands on her hips, she turned in a circle to be certain she hadn't missed anything. "Well, since I've done that, I'd better run by that little jewelry store and see if there's anything appropriate for my mother." She pocketed the receipt, then relieved Nathan of two packages. "How are you holding up?"

"I'm game if you are."

"You're sweet." She leaned over, between packages, to kiss him. "Why don't I buy you an ice-cream cone?"

"Why don't you?"

She grinned at that, thinking he was certainly coming along. "Right after I find something tasteful for my mother," she promised, and she proved as good as her word.

Some fifteen minutes later, she chose an ebony pin crusted with pearls. It was a very mature, very elegant piece in faultless taste.

The purchase showed Nathan two things. First that she glanced only casually at the price, so casually that he was certain she would have bought it no matter what the amount. An impulse buyer she certainly was, but he sensed that once she'd decided an item was right, the dollar amount was unimportant. And second that the pin was both conventional and elegant, making it a far cry from the parrot she'd chosen for her father.

It made him wonder, as she loitered over some of the more colorful pieces in the shop, if her parents were as different as her vision of them.

He'd always believed, perhaps too strongly, that children inherited traits, good and bad. Yet here was Jackie, nothing like a woman who would wear a classically tasteful pin, and also nothing like a man who had spent his adult life wheeling and dealing in the business world.

Moments later, he had other things to worry about. They were out on the street again, and Jackie was making arrangements to rent a bicycle built for two.

"Jack, I don't think this is—"

"Why don't you put those packages in the basket, Nathan?" She patted his hand before paying for the rental.

"Listen, I haven't been on a bike since I was a teenager."

"It'll come back to you." The transaction complete, she turned to him and smiled. "I'll take the front if you're worried."

Perhaps she hadn't meant to bait him, but he didn't believe it. Nathan swung his leg over and settled on the front seat. "Get on," he told her. "And remember, you asked for it."

"I love a masterful man," she cooed. Nathan found his lips twitching at the phony southern accent as he set off.

She'd been right. It did come back to him. They pedaled smoothly, even sedately, across the street to ride along the seawall.

Jackie was glad he'd taken the lead. It gave her the opportunity to daydream and sightsee. Which, she thought with a smile, she would have done even if she'd been steering. This way, she didn't have to worry about running into a parked car or barreling down on pedestrians. Nathan could be trusted to steer true. It was only one more reason she loved him.

Matching her rhythm to his, she watched his shoulders. Strong and dependable. She found those both such lovely words. Strange...she'd never known she would find dependability so fiercely attractive until she'd found it. Found him.

Now he was relaxed, enjoying the sun and the day in it. She could give that to him. Not every day of the week, Jackie mused. He wouldn't always fall in with whatever last-minute plans she cooked up. But often enough, she thought, and wished there wasn't so much space between them so that she could wrap her arms around him and just hug.

He'd never pictured himself biking along the ocean-front—much less enjoying it. The fact was, Nathan rarely even came to this section of town. It was for tourists and teenagers. Being with Jackie made him feel like both. She was showing him new things not only about the city where he'd lived for nearly a decade but about the life he'd had more than thirty years to experience.

Everything about her was unexpected. How could he have known that the unexpected could also be the fresh? For a few hours he hadn't given a thought to Denver or penalty clauses or the responsibilities of tomorrow. He hadn't thought of tomorrow at all.

This was today, and the sun was bright, and the water was a rich blue against the golden sand. There were children squealing as they played in the surf, and there was the smell of oils and lotions. Someone was walking a dog along the beach, and a vendor was hawking nachos.

Across the street, beach towels waved colorfully over rails, making a tawdry little hotel seem exotic. He could smell hot dogs, he realized, and some kind of colored ice was being sold to children so that it would drip sticky down their arms as they slurped it. Oddly enough, he had a sudden yen for it himself.

When he looked up, he spotted the black-and-yellow colors of a kite shaped like a wasp. It had caught the wind and was climbing. A light plane flew over, trailing a flowing message about the special at a local restaurant.

He took it all in, wondering why he'd thought the beach held no magic for him. Perhaps it hadn't when he'd been alone.

On impulse, he signaled Jackie, then stopped.

"You owe me some ice cream."

"So I do." She slipped lithely off the bike, kissed him, then backtracked a few steps to a vendor. She considered, debated and studied her choices, taking a longer and more serious deliberation over ice cream on a stick than she had over a five-hundred-dollar brooch. After weighing the pros and cons, she settled on chocolate and nuts wrapped around a slab of vanilla.

Stuffing her change in her pocket, she turned and saw

Nathan. He was holding a big orange balloon. "Goes with your outfit," he told her, then gently looped the string around her wrist.

She was going to cry. Jackie felt the tears well up. It was only a ball of colorful rubber held by a string, she knew. But as symbols went, it was the best. She knew that when the air had finally escaped she would press the remains between the pages of a book as sentimentally as she would a rose.

"Thanks," she managed, then dutifully handed him the ice cream before she threw her arms around him.

He held her close, trying not to show the awkwardness he was suddenly feeling. How did a man deal with a woman who cried over a balloon? He'd expected her to laugh. Kissing her temple, he reminded himself that she rarely did the expected.

"You're welcome."

"I love you, Nathan."

"I think maybe you do," he murmured. The idea left him both exhilarated and shaken. What was he going to do about her? he wondered as his arms tightened around her. What the hell was he going to do about her, and them?

Looking up, Jackie saw the concern and the doubt in his eyes. She bit back a sigh, touching his face instead. There was time, she told herself. There was still plenty of time.

"Ice cream's melting." She was smiling as she brushed his lips with hers. "Why don't we sit on the wall while we eat it? Then you can change into your new shirt."

He cupped her chin in his hand, lingering over another kiss. He didn't know Justine had used the word *besotted* in describing his feelings for Jackie, but that was precisely what he was.

"I'm not changing shirts on the street."

She smiled again and took his hand.

When their hour was up, they pedaled back. Nathan was wearing his shark.

Chapter 10

From the doorway, Jackie watched Nathan drive off. She lifted her hand as his car headed down the street. For a moment there was only the sound of his fading engine breaking the morning quiet. Then, standing there, she heard the neighborhood noises of children being loaded into cars for school, doors slamming, goodbyes and last-minute instructions being given.

Nice sounds, Jackie thought as she leaned against the doorjamb. Regular everyday sounds that would be repeated morning after morning. There was a solidity to them, and a comfort.

She wondered if wives felt this way, seeing off their husbands after sharing that last cup of coffee and before the workday really began. It was an odd mixture of emotions, the pleasure of watching her man tidily on his way and the regret of knowing it would be hours before he came back.

But she wasn't a wife, Jackie reminded herself as she wandered away from the door without remembering to shut it. It didn't do any good to imagine herself as one. It did less good to regret knowing that Nathan was still far from ready for commitments and wedding rings.

It shouldn't be so important.

Chewing on her bottom lip, she started back upstairs. Mrs. Grange was already scrubbing and mopping the kitchen, and she herself had enough work to do to keep her occupied throughout the day. When Nathan came home, he would be glad to see her, and they'd share the casual talk of couples.

It couldn't be so important.

She was happy, after all, happier with Nathan than she'd ever been before or than she could imagine herself being without him. Since there had never been any major tragedies in her life, that was saying quite a lot. He cared for her, and if there were still restrictions on how much he would allow himself to care, what they had now was more than many people ever had.

He laughed more. It was very gratifying to know she'd given him that. Now, when she put her arms around him, it was a rare thing for her to find him tense. She wondered if he knew he reached for her in his sleep and held her close. She didn't think so. His subconscious had already accepted that they belonged together. That they were together. It would take a bit longer for him to accept that consciously.

So she'd be patient. Until Nathan, Jackie hadn't realized she had such an enormous capacity for patience. It pleased her to be able to find a virtue in herself that, because it had so seldom been tapped, seemed to run free.

He'd changed her. Jackie took her seat in front of her typewriter, thinking Nathan probably didn't realize that, either. She hadn't fully realized it herself until it had already happened. She thought of the future more, without the need for rose-colored glasses. She'd come to appreciate the ability to make plans—not that she wouldn't always enjoy an interesting detour, but she'd come to understand that happiness and good times didn't always hinge on impulse.

She'd begun to look at life a little differently. It had come home to her that a sense of responsibility wasn't necessarily a burden. It could also bring a sense of satisfaction and accomplishment. Seeing something through, even when the pace began to drag and the enthusiasm began to wane, was part of living. Nathan had shown her that.

She wasn't certain she could explain it to him so that he would understand or even believe her. After all, she'd never given anyone reason to believe she could be sensible, dependable and tenacious. Things were different now.

Surprised at her own nerves, she looked down at the padded envelope sitting beside the neatly typed pile of manuscript pages. For the first time in her life, she was ready to put herself on the line. To prove herself, Jackie thought, taking a deep breath. To prove herself to herself first, then to Nathan, then to her family.

There was no guarantee that the agent would accept the proposal, nor, though he'd been gracious and marginally encouraging, that he would find anything appealing in her work. Risks didn't frighten her, Jackie told herself. But still she hesitated, not quite able to take the next step and slip the pages into the envelope.

This risk frightened her. It hurt to admit it, but she was scared to death. It was no longer just a matter of telling an entertaining story from start to finish. It was her future on the line now, the future she had once blithely believed could take care of itself. If she failed now, she had no one to blame but herself.

She couldn't, as she had with so many of her other projects, claim that she'd discovered something that interested her more. Writing was it, win or lose, and somehow, though she knew it was foolish, the success or failure of her work was inevitably tied up with her success or failure with Nathan.

She crossed her fingers tight, eyes closed, and recited the first prayer that came into her head, though "Now I lay me down to sleep" wasn't quite appropriate. This done, Jackie shoved the proposal into the bag. Clutching it to her chest, she ran downstairs.

"Mrs. Grange, I've got to go out for a few minutes. I won't be long."

The housekeeper barely glanced up from her polishing. "Take your time."

It was done within fifteen minutes. Jackie stood in front of the post office, certain she'd just made the biggest mistake of her life. She should have gone over the first chapter again. A dozen glaring errors leaped into her mind, errors that seemed so obvious now that the manuscript was sealed and stamped and handed over to some post office clerk she didn't even know.

It occurred to her that there had been a wonderful angle she hadn't bothered to explore and that her characterization of the sheriff was much too weak. He should have chewed tobacco. That was the answer, the perfect answer. All she had to do was go in and stick a wad of tobacco in his mouth and the book would be a best-seller.

She took a step toward the door, stopped and took a step back. She was being ridiculous. Worse, if she didn't get hold of herself, she was going to be sick. Weak-kneed, she sat on the curb and dropped her head into her hands. Sink or swim, the proposal was going to New York, and it was going today. It amazed her to remember that she'd once thought of celebrating with champagne when she had enough to ship off. She didn't feel like celebrating. She felt like crawling home and burying herself under the covers.

What if she was wrong? Why hadn't she ever considered the fact that she could be totally and completely wrong— about the book, about Nathan, about herself? Only a fool, only a stupid fool, left herself without any route to survival.

She'd poured her heart into that story, then sent it off to a relative stranger who would then have the authority to give a thumbs-up or a thumbs-down without any regard for her as a person. It was business.

She'd given her heart to Nathan. She'd held it out to him in both hands and all but forced him to take it. If he tried to give it back to her, no matter how gently he handled it, it would be cracked and bruised.

There were tears on her cheeks. Feeling them, Jackie let out a little huff of disgust and dragged the heels of her hands over them. What a pitiful sight. A grown woman sitting on a curb crying because things might not work out the way she wanted them to. She sniffled, then rose to her feet. Maybe they wouldn't work out and she'd have to deal with it. But in the meantime she was going to do her damnedest to win.

By noon, Jackie was sitting at the counter, elbows up, looking at Mrs. Grange's latest pictures of her grandchildren while they shared a pasta salad.

"These are great. This one here… Lawrence, right?"

"That's Lawrence. He's three. A pistol."

Jackie studied the little towhead with the smear of what might have been peanut butter on his chin. "Looks like a heartbreaker to me. Do you get to spend much time with them?"

"Oh, now and again. Don't seem enough, though, with grandkids. They grow up faster than your own. This one, Anne Marie, she favors me." A big knuckled finger tapped a snapshot of a little girl in a frilly blue dress. "Hard to believe now—" Mrs. Grange patted an ample hip "—but I was a good-looking woman a few years and a few pounds back."

"You're still a good-looking woman, Mrs. Grange." Jackie poured out more of the fruit drink she'd concocted. "And you have a beautiful family."

Because the compliment had been given easily, Mrs. Grange accepted it. "Families, they make up for a lot. I was eighteen when I ran off to marry Clint. Oh, he was something to look at, let me tell you. Lean as a snake and twice as mean." She chuckled, the way a woman could over an old and almost faded mistake. "I was what you might call swept away."

She took a bite of pasta as she looked back. It didn't occur to her that she was talking about private things to someone she hardly knew. Jackie made it easy to talk. "Girls got no sense at that age, and I wasn't any different. Marry in haste, they say, but who listens?"

"People who say that probably haven't been lucky enough to have been swept away."

Admiring Jackie's logic, Mrs. Grange smiled. "That's true enough, and I can't say I regret it, even though at twenty-four I found myself in a crowded little apartment without a husband, without a penny, and with four little boys wanting their supper. Clinton had walked out on the lot of us, smooth as you please."

"I'm sorry. It must have been awful for you."

"I've had better moments." She turned then, seeing Jackie looking at her not with polite interest but with eyes filled with sympathy and understanding. "Sometimes we get what we ask for, Miss Jack, and I'd asked for Clint Grange, worthless snake that he was."

"What did you do after he'd left?"

"I cried. Spent the night and the better part of a day at it. It felt mighty good, that self-pity, but my boys needed a mother, not some wet-eyed female pining after her man. So I took a look around, figured I'd made enough of a mess of things for a while and decided to fix what I could. That's when I started cleaning houses. Twenty-eight years later, I'm still cleaning them." She looked around the tidy kitchen with a sense of simple satisfaction. "My kids are grown up, and two of them have families of their own. I guess you might say Clint did me a favor, but I don't think I'd thank

him if we happened to run into each other in the checkout
line at the supermarket."

Jackie understood the last of the sentiment, but not the
beginning. If a man had left her high and dry with four children, hanging was too good for him. "How do you figure
he did you a favor?"

"If he'd stayed with me, I'd never have been the same
kind of mother, the same kind of person. I guess you could
say that some people change your life by coming into it,
and others change it by going out." Mrs. Grange smiled
as she finished off her salad. "Course, I don't suppose I'd
shed any tears if I heard old Clinton was lying in a gutter
somewheres begging for loose change."

Jackie laughed and toasted her. "I like you, Mrs. Grange."

"I like you, too, Miss Jack. And I hope you find what
you're looking for with Mr. Powell." She rose then, but hesitated. She'd always been a good mother, but she'd never
been lavish with praise. "You're one of those people who
change lives by coming in. You've done something nice for
Mr. Powell."

"I hope so. I love him a lot." With a sigh, she stacked
Mrs. Grange's snapshots. "That's not always enough, is it?"

"It's better than a stick in the eye." In her gruff way,
she patted Jackie's shoulder, then went about her business.

Jackie thought that over, nodded, then walked upstairs,
where she went to work with a vengeance.

Long after Mrs. Grange had gone home and afternoon had
turned to evening, Nathan found her there. She was hunched
over the machine, posture forgotten, her hair falling into her
face and her bare feet hooked around the legs of the chair.

He watched her, more than a little intrigued. He'd never
really seen her work before. Whenever he'd come up, she'd

somehow sensed his approach and swung around in her chair the moment he'd entered.

Now her fingers would drum on the keys, then stop, drum again, then pause while she stared out of the window as if she'd gone into a trance. She'd begin to type again, frowning at the paper in front of her, then smiling, then muttering to herself.

He glanced over at the pile of pages to her right, unaware that the bulk of them were copies of what she'd mailed that morning. He had an uncomfortable feeling that she was more done than undone by this time. Then he cursed himself for being so selfish. What she was doing was important. He'd understood that since the night she'd spun part of the tale for him. It was wrong of him to wish it wouldn't move so quickly or so well, but he'd come to equate the end of her book with the end of their relationship. Yet he knew, even as he stood in the doorway and watched her, that it was he who would end it, and soon.

It had been a month. Only a month, he thought, dragging a hand through his hair. How had she managed to turn his life upside down in a matter of weeks? Despite all his resolutions, all his plans to the contrary, he'd fallen in love with her. That only made it worse. Loving, he wanted to give her all those pretty, unrealistic promises. Marriage, family, a lifetime. Years of shared days and nights. But all he could give her was disappointment.

It was best, really for the best, that Denver was only two weeks away. Even now the wheels were turning that would keep him at the office and in meetings more and at home less. In twelve days he would get on a plane and head west, away from her. Nathan had come to understand that if he didn't love her, if it were only need now, he might be tempted to make those promises to keep her there.

She deserved better. Despite both of them, he was going to make sure she didn't settle for less.

But there were twelve days left.

Quietly he moved toward her. When her fingers stilled again, he laid his hands on her shoulders. Jackie came off the chair with a yelp.

"I'm sorry," he said, but he had to laugh. "I didn't mean to startle you."

"You didn't. You scared me out of my skin." She sank back into the chair with a hand to her heart. "What are you doing home so early?"

"I'm not. It's after six."

"Oh. No wonder my back feels like it belongs to an eighty-year-old weight lifter."

He began to massage her shoulders. That, too, was something he'd learned from her. "How long have you been at it?"

"I don't know. Lost track. Right there... Mmm." Sighing her approval, she shifted under his hands. "I was going to set an alarm or something after Mrs. Grange left, but Burt Donley rode into town, and I forgot."

"Burt Donley?"

"The cold-blooded hired hand of Samuel Carlson."

"Oh, of course, Burt."

Chuckling, she looked over her shoulder. "Burt murdered Sarah's father, at Carlson's bidding. He and Jake have unfinished business from Laramie. That's when Burt gunned down Jake's best friend—in the back, of course."

"Of course."

"And how was your day?"

"Not as exciting. No major shootouts or encounters with loose women."

"Lucky for you I happen to be feeling very loose." She rose, sliding her body up his until her arms were linked around his neck. "Why don't I go see what I can mix together for dinner? Then we'll talk about it."

"Jack, you don't have to cook for me every night."

"We made a deal."

He stilled her mouth with a kiss, a longer and more intense one than he'd realized he needed. When he drew away, her eyes had that soft, unfocused look he'd come to love. "I'd say all those bets were off. Wouldn't you?"

"I don't mind cooking for you, Nathan."

"I know." She could have no idea how such a simple statement humbled him. "But I'd guess of the two of us you've had the tougher day." He drew her closer, wanting to smell her hair, brush his lips over her temple. He was hardly aware that his hands had slipped under her shirt just to stroke the long line of her back. "I'd offer to go down and throw something together, but I doubt you'd be able to eat it. Over the past few weeks I've learned my cooking's not just bad, it's embarrassing."

"We could send out for pizza."

"An excellent idea." He drew her toward the bed. "In an hour."

"An even better idea," she murmured, and melted into him.

Later, much later, after the sun had set and the cicadas had started their serenade, they sat on the patio, an empty carton between them and wine growing warm in glasses. The silence between them had stretched out, long and comfortable. Lovemaking and food had left them content. There was an ease between that usually came only from years of friendship or from complete understanding.

The moon was round and white and generous with its light. With her legs stretched out and her eyes half closed, Jackie decided she could happily stay where she was for hours. It could be like this, just like this, she thought, for the rest of her life.

"You know, Nathan, I've been thinking."

"Hmm?" He stirred himself enough to look at her. Moonlight did something special to her skin, to her eyes. Though he knew he would remember her best in the sunlight, with energy vibrating through her, there would be times when he would need a memory like this—of Jackie, almost bonelessly relaxed, in the light of a full moon.

"Are you listening?"

"No, I'm looking. There are times you are incredibly lovely."

She smiled, almost shyly, then reached out to take his hands. "Keep that up and I won't be able to think at all."

"Is that all it takes?"

"Do you want to hear my idea or not?"

"I'm never sure if I want to hear your ideas."

"This is a good one. I think we should have a party."

"A party?"

"Yes, you know what a party is, Nathan. A social gathering, often including music, food, drink and a group of people brought together for entertainment purposes."

"I've heard of them."

"Then we've passed the first hurdle." She kissed his hand, but he could tell that her mind was already leaping forward. "You've been back from Europe for weeks now and you haven't seen any of your friends. You do have friends, don't you?"

"One or two."

"There we go, over the second hurdle." Lazily she stretched out her legs, rubbing the arch of her foot over his calf. "As a businessman and a pillar of the community— I'm sure you're a pillar of the community—it's practically your obligation to entertain."

He lifted a brow. "I've never been much of a pillar, Jack."

"That's where you're wrong. Anyone who wears a suit the way you do is an absolute pillar." She grinned at him, knowing she'd ruffled his feathers. "A man of distinction, that's you, darling. A tower of strength and conservatism. A dyed-in-the-wool Republican."

"How do you know I'm a Republican?"

Her smile became sympathetic. "Please, Nathan, let's not debate the obvious. Have you ever owned a foreign car?"

"I don't see what that has to do with it."

"Never mind, your politics are entirely your affair." She patted his hand. "Myself, I'm a political agnostic. I'm not entirely convinced they exist. But we're getting off the subject."

"What else is new?"

"Let's talk party, Nathan." As she spoke, she leaned closer, enthusiasm already bubbling. "You've got those fat little address books at every phone in the house. I'm sure out of them you could find enough convivial bodies to make up a party."

"Convivial bodies?"

"A party's nothing without them. It doesn't have to be elaborate—just a couple dozen people, some nice little canapés and an air of good cheer. It could be a combination welcome-home and bon-voyage party for you."

He glanced over sharply at that. Her eyes were steady and a great deal more serious than her words. So, she was thinking about Denver, too. It was like her not to have mentioned it directly or to have asked questions. His fingers tightened on hers. "When did you have in mind?"

She could smile again. Now that his leaving had been brought up and acknowledged, she could push it firmly to the back of her mind. "How about next week?"

"All right. I have an agency we can call."

"No, a party's personal."

"And a lot of work."

She shook her head. She wasn't able to explain that she needed something to keep her mind occupied. "Don't worry, Nathan. If there's one thing I know how to do, it's throw a party. You take care of contacting your friends. I'll do the rest."

"If that's what you want."

"Very much. Now that that's settled, how about a swim?"

He glanced over at the pool. It was inviting and tempting, but so was sitting doing nothing. "Go ahead. The idea of changing into a suit seems too complicated."

"Who needs a suit?" To prove a point, she rose and shimmied out of her shorts.

"Jack…"

"Nathan," she said, mimicking his tone, "one of the ten great pleasures of life is skinny-dipping in the moonlight." The thin bikinis she wore joined her shorts. Her baggy T-shirt skimmed her thighs. "You have a very private pool here," she continued. "Your neighbors would need a stepladder and binoculars to sneak a peak." Carelessly she pulled the T-shirt over her head and stood, slim and naked. "If they want to that badly, we may as well oblige them."

His mouth went dry. He should have been beyond that by now. Over the past few weeks he'd seen, touched, tasted every inch of her. Yet watching Jackie poised at the edge of the pool, her body gold and gleaming in the moonlight, made his heart thud like a teenager's on a first date.

She rose on her toes, arched and dived cleanly into the water. And surfaced, laughing. "God, I've missed this." Her body glimmered beneath the surface, darker and somehow more lush with the illusion of moonlight and water. "I used to sneak out at one in the morning to swim like this. My mother would have been horrified, even though there was a six-foot wall around the estate and the pool was hidden by trees. There was something wonderfully decadent about swimming nude at one in the morning. Aren't you coming in?"

He was already having trouble breathing, and he only shook his head. If he went in, he wouldn't do much swimming.

"And you said you weren't a pillar of the community." She laughed at him and trailed her fingers through the water. "All right, then, I guess I've got to get tough. It's for your own good." With a sigh, she lifted a hand out of the water. Like a child playing cowboy, she pointed it at him, finger out, thumb up. "Okay, Nathan, get up slow. Don't make any sudden moves."

"Give me a break, Jack."

"This is a hair trigger," she warned him. "Get up, and keep your hands where I can see them."

He couldn't have said why he did it. Maybe it was the full moon. He rose to a more interesting view.

"Okay, strip." She touched her tongue to her top lip. "Slow."

"You really are out of your mind."

"Don't beg, Nathan, it's pitiful." She cocked her thumb back over an invisible hammer. "Do you have any idea what a .38 slug can do to the human body? Take my word for it, it's not a pretty sight."

With a shrug, he pulled off his shirt. It wouldn't hurt to go in wearing his shorts. "You haven't got the guts to use that thing."

"Don't bet on it." But her lips twitched as she struggled with a grin. "Come a step closer with your pants on and I'll blow off a kneecap. Something like that gives a whole new meaning to the word *pain*."

She was crazy, he had no doubt about that. But apparently some of it had rubbed off. Nathan unsnapped his shorts and stepped out of them. She was going to get a surprise when he joined her in the water.

"That's good, very good." Deliberately she took her time evaluating him. "Now the rest."

With his eyes on hers, he stripped off his briefs. "You have no shame."

"Not a bit. Aren't you lucky?" Laughing, she gestured with her imaginary gun. "Into the pool, Nathan. Face the music."

He dived in, no more than an arm's length from her. When he surfaced, Jackie was treading water and smiling. "You dropped your gun."

She glanced down, as if surprised, at her open hand. "So I did."

"Let's see how tough you are unarmed."

He lunged for her, but she was quick. Anticipating him, Jackie dived deep, kicked out and glided under him. When she surfaced, she was six feet away with a smug smile. "Missed," she said lightly, and waited for his next move.

Slowly they circled, eyes locked. Jackie bit her lip, knowing that if she gave in to the laughter she would be sunk in more ways than one. Nathan was as strong a swimmer as she, but she was counting on speed and agility to see her through. Until she was ready to lose.

He advanced, she evaded. He feinted, she adjusted. He maneuvered, she outmaneuvered. For the next few minutes there were only the sounds of insects and lapping water, giving them both a sense of solitude. Suddenly inspired, he brought a hand out of the water, cupping his fingers in his palm, pointing the index and cocking the thumb.

"Look what I found."

That was all it took to have her laughter breaking through. In two long strokes, he had her.

"Cheat. You cheated. Nathan, there's hope for you yet." Giggling, she reached to hug him. Then his hand was hard and fast around her hair. The roughness was so uncharacteristic that her eyes flew to his. What she saw had her breath catching. This time it was her mouth that went dry. "Nathan," she managed before her lips were imprisoned by his.

The need was fiercer, edgier, more frenzied than it had ever been before. He felt as though his body were full of springs that had all been wound too tightly. Against his own, her heart was beating desperately as he dived into her mouth, taking, tasting, devouring all. His teeth scraped her lips, his tongue invaded, tantalized by her breathless moan. Her body, at first taut as wire, went limp against him. They slipped beneath the surface without a thought for air.

The water enveloped them, making their movements slow and sluggish but no less urgent. The sensuous kiss of the cool, night-darkened water flowed around them, then ran off in torrents as they rose above it, still wrapped close.

Her first submission had passed. Now she was as desperate and anxious as he. She clung to him, head thrown back as he brought her up so that he could suckle her damp, water-cooled breasts. With each greedy pull, her stomach contracted and her pulse thudded out the new rhythm. The fingers on his shoulders dug in, leaving thin crescents. Then her mouth was on his again, thirsty.

She took her hands under, then over him, while her mind spun faster than her movements. Their bodies were captured in a slow-motion dream world, but their thoughts, their needs, raced.

Reaching down, he found her, cool and inviting. At his touch, his name burst from her. The sound of it across the quiet moonlight had his madness growing. She clung to him, her hands slipping over his slick body, then grasping for purchase. Her lips were wet and open when he took them again.

Jackie found her back braced against the side of the pool. Trembling with anticipation, she opened for him, then groaned when he filled her. Her hands fell lifelessly in the water, and he was there, holding her, moving in her.

The moonlight was on her face, making it both exotic and beautiful, but he could only press his own into her shoulder and ride the wave.

Chapter 11

Some people were born knowing how to entertain, and Jackie was one of them. The fact that she was using a party as a way of blocking out the knowledge that she had only a few more days until Nathan left didn't mean she was any less determined to make it a success.

She wrote for eight, sometimes ten, hours a day, losing herself in another romance, in another catastrophe. When she wasn't chained to her machine, she was shopping, planning menus, checking off lists and supplies.

She insisted on doing all the cooking herself but had decided to enlist Mrs. Grange to help serve and her son, the future teacher, to tend bar.

She was delighted when Nathan joined her in the kitchen the afternoon of the party, his sleeves rolled up and his mind set on helping her make hors d'oeuvres. Determined he was, and clumsy. Jackie found both traits endearing. Tactfully she buried his attempts on the bottom tray.

Jackie, optimistic about the weather, had planned to set up tables outside so that the guests could wander out among the colored lights she'd hung. Her faith was rewarded when the day remained clear and promised a star-filled, breezy night.

She rarely worried about the success or failure of a party, but this was different. She wanted it to be perfect, to prove to herself and to Nathan that she belonged in his world as much as she belonged in his arms.

She had only a matter of days left before he would fly thousands of miles away from her. It was difficult not to dwell on that, and on the fact that he had never told her what he wanted of her. What he wanted for them. She refused to believe that he still considered permanence impossible.

He'd never told her he loved her. That was a thought that hit her painfully at the oddest times. But he'd shown her in so many ways. Often he'd call her in the middle of the day just to hear her voice. He'd bring her flowers, from his garden or from a roadside stand, just when the ones she'd put in a vase had begun to fade. He'd draw her close, just to hold her after lovemaking, after passion had ebbed and contentment remained.

A woman didn't need words when she had everything else.

The hell she didn't.

Pushing back her gnawing doubts, Jackie told herself that for once she would have to be content with what she had instead of what she wanted.

An hour before the party she began to pamper herself. This was one of her mother's traditions that Jackie approved of. She was using her old room after telling Nathan he'd only be in her way. There was some truth in that, but more, Jackie had discovered she wanted to add a touch of mystery to the evening. She wanted him to see not the step-by-step preparation but the completed woman.

A long, leisurely bubble bath was first on her list. She soaked, the radio playing quietly while she looked out through the skylight over the tub. The only clouds in the sky were as harmless as white spun sugar.

She took time and care with her makeup, shooting for the exotic. When she studied her face from every angle in the mirror, she was satisfied with the results. She indulged in the feminine pleasure of slathering on perfumed cream before she took the dress she'd bought only the day before out of the closet.

Nathan was already downstairs when she started out. She could hear him talking to Mrs. Grange, and she could hear the woman's gruff replies. Always one to enjoy a bit of drama, Jackie put her hand on the rail and started slowly down.

She wasn't disappointed. Nathan glanced up, saw her and stopped in midsentence. Intent on him, she didn't notice the tall sandy-haired man beside Mrs. Grange. Nor did she see his mouth fall open.

Her eyes dominated her face, smudged on the lids with blending tones of bronze. Her hair, a combination of nature and womanly art, was windswept and cunningly tousled. Oversize silver stars glinted at her ears.

When Nathan could drag his gaze away from her face to take in the rest of her, it was another shock to the system.

The dress she'd chosen was stunning, eye-burning white that fell in a narrow column from her breasts to her ankles, leaving her shoulders bare and her arms unadorned but for the dozen silver bracelets that encircled her arm from her wrist almost to her elbow. Smiling, she reached the bottom, then turned in a circle, revealing the slit in the back of the dress that reached to midthigh.

"What do you think?"

"You're stunning."

Finishing the circle, she studied him in turn. No one wore a black suit with quite as much style as Nathan, Jackie thought. It must have been that broad-shouldered, muscled body that gave conservatism a dangerous look. She took a step closer to kiss him. Then, with her hand in his, she turned to Mrs. Grange.

"I really appreciate you helping us out tonight. And this is your son? You must be Charlie."

"Yes, ma'am." He swallowed audibly, then accepted the hand she offered. His palm was sweaty. His mother hadn't told him that Miss Jack was a goddess.

"It's nice to meet you, Charlie. Your mom's told us a lot about you. Shall I show you where we've set up the bar?"

Mrs. Grange gave him an elbow in the ribs. The boy looked as if he had rocks in his head when he stared that way. "I'll show him what he needs to know. Come on, Charlie, get the lead out."

Charlie went with his mother—because she had a death grip on his arm—but sent one last moonstruck look over his shoulder.

"The kid's jaw dropped on his shoes when he saw you."

With a laugh, Jackie tucked her arm through Nathan's. "That's kind of sweet."

"Mine hit the floor."

She looked at him, nearly level with him in her heeled sandals. "That's even sweeter."

"You always manage to surprise me, Jack."

"I hope so."

With his free hand he touched her shoulder, then ran his fingertips down her arm. "This is the first time I remember wishing a party was over before it began." It wasn't her usual scent tonight, but something stunningly sexy and taunting. "What did you do to yourself up there?"

"Tricks of the trade." She had to shift only slightly for her lips to meet his. "It's still me, Nathan."

"I know." His arm curled around her waist to keep her there. "That's why I wish the party was over."

"Tell you what." She slid her hands over his shoulders. "When it is, we'll have one all our own."

"I'm counting on it." He lowered his lips to hers as the doorbell rang.

"Round one," she said. Keeping his hand in hers, she went to answer the door.

Within an hour, the house was milling with people. Most of them were every bit as interested in finding out about the woman in Nathan's life as they were in an evening of socializing. She didn't mind. She was just as curious about them.

She discovered Nathan knew a wide variety of people, from the staunch and stuffy to the easygoing. It took only a smile and a greeting for her to click with Cody Johnson, an architect who had joined Nathan's firm two years before. He favored scuffed boots and faded jeans but had made a concession to formality by tossing on a suit jacket. Since her brother favored the same style and brand, Jackie recognized it as murderously expensive. He clamped a hand over hers, looked her up and down with eyes as brown as her own, then winked.

"I've been wanting to get a look at you."

"Check out the boss's outside interests?"

"Something like that." He still held her hand, but there was nothing flirtatious in the gesture. Jackie had the feeling that Cody got his impressions as much by touch as by sight. "One thing you can never fault Nathan for is his taste. I always figured whenever he looked more than twice at a woman she'd have to be special."

"That seemed like both a compliment and approval."

"You could say that." He didn't often give both so easily. "I'm glad, because Nathan's a good friend. The best. You planning on sticking around?"

Her brow lifted. Though she preferred direct questions, Jackie didn't feel obligated to respond with a direct answer. "You cut right through, don't you?"

"Hate to waste time."

Yes, she decided, she liked Cody Johnson just fine. With

her hand still in his, she looked over and spotted Nathan. "I plan on sticking around."

His lips curved. He had one of those quick, arrogant grins that women found devastating. Because, Jackie thought, a woman could never be sure what he was thinking. "Then why don't I buy you a drink?"

Tucking her arm through his, she headed for the bar. "Have you met Justine Chesterfield?"

His laugh was full and rich. Jackie liked that as much as she did the sun-bronzed hair that fell over his forehead. "Anyone ever tell you you're clear as glass?"

"Hate to waste time."

"I appreciate that." He stopped at the bar and was amused by the way the college boy gaped at his hostess. "She's a nice lady, but a little rich for my blood."

"Is there anyone special?"

"Depends. You got a sister?"

With a laugh, Jackie turned and ordered champagne. Neither of them noticed Nathan watching them with a small, preoccupied frown.

He wasn't a jealous man. Nathan had always considered that one of the most foolish and unproductive emotions. Not only was jealousy the green-eyed monster, it invariably made the affected party look, and act, like an idiot.

He was neither an idiot nor jealous, but watching Jackie with Cody made him feel suspiciously like both. It was not, Nathan discovered, a sensation that could be enjoyed or ignored.

Cody was certainly more her type. Nathan managed to smile at the squeaky-voiced engineer who thought he had his attention. Cody could easily have passed for a gunfighter. Jackie's diamond-in-the-rough Jake Redman. That was Cody, with his loose limbed, rangy build and his sun-bleached hair that always looked as though it were one week past time for the barber. And there was the drawl. Nathan had always considered Cody's slight drawl soothing, but it began to occur to him that a woman might find it exciting. Some women.

Added to that was a deceptively laid-back attitude, a total lack of interest in convention and a restless, unerring eye for quality. Fast cars, late nights and bright lights. That was Cody.

When Nathan saw Jackie glance up and laugh into Cody's wide grin, he considered the potential satisfaction of strangling them both.

Ridiculous. Nathan sipped his drink, then reached for a cigarette. He wasn't fully aware that he rarely wanted—needed—a cigarette these days. Cody was a friend, probably the best friend Nathan had now, or had ever had. And Jackie... What was Jackie?

Lover, friend, companion. A delight and, oddly enough, a rock. It was strange to think of someone who looked and acted like a butterfly as something so solid and secure. She could be loyal when loyalty was deserved and strong when strength was needed. But rock or not, he'd given her no reason to pledge her fidelity. For her own good. He didn't want to cage her in or narrow her horizons.

The hell he didn't.

Cutting off the engineer in midsentence, Nathan made a vague excuse and moved toward Jackie.

She was laughing again, her face glowing with it, her eyes brilliant as they slanted upward over the rim of her champagne flute. "Nathan, you didn't tell me your associate was the kind of man mothers warn their daughters about." But as she spoke, her hand linked casually with Nathan's. It was the kind of ease that spoke of certain intimacy.

"I'm happy to take that as a compliment." Cody was drinking vodka straight up, and he toasted her with the squat glass. "Nice party, boss. I've already complimented you on your taste."

"Thanks. You know there are tables loaded with food outside. Knowing your appetite, I'm surprised you haven't found them."

"I'm on my way." He sent Jackie a final wink, then sauntered off.

"Well, that was certainly a subtle heave-ho," she commented.

"It seemed he was taking up a great deal of your time."

Her head swiveled around, her brows lifted, and then her face glowed again with a fresh smile. "That's nice. That's very, very nice." She brushed her lips lightly over his. "Some women don't care for possessive men. Myself, I like them a lot. To a point."

"I simply meant—"

"Don't spoil it." She kissed him again before she tucked her arm through his. "Well, shall we stroll around looking convivial, or shall we dive into that food before I starve to death?"

He raised her hand to his lips. The quick bout of jealousy, if that was what it was, hadn't caused him to look or act like an idiot. That was one more thing he'd have to rearrange his thinking about.

"We'll dive," he decided. "It's hard to be convivial on an empty stomach."

The evening was a complete success. Cards and calls came in over the next few days complimenting and commenting. Invitations were extended. It should have been a delightful time for Jackie. She had met Nathan's friends and associates and had won them over. But it wasn't Nathan's friends and associates who mattered. The bottom line was Nathan himself, and he was going to Denver.

It was no longer something she could think about later, not when his plane ticket was tucked in his briefcase. She'd been to Denver herself once, to sit on the fifty-yard line at Mile High Stadium and cheer. She'd enjoyed it well enough. Now she hated it, as a city and as a symbol.

He was leaving in a matter of hours, and they'd settled nothing. Once or twice he'd tried to talk to her, but she'd put him off. It was cowardly, but if he was going to brush her out of his life, she wanted every moment she could grab before it happened.

Now she was out of time, but she'd made herself a firm promise. He would at least tell her why. If he didn't want her any longer—wouldn't let himself want her—she would have the reasons.

She braced herself outside the bedroom door, squared her shoulders, then walked in. "I brought you some coffee."

Nathan glanced up from his packing. "Thanks." He'd thought he'd been miserable a few times before in his life. He'd been wrong.

"Need any help with this?" She lifted her own cup and sipped. Somehow it was easier to have serious, life-altering discussions when you were doing something as casual as drinking coffee.

"No. I'm almost finished."

Nodding, she sat on the edge of the bed. If she paced, as she wanted to, it would be easy to slam the cup against the wall and watch it shatter. As she wanted to. "You haven't said how long you'll be out of town."

"That's because I can't be sure." He'd never hated packing before. It had always been just one more small, slightly annoying chore. He hated it now. "It could be three weeks, more likely four, on this first trip. If we don't run into any major complications, I should be able to spot-check it as we go."

She sipped again, but the coffee was bitter. "Should I be here when you get back?"

It was like her to put it that way, not a demand or even a request, but a question. He wanted to say yes, please, yes, but "It's up to you" was what he told her.

"No, it's not. We both know how I feel, what I want. I haven't made a secret out of it." She paused a moment, wondering if she should feel a loss of pride. But none came. "Now it comes down to what you feel and what you want."

Her eyes were so solemn. There was no hint of a smile on her lips. He missed that, already missed that bright, vivid look she wore the way other women wore jewelry. "You mean a lot to me, Jackie." The word *love* was there, in his mind, in his heart, but he couldn't say it. "More than anyone else."

It amazed her that she was almost desperate enough, almost hungry enough, to accept those crumbs and be content. But she lifted a brow and continued watching him. "And?"

He packed another freshly laundered shirt. He wanted to choose the right words, say the right thing. Over and over during the last twenty-four hours he'd imagined what he would say to her, what he would do. In one wildly satisfying fantasy he'd dragged her to the airport with him and they'd flown away together. On a shell pelican.

But this was real. If he couldn't give her anything else, he could give her fairness.

"I can't ask you to stay, to wait, then live your life day by day. That's not what I want for you, Jack."

The hurting came from his honesty. He wouldn't lie or give her what she thought might be the comfort of pretense. "I'd like you to take a step back and tell me what you want for yourself. Is it what you had before, Nathan? Peace and quiet and no complications?"

Wasn't it? But somehow, when she said it, that life no longer sounded settled and comfortable, it sounded stagnant and boring. Yet it was the only one he was sure of. "I can't give you what you want," he said, struggling for calm. "I can't give you marriage and family and a lifetime commitment, because I don't believe in those things, Jack. I'd rather hurt you now than hurt you consistently over the rest of our lives."

She said nothing for a moment, afraid she would say too much. Her heart had gone out to him. There had been more misery in those last few words than she'd known he felt, or could feel. Though she hurt with him, she wasn't sorry she'd dredged it up.

"Was it that bad?" she said quietly. "Were you that unhappy growing up?"

He could have sworn at her for putting her slim, sensitive finger on the core of it. "That's not relevant."

"Oh, it is, and we both know it." She rose. She had to move, just a little, or the tension inside of her was going to explode and shatter her into a million pieces. "Nathan, I won't say you owe me an explanation. People are always saying, 'He owes me,' or 'I owe him.' I've always felt that when you do something for someone, or give something away, that you should do it freely or not at all. So there's no debt." She sat again, calmer, then looked at him again. "But I have to say that I think it's right for you to tell me why."

He fished out a cigarette and lit it as he sat on the opposite end of the bed. "Yes, you're right. You're entitled to reasons." He was silent for a long time, trying to sort out the words, but it wasn't possible to plan them. So he simply began.

"My mother came from a wealthy and established family. She was expected to make a good marriage. A proper marriage. She'd been raised and educated with that in mind."

Jackie frowned a little, but tried to be fair. "That wasn't so unusual a generation ago."

"No, and it was the rule of thumb in her family. My father had more ambition than security, but had earned a reputation as an up-and-comer. He was, I've been told, dynamic and charismatic. When my mother fell in love with him, her family wasn't overjoyed, but they didn't object. Marriage to her gave my father exactly what he wanted. Family name, family backing, a well-bred wife who could entertain properly and give him an heir."

Jackie looked down at her empty cup. "I see," she murmured, and she was beginning to.

"He didn't love her. The marriage was a business decision."

He paused again, studying the column of smoke rising toward the ceiling. Was that the core of it? he wondered. Was that what had damaged his parents, and him, the most? Restless, he moved his shoulders. It was history, ancient history.

"I don't doubt that he had a certain amount of affection for her. He wasn't able, he'd never been able, to give too much of himself. His business took him away from home quite a bit. He was obsessed with making a fortune, with personal and professional success. When I was born, he gave my mother an emerald necklace as a reward for producing a son."

She started to speak, struck by the bitterness in his tone, then closed her mouth. Sometimes it was best only to listen.

"My mother adored him, was almost fanatic about it. As a child I had a nurse, a nanny and a bodyguard. She was terrified of what he might do if anything happened to me. It wasn't so much that she worried about me as a son, but as *his* son. His symbol."

"Oh, Nathan…" she began, but he shook his head.

"She told me in almost those words when I was five, six years old. She told me that and a great deal more once her feelings for him had changed. I rarely saw either of them when I was growing up. She was so determined to be the perfect society wife, and he was always flying off somewhere or another to close a deal. His idea of being a father consisted of periodic checks on my progress in school, lectures on responsibility and family honor. The trouble was, he had no honor himself."

With slow, deliberate motions he crushed out his cigarette. "There were other women. My mother knew and ignored it. He told me once there was nothing serious in those relationships. A man away from home so often required certain comforts."

"He told you?" Jackie demanded, stupidly shocked.

"When I was sixteen. I believe he considered it a heart-to-heart. My mother's feelings for him were dead by that time, and we were living like three polite strangers in the same house."

"Couldn't you have gone to your grandparents?"

"My grandmother was dead. She might have understood. I can't be sure. My grandfather considered the marriage a success. My mother certainly never complained, and my father had lived up to his potential. He would have been horrified if I'd arrived on his doorstep saying I couldn't live in the same house with my own parents. Besides, I had the place to myself a great deal of the time."

Privacy, she thought. She certainly understood his need for privacy. But what would it have done to a young boy to have his privacy in such an unhealthy place? "It must have been terrible for you."

She thought of her own family, wealthy, prestigious, respected. But their house had never been quiet, not the way she imagined Nathan's childhood home. It had never been cold. Hers had been filled with screams of laughter and accusations. With fists raised, the emotion in the threat heatedly real at the moment, then laughed about later.

"Nathan," she began slowly, "did you ever tell them how they made you feel?"

"Once. They were simply appalled with me for my lack of gratitude. And my lack of…graciousness in bringing up the subject. You learn not to beat your head against a wall that isn't going to move and find other ways."

"What other ways?"

"Study, personal ambitions. I can't say they ceased to exist for me as parents, but I shifted priorities. My father was away when I graduated from high school. I went to Europe that summer, so I didn't see him again until I was in college. He'd discovered I was studying architecture and came, he thought, to pull the rug out from under my feet.

"He wanted, as you put it once, for me to follow in his footsteps. He expected it. He demanded it. I'd lived under his thumb for eighteen years, totally cowed by my, and my mother's, perception of him. But something had happened. When I'd decided I wanted to build, the idea, the dream of that, became bigger than he."

"You'd grown up," she murmured.

"Enough, apparently, to stand up to him. He threatened to stop my tuition. I had a responsibility to him and the family business. That's all the family was, you see. A business. My mother was in full agreement. The fact was, once she'd stopped loving him, she couldn't have cared less. For her, I was my father's son."

"Surely that's too harsh, Nathan. Your mother—"

"Told me she hadn't wanted me." He reached for another cigarette, then broke it in half. "She said she believed if I hadn't been born her marriage could have been saved.

Without the responsibility of a child she could have traveled with my father."

Her face had gone very white. She didn't want to believe him. She didn't want to think that anyone could be so cruel to her own child. "They didn't deserve you." Swallowing a lump of tears, she rose to go to him.

"That's not the point." He put his hands out, knowing if she put her arms around him now he would fall apart. He had never spoken of this with anyone before, hadn't wanted to think it through stage by stage. "I made a decision that day I faced my father. I had no family, had never had one and didn't need one. My grandmother had left me enough to get me through college. So I used that, and took nothing from him. What I did from that point, I did on my own, for myself. That hasn't changed."

She let her arms rest at her sides. He wouldn't allow her to comfort him, and as much as her heart ached to, her mind told her that perhaps it wasn't comfort he needed.

"You're still letting them run your life." Her voice wasn't soft now, but angry, angry with him, angry for him. "Their marriage was ugly, so marriage itself is ugly? That's stupid."

"Not marriage itself, marriage for me." Fury hit him suddenly. He'd opened up an old and tender wound for her, yet she still wanted more. "Do you think people only inherit brown eyes or a cleft chin from their parents? Don't you be stupid, Jack. They give us a great deal more than that. My father was a selfish man. I'm a selfish man, but at least I have the common sense to know I can't put myself, you or the children we'd have through that kind of misery."

"Common sense?" The MacNamara temper, famed for generations, leaped out. "You can stand there spouting off that kind of drivel and call it common sense? You haven't got enough sense to fill a teaspoon. For God's sake, Nathan, if your father had been an ax murderer, does that mean you'd be lunging around looking for people to chop up? My father loves raw oysters, and I can't stand to look at them. Does that mean I'm adopted?"

"You're being absurd."

"I'm being absurd? *I'm* being absurd?" With a sound of disgust, she reached for the closest thing at hand—a nineteenth-century Venetian bowl—and smashed it to the floor. "You obviously wouldn't recognize absurd if it shot you between the eyes. I'll tell you what's absurd. Absurd is loving someone and having them love you right back, then refusing to do anything solid about it because maybe, just maybe, it wouldn't work out perfectly."

"I'm not talking about perfect. Damn it, Jack, not that vase."

But it was already a pile of French porcelain shards on the floor. "Of course you're talking about perfect. Perfect's your middle name. Nathan Perfect Powell, projecting his life years into the future, making certain there aren't any loose ends or uneven edges."

"Fine." He swung her around before she could grab something else. "That should be enough right there to show you I'm right about this, about us. I like things done a certain way, I do plan ahead and insist on completing things as carefully as they're begun. You, by your own admission, never finish anything."

Her chin came up. Her eyes were dry. The tears would come later, she knew, torrents of them. "I wondered how long it would take you to throw that in my face. You're right about one thing, Nathan. The world's made up of two kinds of people, the careful and the careless. I'm a careless person and content to be so. But I don't think less of you for being a careful one."

He let out a quiet breath. He wasn't used to fighting,

not unless it was over the quality of materials or working conditions for his men. "I didn't mean that as an insult."

"No? Well, maybe not, but the point's taken. We're not alike, and though I think we're both capable of a certain amount of growth and compromise, we'll never be alike. That doesn't change the fact that I love you and want to spend my life with you." This time she grabbed him, by the shirtfront. "You're not your father, Nathan, and I'm sure as hell not your mother. Don't let them do this to you, to us."

He covered her hands with his. "Maybe if you weren't so important it would be easier to risk it. I could say all right, we want each other, so let's take the chance. But I care for you too much to go into this with two strikes against me."

"You care too much." The tears were going to come, and soon, so she backed away. "Damn you for that, Nathan. For not having the guts to say you love me, even now."

She whirled around and ran out. He heard the front door slam.

Chapter 12

"The masons lost two days with the rain. I'm putting on double shifts."

Nathan stood at the building site, squinting into the sun, which had finally made an appearance. It was cold in Denver. Spring hadn't floated in gently. The few hopeful wildflowers that had poked up had been carelessly trampled over. By next spring, the grounds would be green and trimmed. Looking at the scarred earth and the skeleton of the building, he already saw it.

"Considering the filthy weather you've been having, there's been a lot of progress in just under three weeks." Cody, a Stetson shading his eyes, his booted feet planted wide apart, looked at the beams and girders. Unlike Nathan, he didn't see the finished product. He preferred this stage, when there were still possibilities. "It looks good," he decided. "You, on the other hand, look like hell."

"It's always nice to have you around, Cody." Studying his clipboard, Nathan began a steady and detailed analysis of work completed and work projected. Schedules had to be adjusted, and deadlines met.

"You seem to have everything under control, as usual."

"Yeah." Nathan pulled out a cigarette, cupping his hands over his lighter.

As the flame leaped on, Cody noticed the shadows under Nathan's eyes, the lines of strain that had dug in around his mouth. To Cody's mind, there was only one thing that could make a strong man look battered. That was a woman.

Nathan dropped his lighter back in his pocket. "The building inspector should make his pass through today."

"Bless his heart." Cody helped himself to a cigarette from Nathan's pack. "I thought you were quitting these?"

"Eventually." One of the laborers had a portable radio turned up full. Nathan thought of Jackie blaring music through the kitchen speakers. "Any problems back home?"

"Businesswise? No. But I was about to ask you the same thing."

"I haven't been there, remember? Got an update on the Sydney project?"

"Ready to break ground in about six weeks." He took another drag, then broke the filter off the cigarette. Cody figured if you were going to kill yourself you might as well do it straight out. "You and Jack have a disagreement?"

"Why?"

"Because from the looks of you you haven't had a decent night's sleep since you got out here." He found a bent pack of matches in his pocket, remembered the club that was printed on the front with some fondness, then struck a match. "Want to talk about it?"

"There's nothing to talk about."

Cody merely lifted a brow and drew in more smoke. "Whatever you say, boss."

Nathan swore and pinched at the tension between his eyes. "Sorry."

"Okay." He stood quiet for a time, smoking and watching the men at work. "I could do with some coffee and a plateful of eggs." He pitched the stub of the cigarette into the construction rubble. "Since I'm on an expense account, I'll buy."

"You're a sport, Cody." But Nathan walked back to the pickup truck.

Within ten minutes they were sitting in a greasy little diner where the menu was written on a chalkboard and the waitresses wore holsters and short shocking-pink uniforms. There was a bald man dozing over his coffee at the counter and booths with ashtrays in the shape of saddles. The smell of onions hung stubbornly in the air.

"You always could pick a class joint," Nathan muttered as they slid into a booth, but all he could think of was how Jackie would have enjoyed it.

"It ain't the package, son." Cody settled back and grinned as one of the waitresses shrieked out an order to a stocky, grim-faced man at the grill.

A pot of coffee was plopped down without being asked for. Cody poured it himself and watched the steam rise. "You can keep your fancy French restaurants. Nobody makes coffee like a diner."

Jackie did, Nathan thought, and found he'd lost his taste for it.

Cody grinned up at the frowsy blonde who stopped, pad in hand, by their booth. "That blue plate special. I want two of them."

"Two blue plates," she muttered, writing.

"On one plate, darling," he added.

She looked over her pad and let her gaze roam over him. "I guess you do have a lot to fill up."

"That's the idea. Bring my friend the same."

She turned to study Nathan and decided it was her lucky day. Two hunks at her station, though the dark one looked as if he'd put in a rough night. Or a week of rough nights. She smiled at Nathan, showing crooked incisors. "How do you want your eggs, sweetie?"

"Over light," Cody told her, drawing her attention back

to him. "And don't wring all the grease out of the home fries."

She chuckled and started off, her voice pitched high. "Double up on a couple of blue plates. Flip the eggs but make it easy."

For the first time in weeks, Nathan had the urge to smile. "What is the blue plate?"

"Two eggs, a rasher of bacon, home fries, biscuits and coffee by the barrel." As he took out one of his own cigarettes, Cody stretched his legs to rest his feet on the seat beside Nathan. "So, have you called her?"

It wasn't any use pretending he didn't want to talk about it. If that had been the case, he could have made some excuse and remained on the building site. He'd come because Cody could be counted on to be honest, whether the truth was pretty or not.

"No, I haven't called her."

"So you did have a fight?"

"I don't think you could call it a fight." Frowning, he remembered the china shattering on the floor. "No, you could call it that."

"People in love fight all the time."

Nathan smiled again. "That sounds like something she'd say."

"Sensible woman." He poured a second cup of coffee and noted that Nathan had left his untouched. "From the looks of you, I'd say whatever you two fought about, she won."

"No. Neither of us did."

Cody was silent for a moment, tapping his spoon on the table with the tinny country song playing on the jukebox. "My old man was big on sending flowers whenever he and my mother went at each other. Worked every time."

"This isn't as simple as that."

Cody waited until two heaping plates were set in front

of them. He sent the waitress a cheeky wink, then dug in. "Nathan, I know you're the kind of man who likes to keep things to himself. I respect that. Working with you the last couple of years has been an education for me, in organization and control, in professionalism. But I figure by this time we're more than associates. A man has trouble with a woman, it usually helps if he dumps it out on another man. Not that another man understands women any better. They can just be confused about it together."

A semi pulled up in front of the diner's dusty window, gears groaning. "Jack wanted a commitment. I couldn't give her one."

"Couldn't?" Cody took his time pouring honey on a biscuit. "Isn't the word *wouldn't*?"

"Not in this case. For reasons I don't want to get into, I couldn't give her the marriage and family she wanted. Needed. Jack needed promises. I don't make promises."

"Well, that's for you to decide." Cody scooped up more eggs. "But it seems to me you're not too happy about it. If you don't love her—"

"I didn't say I didn't love her."

"Didn't you? Guess I misunderstood."

"Look, Cody, marriage is impossible enough when people think alike, when they have the same attitudes and habits. When they're as different as Jack and I, it's worse than impossible. She wants a home, kids and all the confusion that goes with it. I'm on the road for weeks at a time, and when I come home I want…" He let his words trail off because he no longer knew. He used to know.

"Yeah, that's a problem, all right," Cody continued as if Nathan weren't staring out of the window. "I guess dragging a woman along, having her to share those nameless hotel rooms and solitary meals, would be inconvenient.

And having one who loved you waiting for you when you got home would be a pain."

Nathan turned back from the window and gave Cody a level look. "It would be unfair to her."

"Probably right. It's better to move on and be unhappy without her than risk being happy with her. Your eggs are getting cold, boss."

"Marriages break up as often as they work out."

"Yeah, the statistics are lousy. Makes you wonder why people keep jumping in."

"You haven't."

"Nope. Haven't found a woman mean enough." He grinned as he shoveled in the last of his eggs. "Maybe I'll look Jack up next week." The sudden deadly fury on Nathan's face had Cody stretching an arm over the back of the booth. "Figure this, Nathan, when a woman puts light into a man's life and he pulls the shade, he's asking for somebody else to enjoy it. Is that what you want?"

"Don't push it, Cody."

"No, I think you've already pushed yourself." He leaned forward again, his face quietly serious. "Let me tell you something, Nathan. You're a good man and a hell of an architect. You don't lie or look for the easy way. You fight for your men and for your principles, but you're not so hardheaded you won't compromise when it's time. You'll still be all of those things without her, but you could be a hell of a lot more with her. She did something for you."

"I know that." He shoved his all-but-untouched meal aside. "I'm worried about what I might do to her. If it were up to me…"

"If it were up to you, what?"

"It comes down to the fact that I'm not better off without her." That was a tough one to bring out in the open, to say plainly and live with. "But she may be better off without me."

"I guess she's the only one who can answer that." He drew out his wallet and riffled through bills. "I figure I know as much about this project here as you."

"What? Yes, so?"

"So I got an airline ticket in my room. Booked to leave day after tomorrow. I'll trade you for your hotel room."

Nathan started to make excuses, to give all the reasons why he was responsible for the project. Excuses, he realized, were all they would be. "Keep it," he said abruptly. "I'm leaving today."

"Smart move." Cody added a generous tip to the bill.

Nathan arrived home at 2:00 a.m. after a frenzied stop-and-go day of traveling. He'd had to route through St. Louis, bump into Chicago, then pace restlessly through O'Hare for two and a half hours waiting for his connection to Baltimore. From there he took his only option, a puddle jumper that touched down hourly.

He was sure she'd be there. He'd kept himself going with that alone. True, she hadn't answered when he'd called, but she could have been out shopping, in the pool, taking a walk. He didn't believe she'd left.

Somewhere in his heart he'd been sure all along that no matter what he'd said or how they'd left things she would be there when he returned. She was too stubborn and too self-confident to give up on him because he'd been an idiot.

She loved him, and when a woman like Jackie loved, she continued to love, for better or for worse. He'd given her worse. Now, if she'd let him, he was going to try for better.

But she wasn't there. He knew it almost from the minute he opened his front door. The house had that same quiet, almost respectful feel it had had before she'd come into it. A lonely feel. Swearing, he took the steps two at a time, calling her.

The bed was empty, made up with Mrs. Grange's no-nonsense tucks. There were no colorful shirts or grubby shoes tossed anywhere. The room was neat as a pin. He detested it on sight. Still unable to accept it, he pulled open the closet. Only his own ordered clothes were there.

Furious with her, as well as himself, he strode into the guest room. And had to accept. She wasn't there, curled under tangled sheets. The clutter of books and papers was gone. So was her typewriter.

He stared for a long time, wondering how he could ever had thought it preferable to come home to order and peace. Tired, he sat on the edge of the bed. Her scent was still there, but it was fading. That was the worst of it, to have a trace of her without the rest.

He lay back on the bed, unwilling to sleep in the one he'd shared with her night after night. She wasn't going to get away with it, he thought, and instantly fell asleep.

"It's worse than pitiful for a grown man to cheat at Scrabble."

"I don't have to cheat." J. D. MacNamara narrowed his eyes and focused them on his daughter. "*Zuckly* is an adjective, meaning graceful. As in 'the ballerina executed a zuckly pirouette.'"

"That's a load of you-know-what," Jackie said, and scowled at him. "I let you get away with *quoho*, Daddy, but this is too much."

"Just because you're a writer now doesn't mean you know every word in the dictionary. Go ahead, look it up, but you lose fifty points if you find it."

Jackie's fingers hovered over the dictionary. She knew her father could lie beautifully, but she also knew he had an uncanny way of coming out on top. With a sigh of disgust, she dropped her hand. "I'll concede. I know how to be a zuckly player."

"That's my girl." Pleased with himself, he began to add points to his score. Jackie lifted her glass of wine and considered him.

J. D. MacNamara was quite a man. But then, she'd always known that. She supposed it was Nathan's description of his own father, his family life, that had made her stand back and appreciate fully what she'd been given. She knew her father had a tough-as-nails reputation in the business world. He derived great pleasure from wheeling and dealing and outwitting competitors. Yet she'd seen the same self-satisfied look on his face after pulling off a multimillion-dollar business coup as she saw on it now as he outscored his daughter in a game of Scrabble.

He just loved life, with all its twists and turns. Perhaps Nathan was right about children inheriting more than eye color, and if she'd inherited that joie de vivre from her father, she was grateful.

"I love you, Daddy, even if you are a rotten cheat."

"I love you, too, Jackie." He beamed at the totals. "But I'm not going to let that interfere with destroying you. Your turn, you know."

Folding up her legs, she propped her elbows and stared owlishly at her letters. The room was gracefully lit, the drapes yet to be drawn as sunset exploded in the western sky. The second parlor, as her mother insisted on calling it, was for family or informal gatherings, but it was a study in elegance and taste.

The rose-and-gray pattern of the Aubusson was picked up prettily in soft floor-length drapes and the upholstery of a curvy sofa. Her mother's prize collection of crystal had been moved out some years before when Jackie and Brandon had broken a candy dish while wrestling over some forgotten disagreement. Patricia had stubbornly left a few dainty pieces of porcelain.

There was a wide window seat in the east wall, where Jackie had hidden playing hide-and-seek as a child and dreamed of her latest crush as a teenager. She'd spent thousands of hours in that room, happy ones, furious ones, tearful ones. It was home. She hadn't fully understood or appreciated that until now.

"What's the matter with you, girl? Writers are supposed to have a way with words."

Her lips twitched a bit. J.D. had already fallen into the habit of calling her a writer several times a day. "Off my case, J.D."

"Hell of a way to talk to your father. Why, I ought to take a strap to you."

She grinned. "You and who else?"

He grinned back. He had a full, generous face with that oh-so-Irish ruddy skin. His eyes were a bright blue even through the glasses he had perched on his nose. He wore a suit because dressing for dinner was expected, but the vest was unbuttoned and the tie pulled crooked. A cigar was clamped between his big teeth, a cigar that Patricia tolerated in dignified silence.

Jackie pushed her letters around. "You know, Daddy, I've just began to think about it, but you and Mother, you're so different."

"Hmm?" He glanced up, distracted from the creative demands of inventing a new word.

"I mean, Mother is so elegant, so well-groomed."

"What am I, a slob?"

"Not exactly." When he frowned, she spread out her letters on the board. "There, *hyfoxal*."

"What the hell is this?" J.D. waved a blunt finger at the word. "No such thing."

"It's from the Latin for sly or cleverly adept. As in 'My father is well-known for his hyfoxal business dealings.'"

In answer, J.D. used a brief four-letter word that would have had his wife clucking her tongue. "Look it up," Jackie invited. "If you want to lose fifty points. Daddy," she said to distract him again, "how do you and Mother stay so happy?"

"I let her do what she does best, she lets me do what I do best. Besides, I'm crazy about the old prude."

"I know." Jackie felt her eyes fill with the tears that never seemed far away these days. "I've been thinking a lot lately about what you've both done for me and the boys. And loving each other might be the most important part of all."

"Jack, why don't you tell me what's on your mind?"

She shook her head but leaned over to stroke his cheek. "I just grew up this spring. Thought you'd like to know."

"And does growing up have anything to do with the man you're in love with?"

"Just about everything. Oh, you'd like him, Daddy. He's strong, sometimes too strong. He's kind and funny in the oddest sorts of ways. He likes me the way I am." The tears threatened again, and she put a hand to her eyes, pressing hard for a moment. "He makes lists for everything and always makes sure that *B* follows *A*. He, uh…" Letting out a long breath, she dropped her hands. "He's the kind of man who opens the door for you, not because he thinks it's the gentlemanly or proper thing to do, but because he is a gentleman. A very gentle man." She smiled again, her tears under control. "Mother would like him, too."

"Then what's the problem, Jackie?"

"He's just not ready for me or for the way we feel about

each other. And I'm not sure how long I can wait for him to get ready."

J.D. frowned a moment. "Want me to give him a kick in the pants?"

That made her laugh. She was up and in his lap, her arms tight around him. "I'll let you know."

Patricia glided into the room, slim and pretty in a silk sheath the same pale blue as her eyes. "John, if the chef continues to throw these disgraceful temper tantrums, you're going to have to speak to him yourself. I'm at my wit's end." She went to the bar, poured a small glass of dry sherry, then settled in a chair. She crossed her legs, which her husband still considered the best on the East Coast, and sipped. "Jackie, I came across a new hairdresser last week. I'm convinced he could do wonders for you."

Jackie grinned and blew her hair out of her eyes. "I love you, Mother."

Instantly, and in the way Jackie had always adored, Patricia's eyes softened. "I love you too, darling. I meant to tell you that your tan is wonderfully flattering, particularly with your coloring, but after all I've been reading lately I'm worried about the long-term effects." Then she smiled in a way that made her look remarkably like her daughter. "It's good to have you home for a little while. The house is always too quiet without you and the boys."

"Won't be seeing too much of her now." J.D. gave her a fatherly pinch on the rump. "Now that she's a big-time author."

"It's only one book," she reminded him, then grinned. "So far."

"It did give me a great deal of satisfaction to mention, very casually, of course, to Honoria that you'd sold your manuscript to Harlequin Historicals." Patricia took a delicate sip as she settled back on the cushions.

"Casual?" J.D. gave a shout of laughter. "She couldn't wait to pick up the phone and brag. Hey, there, what do you think you're doing?"

Jackie turned back from her study of his letters. "Nothing." She gave him a loud kiss on the cheek. "You're doomed, you know. You're never going to be able to use that ridiculous collection."

"We'll see about that." J.D. dumped her off of his lap, then rubbed his palms together. "Sit down and shut up."

"John, really," Patricia said, in a tone that had Jackie running over to hug her. When the doorbell rang, Jackie straightened, but her mother waved her back. "Philip will get the door, Jacqueline. Do fix your hair."

Dutifully Jackie dragged her fingers through it as their graying butler came to the parlor entrance. "I beg your pardon, Mrs. MacNamara, but there's a Nathan Powell here to see Miss Jacqueline."

With a quick squeal, Jackie leaped forward. Her mother's firm command stopped her. "Jacqueline, sit down and pretend you're a lady. Philip will show the man in."

"But—"

"Sit down," J.D. told her. "And shut up."

"Quite," Patricia murmured, then nodded to Philip.

She sat with a thud.

"And I'd take that sulky look off your pointy face," her father suggested. "Unless you want him to turn right around and leave again."

Jackie gritted her teeth, glared arrows at him, then settled down. Maybe they were right, she thought. Just this once, she'd look before she leaped. But when she saw him she would have been out of her chair in an instant if her father's foot hadn't stamped down on hers.

"Jack." There was something strained and husky about his voice, as though he hadn't spoken for days.

"Hello, Nathan." Pulling herself in, she rose easily and offered a hand. "I didn't expect you."

"No, I…" He felt suddenly and completely foolish standing there in a travel-stained suit with a brightly ribboned box under his arm. "I should have called."

"Of course not." As if there had never been any strain between them, or any passion, she tucked her arm through his. "I'd like you to meet my parents. J. D. and Patricia Mac-Namara, Nathan Powell."

J.D. shoved himself to his feet. He'd already made his assessment, and if he'd ever seen a more lovesick, frustrated man before, he couldn't bring it to mind. It was with both sympathy and interest that he offered a hand.

"Pleased to meet you. Admire your work." He shook his hand with a hefty pumping stroke. "Jack's told us all about you. I'll get you a drink."

Nathan managed to nod through these rapid-fire statements before turning to greet Jackie's mother. This was what she would look like in twenty or twenty-five years, Nathan realized with a jolt. Still lovely, with her skin clear as a bell and the grace that only years could add.

"Mrs. MacNamara, I apologize for dropping in on you like this."

"No need for that." But it pleased her that he had the manners to do so. She took stock in much the same way her husband had and saw a breeding and a kindness that she approved of. "Won't you sit down, Mr. Powell?"

"Well, I—"

"Here you are, nothing like a nice shot of whiskey to put hair on your chest." J.D. slapped him on the back as he offered the glass. "So you design buildings? Do any remodeling?"

"Yes, when there's—"

"Good, good. I'd like to talk to you about this building I'd had my eye on. Place is a mess, but it has potential. Now if I—"

"Excuse me." Forgetting his manners, Nathan shoved the glass back in J.D.'s hand and grabbed Jackie's arm. Without another word, he dragged her through the terrace doors he'd spotted.

"Well." Patricia raised both brows as if scandalized and hid her smile in her drink. J.D. merely hooted and downed the whiskey himself.

"Up to planning a wedding, Patty, old girl?"

The air was balmy and full of flowers. The stars were close enough to touch, vying with the moon for brilliance. Nathan noticed none of it as he stopped, dropped his package on a gleaming white table and hauled Jackie into his arms.

She fit perfectly.

"I'm sorry," he managed after a moment. "I was rude to your parents."

"That's all right. We often are." She lifted both hands to his face and studied him. "You look tired."

"No, I'm fine." He was anything but. Searching for lost control, he stepped back. "I wasn't sure you'd be here, either."

"Either?"

"You were gone when I got home, and then I tracked down your apartment, but you weren't there, either, so I came looking here."

Hoping she could take it slowly, she leaned back against the table. "You've been looking for me?"

"For a couple of days."

"I'm sorry. I didn't expect you back from Denver until next week. Your office certainly didn't."

"I came back sooner than— You called my office?"

"Yes. You came back sooner than what, Nathan?"

"Sooner than expected," he said with a snap. "I left Cody in charge, dumped the project in his lap and flew home. You'd gone. You'd left me."

She nearly flew at him, laughing, but decided to play it out. "Did you expect me to stay on?"

"Yes. No. Yes, damn it." He dragged both hands through his hair. "I know I hadn't any right to expect it, but I did. Then, when I got home, the house was empty. I hated it there without you. I can't think without you. That's your fault. You've done something to my brain." He'd begun to pace, which made her lift a brow. The Nathan she'd come to know rarely made unnecessary moves. "Every time I see something I wonder what you'd think about it, what you'd say. I couldn't even eat a blue plate special without thinking about you."

"That's really dreadful." She drew a breath. It needed to be asked. "Do you want me back, Nathan?"

There was fury in his eyes when he turned, a kind of vivid, blazing fury that made her want to launch herself into his arms again. "Do you want me to crawl?"

"Let me think about it." She touched the bow on the package, wondering what was inside. Wondering was almost as good as knowing. "You deserve to crawl a bit, but I don't have the heart for it." She smiled at him, her hands folded neatly. "I hadn't gone anywhere, Nathan."

"You'd cleared out. The place was tidy as a tomb."

"Didn't you look in the closet?"

Impatience shimmered, then stilled. "What do you mean?"

"I mean, I hadn't left. My clothes are still in the guest room. I couldn't sleep in your bed without you, so I moved, but I didn't leave." She touched his face again, gently. "I had no intention of letting you ruin your life."

He grabbed her hand as if it were a lifeline. "Then why are you here and not there?"

"I wanted to see my parents. Partly because of the things you'd told me. It made me realize I needed to see them, to thank them somehow for being as wonderful as they are. And partly because I wanted to tell them I'd finally done something from beginning to end." Her fingers curved nervously over his. "I sold my book."

"Sold it? I didn't know you'd sent it in."

"I didn't want to tell you. I didn't want you to be disappointed in me if it didn't work."

"I wouldn't have been." He drew her close. Her scent, so needed, was all around him. It was only then that he understood that you could come home even without the familiar walls. "I'm happy for you. I'm proud of you. I wish... I wish I'd been here."

"This is something I had to do, this first time, by myself." She shifted back, not out of his arms, but circled by them. "I'd like you to be around the next time."

His fingers tensed on the back of her waist, and his eyes went dark. Jake's look, she thought yet again, giddy with love for him. "It's that easy? All I had to do was walk in and ask?"

"That's all you've ever had to do."

"I don't deserve you."

She smiled. "I know."

With a laugh, he swung her in a circle, then brought her down to crush his lips to hers in a long, breathless kiss. "I came prepared to make all kinds of offers and promises. You aren't going to ask for any."

"That's not to say I wouldn't like to hear them." She laid her head on his shoulder. "Why don't you tell me what you've got in mind?"

"I want you, but I want it to be right. No long separations, no broken promises. I'm doing something I should have done a year ago and making Cody a partner."

When she drew her head back, he noticed that her eyes could be as shrewd as her father's. "That's an excellent decision."

"A personal one, as well as a business one. I'm learning, Jack."

"I can see that."

"Between the two of us, the pressure will lighten enough to make it possible to start a family, a real family. I don't know what kind of husband I'll make, or father, but—"

She touched her fingers to his lips. "We'll find out together."

"Yes." Reaching up, he took her hands again. "I'll still have to travel some, but I hope you'll agree to come with me whenever you can."

"Just try to stop me."

"And you'll be there to make certain I don't forget that marriage and family come first."

She turned her face into his throat. "You can count on it."

"I'm doing this backward. I do that a lot since I met you." He ran his hands down her arms, then drew her away. "I wanted to tell you that since I found you everything changed for me. Losing you would be worse than losing my eyes or my arms, because without you I can't see or touch anything. I need you in my life, I want you to share it all with me. We can learn from each other, make mistakes together, and I love you more than I know how to say."

"I think you said it very nicely." She sniffled, then shook her head. "I don't want to cry. I look really awful when I cry, and I want to be beautiful tonight. Let me have my present, will you, before I start babbling?"

"I like it when you babble." He pressed a kiss to her

brow, to her temple, to the dimple at the corner of her mouth. "Oh, God, I do owe cousin Fred."

Jackie gave a watery laugh. "He's trying to find a buyer for twenty-five acres of swampland."

"Sold." He caught her face in his hands again, just to look, just to touch what was more real to him than his own heart. "I do love you, Jack."

"I know, but you can repeat yourself all you want."

"I intend to, but first I think you should have this." He picked up the package and offered it to her. "I wanted you to have something that would show you, if I couldn't make myself clear, how I felt about you. How you'd given me hope for a future I never believed in."

She dragged the heels of her hands under her eyes. "Well, let's see. Diamonds are forever, but I've always had a fondness for colored stones." She ripped at the paper ruthlessly, then pulled out her gift.

For a moment she was speechless, standing in the moonlight, her cheeks still gleaming with tears. In her hands was a shell-covered pelican. When she looked at him again, her eyes were drenched. "Nobody understands me the way you do."

"Don't change," he murmured, holding her close again with the tacky bird between them. "Let's go home, Jack."

* * * * *

LAWLESS

To Ruth, Marianne and Jan,
for taking me to Silverado.

Chapter 1

He wanted a drink. Whiskey, cheap and warm. After six weeks on the trail, he wanted the same kind of woman. Some men usually managed to get what they wanted. He was one of them. Still, the woman could wait, Jake decided as he leaned against the bar. The whiskey couldn't.

He had another ninety long, dusty miles to go before he got home. If anybody could call a frying pan like Lone Bluff home. Some did, Jake thought as he signaled for a bottle and took his first gut-clenching gulp. Some had to.

For himself, home was usually the six feet of space where his shadow fell. But for the past few months Lone Bluff had been as good a place as any. He could get a room there, a bath and a willing woman, all at a reasonable price. It was a town where a man could avoid trouble—or find it, depending on his mood.

For now, with the dust of the trail still scratchy in his throat and his stomach empty except for a shot of whiskey, Jake was just too tired for trouble. He'd have another drink, and whatever passed for a meal in this two-bit town blown up from the desert, then he'd be on his way.

The afternoon sunlight poured in over the swinging doors at the saloon's entrance. Someone had tacked a picture of a woman in red feathers to the wall, but that was the extent of the female company. Places like this didn't run to providing women for their clientele. Just to liquor and cards.

Even towns like this one had a saloon or two. A man

could depend upon it, the way he could depend on little else. It wasn't yet noon, and half the tables were occupied. The air was thick with the smoke from the cigars the bartender sold, two for a penny. The whiskey went for a couple of bits and burned a line of fire straight from the throat to the gut. If the owner had added a real woman in red feathers, he could have charged double that and not heard a single complaint.

The place stank of whiskey, sweat and smoke. But Jake figured he didn't smell too pretty himself. He'd ridden hard from New Mexico, and he would have ridden straight through to Lone Bluff except he'd wanted to rest his horse and fill his own stomach with something other than the jerky in his saddlebags.

Saloons always looked better at night, and this one was no exception. Its bar was grimy from hundreds of hands and elbows, dulled by spilled drinks, scarred by matchtips. The floor was nothing but hard-packed dirt that had absorbed its share of whiskey and blood. He'd been in worse, Jake reflected, wondering if he should allow himself the luxury of rolling a cigarette now or wait until after a meal.

He could buy more tobacco if he had a yearning for another. There was a month's pay in his pocket. And he'd be damned if he'd ever ride cattle again. That was a life for the young and stupid—or maybe just the stupid.

When his money ran low he could always take a job riding shotgun on the stage through Indian country. The line was always looking for a man who was handy with a gun, and it was better than riding at the back end of a steer. It was the middle of 1875 and the easterners were still coming—looking for gold and land, following dreams. Some of them stopped in the Arizona Territory on their way to California because they ran out of money or energy or time.

Their hard luck, Jake thought as he downed his second

whiskey. He'd been born here, and he still didn't figure it was the most hospitable place on the map. It was hot and hard and stingy. It suited him just fine.

"Redman?"

Jake lifted his eyes to the dingy glass behind the bar. He saw the man behind him. Young, wiry and edgy. His brown hat was tipped down low over his eyes, and sweat glistened on his neck. Jake nearly sighed. He knew the type too well. The kind that went out of his way looking for trouble. The kind that didn't know that if you hung around long enough it found you, anyway.

"Yeah?"

"Jake Redman?"

"So?"

"I'm Barlow, Tom Barlow." He wiped his palms on his thighs. "They call me Slim."

The way he said it, Jake was sure the kid expected the name to be recognized…shuddered over. He decided the whiskey wasn't good enough for a third drink. He dropped some money on the bar, making sure his hands were well clear of his guns.

"There a place where a man can get a steak in this town?" Jake asked the bartender.

"Down to Grody's." The man moved cautiously out of range. "We don't want any trouble in here."

Jake gave him a long, cool look. "I'm not giving you any."

"I'm talking to you, Redman." Barlow spread his legs and let his hand hover over the butt of his gun. A mean-looking scar ran across the back of his hand from his index finger to his wrist. He wore his holster high, a single rig with the leather worn smooth at the buckle. It paid to notice details.

Easy, moving no more than was necessary, Jake met his eyes. "Something you want to say?"

"You got a reputation for being fast. Heard you took out Freemont in Tombstone."

Jake turned fully. As he moved, the swinging door flew back. At least one of the saloon's customers had decided to move to safer ground. The kid was packing a .44 Colt, its black rubber grip well tended. Jake didn't doubt there were notches in it. Barlow looked like the type who would take pride in killing.

"You heard right."

Barlow's fingers curled and uncurled. Two men playing poker in the corner let their hands lie to watch and made a companionable bet on the higher-stakes game in front of them. "I'm faster. Faster than Freemont. Faster than you. I run this town."

Jake glanced around the saloon, then back into Barlow's dark, edgy eyes. "Congratulations." He would have walked away, but Barlow shifted to block him. The move had Jake narrowing his eyes. The look came into them, the hard, flat look that made a smart man give way. "Cut your teeth on somebody else. I want a steak and a bed."

"Not in my town."

Patience wasn't Jake's long suit, but he wasn't in the mood to waste time on a gunman looking to sharpen his reputation. "You want to die over a piece of meat?"

Jake watched the grin spread over Barlow's face. He didn't think he was going to die, Jake thought wearily. His kind never did.

"Why don't you come find me in about five years?" Jake told him. "I'll be happy to put a bullet in you."

"I found you now. After I kill you, there won't be a man west of the Mississippi who won't know Slim Barlow."

For some—for many—no other reason was needed to

draw and fire. "Make it easy on both of us." Jake started for the doors again. "Just tell them you killed me."

"I hear your mother was a squaw." Barlow grinned when Jake stopped and turned again. "Guess that's where you got that streak of yellow."

Jake was used to rage. It could fill a man from stomach to brain and take over. When he felt it rising up, he clamped down on it. If he was going to fight—and it seemed inevitable—he preferred to fight cold.

"My grandmother was Apache."

Barlow grinned again, then wiped his mouth with the back of his left hand. "That makes you a stinking breed, don't it? A stinking yellow breed. We don't want no Indians around here. Guess I'll have to clean up the town a little."

He went for his gun. Jake saw the move, not in Barlow's hands but in his eyes. Cold and fast and without regret, Jake drew his own. There were those who saw him who said it was like lightning and thunder. There was a flash of steel, then the roar of the bullet. He hardly moved from where he stood, shooting from the hip, trusting instinct and experience. In a smooth, almost careless movement, he replaced his gun. Tom they-call-me-Slim Barlow was sprawled on the barroom floor.

Jake passed through the swinging doors and walked to his horse. He didn't know whether he'd killed his man or not, and he didn't care. The whole damn mess had ruined his appetite.

Sarah was mortally afraid she was going to lose the miserable lunch she'd managed to bolt down at the last stop. How anyone—*anyone*—survived under these appalling conditions, she'd never know. The West, as far as she could see, was only fit for snakes and outlaws.

She closed her eyes, patted the sweat from her neck with

her handkerchief, and prayed that she'd make it through the next few hours. At least she could thank God she wouldn't have to spend another night in one of those horrible stage depots. She'd been afraid she would be murdered in her bed. If one could call that miserable sheetless rope cot a bed. And privacy? Well, there simply hadn't been any.

It didn't matter now, she told herself. She was nearly there. After twelve long years, she was going to see her father again and take care of him in the beautiful house he'd built outside Lone Bluff.

When she'd been six, he'd left her in the care of the good sisters and gone off to make his fortune. There had been nights, many nights, when Sarah had cried herself to sleep from missing him. Then, as the years had passed, she'd had to take out the faded daguerreotype to remember his face. But he'd always written to her. His penmanship had been strained and childish, but there had been so much love in his letters. And so much hope.

Once a month she'd received word from her father from whatever point he'd stopped at on his journey west. After eighteen months, and eighteen letters, he'd written from the Arizona Territory, where he'd settled, and where he would build his fortune.

He'd convinced her that he'd been right to leave her in Philadelphia, in the convent school, where she could be raised and educated as a proper young lady should. Until, Sarah remembered, she was old enough to travel across the country to live with him. Now she was nearly eighteen, and she was going to join him. Undoubtedly the house he'd built, however grand, required a woman's touch.

Since he'd never married again, Sarah imagined her father a crusty bachelor, never quite certain where his clean collars were or what the cook was serving for dinner. She'd soon fix all that.

A man in his position needed to entertain, and to entertain he needed a hostess. Sarah Conway knew exactly how to give an elegant dinner party and a formal ball.

True, what she'd read of the Arizona Territory was distressing, to say the least. Stories of ruthless gunmen and wild Indians. But, after all, this was 1875. Sarah had no doubt that even so distant a place as Arizona was under control by this time. The reports she'd read had obviously been exaggerated to sell newspapers and penny dreadfuls.

They hadn't exaggerated about the climate.

She shifted for a better position. The bulk of the woman beside her, and her own corset, gave her little room for relief. And the smell. No matter how often Sarah sprinkled lavender water on her handkerchief, there was no escaping it. There were seven passengers, crammed all but elbow-to-knee inside the rattling stagecoach. It was airless, and that accentuated the stench of sweat and foul breath and whatever liquor it was that the man across from her continued to drink. Right from the bottle. At first, his pockmarked face and grimy neckcloth had fascinated her. But when he'd offered her a drink, she had fallen back on a woman's best defense. Her dignity.

It was difficult to look dignified when her clothes were sticking to her and her hair was drooping beneath her bonnet. It was all but impossible to maintain her decorum when the plump woman beside her began to gnaw on what appeared to be a chicken leg. But when Sarah was determined, she invariably prevailed.

The good sisters had never been able to pray or punish or lecture her stubbornness out of her. Now, with her chin slightly lifted and her body braced against the bouncing sway of the coach, she kept her eyes firmly shut and ignored her fellow passengers.

She'd seen enough of the Arizona landscape, if one could

call it that. As far as she could see, the entire territory was nothing but miles of sunbaked desert. True, the first cacti she'd seen had been fascinating. She'd even considered sketching a few of them. Some were as big as a man, with arms that stretched up to the sky. Others were short and squat and covered with hundreds of dangerous-looking needles. Still, after she'd seen several dozen of them, and little else, they'd lost their novelty.

The rocks were interesting, she supposed. The buttes and flat-topped mesas growing out of the sand had a certain rugged charm, particularly when they rose up into the deep, endless blue of the sky. But she preferred the tidy streets of Philadelphia, with their shops and tearooms.

Being with her father would make all the difference. She could live anywhere, as long as she was with him again. He'd be proud of her. She needed him to be proud of her. All these years she'd worked and learned and practiced so that she could become the proper, well-educated young lady he wanted his daughter to be.

She wondered if he'd recognize her. She'd sent him a small, framed self-portrait just last Christmas, but she wasn't certain it had been a truly good likeness. She'd always thought it was too bad she wasn't pretty, in the soft, round way of her dear friend Lucilla. Still, her complexion was good, and Sarah comforted herself with that. Unlike Lucilla, she never required any help from the little pots of rouge the sisters so disapproved of. In fact, there were times she thought her complexion just a bit too healthy. Her mouth was full and wide when she would have preferred a delicate Cupid's bow, and her eyes were an unremarkable brown rather than the blue that would have suited her blond hair so much better. Still, she was trim and neat—or she had been neat before she'd begun this miserable journey.

It would all be worthwhile soon. When she greeted her

father and they settled into the lovely house he'd built. Four bedrooms. Imagine. And a parlor with windows facing west. Delightful. Undoubtedly, she'd have to do some re-decorating. Men never thought about such niceties as curtains and throw rugs. She'd enjoy it. Once she had the glass shining and fresh flowers in the vases he would see how much he needed her. Then all the years in between would have been worthwhile.

Sarah felt a line of sweat trickle down her back. The first thing she wanted was a bath—a nice, cool bath laced with the fragrant lilac salts Lucilla had given her as a parting gift. She sighed. She could almost feel it, her body free of the tight corset and hot clothes, the water sliding over her skin. Scented. Delicious. Almost sinful.

When the coach jolted, Sarah was thrown against the fat woman to her left. Before she could right herself, a spray of rotgut whiskey soaked her skirts.

"Sir!" But before she could lecture him she heard the shot, and the screams.

"Indians!" The chicken leg went flying, and the fat woman clutched Sarah to her bosom like a shield. "We're all going to be murdered."

"Don't be absurd." Sarah struggled to free herself, not certain if she was more annoyed by the sudden dangerous speed of the coach or the spot of chicken grease on her new skirt. She leaned toward the window to call to the driver. As she did, the face of the shotgun rider slid into view, inches from hers. He hung there, upside down, for seconds only. But that was long enough for Sarah to see the blood trickling from his mouth, and the arrow in his heart. Even as the woman beside her screamed again, his body thudded to the ground.

"Indians!" she shouted again. "God have mercy."

"Apaches," the man with the whiskey said as he finished

off the bottle. "Must've got the driver, too. We're on a run-away." So saying, he drew his gun, made his way to the opposite window and began firing methodically.

Dazed, Sarah continued to stare out the window. She could hear screams and whoops and the thunder of horses' hooves. Like devils, she thought dully. They sounded like devils. That was impossible. Ridiculous. The United States was nearly a century old. Ulysses S. Grant was president. Steamships crossed the Atlantic in less than two weeks. Devils simply didn't exist in this day and age.

Then she saw one, bare chested, hair flying, on a tough paint pony. Sarah looked straight into his eyes. She could see the fever in them, just as she could see the bright streaks of paint on his face and the layer of dust that covered his gleaming skin. He raised his bow. She could have counted the feathers in the arrow. Then, suddenly, he flew off the back of his horse.

It was like a play, she thought, and she had to pinch herself viciously to keep from swooning.

Another horseman came into view, riding low, with pistols in both hands. He wore a gray hat over dark hair, and his skin was nearly as dark as that of the Apache she'd seen. In his eyes, as they met hers, she saw not fever, but ice.

He didn't shoot her, as she'd been almost certain he would, but fired over his shoulder, using his right hand, then his left, even as an arrow whizzed by his head.

Amazing, she thought as a thudding excitement began to race with her terror. He was magnificent—sweat and grime on his face, ice in his eyes, his lean, tense body glued to the racing horse. Then the fat lady grabbed her again and began to wail.

Jake fired behind him, clinging to the horse with his knees as easily as any Apache brave. He'd caught a glimpse of the passengers, in particular a pale, dark-eyed girl in a dark blue bonnet. His Apache cousins would've enjoyed that one, he thought dispassionately as he holstered his guns.

He could see the driver, an arrow piercing one shoulder, struggling to regain control of the horses. He was doing his best, despite the pain, but he wasn't strong enough to shove the brake down. Swearing, Jake pushed his horse on until he was close enough to the racing coach to gain a handhold.

For one endless second he hung by his fingers alone. Sarah caught a glimpse of a dusty shirt and one powerful forearm, a long, leather-clad leg and a scarred boot. Then he was up, scrambling over the top of the coach. The woman beside her screamed again, then fainted dead away when they stopped. Too terrified to sit, Sarah pushed open the door of the coach and climbed out.

The man in the gray hat was already getting down. "Ma'am," he said as he moved past her.

She pressed a hand to her drumming heart. No hero had ever been so heroic. "You saved our lives," she managed, but he didn't even glance her way.

"Redman." The passenger who'd drunk the whiskey stepped out. "Glad you stopped by."

"Lucius." Jake picked up the reins of his horse and proceeded to calm him. "There were only six of them."

"They're getting away," Sarah blurted out. "Are you just going to let them get away?"

Jake looked at the cloud of dust from the retreating horses, then back at Sarah. He had time now for a longer, more interested study. She was tiny, with *East* stamped all over her pretty face. Her hair, the color of honeycombs, was tumbling down from her bonnet. She looked as if she'd just stepped out of the schoolroom, and she smelled like a cheap saloon. He had to grin.

"Yep."

"But you can't." Her idea of a hero was rapidly crumbling. "They killed a man."

"He knew the chance he was taking. Riding the line pays good."

"They murdered him," Sarah said again, as if she were speaking to a very dull pupil. "He's lying back there with an arrow through his heart." When Jake said nothing, just walked his horse to the back of the coach, Sarah followed him. "At least you can go back and pick up that poor man's body. We can't just leave him there."

"Dead's dead."

"That's a hideous thing to say." Because she felt ill, Sarah dragged off her bonnet and used it to fan hot air around her face. "The man deserves a decent burial. I couldn't possibly— What are you doing?"

Jake spared her a glance. Mighty pretty, he decided. Even prettier without the bonnet hiding her hair. "Hitching my horse."

She dropped her arm to her side. She no longer felt ill. She was certainly no longer impressed. She was furious. "Sir, you appear to care more about that horse than you do about the man."

He stooped under the reins. For a moment they stood face-to-face, with the sun beating down and the smell of blood and dust all around them. "That's right, seeing as the man's dead and my horse isn't. I'd get back inside, ma'am. It'd be a shame if you were still standing here when the Apaches decide to come back."

That made her stop and look around uneasily. The desert was still, but for the cry of a bird she didn't recognize as a vulture. "I'll go back and get him myself," she said between her teeth.

"Suit yourself." Jake walked to the front of the coach.

"Get that stupid woman inside," he told Lucius. "And don't give her any more to drink."

Sarah's mouth fell open. Before she could retaliate, Lucius had her by the arm. "Now, don't mind Jake, miss. He just says whatever he damn pleases. He's right, though. Those Apaches might turn back this way. We sure don't want to be sitting here if they do."

With what little dignity she had left, Sarah stepped back into the coach. The fat woman was still sobbing, leaning heavily against a tight-lipped man in a bowler. Sarah wedged herself into her corner as the stage jumped forward again. Securing her bonnet, she frowned at Lucius.

"Who is that horrible man?"

"Jake?" Lucius settled back. There was nothing he liked better than a good fight, particularly when he stayed alive to enjoy it. "That's Jake Redman, miss. I don't mind saying we was lucky he passed this way. Jake hits what he aims at."

"Indeed." She wanted to be aloof, but she remembered the murderous look in the Apache's eyes when he'd ridden beside the window. "I suppose we do owe him our gratitude, but he seemed cold-blooded about it."

"More'n one says he's got ice in his veins. Along with some Apache blood."

"You mean he's… Indian?"

"On his grandmother's side, I hear." Because his bottle was empty, Lucius settled for a plug of tobacco. He tucked it comfortably in his cheek. "Wouldn't want to cross him. No, ma'am, I sure wouldn't. Mighty comforting to know he's on your side when things heat up."

What kind of man killed his own kind? With a shiver, Sarah fell silent again. She didn't want to think about it.

On top of the stage, Jake kept the team to a steady pace. He preferred the freedom and mobility of having a single horse under him. The driver held a hand to his wounded shoulder and refused the dubious comfort of the coach.

"We could use you back on the line," he told Jake.

"Thinking about it." But he was really thinking about the little lady with the big brown eyes and the honey-colored hair. "Who's the girl? The young one in blue?"

"Conway. From Philadelphia." The driver breathed slow and easy against the pain. "Says she's Matt Conway's daughter."

"That so?" Miss Philadelphia Conway sure as hell didn't take after her old man. But Jake remembered that Matt bragged about his daughter back east from time to time. Especially after he started a bottle. "Come to visit her father?"

"Says she's come to stay."

Jake gave a quick, mirthless laugh. "Won't last a week. Women like that don't."

"She's planning on it." With a jerk of his thumb, the driver indicated the trunks strapped to the coach. "Most of that's hers."

With a snort, Jake adjusted his hat. "Figures."

Sarah caught her first glimpse of Lone Bluff from the stagecoach window. It spread like a jumble of rock at the base of the mountains. Hard, cold-looking mountains, she thought with a shudder, fooled—as the inexperienced always were—into thinking they were much closer than they actually were.

She'd forgotten herself enough to crane her head out. But she couldn't get another look at Jake Redman unless she pushed half her body through the opening. She really wasn't interested anyway, she assured herself. Unless it was purely for entertainment purposes. When she wrote back to Lucilla and the sisters, she wanted to be able to describe all the local oddities.

The man was certainly odd. He'd ridden like a warrior one moment, undoubtedly risking his life for a coachful of strangers. Then, the next minute, he'd dismissed his Christian duty and left a poor soul beside a lonely desert road. And he'd called her stupid.

Never in her life had anyone ever accused Sarah Conway of being stupid. In fact, both her intelligence and her breeding were widely admired. She was well-read, fluent in French and more than passably accomplished on the pianoforte.

Taking the time to retie her bonnet, Sarah reminded herself that she hardly needed approval from a man like Jake Redman. After she was reunited with her father and took her place in the local society, it was doubtful she'd ever see him again.

She'd thank him properly, of course. Sarah drew a fresh handkerchief from her reticule and blotted her temples. Just because he had no manners was no excuse to forget her own. She supposed she might even ask her father to offer him some monetary reward.

Pleased with the idea, Sarah looked out the window again. And blinked. Surely this wasn't Lone Bluff. Her father would never have settled in this grimy excuse for a town. It was no more than a huddle of buildings and a wide patch of dust that served as a road. They passed two saloons side by side, a dry goods store and what appeared to be a rooming house. Slack-legged horses were hitched to posts, their tails switching lazily at huge black flies. A handful of young boys with dirty faces began to race alongside the coach, shouting and firing wooden pistols. Sarah saw two women in faded gingham walking arm in arm on some wooden planks that served as a sidewalk.

When the coach stopped, she heard Jake call out for a doctor. Passengers were already streaming out through the doors on both sides. Resigned, Sarah stepped out and shook out her skirts.

"Mr. Redman." The brim of her bonnet provided inadequate shade. She was forced to lift her hand over her eyes. "Why have we stopped here?"

"End of the line, ma'am." A couple of men were already lifting the driver down, so he swung himself around to unstrap the cases on top of the coach.

"End of the line? But where are we?"

He paused long enough to glance down at her. She saw then that his eyes were darker than she'd imagined. A smoky slate gray. "Welcome to Lone Bluff."

Letting out a long, slow breath, she turned. Sunlight treated the town cruelly. It showed all the dirt, all the wear, and it heightened the pungent smell of horses.

Dear God, so this was it. The end of the line. The end of her line. It didn't matter, she told herself. She wouldn't be living in town. And surely before long the gold in her father's mine would bring more people and progress. No, it didn't matter at all. Sarah squared her shoulders. The only thing that mattered was seeing her father again.

She turned around in time to see Jake toss one of her trunks down to Lucius.

"Mr. Redman, please take care of my belongings."

Jake hefted the next case and tossed it to a grinning Lucius. "Yes, ma'am."

Biting down on her temper, she waited until he jumped down beside her. "Notwithstanding my earlier sentiments, I'm very grateful to you, Mr. Redman, for coming to our aid. You proved yourself to be quite valiant. I'm sure my father will want to repay you for seeing that I arrived safely."

Jake didn't think he'd ever heard anyone talk quite so fine since he'd spent a week in St. Louis. Tipping back his hat, he looked at her, long enough to make Sarah flush. "Forget it."

Forget it? Sarah thought as he turned his back and walked away. If that was the way the man accepted gratitude, she certainly would. With a sweep of her skirts she moved to the side of the road to wait for her father.

Jake strode into the rooming house with his saddlebag slung over his shoulder. It was never particularly clean, and it always smelled of onions and strong coffee. There were a couple of bullet holes in the wall. He'd put one of them there personally. Since the door was propped open, flies buzzed merrily in and out of the cramped entrance.

"Maggie." Jake tipped his hat to the woman who stood at the base of the stairs. "Got a room?"

Maggie O'Rourke was as tough as one of her fried steaks. She had iron-gray hair pinned back from a face that should have been too skinny for wrinkles. But wrinkles there were, a maze of them. Her tiny blue eyes seemed to peek out of the folds of a worn blanket. She ran her business with an iron fist, a Winchester repeater and an eye for a dollar.

She took one look at Jake and successfully hid her pleasure at seeing him. "Well, look what the cat dragged in," she said, the musical brogue of her native country still evident in her thin voice. "Got the law on your tail, Jake, or a woman?"

"Neither." He kicked the door shut with his boot, wondering why he always came back here. The old woman never gave him a moment's peace, and her cooking could kill a man. "You got a room, Maggie? And some hot water?"

"You got a dollar?" She held out her thin hand. When Jake dropped a coin into it, she tested it with the few good teeth she had left. It wasn't that she didn't trust Jake. She did. She just didn't trust the United States government. "Might as well take the one you had before. No one's in it."

"Fine." He started up the steps.

"Ain't had too much excitement since you left. Couple drifters shot each other over at the Bird Cage. Worthless pair, the both of them. Only one dead, though. Sheriff sent the other on his way after the doc patched him up. Young Mary Sue Brody got herself in trouble with that Mitchell boy. Always said she was a fast thing, that Mary Sue. Had a right proper wedding, though. Just last month."

Jake kept walking, but that didn't stop Maggie. One of the privileges in running a rooming house was giving and receiving gossip.

"What a shame about old Matt Conway."

That stopped him. He turned. Maggie was still at the base of the steps, using the edge of her apron to swipe half-heartedly at the dust on the banister. "What about Matt Conway?"

"Got himself killed in that worthless mine of his. A cave-in. Buried him the day before yesterday."

Chapter 2

The heat was murderous. A plume of thin yellow dust rose each time a rider passed, then hung there to clog the still air. Sarah longed for a long, cool drink and a seat in the shade. From the looks of things, there wasn't a place in town where a lady could go to find such amenities. Even if there were, she was afraid to leave her trunks on the side of the road and risk missing her father.

She'd been so sure he would be waiting for her. But then, a man in his position could have been held up by a million things. Work at the mine, a problem with an employee, perhaps last-minute preparations for her arrival.

She'd waited twelve years, she reminded herself, resisting the urge to loosen her collar. She could wait a little longer.

A buckboard passed, spewing up more dust, so that she was forced to lift a handkerchief to her mouth. Her dark blue traveling skirt and her neat matching jacket with its fancy black braid were covered with dust. With a sigh, she glanced down at her blouse, which was drooping hopelessly and now seemed more yellow than white. It wasn't really vanity. The sisters had never given her a chance to develop any. She was concerned that her father would see her for the first time when she was travel-stained and close to exhaustion. She'd wanted to look her best for him at this first meeting. All she could do now was retie the bow at her chin, then brush hopelessly at her skirts.

She looked a fright. But she'd make it up to him. She would wear her brand-new white muslin gown for dinner tonight, the one with the charming rosebuds embroidered all over the skirt. Her kid slippers were dyed pink to match. He'd be proud of her.

If only he'd come, she thought, and take her away from here.

Jake crossed the street after losing the battle he'd waged with himself. It wasn't his business, and it wasn't his place to tell her. But for the past ten minutes he'd been watching her standing at the side of the road, waiting. He'd been able to see, too clearly, the look of hope that sprang into her eyes each time a horse or wagon approached. Somebody had to tell the woman that her father wasn't going to meet her.

Sarah saw him coming. He walked easily, despite the guns at his sides. As if they had always been there. As if they always would be. They rode low on his hips, shifting with his movements. And he kept his eyes on her in a way that she was certain a man shouldn't keep his eyes on a woman—unless she was his own. When she felt her heart flutter, she automatically stiffened her backbone.

It was Lucilla who was always talking about fluttering hearts. It was Lucilla who painted romantic pictures of lawless men and lawless places. Sarah preferred a bit more reality in her dreams.

"Ma'am." He was surprised that she hadn't already swooned under the power of the afternoon sun. Maybe she was tougher than she looked, but he doubted it.

"Mr. Redman." Determined to be gracious, she allowed her lips to curve ever so slightly at the corners.

He tucked his thumbs into the pockets of his pants. "I got some news about your father."

She smiled fully, beautifully, so that her whole face lit

up with it. Her eyes turned to gold in the sunlight. Jake felt the punch, like a bullet in the chest.

"Oh, did he leave word for me? Thank you for letting me know. I might have waited here for hours."

"Ma'am—"

"Is there a note?"

"No." He wanted to get this done, and done quickly. "Matt's dead. There was an accident at his mine." He was braced for weeping, for wild wailing, but her eyes filled with fury, not tears.

"How dare you? How dare you lie to me about something like that?" She would have brushed past him, but Jake clamped a hand over her arm. Sarah's first reaction was simple indignation at being manhandled. Then she looked up at him, really looked, and said nothing.

"He was buried two days ago." He felt her recoil, then go still. The fury drained from her eyes, even as the color drained from her cheeks. "Don't go fainting on me."

It was true. She could see the truth on his face as clearly as she could see his distaste at being the one to tell her. "An accident?" she managed.

"A cave-in." He was relieved that she wasn't going to faint, but he didn't care for the glassy look in her eyes. "You'll want to talk to the sheriff."

"The sheriff?" she repeated dully.

"His office is across the street."

She just shook her head and stared at him. Her eyes *were* gold, Jake decided. The color of the brandy he sometimes drank at the Silver Star. Right now they were huge and full of hurt. He watched her bite down on her bottom lip in a gesture he knew meant she was fighting not to let go of the emotions he saw so clearly in her eyes.

If she'd fainted, he'd happily have left her on the road in

the care of whatever woman happened to pass by. But she was hanging on, and it moved something in him.

Swearing, Jake shifted his grip from her arm to her elbow and guided her across the street. He was damned if he could figure out how he'd elected himself responsible.

Sheriff Barker was at his desk, bent over some paperwork and a cup of sweetened coffee. He was balding rapidly. Every morning he took the time to comb what hair he had left over the spreading bare spot on top of his head. He had the beginnings of a paunch brought on by his love of his wife's baking. He kept the law in Lone Bluff, but he didn't worry overmuch about the order. It wasn't that he was corrupt, just lazy.

He glanced up as Jake entered. Then he sighed and sent tobacco juice streaming into the spittoon in the corner. When Jake Redman was around, there was usually work to be done.

"So you're back." The wad of tobacco gave Barker a permanently swollen jaw. "Thought you might take a fancy to New Mexico." His brows lifted when Jake ushered Sarah inside. There was enough gentleman left in him to bring him to his feet. "Ma'am."

"This is Matt Conway's daughter."

"Well, I'll be damned. Begging your pardon, ma'am. I was just fixing to send you a letter."

"Sheriff." She had to pause a moment to find her balance. She would not fall apart, not here, in front of strangers.

"Barker, ma'am." He came around the desk to offer her a chair.

"Sheriff Barker." Sarah sat, praying she'd be able to stand again. "Mr. Redman has just told me that my father…" She couldn't say it. No matter how weak or cowardly it might be, she just couldn't say the words.

"Yes, ma'am. I'm mighty sorry. Couple of kids wandered on up by the mine playing games and found him. Appears he was working the mine when some of the beams gave way." When she said nothing, Barker cleared his throat and opened the top drawer of his desk. "He had this watch on him, and his tobacco." He'd had his pipe, as well, but since it had been broken—like most of Conway's bones— Barker hadn't thought anyone would want it. "We figured he'd want to be buried with his wedding ring on."

"Thank you." As if in a trance, she took the watch and the tobacco pouch from him. She remembered the watch. The tears almost won when she remembered how he'd taken it out to check the time before he'd left her in Mother Superior's lemony-smelling office. "I want to see where he's buried. My trunks will need to be taken out to his house."

"Miss Conway, if you don't mind me offering some advice, you don't want to stay way out there. It's no place for a young lady like you, all alone and all. My wife'll be happy to have you stay with us for a few days. Until the stage heads east again."

"It's kind of you to offer." She braced a hand on the chair and managed to stand again. "But I'd prefer to spend the night in my father's house." She swallowed and discovered that her throat was hurtfully dry. "Is there… Do I owe you anything for the burial?"

"No, ma'am. We take care of our own around here."

"Thank you." She needed air. With the watch clutched in her hand, she pushed through the door. Leaning against a post, she tried to catch her breath.

"You ought to take the sheriff up on his offer."

She turned her head to give Jake an even look. She could only be grateful that he made her angry enough to help her hold off her grief. He hadn't offered a word of sympathy. Not one. Well, she was glad of it.

"I'm going to stay in my father's house. Will you take me?"

He rubbed a hand over his chin. He hadn't shaved in a week. "I've got things to do."

"I'll pay you," she said quickly when he started to walk away.

He stopped and looked back at her. She was determined, all right. He wanted to see how determined. "How much?"

"Two dollars." When he only continued to look at her, she said between her teeth, "Five."

"You got five?"

Disgusted, Sarah dug in her reticule. "There."

Jake looked at the bill in her hand. "What's that?"

"It's five dollars."

"Not around here it ain't. Around here it's paper."

Sarah pushed the bill back into her reticule and pulled out a coin. "Will this do?"

Jake took the coin and turned it over in his hand, then stuck it in his pocket. "That'll do fine. I'll get a wagon."

Miserable man, she thought as he strode away. She hated him. And hated even more the fact that she needed him.

During the long, hot ride in the open wagon, she said nothing. She no longer cared about the desolation of the landscape, the heat or the cold-bloodedness of the man beside her. Her emotions seemed to have shriveled up inside her. Every mile they'd gone was just another mile behind her.

Jake Redman didn't seem to need conversation. He drove in silence, armed with a rifle across his lap, as well as the pistols he carried. There hadn't been trouble out here in quite some time, but the attack on the coach had warned him that that could change.

He'd recognized Strong Wolf in the party that had attacked the stage. If the Apache brave had decided to raid in the area, he would hit the Conway place sooner or later.

They passed no one. They saw only sand and rock and a hawk out hunting.

When he reined the horses in, Sarah saw nothing but a small adobe house and a few battered sheds on a patch of thirsty land.

"Why are we stopping here?"

Jake jumped down from the wagon. "This is Matt Conway's place."

"Don't be ridiculous." Because it didn't appear that he was going to come around and assist her, Sarah struggled down herself. "Mr. Redman, I paid you to take me to my father's home and I expect you to keep the bargain."

Before she could stop him, he dumped one of her trunks on the ground. "What do you think you're doing?"

"Delivering your luggage."

"Don't you take another piece off that wagon." Surprising them both, Sarah grabbed his shirt and pulled him around to face her. "I insist you take me to my father's house immediately."

She wasn't just stupid, Jake thought. She was irritating. "Fine." He clipped her around the waist and hauled her over his shoulder.

At first she was too shocked to move. No man had ever touched her before. Now this, this *ruffian* had his hands all over her. And they were alone. Totally alone. Sarah began to struggle as he pushed open the door of the hut. Before she could draw the breath to scream, he was dropping her to her feet again.

"That good enough for you?"

She stared at him, visions of a hundred calamities that could befall a defenseless woman dancing in her brain. She stepped back, breathing hard, and prayed she could reason with him. "Mr. Redman, I have very little money of my own—hardly enough worth stealing."

Something came into his eyes that had her breath stopping altogether. He looked more than dangerous now. He looked fatal. "I don't steal." The light coming through the low doorway arched around him. She moistened her lips.

"Are you going to kill me?"

He nearly laughed. Instead, he leaned against the wall. Something about her was eating at him. He didn't know what or why, but he didn't like it. Not one damn bit.

"Probably not. You want to take a look around?" She just shook her head. "They told me he was buried around back, near the entrance of the mine. I'll go check on Matt's horses and water the team."

When he left, she continued to stare at the empty doorway. This was madness. Did the man expect her to believe her father had lived here, like this? She had letters, dozens of them, telling her about the house he'd been building, the house he'd finished, the house that would be waiting for her when she was old enough to join him.

The mine. If the mine was near, perhaps she could find someone there she could speak with. Taking a cautious look out the doorway, Sarah hurried out and rounded the house.

She passed what might have been the beginnings of a small vegetable garden, withered now in the sun. There was a shed that served as a stable and an empty paddock made of a few rickety pieces of wood. She walked beyond it to where the ground began to rise with the slope of the mountain.

The entrance to the mine was easily found, though it was hardly more than a hole in the rock wall. Above it was a crudely etched plank of wood.

SARAH'S PRIDE

She felt the tears then. They came in a rush that she had to work hard to hold back. There were no workmen here, no carts shuttling along filled with rock, no picks hacking out gold. She saw it for what it was, the dream of a man who had had little else. Her father had never been a successful prospector or an important landowner. He'd been a man digging in rock and hoping for the big strike.

She saw the grave then. They had buried him only a few yards from the entrance. Someone had been kind enough to fashion a cross and carve his name on it. She knelt and ran her palm along the rubble that covered him.

He'd lied. For twelve years he'd lied to her, telling her stories about rich veins and the mother lode. He'd spun fantasies about a big house with a parlor and fine wooden floors. Had he needed to believe it? When he'd left her he'd made her a promise.

"You'll have everything your heart desires, my sweet, sweet Sarah. Everything your mother would have wanted for you."

He had kept his promise—except for one thing. One vital thing. He hadn't given her himself. All those years, all she'd really wanted had been her father.

He'd lived like this, she thought, in a mud house in the middle of nowhere, so that she could have pretty dresses and new stockings. So that she could learn how to serve tea and waltz. It must have taken nearly everything he'd managed to dig out of the rock to keep her in school back east.

Now he was dead. She could barely remember his face, and he was dead. Lost to her.

"Oh, Papa, didn't you know how little it mattered?" Lying across the grave, she let the tears come until she'd wept her heart clean.

She'd been gone a long time. Too long, Jake thought. He was just about to go after her when he saw her coming over the rise from the direction of the old mine. She paused there, looking down at the house her father had lived in for more than a decade. She'd taken off her bonnet, and she was holding it by the ribbons. For a moment she stood like a statue in the airless afternoon, her face marble-pale, her body slim and elegant. Her hair was pinned up, but a few tendrils had escaped to curl around her face. The sun slanted over it so that it glowed richly, reminding him of the hide of a young deer.

Jake blew out the last of the smoke from the cigarette he'd rolled. She was a hell of a sight, silhouetted against the bluff. She made him ache in places he didn't care to think about. Then she saw him. He could almost see her chin come up as she started down over the rough ground. Yeah, she was a hell of a sight.

"Mr. Redman." The grief was there in her red-rimmed eyes and her pale cheeks, but her voice was strong. "I apologize for the scene I caused earlier."

That tied his tongue for a moment. The way she said it, they might have been talking over tea in some cozy parlor. "Forget it. You ready to go back?"

"I beg your pardon?"

He jerked his thumb toward the wagon. Sarah noted that all her trunks were neatly stacked on it again. "I said, are you ready to go back?"

She glanced down at her hands. Because the palms of her gloves were grimy, she tugged them off. They'd never be the same, she mused. Nothing would. She drew a long, steadying breath.

"I thought you understood me. I'm staying in my father's house."

"Don't be a fool. A woman like you's got no business out here."

"Really?" Her eyes hardened. "Be that as it may, I'm not leaving. I'd appreciate it if you'd move my trunks inside." She breezed by him.

"You won't last a day."

She stopped to look over her shoulder. Jake was forced

to admit that he'd faced men over the barrel of a gun who'd had less determination in their eyes. "Is that your opinion, Mr. Redman?"

"That's a fact."

"Would you care to wager on it?"

"Look, Duchess, this is hard country even if you're born to it. Heat, snakes, mountain lions—not to mention Apaches."

"I appreciate you pointing all that out, Mr. Redman. Now my luggage."

"Damn fool woman," he muttered as he strode over to the wagon. "You want to stay out here, hell, it don't matter to me." He hefted a trunk into the house while Sarah stood a few feet back with her hands folded.

"Your language, Mr. Redman, is quite unnecessary."

He only swore with more skill as he carried in the second trunk. "Nobody's going to be around when it gets dark and you change your mind."

"I won't change my mind, but thank you so much for your concern."

"No concern of mine," he muttered, ignoring her sarcasm. He scooped up the rest of her boxes and dumped them inside the doorway. "Hope you got provisions in there, as well as fancy dresses."

"I assure you I'll be fine." She walked to the doorway herself and turned to him. "Perhaps you could tell me where I might get water."

"There's a stream half a mile due east."

Half a mile? she thought, trying not to show her dismay. "I see." Shading her eyes, she looked out. Jake mumbled another oath, took her by the shoulders and pointed in the opposite direction. "That way's east, Duchess."

"Of course." She stepped back. "Thank you again, Mr.

Redman, for all your help. And good day," she added before she closed the door in his face.

She could hear him swearing at her as he unhitched the horses. If she hadn't been so weary, she might have been amused. She was certainly too exhausted to be shocked by the words he used. If she was going to stay, she was going to have to become somewhat accustomed to rough manners. She peeled off her jacket. And, she was going to stay.

If this was all she had left, she was going to make the best of it. Somehow.

She moved to the rounded opening beside the door that served as a window. From there she watched Jake ride away. He'd left her the wagon and stabled the rented horses with her father's two. For all the good it did her, Sarah thought with a sigh. She hadn't the vaguest idea of how to hitch a team, much less how to drive one.

She continued to watch Jake until he was nothing but a cloud of dust fading in the distance. She was alone. Truly alone. She had no one, and little more than nothing.

No one but herself, she thought. And if she had only that and a mud hut, she'd find a way to make the best of it. Nobody—and certainly not Jake Redman—was going to frighten her away.

Turning, she unbuttoned her cuffs and rolled up her sleeves. The good sisters had always claimed that simple hard work eased the mind and cleansed the soul. She was about to put that claim to the test.

She found the letters an hour later. When she came across them in the makeshift loft that served as a bedroom she wiped her grimy hands as best as she could on the embroidered apron she'd dug out of one of her trunks.

He'd kept them. From the first to the last she'd written, her father had kept her letters to him. The tears threatened again, but she willed them back. Tears would do neither of them any good now. But, oh, it helped more than she could ever have explained that he'd kept her letters. To know now, when she would never see him again, that he had thought of her as she had thought of him.

He must have received the last, the letter telling him she was coming to be with him, shortly before his death. Sarah hadn't mailed it until she'd been about to board the train. She'd told herself it was because she wanted to surprise him, but she'd also wanted to be certain he wouldn't have time to forbid her to come.

Would you have, Papa? she wondered. Or would you finally have been willing to share the truth with me? Had he thought her too weak, too fragile, to share the life he'd chosen? Was she?

Sighing, she looked around. Four bedrooms, and a parlor with the windows facing west, she thought with a quiet laugh. Well, according to Jake Redman, the window did indeed face west. The house itself was hardly bigger than the room she'd shared with Lucilla at school. It was too small, certainly, for all she'd brought with her from Philadelphia, but she'd managed to drag the trunks into one corner. To please herself, she'd taken out a few of her favorite things—one of her wildflower sketches, a delicate blue glass perfume bottle, a pretty petit-point pillow and the china-faced doll her father had sent her for her twelfth birthday.

They didn't make it home, not yet. But they helped.

Setting the letters back in the tin box beside the bed, she rose. She had practical matters to think about now. The first was money. After paying the five dollars, she had only twenty dollars left. She hadn't a clue to how long that would keep her, but she doubted it would be very long. Then there was food. That was of more immediate concern. She'd found some flour, a few cans of beans, some lard and a bottle of whiskey. Pressing a hand to her stom-

ach, Sarah decided she'd have to make do with the beans.
All she had to do now was to figure out how to start a fire
in the battered-looking stove.

She found a few twigs in the wood box, and a box of
matches. It took her half an hour, a lot of frustration and a
few words the sisters would never have approved of before
she was forced to admit she was a failure.

Jake Redman. Disgusted, she scowled at the handful of
charred twigs. The least the man could have done was to
offer to start a cook fire for her and fetch some water. She'd
already made the trip down to the stream and back once,
managing to scrounge out half a bucket from its stingy
trickle.

She'd eat the beans cold. She'd prove to Jake Redman
that she could do very well for herself, by herself.

Sarah unsheathed her father's bowie knife, shuddered
once at the sight of the vicious blade, then plunged it into
the lid of the can until she'd made an opening. Too hungry to care, she sat beside the small stone hearth and devoured the beans.

She'd think of it as an adventure, she told herself. One
she could write about to her friends in Philadelphia. A better one, she decided as she looked around the tiny, clean
cabin, than those in the penny dreadfuls Lucilla had gotten from the library and hidden in their room.

In those, the heroine had usually been helpless, a victim
waiting for the hero to rescue her in any of a dozen dashing
manners. Sarah scooped out more beans. Well, she wasn't
helpless, and as far as she could tell there wasn't a hero
within a thousand miles.

No one would have called Jake Redman heroic—though
he'd certainly looked it when he'd ridden beside the coach.
He was insulting and ill-mannered. He had cold eyes and a
hot temper. Hardly Sarah's idea of a hero. If she had to be

rescued—and she certainly didn't—she'd prefer someone smoother, a cavalry officer, perhaps. A man who carried a saber, a gentleman's weapon.

When she'd finished the beans, she hiccuped, wiped her mouth with the back of her hand and leaned back against the hearth only to lose her balance when a stone gave way. Nursing a bruised elbow, she shifted. She would have replaced the stone, but something caught her eye. Crouching again, she reached into the small opening that was now exposed and slowly pulled out a bag.

With her lips caught tight between her teeth, she poured gold coins into her lap. Two hundred and thirty dollars. Sarah pressed both hands to her mouth, swallowed, then counted again. There was no mistake. She hadn't known until that moment how much money could mean. She could buy decent food, fuel, whatever she needed to make her way.

She poured the coins back into the bag and dug into the hole again. This time she found the deed to Sarah's Pride.

What an odd man he must have been, she thought. To hide his possessions beneath a stone.

The last and most precious item she discovered in the hiding place was her father's journal. It delighted her. The small brown book filled with her father's cramped handwriting meant more to Sarah than all the gold coins in Arizona. She hugged it to her as she'd wanted to hug her father. Before she rose with it, she replaced the gold and the deed under the stone.

She would read about one of his days each evening. It would be like a gift, something that each day would bring her a little closer to this man she'd never really known. For now she would go back to the stream, wash as best she could and gather water for the morning.

Jake watched her come out of the cabin with a pail in

one hand and a lantern in the other. He'd made himself as comfortable as he needed to be among the rocks. There had been enough jerky and hardtack in his saddlebag to make a passable supper. Not what he'd planned on, exactly, but passable.

He'd be damned if he could figure out why he'd decided to keep an eye on her. The lady wasn't his problem. But even as he'd been cursing her and steering his horse toward town, he'd known he couldn't just ride off and leave her there alone.

Maybe it was because he knew what it was to lose everything. Or because he'd been alone himself for more years then he cared to remember. Or maybe, damn her, it had something to do with the way she'd looked coming down that bluff with her bonnet trailing by the ribbons and tears still drying on her face.

He hadn't thought he had a weak spot. Certainly not where women were concerned. He shoved himself to his feet. He just didn't have anything better to do.

He stayed well behind her. He knew how to move silently, over rock, through brush, in sunlight or in the dark of the moon. That was both a matter of survival and a matter of blood. In his youth he'd spent some years with his grandmother's people and he'd learned more than any white man could have learned in a lifetime about tracking without leaving a mark, about hunting without making a sound.

As for the woman, she was still wearing that fancy skirt with the bustle and shoes that were made for city sidewalks rather than rough ground. Twice Jake had to stop and wait, or even at a crawl he'd have caught up with her.

Probably break an ankle before she was through, he thought. That might be the best thing that could happen to her. Then he'd just cart her on back to town. Couldn't say he'd mind too much picking her up again. She felt good—maybe too good. He had to grin when she shrieked and landed on her fancy bustle because a rabbit darted across her path.

Nope, the pretty little duchess from Philadelphia wasn't going to last a day.

With a hand to her heart, Sarah struggled to her feet. She'd never seen a rabbit that large in her life. With a little sound of distress, she noted that she'd torn the hem of her skirt. How did the women out here manage? she wondered as she began to walk again. In this heat, a corset felt like iron and a fashionable skirt prevented anything but the most delicate walking.

When she reached the stream, she dropped down on a rock and went to work with her buttonhook. It was heaven, absolute heaven, to remove her shoes. There was a blister starting on her heel, but she'd worry about that later. Right now all she could think about was splashing some cool water on her skin.

She glanced around cautiously. There couldn't be anyone there. The sensation of being watched was a natural one, she supposed, when a woman was alone in the wilderness and the sun was going down. She unpinned the cameo at her throat and placed it carefully in her skirt pocket. It was the one thing she had that had belonged to her mother.

Humming to keep herself company, she unbuttoned her blouse and folded it over a rock. With the greatest relief, she unfastened her corset and dropped it on top of the blouse. She could breathe, really breathe, for the first time all day. Hurrying now, she stripped down to her chemise, then unhooked her stockings.

Glorious. She closed her eyes and let out a low sound of pleasure when she stepped into the narrow, ankle-deep stream. The water, trickling down from the mountains, was cold and clear as ice.

What the hell did she think she was doing? Jake let out a

low oath and averted his eyes. He didn't need this aggravation. Who would have thought the woman would strip down and play in the water with the night coming on? He glanced back to see her bend down to splash her face. There was nothing between the two of them but shadows and sunlight.

Water dampened the cotton she wore so that it clung here and there. When she bent to scoop up more water, the ruffles at the bodice sagged to tease him. Crouching behind the rock, he began to curse himself instead of her.

His own fault. Didn't he know minding your own business, and only your own, was the best way to get by? He'd just had to be riding along when the Apaches had hit the stage. He'd just had to be the one to tell her about her father. He'd just had to feel obliged to drive her out here. And then to stay.

What he should be doing was getting good and drunk at Carlotta's and spending the night in a feather bed wrestling with a woman. The kind of woman who knew what a man needed and didn't ask a bunch of fool questions. The kind of woman, Jake thought viciously, who didn't expect you to come to tea on Sunday.

He glanced back to see that one of the straps of Sarah's chemise had fallen down her arm and that her legs were gleaming and wet. Her shoulders were pale and smooth and bare.

Too long on the trail, Jake told himself. Too damn long, when a man started to hanker after skinny city women who didn't know east from west.

Sarah filled the pail as best she could, then stepped out of the stream. It was getting dark much more quickly than she'd expected. But she felt almost human again. Even the thought of the corset made her ribs ache, so she ignored it. After slipping on her blouse, she debated donning her shoes and stockings again. There was no one to see or disapprove.

Instead, she hitched on her skirt and made a bundle of the rest. With the water sloshing in the pail, she made her way gingerly along the path.

She had to fight the urge to hurry. With sunset, the air was cooling rapidly. And there were sounds. Sounds she didn't recognize or appreciate. Hoots and howls and rustles. Stones dug into her bare feet, and the lantern spread more shadow than light. The half mile back seemed much, much longer than it had before.

Again she had the uncomfortable sensation that someone was watching her. Apaches? Mountain lions? Damn Jake Redman. The little adobe dwelling looked like a haven to her now. Half running, she went through the door and bolted it behind her.

The first coyote sent up a howl to the rising moon.

Sarah shut her eyes. If she lived through the night, she'd swallow her pride and go back to town.

In the rocks not far away, Jake bedded down.

Chapter 3

Soon after sunrise, Sarah awoke, stiff and sore and hungry. She rolled over, wanting to cling to sleep until Lucilla's maid brought the morning chocolate. She'd had the most awful dream about some gray-eyed man carrying her off to a hot, desolate place. He'd been handsome, the way men in dreams were supposed to be, but in a rugged, almost uncivilized way. His skin had been like bronze, taut over his face. He'd had high, almost exotic cheekbones, and the dark shadow of a beard. His hair had been untidy and as black as coal—but thick, quite thick, as it had swept down past his collar. She'd wondered, even in the dream, what it would be like to run her hands through it.

There had been something familiar about him, almost as if she'd known him. In fact, when he'd forced her to kiss him, a name had run through her mind. Then he hadn't had to force her any longer.

Drowsy, Sarah smiled. She would have to tell Lucilla about the dream. They would both laugh about it before they dressed for the day. Lazily she opened her eyes.

This wasn't the rose-and-white room she used whenever she visited Lucilla and her family. Nor was it the familiar bedroom she had had for years at school.

Her father's house, she thought, as everything came back to her. This was her father's house, but her father was dead. She was alone. With an effort, she resisted the urge to bury her face in the pillow and weep again. She had to decide what to do, and in order to decide she had to think clearly.

For some time last night she'd been certain the best thing would be for her to return to town and use the money she had found to book passage east again. At best, Lucilla's family would welcome her. At worst, she could return to the convent. But that had been before she'd begun reading her father's journal. It had taken only the first two pages, the only two she'd allowed herself, to make her doubt.

He'd begun the journal on the day he'd left her to come west. The love and the hope he'd felt had been in every word. And the sadness. He'd still been raw with grief over the death of Sarah's mother.

For the first time she fully understood how devastated he had been by the loss of the woman they'd both shared so briefly. And how inadequate he'd felt at finding himself alone with a little girl. He'd made a promise to his wife on her deathbed that he would see that their daughter was well cared for.

She remembered the words her father had written on the yellowed paper.

She was leaving me. There was nothing I could do to stop it. Toward the end there was so much pain I prayed for God to take her quickly. My Ellen, my tiny, delicate Ellen. Her thoughts were all for me, and our sweet Sarah. I promised her. The only comfort I could give was my promise. Our daughter would have everything Ellen wanted for her. Proper schooling and church on Sunday. She would be raised the way my Ellen would have raised her. Like a lady. One day she'd have a fine house and a father she could be proud of.

He'd come here to try, Sarah thought as she tossed back the thin blanket. And she supposed he'd done as well as he could. Now she had to figure what was best. And if she was going to think, first she needed to eat.

After she'd dressed in her oldest skirt and blouse, she took stock of the cupboard again. She could not, under any circumstances, face another meal of cold beans. Perhaps he had a storage cellar somewhere, a smokehouse, anything. Sarah pushed open the door and blinked in the blinding sunlight.

At first she thought it was a mirage. But mirages didn't carry a scent, did they? This one smelled of meat roasting and coffee brewing. And what she saw was Jake Redman sitting cross-legged by a fire ringed with stones. Gathering up her skirt, she forgot her hunger long enough to stride over to him.

"What are you doing here?"

He glanced up and gave her the briefest of nods. He poured coffee from a small pot into a dented tin cup. "Having breakfast."

"You rode all the way out here to have breakfast?" She didn't know what it was he was turning on the spit, but her stomach was ready for just about anything.

"Nope." He tested the meat and judged it done. "Never left." He jerked his head in the direction of the rocks. "Bedded down over there."

"There?" Sarah eyed the rocks with some amazement. "Whatever for?"

He looked up again. The look in his eyes made her hands flutter nervously. It made her feel, though it was foolish, that he knew how she looked stripped down to her chemise. "Let's say it was a long ride back to town."

"I hardly expect you to watch over me, Mr. Redman. I explained that I could take... What is that?"

Jake was eating with his fingers and with obvious enjoyment. "Rabbit."

"Rabbit?" Sarah wrinkled her nose at the idea, but her stomach betrayed her. "I suppose you trapped it on my property."

So it was her property already. "Might've."

"If that's the case, the least you could do is offer to share."

Jake obligingly pulled off a hunk of meat. "Help yourself."

"Don't you have any... Never mind." When in Rome, Sarah decided. Taking the meat and the coffee he offered, she sat down on a rock.

"Get yourself some supper last night?"

"Yes, thank you." Never, never in her life, had she tasted anything better than this roast rabbit in the already-sweltering morning. "You're an excellent cook, Mr. Redman."

"I get by." He offered her another hunk. This time she didn't hesitate.

"No, really." She caught herself talking with her mouth full, and she didn't care. "This is delightful." Because she doubted that his saddlebags held any linens, she licked her fingers.

"Better than a can of cold beans, anyway."

She glanced up sharply, but he wasn't even looking at her. "I suppose." She'd never had breakfast with a man before, and she decided it would be proper to engage in light conversation. "Tell me, Mr. Redman, what is your profession?"

"Never gave it much thought."

"But surely you must have some line of work."

"Nope." He leaned back against a rock and, taking out his pouch of tobacco, proceeded to roll a cigarette. She looked as fresh and neat as a daisy, he thought. You'd have thought she'd spent the night in some high-priced hotel instead of a mud hut.

Apparently making conversation over a breakfast of roasted rabbit took some skill. Patiently she smoothed her skirts and tried again. "Have you lived in Arizona long?"

"Why?"

"I—" The cool, flat look he sent her had her fumbling. "Simple curiosity."

"I don't know about back in Philadelphia." Jake took out a match, scraped it on the rock and lit the twisted end of his cigarette, studying her all the while. "But around here people don't take kindly to questions."

"I see." Her back had stiffened. She'd never encountered anyone to whom rudeness came so easily. "In a civilized society, a casual question is merely a way to begin a conversation."

"Around here it's a way to start a fight." He drew on the cigarette. "You want to fight with me, Duchess?"

"I'll thank you to stop referring to me by that name."

He grinned at her again, but lazily, the brim of his hat shadowing his eyes. "You look like one, especially when you're riled."

Her chin came up. She couldn't help it. But she answered him in calm, even tones. "I assure you, I'm not at all riled. Although you have, on several occasions already, been rude and difficult and annoying. Where I come from, Mr. Redman, a woman is entitled to a bit more charm and gallantry from a man."

"That so?" Her mouth dropped open when he slowly drew out his gun. "Don't move."

Move? She couldn't even breathe. She'd only called him rude and, sweet Mary, he was going to shoot her. "Mr. Redman, I don't—"

The bullet exploded against the rock a few inches away

from her. With a shriek, she tumbled into the dirt. When she found the courage to look up, Jake was standing and lifting something dead and hideous from the rock.

"Rattler," he said easily. When she moaned and started to cover her eyes, he reached down and hauled her to her feet. "I'd take a good look," he suggested, still holding the snake in front of her. "If you stay around here, you're going to see plenty more."

It was the disdain in his voice that had her fighting off the swoon. With what little voice she had left, she asked, "Would you kindly dispose of that?"

With a muttered curse, he tossed it aside, then began to smother the fire. Sarah felt her breakfast rising uneasily and waited for it to settle. "It appears you saved my life."

"Yeah, well, don't let it get around."

"I won't, I assure you." She drew herself up straight, hiding her trembling hands in the folds of her skirts. "I appreciate the meal, Mr. Redman. Now, if you'll excuse me, I have a number of things to do."

"You can start by getting yourself into the wagon. I'll drive you back to town."

"I appreciate the offer. As a matter of fact, I would be grateful. I need some supplies."

"Look, there's got to be enough sense in that head of yours for you to see you don't belong out here. It's a two-hour drive into town. There's nothing out here but rattlers and coyotes."

She was afraid he was right. The night she'd spent in the cabin had been the loneliest and most miserable of her life. But somewhere between the rabbit and the snake she'd made up her mind. Matt Conway's daughter wasn't going to let all his efforts and his dreams turn to dust. She was staying, Lord help her.

"My father lived here. This place was obviously important to him. I intend to stay." She doubted Jake Redman had enough heart to understand her reasons. "Now, if you'd be good enough to hitch up the wagon, I'll go change."

"Change what?"

"Why, my dress, of course. I can hardly go into town like this."

He cast a glance over her. She already looked dolled-up enough for a church social in her crisp white blouse and gingham skirt. He'd never known gingham to look quite so good on a woman before.

"Lone Bluff ain't Philadelphia. It ain't anyplace. You want the wagon hitched, I'll oblige you, but you'd better watch how it's done, because there's not going to be anyone around to do it for you next time." With that, he slung his saddlebags over his shoulder and walked away.

Very well, she thought after one last deep breath. He was quite right. It was time she learned how to do things for herself. The sooner she learned, the sooner she'd have no more need of him.

With her head held high, she followed him. She watched him guide the team out. It seemed easy enough. You simply hooked this and tied that and the deed was done. Men, she thought with a little smile. They always exaggerated the most basic chores.

"Thank you, Mr. Redman. If you'll wait just a moment, I'll be ready to go."

Didn't the woman know anything? Jake tipped his hat forward. He'd driven her out of town yesterday. If he drove her back this morning her reputation would be ruined. Even Lone Bluff had its standards. Since she'd decided to stay, at least temporarily, she'd need all the support she could get from the town women.

"I got business of my own, ma'am."

"But—" He was already moving off to saddle his own horse. Setting her teeth, Sarah stamped inside. She added another twenty dollars to what she carried in her reticule. As an afterthought she took down the rifle her father had left on the wall. She hadn't the least idea how to use it, was certain she wouldn't be able to in even the most dire circumstances, but she felt better having it.

Jake was mounted and waiting when she came out. "The road will lead you straight into town," he told her as she fastened her bonnet. "If you give Lucius a dollar he'll drive back out with you, then take the wagon and team back to the livery. Matt's got two horses of his own in the stables. Someone from town's been keeping an eye on them."

"A dollar." As if it were spun glass, she set the rifle in the wagon. "You charged me five."

He grinned at her. "I'm not Lucius." With a tip of his hat, he rode off.

It didn't take her long to climb up into the wagon. But she had to gather her courage before she touched the reins. Though she considered herself an excellent horsewoman, she'd never driven a team before. You've ridden behind them, she reminded herself as she picked up the reins. How difficult can it be?

She took the horses—or they took her—in a circle three times before she managed to head them toward the road.

Jake sat on his horse and watched her from a ridge. It was the best laugh he'd had in months.

By the time she reached Lone Bluff, Sarah was sweating profusely, her hands felt raw and cramped and her lower back was on fire. In front of the dry goods store she climbed down on legs that felt like water. After smoothing her skirts and patting her forehead dry, she spotted a young boy whittling a stick.

"Young man, do you know a man named Lucius?"

"Everybody knows old Lucius."

Satisfied, Sarah drew a coin out of her bag. "If you can find Lucius and tell him Miss Sarah Conway wishes to see him, you can have this penny."

The boy eyed it, thinking of peppermint sticks. "Yes, ma'am." He was off at a run.

At least children seemed about the same, east or west.

Sarah entered the store. There were several customers milling around, looking over the stock and gossiping. They all stopped to stare at Sarah before going back to their business. The young woman behind the counter came around to greet her.

"Good morning. May I help you?"

"Yes, I'm Sarah Conway."

"I know." When the pretty brunette smiled, dimples flashed in her cheeks. She was already envying Sarah her bonnet. "You arrived on the stage yesterday. I'm very sorry about your father. Everyone liked Matt."

"Thank you." Sarah found herself smiling back. "I'm going to need a number of supplies."

"Are you really going to stay out there, at Matt's place? Alone?"

"Yes. At least for now."

"I'd be scared to death." The brunette gave her an appraising look, then offered a hand. "I'm Liza Cody. No relation."

"I beg your pardon?"

"To Buffalo Bill. Most people ask. Welcome to Lone Bluff."

"Thank you."

With Liza's help, Sarah began to gather supplies and introductions. Within twenty minutes she'd nodded to half the women in Lone Bluff, been given a recipe for biscuits and been asked her opinion of the calico fabric just arrived from St. Joe.

Her spirits rose dramatically. Perhaps the women dressed less fashionably than their counterparts in the East, but they made her feel welcome.

"Ma'am."

Sarah turned to see Lucius, hat in hand. Beside him, the young boy was nearly dancing in anticipation of the penny. The moment it was in his hand, he raced to the jars of hard candy and began to negotiate.

"Mr...."

"Just Lucius, ma'am."

"Lucius, I was told you might be willing to drive my supplies back for me, then return the wagon and team to the livery."

He pushed his chaw into his cheek and considered. "Well, now, maybe I would."

"I'd be willing to give you a dollar for your trouble."

He grinned, showing a few yellowed—and several missing—teeth. "Glad to help, Miss Conway."

"Perhaps you'd begin by loading my supplies."

Leaving him to it, Sarah turned back to Liza. "Miss Cody."

"Liza, please."

"Liza, I wonder if you might have any tea, and I would dearly love some fresh eggs."

"Don't get much call for tea, but we've got some in the back." Liza opened the door to the rear storeroom. Three fat-bellied puppies ran out. "John Cody, you little monster. I told you to keep these pups outside."

Laughing, Sarah crouched down to greet them. "Oh, they're adorable."

"One's adorable, maybe," Liza muttered. As usual, her young brother was nowhere in sight when she needed him. "Three's unmanageable. Just last night they chewed through a sack of meal. Pop finds out, he'll take a strap to Johnny."

A brown mutt with a black circle around his left eye jumped into Sarah's lap. And captured her heart. "You're a charmer, aren't you?" She laughed as he bathed her face.

"A nuisance is more like it."

"Will you sell one?"

"Sell?" Liza stretched to reach the tea on a high shelf. "My pop'd pay you to take one."

"Really?" With the brown pup cradled in her arms, Sarah stood again. "I'd love to have one. I could use the company."

Liza added the tea and eggs to Sarah's total. "You want that one, you take it right along." She grinned when the pup licked Sarah's face again. "He certainly seems taken with you."

"I'll take very good care of him." Balancing the dog, she took out the money to pay her bill. "Thank you for everything."

Liza counted out the coins before she placed them in the cash drawer and took out Sarah's change. Pop would be pleased, she thought. Not only because of the pup, but because Miss Conway was a cash customer. Liza was pleased because Sarah was young and pretty and would surely know everything there was to know about the latest fashions.

"It's been nice meeting you, Miss Conway."

"Sarah."

Liza smiled again and walked with Sarah to the door. "Maybe I'll ride out and see you, if you don't mind."

"I'd love it. Any time at all."

Abruptly Liza lifted a hand to pat her hair. "Good morning, Mr. Carlson."

"Liza, you're looking pretty as ever." She blushed and fluttered, though Carlson's eyes were on Sarah.

"Samuel Carlson, this is Sarah Conway."

"Delighted." Carlson's smile made his pale, handsome

face even more attractive. It deepened the already-brilliant blue of his eyes. When he lifted Sarah's hand to his lips in a smooth, cavalier gesture, she was doubly glad she'd come into town.

Apparently Lone Bluff had some gentlemen after all. Samuel Carlson was slim and well dressed in a beautiful black riding coat and a spotless white shirt. His trim mustache was the same rich brown as his well-groomed hair. He had, as a gentleman should, swept off his hat at the introduction. It was a particularly fine hat, Sarah thought, black like his coat, with a silver chain for a band.

"My deepest sympathies for your loss, Miss Conway. Your father was a fine man and a good friend."

"Thank you. It's been comforting for me to learn he was well thought of."

The daughter was certainly a pretty addition to a dust hole like Lone Bluff, he thought. "Word around town is that you'll be staying with us for a while." He reached over to scratch the puppy's ears and was rewarded with a low growl.

"Hush, now." Sarah smiled an apology. "Yes, I've decided to stay. At least for the time being."

"I hope you'll let me know if there's anything I can do to help." He smiled again. "Undoubtedly life here isn't what you're used to."

The way he said it made it clear that it was a compliment. Mr. Carlson was obviously a man of the world, and of some means. "Thank you." She handed the puppy to Lucius and was gratified when Carlson assisted her into the wagon. "It was a pleasure to meet you, Mr. Carlson."

"The pleasure was mine, Miss Conway."

"Goodbye, Liza. I hope you'll come and visit soon." Sarah settled the puppy on her lap. She considered it just her bad luck that she glanced across the street at that moment.

Jake was there, one hand hooked in his pocket, leaning against a post, watching. With an icy nod, she acknowledged him, then stared straight ahead as Lucius clucked to the horses.

When the wagon pulled away, the men studied each other. There was no nod of acknowledgment. They simply watched, cool and cautious, across the dusty road.

Sarah felt positively triumphant. As she stored her supplies, the puppy circled her legs, apparently every bit as pleased as she with the arrangement. Her nights wouldn't be nearly so lonely now, with the dog for company. She'd met people, was perhaps even on the way to making friends. Her cupboard was full, and Lucius had been kind enough to show her how to fire up the old cookstove.

Tonight, after supper, she was going to write to Lucilla and Mother Superior. She would read another page or two from her father's journal before she curled up under the freshly aired blanket.

Jake Redman be damned, she thought as she bent to tickle the pup's belly. She was making it.

With a glass of whiskey at his fingertips, Jake watched Carlotta work the room. She sure was something. Her hair was the color of gold nuggets plucked from a riverbed, and her lips were as red as the velvet drapes that hung in her private room.

She was wearing red tonight, something tight that glittered as it covered her long, curvy body and clung to her smooth white breasts. Her shoulders were bare. Jake had always thought that a woman's shoulders were enough to drive a man to distraction.

He thought of Sarah, standing ankle-deep in a stream with water glistening on her skin.

He took another gulp of whiskey.

Carlotta's girls were dressed to kill, as well. The men in the Silver Star were getting their money's worth. The piano rang out, and the whiskey and the laughter poured.

The way he figured it, Carlotta ran one of the best houses in Arizona. Maybe one of the best west of the Mississippi. The whiskey wasn't watered much, and the girls weren't bad. A man could almost believe they enjoyed their work. As for Carlotta, Jake figured she enjoyed it just fine.

Money came first with her. He knew, because she'd once had enough to drink to tell him that she took a healthy cut of all her girls' pay. If the man one of her girls was with decided to slip her a little extra, that was just fine with Carlotta. She took a cut of that, as well.

She had dreams of moving her business to San Francisco and buying a place with crystal chandeliers, gilt mirrors and red carpets. Carlotta favored red. But for now, like the rest of them, Carlotta was stuck in Lone Bluff.

Tipping back more whiskey, Jake watched her. She moved like a queen, her full red lips always smiling, her cool blue eyes always watching. She was making sure her girls were persuading the men to buy them plenty of drinks. What the bartender served the working girls was hardly more than colored water, but the men paid, and paid happily, before they moved along to one of the narrow rooms upstairs.

Hell of a business, Jake thought as he helped himself to one of the cigars Carlotta provided for her paying customers. She had them shipped all the way from Cuba, and they had a fine, rich taste. Jake had no doubt she added to the price of her whiskey and her girls to pay for them. Business was business.

One of the girls sidled over to light the cigar for him. He just shook his head at the invitation. She was warm and ripe and smelled like a bouquet of roses. For the life of him he couldn't figure out why he wasn't interested.

"You're going to hurt the girls' feelings." Perfume trailing behind her, Carlotta joined Jake at the table. "Don't you see anything you like?"

He tipped his chair back against the wall. "See plenty I like."

She laughed and lifted a hand in a subtle signal. "You going to buy me a drink, Jake?" Before he could answer, one of the girls was bringing over a new bottle and a glass. No watered-down liquor for Carlotta. "Haven't seen you around in a while."

"Haven't been around."

Carlotta took a drink and let it sweep through her system. She'd take liquor over a man any day. "Going to stay around?"

"Might."

"Heard there was a little trouble on the stage yesterday. It's not like you to do good deeds, Jake." She drank again and smiled at him. In a movement as smooth as the liquor she drank, she dropped a hand to his thigh. "That's what I like about you."

"Just happened to be there."

"Also heard Matt Conway's daughter's in town." Smiling, she took the cigar from him and took a puff. "You working for her?"

"Why?"

"Word around is that you drove her on out to his place." She slowly blew out a stream of smoke from between her painted lips. "Can't see you digging in rock for gold, Jake, when it's easier just to take it."

"Far as I remember, there was never enough gold in that rock to dig for." He took the cigar back and clamped it between his teeth. "You know different?"

"I only know what I hear, and I don't hear much about Conway." She poured a second drink and downed it. She didn't want to talk about Matt Conway's mine or about what she knew. Something in the air tonight, she decided. Made her restless. Maybe she needed more than whiskey after all. "Glad you're back, Jake. Things have been too quiet around here."

Two men hankering after the same girl started to scuffle. Carlotta's tall black servant tossed them both out. She just smiled and poured a third drink. "If you're not interested in any of my girls, we could make other arrangements." She lifted the small glass in a salute before she knocked it back. "For old times' sake."

Jake looked at her. Her eyes glittered against her white skin. Her lips were parted. Above the flaming red of her dress, her breasts rose and fell invitingly. He knew what she could do to a man, with a man, when the mood was on her. It baffled and infuriated him that she didn't stir him in the least.

"Maybe some other time." He rose and, after dropping a few coins on the table, strolled out.

Carlotta's eyes hardened as she watched him. She only offered herself to a privileged few. And she didn't like to be rejected.

With the puppy snoozing at her feet, Sarah closed her father's journal. He'd written about an Indian attack on the wagon train and his own narrow escape. In simple, often stark terms, he'd written of the slaughter, the terror and the waste. Yet even after that he'd gone on, because he'd wanted to make something of himself. For her.

Shivering a bit despite her shawl, she rose to replace the book beneath the stone. If she had read those words while

still in Philadelphia, she would have thought them an ex-
aggeration. She was coming to know better.

With a half sigh, she looked down at her hands. They
were smooth and well tended. They were, she was afraid,
woefully inadequate to the task of carving out a life here.

It was only the night that made her feel that way, Sarah
told herself as she moved to check the bolt on the door.
She'd done all she could that day, and it had been enough.
She'd driven to town alone, stocked the cabin and replanted
the vegetable garden. Her back ached enough to tell her
she'd put in a full day. Tomorrow she'd start again.

The lonely howl of a coyote made her heart thud. Gathering the puppy to her breast, she climbed up for bed.

She was in her night shift when the dog started to bark
and growl. Exasperated, she managed to grab him before
he could leap from the loft.

"You'll break your neck." When he strained against her
hold and continued to yelp, she took him in her arms. "All
right, all right. If you have to go out, I'll let you out, but you
might have let me know before I went to bed." Nuzzling
him, she climbed down from the loft again. She saw the fire
through the window and ran to the door. "Oh, my God."

The moment she yanked it open the puppy ran out, barking furiously. With her hands to her cheeks, Sarah watched
the fire rise up and eat at the old, dry wood of the shed. A
scream, eerily like a woman's, pierced the night.

Her father's horses. Following instinct alone, she ran.

The horses were already wild-eyed, stamping and
screaming in their stalls. Muttering a prayer, Sarah dragged
the first one out and slapped its flank. The fire was moving fast, racing up the walls and onto the roof. The hay had
already caught and was burning wildly.

Eyes stinging from the smoke, she groped her way to
the second stall. Coughing, swearing, she fought the ter-

rified horse as it reared and shoved against her. Then she screamed herself when a flaming plank fell behind her. Fire licked closer and closer to the hem of her shift.

Whipping off her shawl, she tossed it over the horse's eyes and dragged them both out of the shed.

Blinded by smoke, she crawled to safety. Behind her she could hear the walls collapse, could hear the roar of flames consuming wood. Gone. It was gone. She wanted to beat her fists in the dirt and weep.

It could spread. The terror of that had her pushing up onto her hands and knees. Somehow she had to prevent the fire from spreading. She caught the sound of a horse running hard and had nearly gained her feet when something slammed into her.

Chapter 4

The night was clear, with a sharp-edged half-moon and white pinpoint stars. Jake rode easily, arguing with himself.

It was stupid, just plain stupid, for him to be heading out when he could be snuggled up against Carlotta right this minute. Except Carlotta didn't snuggle. What she did was more like devouring. With her, sex was fast and hot and uncomplicated. After all, business was business.

At least he knew what Carlotta was and what to expect from her. She used men like poker chips. That was fine with Jake. Carlotta wouldn't expect posies or boxes of chocolates or Sunday calls.

Sarah Conway was a whole different matter. A woman like that wanted a man to come courting wearing a stiff collar. And probably a tie. He snorted and kicked his mount into a trot. You'd have to see that your boots were shined so you could sit around making fancy talk. With her, sex would be… He swore viciously, and the mustang pricked up his ears. You didn't have sex with a woman like that. You didn't even think about it. And even if you did…

Well, he just wasn't interested.

So what the hell was he doing riding out to her place in the middle of the night?

"Stupid," he muttered to his horse.

Overhead, a nighthawk dived and killed with hardly a sound. Life was survival, and survival meant ruthlessness. Jake understood that, accepted it. But Sarah… He shook his head. Survival to her was making sure her ribbons matched her dress.

The best thing he could do was to turn around now and head back to town. Maybe ride right on through town and go down to Tombstone for a spell. He could pick up a job there if he had a mind to. Better yet, he could travel up to the mountains, where the air was cool and smelled of pine. There wasn't anything or anyone holding him in Lone Bluff. He was a free agent, and that was the way he intended to stay.

But he didn't turn his horse around.

When he got back from the mountains, he mused—if he got back—Miss Sarah Conway, with her big brown eyes and her white shoulders, would be long gone. Just plain stubbornness was keeping her here now, anyway. Even stubbornness had to give way sometime. If she was gone, maybe he'd stop having this feeling that he was about to make a big mistake.

As far as he could see, the biggest mistakes men made were over three things—money, whiskey and women. None of the three had ever meant enough to him to worry or fight over. He didn't plan on changing that.

Even if this woman *was* different. Somehow. That was what bothered him the most. He'd always been able to figure people. It had helped keep him alive all these years. He couldn't figure Sarah Conway, or what it was about her that made him want to see that she was safe. Maybe he was getting soft, but he didn't like to think so.

He couldn't help feeling for her some, traveling all this way just to find out her father was dead. And he had to admire the way she was sticking it out, staying at the old mine. It was stupid, he mused, but you had to admire it.

With a shrug, he kept riding. He was nearly to the Conway place, anyway. He might as well take a look and make sure she hadn't shot her foot off with her daddy's rifle.

He smelled the fire before he saw it. His head came up, like a wolf's when it scents an enemy. In a similar move, the mustang reared and showed the whites of his eyes. When he caught the first flicker of flame, he kicked the horse into a run. What had the damn fool woman done now?

There had only been a few times in his life when he had experienced true fear. He didn't care for the taste of it. And he tasted it now, as his mind conjured up the image of Sarah trapped inside the burning house, the oil she'd undoubtedly spilled spreading the fire hot and fast.

Another image came back to him, an old one, an image of fire and weeping and gunplay. He'd known fear then, too. Fear and hate, and an anguish he'd sworn he'd never feel again.

There was some small relief when he saw that it was the shed burning and not the house. The heat from it roared out as the last of the roof collapsed. He slowed his horse when he spotted two riders heading up into the rocks. His gun was already drawn, his blood already cold, before he saw Sarah lying on the ground. His horse was still moving when he slid from the saddle and ran to her.

Her face was as pale as the moon, and she smelled of smoke. As he knelt beside her, a small brown dog began to snarl at him. Jake brushed it aside when it nipped him.

"If you were going to do any guarding, you're too late."

His mouth set in a grim line, he pressed a hand to her heart. Something moved in him when he felt its slow beat. Gently he lifted her head. And felt the blood, warm on his fingers. He looked up at the rocks again, his eyes narrowed and icy. As carefully as he could, he picked her up and carried her inside.

There was no place to lay her comfortably but the cot.

The puppy began to whine and jump at the ladder after Jake carried her up. Jake shushed him again and, grateful that Sarah had at least had the sense to bring in fresh water, prepared to dress her wound.

Dazed and aching, Sarah felt something cool on her head. For a moment she thought it was Sister Angelina, the soft-voiced nun who had nursed her through a fever when she had been twelve. Though she hurt, hurt all over, it was comforting to be there, safe in her own bed, knowing that someone was there to take care of her and make things right again. Sister would sometimes sing to her and would always, when she needed it, hold her hand.

Moaning a little, Sarah groped for Sister Angelina's hand. The one that closed over hers was as hard as iron. Confused, fooled for a minute into thinking her father had come back for her, Sarah opened her eyes.

At first everything was vague and wavering, as though she were looking through water. Slowly she focused on a face. She remembered the face, with its sharp lines and its taut, bronzed skin. A lawless face. She'd dreamed of it, hadn't she? Unsure, she lifted a hand to it. It was rough, unshaven and warm. Gray eyes, she thought dizzily. Gray eyes and a gray hat. Yes, she'd dreamed of him.

She managed a whisper. "Don't. Don't kiss me."

The face smiled. It was such a quick, flashing and appealing smile that she almost wanted to return it. "I guess I can control myself. Drink this."

He lifted the cup to her lips, and she took a first greedy sip. Whiskey shot through her system. "That's horrible. I don't want it."

"Put some color back in your cheeks." But he set the cup aside.

"I just want to…" But the whiskey had shocked her brain enough to clear it. Jake had to hold her down to keep her from scrambling out of bed. Her shift tangled around her knees and drooped over one shoulder.

"Hold on. You stand up now, you're going to fall on that pretty face of yours."

"Fire." She coughed, gasping from the pain in her throat. To balance herself, she grabbed him, then dropped her head weakly on his chest. "There's a fire."

"I know." Relief and pleasure surged through him as he stroked her hair. Her cheek was nestled against his heart as if it belonged there. "It's pretty well done now."

"It might spread. I've got to stop it."

"It's not going to spread." He eased her back with a gentleness that would have surprised her if she'd been aware of it. "Nothing to feed it, no wind to carry it. You lost the shed, that's all."

"I got the horses out," she murmured. Her head was whirling and throbbing. But his voice—his voice and the stroke of his hands soothed her everywhere. Comforted, she let her eyes close. "I wasn't sure I could."

"You did fine." Because he wanted to say more and didn't know how, he passed the cloth over her face. "You'd better rest now."

"Don't go." She reached for his hand again and brought it to her cheek. "Please don't go."

"I'm not going anywhere." He brushed the hair away from her face while he fought his own demons. "Go on to sleep." He needed her to. If she opened her eyes and looked at him again, if she touched him again, he was going to lose.

"The puppy was barking. I thought he needed to go out, so I—" She came to herself abruptly. He could see it in the way her eyes flew open. "Mr. Redman! What are you doing here? Here," she repeated, scandalized, as she glanced around the loft. "I'm not dressed."

He dropped the cloth back in the bowl. "It's been a trial

not to notice." She was coming back, all right, he thought as he watched her eyes fire up. It was a pleasure to watch it. With some regret, he picked up the blanket and tossed it over her. "Feel better?"

"Mr. Redman." Her voice was stiff with embarrassment. "I don't entertain gentlemen in my private quarters."

He picked up the cup of whiskey and took a drink himself. Now that she seemed back to normal, it hit him how scared he'd been. Bone-scared. "Ain't much entertaining about dressing a head wound."

Sarah pushed herself up on her elbows, and the room reeled. With a moan, she lifted her fingers to the back of her neck. "I must have hit my head."

"Must have." He thought of the riders, but said nothing. "Since I picked you up off the ground and carted you all the way up here, don't you figure I'm entitled to know what happened tonight?"

"I don't really know." With a long sigh, she leaned back against the pillow she'd purchased only that morning. He was entitled to the story, she supposed. In any case, she wanted to tell someone. "I'd already retired for the night when the puppy began to bark. He seemed determined to get out, so I climbed down. I saw the fire. I don't know how it could have started. It was still light when I fed the stock, so I never even had a lamp over there."

Jake had his own ideas, but he bided his time. Sarah lifted a hand to her throbbing head and allowed herself the luxury of closing her eyes. "I ran over to get the horses out. The place was going up so fast. I've never seen anything like it. The roof was coming down, and the horses were terrified. They wouldn't come out. I'd read somewhere that horses are so frightened by fire they just panic and burn alive. I couldn't have stood that."

"So you went in after them."

"They were screaming." Her brows drew together as she remembered. "It sounded like women screaming. It was horrible."

"Yeah, I know." He remembered another barn, another fire, when the horses hadn't been so lucky.

"I remember falling when I got out the last time. I think I was choking on the smoke. I started to get up. I don't know what I was going to do. Then something hit me, I guess. One of the horses, perhaps. Or perhaps I simply fell again." She opened her eyes and studied him. He was sitting on her bed, his hair disheveled and his eyes dark and intense. Beautiful, she thought. Then she wondered if she was delirious. "Then you were here. Why are you here?"

"Riding by this way. Saw the fire." He looked into the cup of whiskey. If he was going to sit here much longer, watching what the lamplight did to her skin, he was going to need more than a cupful. "I also saw two riders heading away."

"Away?" Righteous indignation had her sitting up again, despite the headache. "You mean someone was here and didn't try to help?"

Jake gave her a long, even look. She looked so fragile, like something you put behind glass in a parlor. Fragile or not, she had to know what she was up against. "I figure they weren't here to help." He watched as the realization seeped in. There was a flicker of fear. That was what he'd expected. What he hadn't counted on and was forced to admire was the passion in her eyes.

"They came on my land? Burned down my shed? Why?"

She'd forgotten that she was wearing no more than a shift, forgotten that it was past midnight and that she was alone with a man. She sat up, and the blanket dropped to pool at her waist. Her small, round breasts rose and fell with her temper. Her hair was loose. He'd never seen it that way before. Until that moment he hadn't taken the time or the trouble to really look. A man's hands could get lost in hair like that. The thought ran through his mind and was immediately banished. It glowed warm in the lamplight, sliding over her right shoulder and streaming down her back. Anger had brought the color back to her face and the golden glow back to her eyes.

He finished off the whiskey, reminding himself that he'd do well to keep his mind on the business at hand. "Seems logical to figure they wanted to give you some trouble, maybe make you think twice about keeping this place."

"That doesn't make any sense." She leaned forward. Jake shifted uncomfortably when her thin lawn gown gapped at the throat. "Why should anyone care about an adobe house and a few sagging sheds?"

Jake set the cup down again. "You forgot the mine. Some people'll do a lot more than set a fire for gold."

With a sound of disgust, Sarah propped her elbows on her knees. "Gold? Do you think my father would have lived like this if there'd been any significant amount of gold?"

"If you believe that, why are you staying?"

The brooding look left her eyes as she glanced back at him. "I don't expect you to understand. This is all I have. All I have left of my father is this place and a gold watch." She took the watch from the tilting table beside the bed and closed her hand around it. "I intend to keep what's mine. If someone's played a nasty joke—"

Jake interrupted her. "Might've been a joke. It's more likely somebody thinks this place is worth more than you say. Trying to burn horses alive and hitting women isn't considered much of a joke. Even out here."

She lifted a hand to the wound on her head. He was saying someone had struck her. And he was right, she acknowledged with a quick shudder. He was undoubtedly right. "No one's going to scare me off my land. Tomorrow I'll report this incident to the sheriff, and I'll find a way to protect my property."

"Just what way is that?"

"I don't know." She tightened her grip on the watch. The look in her eyes said everything. "But I'll find it."

Maybe she would, he thought. And maybe, since he didn't care much for people setting fires, he'd help her. "Someone might be offering to buy this place from you," Jake murmured, thinking ahead.

"I'm not selling. And I'm not running. If and when I return to Philadelphia, it will be because I've decided that's what I want to do, not because I've been frightened away."

That was an attitude he could respect. "Fair enough. Since it appears you're going to have your hands full tomorrow, you'd best get some sleep."

"Yes." Sleep? How could she possibly close her eyes? What if they came back?

"If it's all the same to you, I'll bunk down outside."

Her eyes lifted to his and held them. The quiet understanding in them made her want to rest her head on his shoulder. He'd take care of her. She had only to ask. But she couldn't ask.

"Of course, you're welcome to. Mr. Redman…" She remembered belatedly to drag the blanket up to her shoulders. "I'm in your debt again. It seems you've come to my aid a number of times in a very short acquaintance."

"I didn't have to go out of my way much." He started to rise, then thought better of it. "I got a question for you."

Because she was feeling awkward again, she offered him a small, polite smile. "Yes?"

"Why'd you ask me not to kiss you?"

Her fingers tightened on the blanket. "I beg your pardon?"

"When you were coming to, you took a good, long look at me, and then you told me not to kiss you."

She could feel the heat rising to her cheeks. Dignity, she told herself. Even under circumstances like these, a woman must keep her dignity. "Apparently I wasn't in my right senses."

He thought that through and then unnerved her by smiling. For his own satisfaction, he reached out to touch the ends of her hair. "A man could take that two ways."

She sputtered. The lamplight shifted across his face. Light, then shadow. It made him look mysterious, exciting. Forbidden. Sarah found it almost as difficult to breathe as she did when her stays were too tight. "Mr. Redman, I assure you—"

"It made me think." He was close now, so close that she could feel his breath flutter over her lips. They parted, seemingly of their own volition. He took the time—a heartbeat, two—to flick his gaze down to them. "Maybe you've been wondering about me kissing you."

"Certainly not." But her denial lacked the ring of truth. They both knew it.

"I'll have to give it some thought myself." The trouble was, he'd been giving it too much thought already. The way she looked right now, with her hair loose around her shoulders and her eyes dark, just a little scared, made him not want to think at all. He knew that if he touched her, head wound or not, he'd climb right in the bed with her and take whatever he wanted.

He was going to kiss her. Her head swam with the idea. He had only to lean closer and his mouth would be on hers. Hard. Somehow she knew it would be hard, firm, masterful. He could take her in his arms right now and there would be nothing she could do about it. Maybe there was nothing she wanted to do about it.

Then he was standing. For the first time she noticed that
he had to stoop so that his head didn't brush the roof. His
body blocked the light. Her heart was thudding so hard
that she was certain he must hear it. For the life of her,
she couldn't be sure if it was fear or excitement. Slowly he
leaned over and blew out the lamp.

In the dark, he moved down from the loft and out into
the night.

Shivering, Sarah huddled under the blanket. The man
was— She didn't have words to describe him. The only
thing she was certain of was that she wouldn't sleep a wink.

She went out like a light.

When Sarah woke, her head felt as though it had been
split open and filled with a drum-and-bugle corps. Moaning, she sat on the edge of the cot and cradled her aching
head in her hands. She wished she could believe it had all
been a nightmare, but the pounding at the base of her skull,
and the rust-colored water in the bowl, said differently.

Gingerly she began to dress. The best she could do for
herself at the moment was to see how bad the damage was
and pray the horses came back. She doubted she could afford two more on her meager budget. In deference to her
throbbing head, she tied her hair back loosely with a ribbon.
Even the thought of hairpins made her grimace.

The power of the sun had her gasping. Small red dots
danced in front of her eyes and her vision wavered and
dimmed. She leaned against the door, gathering her
strength, before she stepped out.

The shed was gone. In its place was rubble, a mass of
black, charred wood. Determined, Sarah crossed over to
it. She could still smell the smoke. If she closed her eyes
she could hear the terrifying sound of fire crackling over

dry wood. And the heat. She'd never forget the heat—the intensity of it, the meanness of it.

It hadn't been much of a structure, but it had been hers. In a civilized society a vandal was made to pay for the destruction of property. Arizona Territory or Philadelphia, she meant to see that justice was done here. But for now she was alone.

Alone. She stood in the yard and listened. Never before had she heard such quiet. There was a trace of wind, hot and silent. It lacked the strength to rustle the scrub that pushed its way through the rocks. The only sound she heard was the quick breathing of the puppy, who was sitting on the ground at her feet.

The horses had run off. So, Sarah thought as she turned in a circle, had Jake Redman. It was better that way, she decided—because she remembered, all too clearly, the way she had felt when he had sat on the cot in the shadowy lamplight and touched her hair. Foolish. It was hateful to admit it, but she'd felt foolish and weak and, worst of all, willing.

There was no use being ashamed of it, but she considered herself too smart to allow it to happen again. A man like Jake Redman wasn't the type a woman could flirt harmlessly with. Perhaps she didn't have a wide and worldly experience with men, but she recognized a dangerous one when she saw him.

There were some, she had no doubt, who would be drawn to his kind. A man who killed without remorse or regret, who came and went as he pleased. But not her. When she decided to give her heart to a man, it would be to one she understood and respected.

With a sigh, she bent down to soothe the puppy, who was whimpering at her feet. There was a comfort in the way he nuzzled his face against hers. When she fell in love and married, Sarah thought, it would be to a man of dignity and breeding, a man who would cherish her, who would protect her, not with guns and fists but with honor. They would be devoted to each other, and to the family they made between them. He would be educated and strong, respected in the community.

Those were the qualities she'd been taught a woman looked for in a husband. Sarah stroked the puppy's head and wished she could conquer this strange feeling that what she'd been taught wasn't necessarily true.

What did it matter now? As things stood, she had too much to do to think about romance. She had to find a way to rebuild the shed. Then she'd have to bargain for a new wagon and team. She stirred some of the charred wood with the toe of her shoe. She was about to give in to the urge to kick it when she heard horses approaching.

Panic came first and had her spinning around, a cry for help on her lips. The sunbaked dirt and empty rocks mocked her. The Lord helped those who help themselves, she remembered, and raced into the house with the puppy scrambling behind her.

When she came out again her knees were trembling, but she was carrying her father's rifle in both hands.

Jake took one look at her, framed in the doorway, her eyes mirroring fear and fury. It came to him with a kind of dull, painful surprise that she was the kind of woman a man would die for. He slid from his horse.

"I'd be obliged, ma'am, if you'd point that someplace else."

"Oh." She nearly sagged with relief. "Mr. Redman. I thought you'd gone." He merely inclined his head and took another meaningful look at the rifle. "Oh," she said again, and lowered it. She felt foolish, not because of the gun but because when she'd looked out and seen him all her thoughts about what she wanted and didn't want had shifted ground. There he was, looking dark and reckless, with guns gleaming at his hip. And there she was, fighting back a driving instinct to run into his arms.

"You...found the horses."

He took his time tying the team to a post before he approached her. "They hadn't gone far." He took the rifle from her and leaned it against the house. The stock was damp from her nervous hands. But he'd seen more than nerves in her eyes. And he wondered.

"I'm very grateful." Because she felt awkward, she leaned down to gather the yapping puppy in her arms. Jake still hadn't shaved, and she remembered how his face had felt against the palm of her hand. Fighting a blush, she curled her fingers. "I'm afraid I don't know what to do with them until I have shelter again."

What was going on in that mind of hers? Jake wondered. "A lean-to would do well enough for the time being. Just need to rig one over a corner of the paddock."

"A lean-to, yes." It was a relief to deal with something practical. Her mind went to work quickly. "Mr. Redman, have you had breakfast?"

He tipped his hat back on his head. "Not to speak of."

"If you could fashion a temporary shelter for the horses, I'd be more than glad to fix you a meal."

He'd meant to do it anyway, but if she wanted to bargain, he'd bargain. "Can you cook?"

"Naturally. Preparing meals was a very important part of my education."

He wanted to touch her hair again. And more. Instead, he hooked his thumb in his pocket. "I ain't worried about you preparing a meal. Can you cook?"

She tried not to sigh. "Yes."

"All right, then."

When he walked away and didn't remount his horse,

Sarah supposed a deal had been struck. "Mr. Redman?" He stopped to look over his shoulder. "How do you prefer your eggs?"

"Hot," he told her, then continued on his way.

She'd give him hot, Sarah decided, rattling pans. She'd give him the best damn breakfast he'd ever eaten. She took a long breath and forced herself to be calm. His way of talking was beginning to rub off on her. That would never do.

Biscuits. Delighted that she'd been given a brand-new recipe only the day before, she went to work.

Thirty minutes later, Jake came in to stand in the doorway. The scents amazed him. He'd expected to find the frying pan smoking with burnt eggs. Instead, he saw a bowl of fresh, golden-topped biscuits wrapped in a clean bandanna. Sarah was busy at the stove, humming to herself. The pup was nosing into corners, looking for trouble.

Jake had never thought much about a home for himself, but if he had it would have been like this. A woman in a pretty dress humming by the stove, the smells of good cooking rising in the air. A man could do almost anything if the right woman was waiting for him.

Then she turned. One look at her face, the elegance of it, was a reminder that a man like him didn't have a woman like her waiting for him.

"Just in time." She smiled, pleased with herself. Conquering the cookstove was her biggest accomplishment to date. "There's fresh water in the bowl, so you can wash up." She began to scoop eggs onto an ironstone plate. "I'm afraid I don't have a great deal to offer. I'm thinking of getting some chickens of my own. We had them at school, so I know a bit about them. Fresh eggs are such a comfort, don't you think?"

He lifted his head from the bowl, and water dripped down from his face. Her cheeks were flushed from cooking, and her sleeves were rolled up past her elbows, revealing slender, milk-white arms. Comfort was the last thing on his mind. Without speaking, he took his seat.

Sarah wasn't sure when he made her more nervous, when he spoke to her or when he lapsed into those long silences and just looked. Gamely she tried again. "Mrs. Cobb gave me the recipe for these biscuits yesterday. I hope they're as good as she claimed."

Jake broke one, and the steam and fragrance poured out. Watching her, he bit into it. "They're fine."

"Please, Mr. Redman, all this flattery will turn my head." She scooped up a forkful of eggs. "I was introduced to several ladies yesterday while I was buying supplies. They seem very hospitable."

"I don't know much about the ladies in town." At least not the kind Sarah was speaking of.

"I see." She took a bite of biscuit herself. It was more than fine, she thought with a pout. It was delicious. "Liza Cody—her family runs the dry goods store. I found her very amiable. She was kind enough to let me have one of their puppies."

Jake looked down at the dog, who was sniffing at his boot and thumping his tail. "That where you got this thing?"

"Yes. I wanted the company."

Jake broke off a bite of biscuit and dropped it to the dog, ignoring Sarah's muttered admonition about feeding animals from the table. "Scrawny now, but he's going to be a big one."

"Really?" Intrigued, she leaned over to look. "How can you tell?"

"His paws. He's clumsy now because they're too big for him. He'll grow into them."

"I fancy it's to my advantage to own a large dog."

"Didn't do you much good last night," he pointed out,

but pleased both the pup and Sarah by scratching between the dog's floppy ears. "You give him a name yet?"

"Lafitte."

Jake paused with his fork halfway to his lips. "What the hell kind of name is that for a dog?"

"After the pirate. He had that black marking around his eye, like a patch."

"Pretty fancy name for a mutt," Jake said over a mouthful of eggs. "Bandit's better."

Sarah lifted a brow. "I'd certainly never give him a name like that."

"A pirate's a bandit, isn't he?" Jake dived into another biscuit.

"Be that as it may, the name stands."

Chewing, Jake looked down at the puppy, who was groveling a bit, obviously hoping for another handout. "Bet it makes you feel pretty stupid, doesn't it, fella?"

"Would you care for more coffee, Mr. Redman?" Frustrated, Sarah rose and, wrapping a cloth around the handle, took the pot from the stove. Without waiting for an answer, she stood beside Jake and poured.

She smelled good, he thought. Soft. Kind of subtle, like a field of wildflowers in early spring. At the ends of her stiff white sleeves, her hands were delicate. He remembered the feel of them on his cheek.

"They taught you good," he muttered.

"I beg your pardon?" She looked down at him. There was something in his eyes, a hint of what she'd seen in them the night before. It didn't make her nervous, as she'd been certain it would. It made her yearn.

"The cooking." Jake put a hand over hers to straighten the pot and keep the coffee from overflowing the cup. Then he kept it there, feeling the smooth texture of her skin and the surprisingly rapid beating of her pulse. She didn't back away, or blush, or snatch her hand from his. Instead, she simply looked back at him. The question in her eyes was one he wanted badly to answer.

She moistened her lips but kept her eyes steady. "Thank you. I'm glad you enjoyed it."

"You take too many chances, Sarah." Slowly, when he was certain she understood his meaning, he removed his hand.

With her chin up, she returned the pot to the stove. How dare he make her feel like that, then toss it back in her face? "You don't frighten me, Mr. Redman. If you were going to hurt me, you would have done so by now."

"Maybe, maybe not. Your kind wears a man down."

"My kind?" She turned, the light of challenge in her eyes. "Just what kind would that be?"

"The soft kind. The soft, stubborn kind who's right on the edge of stepping into a man's arms."

"You couldn't be more mistaken." Her voice was icy now in defense against the blood that had heated at his words. "I haven't any interest in being in your arms, or any man's. My only interest at the moment is protecting my property."

"Could be I'm wrong." He rocked back in his chair. She was a puzzle, all right, and he'd never known how pleasurable it could be to get a woman's dander up. "We'll both find out sooner or later. Meanwhile, just how do you plan to go about protecting this place?"

Not much caring whether he was finished or not, she began to stack the plates. "I'm going to alert the sheriff, of course."

"That's not going to hurt, but it's not going to help much, either, if you get more trouble out here. The sheriff's ten miles away."

"Just what do you suggest?"

He'd already given it some thought, and he had an answer. "If I were you, I'd hire somebody to help out around here. Somebody who can give you a hand with the place, and who knows how to use a gun."

A thrill sprinted through her. She managed, just barely, to keep her voice disinterested. "Yourself, I suppose."

He grinned at her. "No, Duchess, I ain't looking for that kind of job. I was thinking of Lucius."

Frowning, she began to scrub out the frying pan. "He drinks."

"Who doesn't? Give him a couple of meals and a place to bunk down and he'll do all right for you. A woman staying out here all alone's just asking for trouble. Those men who burned your shed last night might've done more to you than give you a headache."

His meaning was clear enough, clearer still because she'd thought of that possibility herself. She'd prefer him—though only because she knew he was capable, she assured herself. But she did need someone. "Perhaps you're right."

"No perhaps about it. Someone as green as you doesn't have the sense to do more than die out here."

"I don't see why you have to insult me."

"The plain truth's the plain truth, Duchess."

Teeth clenched, she banged dishes. "I told you not to—"

"I got a question for you," he said, interrupting her easily. "What would you have done this morning if it hadn't been me bringing back the horses?"

"I would have defended myself."

"You ever shot a Henry before?"

She gave him a scandalized look. "Why in the world would I have shot anyone named Henry?"

With a long sigh, he rose. "A Henry rifle, Duchess. That's what you were pointing at my belt buckle before you fixed my eggs."

Sarah wiped the pan clean, then set it aside. "No, I haven't actually fired one, but I can't imagine it's that complicated. In any case, I never intended to shoot it."

"What did you have in mind? Dancing with it?"

She snatched up a plate. "Mr. Redman, I'm growing weary of being an amusement to you. I realize that someone like you thinks nothing of shooting a man dead and walking away. I, however, have been taught—rightfully—that killing is a sin."

"You're wrong." Something in his voice had her turning toward him again. "Surviving's never a sin. It's all there is."

"If you believe that, I'm sorry for you."

He didn't want her pity. But he did want her to stay alive. Moving over, he took the plates out of her hands. "If you see a snake, are you going to kill it or stand there and let it bite you?"

"That's entirely different."

"You might not think it's so different if you stay out here much longer. Where's the cartridges for the rifle?"

Wiping her hands on her apron, Sarah glanced at the shelf behind her. Jake took the cartridges down, checked them, then gripped her arm. "Come on. I'll give you a lesson."

"I haven't finished cleaning the dishes."

"They'll keep."

"I never said I wanted lessons," she told him as he pulled her outside.

"If you're going to pick up a gun, you ought to know how to use it." He hefted the rifle and smiled at her. "Unless you're afraid you can't learn."

Sarah untied her apron and laid it over the rail. "I'm not afraid of anything."

Chapter 5

He'd figured a challenge would be the best way to get her cooperation. Sarah marched along beside him, chin up, eyes forward. He didn't think she knew it, but when she'd held the rifle that morning she'd been prepared to pull the trigger. He wanted to make sure that when she did she hit what she aimed at.

From the rubble of the burned shed, Jake selected a few pieces of charred wood and balanced three of them against a pile of rocks.

"First thing you do is learn how to load it without shooting off your foot." Jake emptied the rifle's chamber, then slowly reloaded. "You've got to have respect for a weapon, and not go around holding it like you were going to sweep the porch with it."

To prove his point, he brought the rifle up, sighted in and fired three shots. The three pieces of scrap wood flew backward in unison. "Bullets can do powerful damage to a man," he told her as he lowered the gun again.

She had to swallow. The sound of gunfire still echoed. "I'm aware of that, Mr. Redman. I have no intention of shooting anyone."

"Most people don't wake up in the morning figuring on it." He went to the rocks again. This time he set up the largest piece of wood. "Unless you're planning on heading back to Philadelphia real soon, you'd better learn how to use this."

"I'm not going anywhere."

With a nod, Jake emptied the rifle and handed her the ammo. "Load it."

She didn't like the feel of the bullets in her hands. They were cold and smooth. Holding them, she wondered how anyone could use them against another. Metal against flesh. No, it was inconceivable.

"You going to play with them or put them in the gun?"

Because he was watching her, Sarah kept her face impassive and did as he told her.

He pushed the barrel away from his midsection. "You're a quick study."

It shouldn't have pleased her, but she felt the corners of her mouth turn up nonetheless. "So I've been told."

Unable to resist, he brushed the hair out of her eyes. "Don't get cocky." Stepping behind her, he laid the gun in her hands, then adjusted her arms. "Balance it and get a good grip on it."

"I am," she muttered, wishing he wouldn't stand quite so close. He smelled of leather and sweat, a combination that, for reasons beyond her comprehension, aroused her. One hand was firm on her arm, the other on her shoulder. Hardly a lover's touch, and yet she felt her system respond as it had never responded to the gentle, flirtatious hand-holding she'd experienced in Philadelphia. She had only to lean back the slightest bit to be pressed close against him.

Not that she wanted to be. She shifted, then grumbled under her breath when he pushed her into place again.

"Hold still. Not stiff, woman, still," he told her when her body went rigid at his touch.

"There's no need to snap at me."

"You stand like that when you fire, you're going to get a broken shoulder. Loosen up. You see the sight?"

"That little thing sticking up there?"

He closed his eyes for a moment. "Yeah, that little thing sticking up there. Use it to sight in the target. Bring the stock up some." He leaned over. Sarah pressed her lips together when his cheek brushed hers. "Steady," he murmured, resisting the urge to turn his face into her hair. "Wrap your finger around the trigger. Don't jerk it, just pull it back, slow and smooth."

She shut her eyes and obeyed. The rifle exploded in her hands and would have knocked her flat on her back if he hadn't been there to steady her. She screamed, afraid she'd shot herself.

"Missed."

Breathing hard, Sarah whirled around. Always a cautious man, Jake took the rifle from her. "You might have warned me." She brought her hand up to nurse her bruised shoulder. "It felt like someone hit me with a rock."

"It's always better to find things out firsthand. Try it again."

With her teeth clenched, Sarah took the rifle and managed to get back into position.

"This time use your arm instead of your shoulder to balance it. Lean in a bit."

"My ears are ringing."

"You'll get used to it." He put a steadying hand on her waist. "It helps if you keep your eyes open. Sight low. Good. Now pull the trigger."

This time she was braced for the kick and just staggered a little. Jake kept a hand at her waist and looked over her head. "You caught a corner of it."

"I did?" She looked for herself. "I did!" Laughing, she looked over her shoulder at him. "I want to do it again." She lifted the rifle and didn't complain when Jake pushed the barrel three inches to the right. She kept her eyes wide open this time as she pressed her finger down on the trigger. She let out a whoop when the wood flew off the rocks. "I hit it."

"Looks like."

"I really hit it. Imagine." When he took the gun from her, she shook her hair back and laughed. "My arm's tingling."

"It'll pass." He was surprised he could speak. The way she looked when she laughed made his throat slam shut. He wasn't a man for pretty words, not for saying them or for thinking them. But just now it ran through his head that she looked like an angel in the sunlight, with her hair the color of wet wheat and her eyes like gold dust.

And he wanted her, as he'd wanted few things in his life. Slowly, wanting to give himself time to regain control, he walked over to the rocks to pick up the target. She had indeed hit it. The hole was nearly at the top, and far to the right of center, but she'd hit it. He walked back to drop the wood in Sarah's hands and watched her grin about it.

"Trouble is, most things you shoot at don't sit nice and still like a block of wood."

He was determined to spoil it for her, Sarah thought, studying his cool, unreadable eyes. The man was impossible to understand. One moment he was going to the trouble to teach her how to shoot the rifle, and the next he couldn't even manage the smallest of compliments because she'd learned well. The devil with him.

"Mr. Redman, it's very apparent that nothing I do pleases you." She tossed the block of wood aside. "Isn't it fortunate for both of us that it doesn't matter in the least?" With that she gathered up her skirts and began to stamp back toward the house. She managed no more than a startled gasp as he spun her around.

She knew that look, she thought dazedly as she stared at him. It was the same one she'd first seen on his face, when he'd ridden beside the stage, firing his pistol over his shoulder. She hadn't a clue as to how to deal with him now, so she took the only option that came to mind.

"Take your hands off me."

"I warned you, you took too many chances." His grip only tightened when she tried to shrug him off. "It's not smart to turn your back on a man who's holding a loaded gun."

"Did you intend to shoot me in the back, Mr. Redman?" It was an unfair remark, and she knew it. But she wanted to get away from him, quickly, until that look faded from his eyes. "I wouldn't put that, or anything else, past you. You're the rudest, most ill-mannered, most ungentlemanly man I've ever met. I'll thank you to get back on your horse and ride off my land."

He'd resisted challenges before, but he'd be damned if he'd resist this one. From the first time he'd seen her she'd started an itch in him. It was time he scratched it.

"Seems to me you need another lesson, Duchess."

"I neither need nor want anything from you. And I won't be called by that ridiculous name." Her breath came out in a whoosh when he dragged her against him. He saw her eyes go wide with shock.

"Then I won't call you anything." He was still holding the rifle. With his eyes on hers, he slid his hand up her back to gather up her hair. "I don't much like talking, anyway."

She fought him. At least she needed to believe she did. Despite her efforts, his mouth closed over hers. In that instant the sun was blocked out and she was plunged, breathless, into the deepest, darkest night.

His body was like iron. His arm bonded her against him so that she had no choice, really no choice, but to absorb the feel of him. He made her think of the rifle, slim and hard and deadly. Through the shock, the panic and the excitement she felt the fast, uneven beating of his heart against hers.

Her blood had turned into some hot, foreign liquid that made her pulse leap and her heart thud. The rough stubble of his beard scraped her face, and she moaned. From the pain, she assured herself. It couldn't be from pleasure.

And yet... Her hands were on his shoulders, holding on now rather than pushing away.

He wondered if she knew she packed a bigger kick than her father's rifle. He'd never known that anything so sweet could be so potent. That anything so delicate could be so strong. She had him by the throat and didn't even know it. And he wanted more. In a move too desperate to be gentle, he dragged her head back by the hair.

She gasped in the instant he allowed her to breathe, dragging in air, unaware that she'd been stunned into holding her breath. Then his mouth was on hers again, his tongue invading, arousing in a way she hadn't known she could be aroused, weakening in a way she hadn't believed she could be weakened.

She moaned again, but this time there was no denying the pleasure. Tentatively, then boldly, she answered the new demand. Savoring the hot, salty taste of his lips, she ran her hands along the planes of his face and into his hair. Glorious. No one had ever warned her that a kiss could make the body burn and tremble and yearn. A sound of stunned delight caught in her throat.

The sound lit fires in him that he knew could never be allowed to burn free. She was innocent. Any fool could see that. And he...he hadn't been innocent since he'd drawn his first breath. There were lines he crossed, laws he broke. But this one had to be respected. He struggled to clear his mind, but she filled it. Her arms were around his neck, pulling him closer, pulling him in. And her mouth... Sweet Lord, her mouth. His heart was hammering in his head, in his loins…all from the taste of her. Honeyed whiskey. A man could drown in it.

Afraid he would, and even more afraid he'd want to, he pushed her away. Her eyes were dark and unfocused—the way they'd been last night, when she'd started to come to. It gave him some satisfaction to see it, because he felt as though he'd been knocked cold, himself.

"Like I said, you learn fast, Sarah." His hand was shaking. Infuriated, he curled it into a fist. He had a flash, an almost painful one, of what it would be like to drag her to the ground and take everything from her. Before he could act, one way or the other, he heard the sound of an approaching wagon. "You got company coming." He handed her the rifle and walked away.

What had he done to her? Sarah put a hand to her spinning head. He'd…he'd forced himself on her. Forced her until…until he hadn't had to force her any longer. Until it had felt right to want him. Until wanting him had been all there was.

Just like the dream. But this wasn't a dream, Sarah told herself, straightening her shoulders. It was more than real, and now he was walking away from her as if it hadn't mattered to him in the least. Pride was every bit as dangerous an emotion as anger.

"Mr. Redman."

When he turned, he saw her standing there with the rifle. If the look in her eyes meant anything, she'd have dearly loved to use it.

"Apparently you take chances, too." She tilted her head. There was challenge in the gesture, as well as a touch of fury and a stab of hurt. "This rifle's still loaded."

"That's right." He touched the brim of his hat in a salute. "It's a hell of a lot harder to pull the trigger when you're aiming at flesh and blood, but go ahead. It'd be hard to miss at this range."

She wished she could. She wished she had the skill to put a bullet between his feet and watch him jump. Lifting her chin, she walked toward the house. "The difference between you and me, Mr. Redman, is that I still have morals."

"There's some truth in that." He strode easily beside her. "Seeing as you fixed me breakfast and all, why don't you call me Jake?" He swung up into the saddle as a buggy rumbled into the yard.

"Sarah?" With her hands still on the reins, Liza cast an uncertain glance at her new friend, then at the man in the saddle. She knew she wasn't supposed to approve of men like Jake Redman. But she found it difficult not to when he looked so attractive and exciting. "I hope you don't mind us coming out." A young boy jumped out of the buggy and began to chase the puppy, who was running in circles.

"Not at all. I'm delighted." Sarah shaded her eyes with her hand so that she could see Jake clearly. "Mr. Redman was just on his way."

"Those sure are some pretty guns you got there, mister." Young John Cody put a hand on the neck of Jake's gray mustang and peered up at the smooth wooden grip of one of the Colt .45s he carried. He knew who Jake Redman was—he'd heard all the stories—but he'd never managed to get this close before.

"Think so?" Ignoring the two women, Jake shifted in his saddle to get a better look at the boy. No more than ten, he figured, with awe in his eyes and a smudge of dirt on his cheek.

"Yessiree. I think that when you slap leather you're just about the fastest there is, maybe in the whole world."

"John Cody." Liza stayed in the buggy, wringing her hands. "You oughtn't to bother Mr. Redman."

Jake shot her a quick, amused look. Did she think he'd shoot the kid for talking to him? "No bother, ma'am." He glanced down at Johnny again. "You can't believe everything you hear."

But Johnny figured he knew what was what. "My ma says that since you saved that stage there's probably some good in you somewhere."

This time Liza called her brother's name in a strained, desperate whisper. Jake had to grin. He shifted his attention to Sarah long enough to see that she was standing as stiff as a rod, with one eyebrow arched.

"That's right kind of her. I'll tell the sheriff about your trouble... Miss Conway. I reckon he'll be out to see you."

"Thank you, Mr. Redman. Good day."

He tipped his hat to her, then to Liza. "See you around, Johnny." He turned his horse in a half circle and rode away.

"Yessir," Johnny shouted after him. "Yessiree."

"John Cody." Liza collected herself enough to climb out of the buggy. Johnny just grinned and raced off after the puppy again, firing an imaginary Peacemaker. "That's my brother."

"Yes, I imagined it was."

Liza gave Johnny one last look of sisterly disgust before going to Sarah. "Ma's tending the store today. She wanted you to have this. It's a loaf of her cinnamon bread."

"Oh, how kind of her." One whiff brought memories of home. "Can you stay?"

Liza gave Sarah the bread and a quick, dimpled smile. "I was hoping I could."

"Come in, please. I'll fix us some tea."

While Sarah busied herself at the stove, Liza looked around the tiny cabin. It was scrubbed clean as a whistle. "It's not as bad as I thought it would be." Instantly she lifted a hand to her mouth. "I'm sorry. Ma always says I talk too much for my own good."

"That's all right." Sarah got out two tin cups and tried not to wish they were china. "I was taken by surprise myself."

At ease again, Liza sat at the table. "I didn't expect to run into Jake Redman out here."

Sarah brought the knife down into the bread with a thwack. "Neither did I."

"He said you had trouble."

Unconsciously Sarah lifted a finger to her lips. They were still warm from his, and they tingled as her arms had from the kick of the Henry. She had trouble, all right. Since she couldn't explain the kiss to herself, she could hardly explain it to Liza. "Someone set fire to my shed last night."

"Oh, Sarah, no! Who? Why?"

"I don't know." She brought the two cups to the table. "Fortunately, Mr. Redman happened to be riding by this way."

"Do you think he might have done it?"

Sarah's brow rose as she considered the possibility. She remembered the way he'd bathed her face and tended her hurts. "No, I'm quite certain he didn't. I believe Mr. Redman takes a more direct approach."

"I guess you're right about that. I can't say he's started any trouble here in Lone Bluff, but he's finished some."

"What do you know about him?"

"I don't think anyone knows much. He rode into town about six months ago. Of course, everybody's heard of Jake Redman. Some say he's killed more than twenty men in gunfights."

"Killed?" Stunned, Sarah could only stare. "But why?"

"I don't know if there always is a why. I did hear that some rancher up north hired him on. There'd been trouble...rustling, barn-burning."

"Hired him on," Sarah murmured. "To kill."

"That's what it comes down to, I suppose. I do know that plenty of people were nervous when he rode in and took a room at Maggie O'Rourke's." Liza broke off a corner of the slice of bread Sarah had served her. "But he didn't seem to be looking for trouble. About two weeks later he found it, anyway."

A hired killer, Sarah thought, her stomach churning. And she'd kissed him, kissed him in a way no lady kissed a man who wasn't her husband. "What happened?"

"Jim Carlson was in the Bird Cage. That's one of the saloons in town."

"Carlson?"

"Yes, he's Samuel Carlson's brother. You wouldn't know it," Liza continued, pursing her lips. "Jim's nothing like Samuel. Full of spit, that one. Likes to brag and swagger and bully. Cheats at cards, but nobody had the nerve to call him on it. Until Jake." Liza drank more tea and listened with half an ear to her brother's war whoops in the yard. "The way I heard it, there were some words over the card table. Jim was drunk and a little careless with his dealing. Once Jake called him on it, some of the other men joined in. Word is, Jim drew. Everybody figured Jake would put a bullet in him there and then, but he just knocked him down."

"He didn't shoot him?" She felt a wave of relief. Perhaps he wasn't what people said he was.

"No. At least, the way I heard it, Jake just knocked him silly and gave Jim's gun to the bartender. Somebody had already hightailed it for the sheriff. By the time he got there, Jake was standing at the bar having himself a drink and Jim was picking himself up off the floor. I think Barker was going to put Jim in a cell for the night until he sobered up. But when he took hold of him, Jim pulled the gun from the sheriff's holster. Instead of getting a bullet in the back,

Jake put one in Jim Carlson, then turned around and finished his drink."

Dead's dead. "Did he kill him?"

"No, though there's some in town wished he had. The Carlsons are pretty powerful around here, but there were enough witnesses, the sheriff included, to call it self-defense."

"I see." But she didn't understand the kind of justice that had to be meted out with guns and bullets. "I'm surprised Jake—Mr. Redman—hasn't moved on."

"He must like it around here. What about you? Doesn't it scare you to stay out here alone?"

Sarah thought of her first night, shivering under the blanket and praying for morning. "A little."

"After living back east." Liza gave a sigh. To her, Philadelphia sounded as glamorous and foreign as Paris or London. "All the places you've seen, the pretty clothes you must have worn."

Sarah struggled with a quick pang of homesickness. "Have you ever been east?"

"No, but I've seen pictures." Liza eyed Sarah's trunks with longing. "The women wear beautiful clothes."

"Would you like to see some of mine?"

Liza's face lit up. "I'd love to."

For the next twenty minutes Liza oohed and aahed over ruffles and lace. Her reaction caused Sarah to appreciate what she had always taken for granted. Crouched on the cabin floor, they discussed important matters such as ribbons and sashes and the proper tilt of a bonnet while Johnny was kept occupied with a hunk of bread and the puppy.

"Oh, look at this one." Delighted, Liza rose, sweeping a dress in front of her. "I wish you had a looking glass."

It was the white muslin with the rosebuds on the skirt. The dress she'd planned to wear for her first dinner with her father. He'd never see it now. She glanced at the trunks.

Or any of the other lovely things he'd made certain she had in her life.

"What's wrong?" With the dress still crushed against her, Liza stepped forward. "You look so sad."

"I was thinking of my father, of how hard he worked for me."

Liza's fascination with the clothes was immediately outweighed by her sympathy. "He loved you. Often when he came in the store he'd talk about you, about what you'd written in one of your letters. I remember how he brought in this picture of you, a drawing in a little frame. He wanted everyone to see how pretty you were. He was so proud of you, Sarah."

"I miss him." With a shake of her head, Sarah blinked back tears. "It's strange, all those years we were separated. Sometimes I could barely remember him. But since I've been here I seem to know him better, and miss him more."

Gently Liza laid a hand on her shoulder. "My pa sure riles me sometimes, but I guess I'd about die if anything happened to him."

"Well, at least I have this." She looked around the small cabin. "I feel closer to him here. I like to think about him sitting at that table and writing to me." After a long breath she managed to smile. "I'm glad I came."

Liza held out a hand. "So am I."

Rising, Sarah fluffed out the sleeves of the dress Liza was holding. "Now, let me be your looking glass. You're taller and curvier than I…" With her lips pursed, she walked in a circle around Liza. "The neckline would flatter you, but I think I'd do away with some of the ruffles in the bodice. A nice pink would be your color. It would show off your hair and eyes."

"Can you imagine me wearing a dress like that?" Closing her eyes, Liza turned in slow circles. "It would have to be at a dance. I'd have my hair curled over my shoulder and wear a velvet ribbon around my throat. Will Metcalf's eyes would fall right out."

"Who's Will Metcalf?"

Liza opened her eyes and giggled. "Just a man. He's a deputy in town. He'd like to be my beau." Mischief flashed across her face. "I might decide to let him."

"Liza loves Will," Johnny sang through the window.

"You hush up, John Cody." Rushing to the window, Liza leaned out. "If you don't, I'll tell Ma who broke Grandma's china plate."

"Liza loves Will," he repeated, unconcerned, then raced off with the puppy.

"Nothing more irritating than little brothers," she muttered. With a sigh of regret, she replaced the dress in the trunk.

Tapping a finger on her lips, Sarah came to a quick decision. She should have thought of it before, she reflected. Or perhaps it had been milling around in her mind all along. "Liza, would you like a dress like that...in pink, like that pretty muslin I saw in your store yesterday?"

"I guess I'd think I'd gone to heaven."

"What if I made it for you?"

"Made it for me?" Wide-eyed, Liza looked at the trunk, then back at Sarah. "Could you?"

"I'm very handy with a needle." Caught up in the idea, Sarah pushed through her trunks to find her measuring tape. "If you can get the material, I'll make the dress. If you like it, you can tell the other women who come in your store."

"Of course." Obediently Liza lifted her arms so that Sarah could measure her. "I'll tell everyone."

"Then some of those women might want new dresses,

fashionable new dresses." Looking up, she caught the gleam of understanding in Liza's eyes.

"You bet they would."

"You get me that material and I'll make you a dress that will have Will Metcalf standing on his head."

Two hours later Sarah was pouring water over her vegetable garden. In the heat of the afternoon, with her back smarting from the chores and sun baking the dirt almost as fast as she could dampen it, she wondered if it was worth it. A garden out here would require little less than a miracle. And she would much prefer flowers.

You couldn't eat flowers, she reminded herself, and poured the last of the water out. Now she would have to walk back to the stream and fill the pail again to have water for cooking and washing.

A bath, she thought as she wiped the back of her hand over her brow. What she wouldn't give for a long bath in a real tub.

She heard the horses. It pleased her to realize that she was becoming accustomed to the sound—or lack of sound—that surrounded her new home. With her hand shading her eyes, she watched two riders come into view. It wasn't until she recognized one as Lucius that she realized she'd been holding her breath.

"Lafitte!" she called, but the dog continued to race around the yard, barking.

"Miss Conway." Sheriff Barker tipped his hat and chuckled at the snarling pup. "Got yourself a fierce-looking guard dog there."

"Makes a ruckus, anyhow," Lucius said, swinging down from his horse. Lafitte sprang at him, gripping the bottom of his pant leg with sharp puppy teeth. Bending, Lucius snatched him up by the cuff of the neck. "You mind your manners, young fella." The second he was on the ground again, Lafitte ran to hide behind Sarah's skirts.

"Heard you had some trouble out here." Barker nodded toward the remains of the shed. "This happen last night?"

"That's right. If you'd like to come inside, I was just about to get some water. I'm sure you'd like some coffee after your ride."

"I'll fetch you some water, miss," Lucius said, taking the pail from her. "Hey, boy." He grinned down at the pup. "Why don't you come along with me? I'll keep you out of trouble." After a moment's hesitation, Lafitte trotted along after him.

"Are you thinking about hiring him on?"

With her lip caught between her teeth, Sarah watched Lucius stroll off. "I was considering it."

"You'd be smart to do it." Barker took out a bandanna and wiped his neck. "Lucius has a powerful affection for the bottle, but it doesn't seem to bother him. He's honest. Did some soldiering a while back. He's amiable enough, drunk or sober."

Sarah managed a smile. "I'll take that as a recommendation, Sheriff Barker."

"Well, now." The sheriff looked back at the shed. "Why don't you tell me what happened here?"

As clearly as she could, Sarah told him everything she knew. He listened, grunting and nodding occasionally. Everything she said jibed with the story Jake had given him. But she didn't add, because she didn't know, that Jake had followed the trail of two riders into the rocks, where he'd discovered the ashes of a campfire.

"Any reason you can think of why somebody'd want to do this?"

"None at all. There's nothing here that could mean anything to anyone other than myself. Did my father have any enemies?"

Barker spit tobacco juice in the dirt. "I wouldn't think so right off. I got to tell you, Miss Conway, there ain't much I can do. I'll ask some questions and poke around some. Could be some drifters passed through and wanted to raise some hell. Begging your pardon." But he didn't think so.

"I'd wondered the same myself."

"You'll feel safer having old Lucius around."

She glanced over to see him coming back with the pail and the puppy. "I suppose you're right." But he didn't look like her idea of a protector. It was unfortunate for her that her idea of one had taken the form of Jake Redman. "I'm sure we'll do nicely," she said with more confidence than she felt.

"I'll ride out now and again and see how you're getting on." Barker pulled himself onto his horse. "You know, Miss Conway, Matt tried to grow something in that patch of dirt for as long as I can recollect." He spit again. "Never had any luck."

"Perhaps I'll have better. Good afternoon, Sheriff."

"Good day, ma'am." He lifted a hand to Lucius as he turned for home.

Chapter 6

Within a week Sarah had orders for six dresses. It took all her creativity and skill to fashion them, using her wardrobe and her imagination instead of patterns. She set aside three hours each day and three each evening for sewing. Each night when she climbed up to bed her eyes and fingers ached. Once or twice, when the exhaustion overwhelmed her, she wept herself to sleep. The grief for her father was still too raw, the country surrounding her still too rugged.

But there were other times, and they were becoming more common, when she fell asleep with a sense of satisfaction. In addition to the dresses, she'd made pretty yellow curtains for the windows and a matching cloth for the table. It was her dream, when she'd saved enough from her sewing, to buy planks for a real floor. In the meantime, she made do with what she had and was more grateful than she'd ever imagined she could be for Lucius.

He'd finished building a new shed and he was busy repairing the other outbuildings. Though he'd muttered about it, he'd agreed to build Sarah the chicken coop she wanted. At night he was content to sleep with the horses.

Sometimes he watched, tickling Lafitte's belly, as she took her daily rifle practice.

She hadn't seen Jake Redman since the day he'd given her a shooting lesson. Just as well, Sarah told herself as she pulled on her gloves. There was no one she wanted to see less. If she thought about him at all—and she hated to admit she had—it was with disdain.

A hired gun. A man with no loyalty or morals. A drifter, moving from place to place, always ready to draw his weapon and kill. To think she'd almost begun to believe there was something special about him, something good and admirable. He'd helped her, there was no denying that. But he'd probably done so out of sheer boredom. Or perhaps, she thought, remembering the kiss, because he wanted something from her. Something, she was ashamed to admit, she had nearly been willing to give.

How? Sarah picked up her hand mirror and studied her face, not out of vanity but because she hoped to see some answers there. How had he managed to make her feel that way in just a few short days, with just one embrace? Now, time after time, in the deepest part of the night, she brought herself awake because she was dreaming of him. Remembering, she thought, experiencing once again that stunning moment in the sun when his mouth had been on hers and there had been no doubt in her mind that she belonged there.

A momentary madness, she told herself, placing the mirror facedown on the table. Sunstroke, perhaps. She would never, could never, be attracted to a man who lived his life the way Jake Redman lived his.

It was time to forget him. Perhaps he had already moved on and she would never see him again. Well, it didn't matter one way or the other. She had her own life to see to now, and with a little help from Liza it appeared she had her own business. Picking up the three bundles wrapped in brown paper, Sarah went outside.

"You real sure you don't want me to drive you to town, Miss Conway?"

Sarah put the wrapped dresses in the back of the wagon while Lucius stood at the horses' heads. "No, thank you, Lucius."

She was well aware that her driving skills were poor at

best, but she'd bartered for the wagon with the owner of the livery stable. He had two daughters that she'd designed gingham frocks for, and she intended to deliver them herself. For Lucius she had a big, sunny smile.

"I was hoping you'd start on the chicken coop today. I'm going to see if Mrs. Miller will sell me a dozen young chicks."

"Yes'm." Lucius shuffled his feet and cleared his throat. "Going to be a hot, dry day."

"Yes." What day wasn't? "I have a canteen, thank you."

He waited until Sarah had gained the seat and smoothed out her skirts. "There's just one thing, Miss Conway."

Anxious to be on her way, Sarah took the reins. "Yes, Lucius, what is it?"

"I'm plumb out of whiskey."

Her brow rose, all but disappearing under the wispy bangs she wore. "And?"

"Well, seeing as you're going into town and all, I thought you could pick some up for me."

"I? You can hardly expect me to purchase whiskey."

He'd figured on her saying something of the kind. "Maybe you could get somebody to buy a bottle for you." He gave her a gap-toothed smile and was careful not to spit. "I'd be obliged."

She opened her mouth, ready to lecture him on the evils of drink. With a sigh, she shut it again. The man worked very hard for very little. It wasn't her place to deny him his comforts, whatever they might be.

"I'll see what can be done."

His grizzled face brightened immediately. "That's right kind of you, miss. And I sure will get started on that coop." Relieved, he spit in the dirt. "You look real pretty today, miss. Just like a picture."

Her lips curved. If anyone had told her a week ago that

she would grow fond of a smelly, whiskey-drinking crea-
ture like Lucius, she'd have thought them mad. "Thank you.
There's chicken and fresh bread in the cabin." She held her
breath and snapped the reins.

Sarah had dressed very carefully for town. If she was
going to interest the ladies in ordering fashionable clothes
from her, then it was wise to advertise. Her dress was a particularly flattering shade of moss green with a high neckline she'd graced with her cameo. The trim of rose-colored
ribbon and the rows of flounces at the skirt made it a bit
flirtatious. She'd added a matching bonnet, tilted low as
much for dash as for added shade. She felt doubly pleased
with her choice when her two young customers came running out of the livery and goggled at it.

Sarah left them to race home and try on their new
dresses while she completed her errands.

"Sarah." Liza danced around the counter of the dry
goods store to take both of her hands. "Oh, what a wonderful dress. Every woman in town's going to want one like it."

"I was hoping to tempt them." Laughing, Sarah turned
in a circle. "It's one of my favorites."

"I can see why. Is everything all right with you? I haven't
been able to get away for days."

"Everything's fine. There's been no more trouble." She
wandered over to take a look at the bolts of fabric. "I'm certain it was just an isolated incident. As the sheriff said, it
must have been drifters." Glancing over, she smiled. "Hello,
Mrs. Cody," she said as Liza's mother came in from the
stockroom.

"Sarah, it's nice to see you, and looking so pretty, too."

"Thank you. I've brought your dress."

"Well, that was quick work." Anne Cody took the package in her wide, capable hands and went immediately to
the cash drawer.

"Oh, I don't want you to pay for it until you look and make sure it's what you wanted."

Anne smiled, showing dimples like her daughter's. "That's good business. My Ed would say you've got a head on your shoulders. Let's just take a look, then." As she unwrapped the package, two of her customers moved closer to watch.

"Why, Sarah, it's lovely." Clearly pleased, Anne held it up. The dress was dove gray, simple enough to wear for work behind the counter, yet flatteringly feminine, with touches of lace at the throat and sleeves. "My goodness, honey, you've a fine hand with a needle." Deliberately she moved from behind the counter so that the rest of her customers could get the full effect. "Look at this work, Mrs. Miller. I'll swear you won't see better."

Grinning, Liza leaned over to whisper in Sarah's ear. "She'll have a dozen orders for you in no time. Pa always says Ma could sell a legless man new boots."

"Here you are, Sarah." Anne passed her the money. "It's more than worth every penny."

"Young lady." Mrs. Miller peered through her spectacles at the stitches in Anne's new dress. "I'm going to visit my sister in Kansas City next month. I think a traveling suit of this same fabric would be flattering to me."

"Oh, yes, ma'am." Sarah beamed, ignoring the fact that very little would be flattering to Mrs. Miller's bulky figure. "You have a good eye for color. This fabric trimmed in purple would be stunning on you."

By the time she was finished, Sarah had three more orders and an armful of fabric. With one hand muffling her giggles, Liza walked out with her. "Imagine you talking that old fuddy-duddy Mrs. Miller into two dresses."

"She wants to outshine her sister. I'll have to make sure she does."

"It won't be easy, considering what you have to work with. And she's overcharging you for those chicks."

"That's all right." Sarah turned with a grin. "I'm going to overcharge her for the dresses. Do you have time to walk with me? I'd like to go down and see if this blue-and-white stripe takes Mrs. O'Rourke's fancy."

They started down the walkway. After only a few steps, Liza stopped and swept her skirts aside. Sarah watched the statuesque woman approach. In all her life she'd never seen hair that color. It gleamed like the brass knob on Mother Superior's office door. The vivid blue silk dress she wore was too snug at the bodice and entirely too low for day wear. Smooth white breasts rose out of it, the left one adorned with a small beauty mark that matched another at the corner of her red lips. She carried an unfurled parasol and strolled, her hips swaying shamelessly.

As she came shoulder-to-shoulder with Sarah, the woman stopped and looked her up and down. The tiny smile she wore became a smirk as she walked on, rolling her hips.

"My goodness." Sarah could think of little else to say as she rubbed her nose. The woman's perfume remained stubbornly behind.

"That was Carlotta. She runs the Silver Star."

"She looks...extraordinary."

"Well, she's a—you know."

"A what?"

"A woman of ill repute," Liza said in a whisper.

"Oh." Sarah's eyes grew huge. She'd heard, of course. Even in Philadelphia one heard of such women. But to actually pass one on the street... "Oh, my. I wonder why she looked at me that way."

"Probably because Jake Redman's been out your way a couple times. Jake's a real favorite with Carlotta." She shut her mouth tight. If her mother heard her talking that way she'd be skinned alive.

"I should have known." With a toss of her head Sarah started to walk again. For the life of her she didn't know why she felt so much like crying.

Mrs. O'Rourke greeted her with pleasure. Not only had it been a year since she'd had a new dress, she was determined to know all there was to know about the woman who was keeping Jake so churned up.

"I thought you might like this striped material, Mrs. O'Rourke."

"It's right nice." Maggie fingered the cotton with a large, reddened hand. "No doubt it'll make up pretty. Michael… my first husband was Michael Bailey, he was partial to a pretty dress. Died young, did Michael. Got a little drunk and took the wrong horse. Hung him for a horse thief before he sobered up."

Not certain what response was proper, Sarah murmured something inaudible. "I'm sure the colors would flatter you."

Maggie let out a bray of laughter. "Girl, I'm past the age where I care about being flattered. Buried me two husbands. Mr. O'Rourke, rest his soul, was hit by lightning back in '63. The good Lord doesn't always protect fools and drunkards, you know. Save me, I'm not in the market for another one. The only reason a woman decks herself out is to catch a man or keep one." She ran her shrewd eyes over Sarah. "Now you've got a rig on this day, you do."

Deciding to take the remark as a compliment, Sarah offered a small smile. "Thank you. If you'd prefer something else, I could—"

"I wasn't saying I didn't like the goods."

"Sarah can make you a very serviceable dress, Mrs. O'Rourke," Liza put in. "My ma's real pleased with hers.

Mrs. Miller's having her make up two for her trip to Kansas City."

"That so?" Maggie knew what a pinchpenny the Miller woman was. "I reckon I could do with a new dress. Nothing fancy, mind. I don't want any of my boarders getting ideas in their heads." She let out a cackle.

"If a man got ideas about you, Maggie, he'd lose them quick enough after a bowl of your stew."

Sarah's fingers curled into her palms when she heard Jake's voice. Slowly, her body braced, she turned to face him. He was halfway down the stairs.

"Some men want something more from a woman than a bowl of stew," Maggie told him, and cackled again. "You ladies want to be wary of a man who smiles like that," she added, pointing a finger at Jake. "I ought to know, since I married two of them." As she spoke, she watched the way Jake and Sarah looked at each other. Someone had lit a fire there, she decided. She wouldn't mind fanning it a bit. "Liza, all this talk about cooking reminds me. I need another ten pounds of flour. Run on up and fetch it for me. Have your ma put it on my account."

"Yes, ma'am."

Anxious to be off, Sarah picked up the bolt of material again. "I'll get started on this right away, Mrs. O'Rourke."

"Hold on a minute. I've got a dress upstairs you can use for measuring. Needs some mending, too. I'm no hand with a needle. Liza, I can use two pounds of coffee." She motioned at the girl with the back of her hand. "Go on, off with you."

"I'll just be a minute," Liza promised as she walked out the door. Pleased with her maneuvering, Maggie started up the stairs.

"You're about as subtle as a load of buckshot," Jake murmured to her.

With the material still in her hands, Sarah watched Jake approach her. Though she was standing in the center of the room, she had the oddest sensation that her back was against the wall. He was staring at her in that way he had that made her stomach flutter and her knees shake. She promised herself that if he touched her, if he even looked as though he might touch her, she would slap him hard enough to knock his hat off.

He had images of touching her. Of tasting her. Of rolling around on the ground and filling himself with her. Seeing her now, looking like some flower that had sprung up out of the sand, he had to remind himself that they could only be images.

He figured that was no reason he couldn't needle her a bit.

"Morning, Duchess. You come by to see me?"

"Certainly not."

He couldn't help but enjoy the way her eyes fired up. Casually he brushed a finger over the fabric she held and felt her jolt. "Mighty pretty, but I like the dress you've got on better."

"It isn't for me." There was no reason in the world she should feel flattered, Sarah reminded herself. No reason at all. "Mrs. O'Rourke expressed interest in having a dress made."

"So you sew, too." His gaze traveled over her face, lingering on her mouth too long for comfort. "You're full of surprises."

"It's an honest way to make a living." Deliberately she looked down at the gun on his hip. "It's a pity not everyone can say the same."

It was difficult to say what the cool, disapproving tone made him feel. Rage, familiar and bitter-tasting. Futility, with its cold, hollow ring. Both emotions and flickers of others showed in his eyes as he stared down at her.

"So you heard about me," he said before she could follow her first impulse and lay a soothing hand on his arm. "I'm a dangerous man, Sarah." He took her chin in his hand so that her eyes stayed on his. "I draw my gun and leave women widows and children orphans. The smell of gunsmoke and death follows me wherever I go. I got Apache blood in my veins, so I don't look on killing the way a white man might. I put a bullet in a man the same way a wolf rips out throats. Because it's what I was made for. A woman like you had best keep her distance."

She heard the fury licking at his words. More, she heard frustration, a deep, raw frustration. Before he could reach the door, she was calling after him.

"Mr. Redman. Mr. Redman, please." Gathering up her skirts, she hurried after him. "Jake."

He stopped and turned as she came through the doorway. They were outside only a step, but that was enough to have the heat and dust rising around them.

"You'd do better to stay inside until Maggie comes down for you."

"Please, wait." She laid a hand on his arm. "I don't understand what you do, or who you are, but I do know you've taken the trouble to be a help to me. Don't tell me to forget it," she said quickly. "Because I won't."

"You've got a talent for tying a man up in knots," he murmured.

"I don't mean—"

"No, I don't reckon you do. Anything else you want to say?"

"Actually, I—" She broke off when she heard a burst of wild laughter from the next building. As she looked, a man was propelled headfirst through a pair of swinging doors.

He landed in a heap in the dust of the road. Even as Sarah started forward, Jake shifted to block her.

"What do you think you're doing?"

"That man might be hurt."

"He's too drunk to be hurt."

Her eyes wide, Sarah looked past Jake's shoulder and saw the drunk struggle to his feet and stagger back inside. "But it's the middle of the day."

"Just as easy to get drunk in the daylight as it is when the sun's down."

Her lips primmed. "It's just as disgraceful." Whiskey might be the work of the devil, Sarah thought, but she had promised Lucius. "I wonder if I might ask you another favor?"

"You can ask."

"I need a bottle of whiskey."

Jake took off his hat and smoothed back his hair, then replaced the hat. "I thought you didn't care for it much."

"It's not for me. It's for Lucius." She was certain she heard the sound of breaking glass from the neighboring saloon as she reached for her reticule. "I'm afraid I don't know the price."

"Lucius is good for it. Go back inside," he told her, then passed through the swinging doors.

"Quite a man, isn't he?"

Sarah lifted a hand to her heart. "Mrs. O'Rourke, you startled me."

Grinning, Maggie stepped outside. "Your mind was elsewhere." She handed Sarah a bundle. "Good-looking, Jake is. Strong back, good hands. A woman can hardly ask for more." Maggie glanced over as the din from the saloon grew louder. "You don't have a fella back east, do you?"

"A what?" Distracted, Sarah inched closer to the saloon.

She hated to admit it, but she was dying to see inside. "Oh, no. At least there was no one I cared for enough to marry."

"A smart woman knows how to bring a man around to marriage and make him think it was his idea all along. You take Jake—" Maggie broke off when Sarah squealed. Two men burst through the swinging doors and rolled into the street, fists flying.

"My goodness." Her mouth hanging open, Sarah watched the two men kick and claw and pummel each other.

"I thought I told you to go inside." Jake strolled out, carrying a bottle of whiskey by the neck.

"I was just— Oh!" She saw blood fly as a fist connected with a nose. "This is dreadful. You have to stop them."

"Like hell I do. Where's your wagon?"

"But you must," Sarah insisted. "You can't simply stand here and watch two men beat each other like this."

"Duchess, if I try to break that up, both of them are going to start swinging at me." He passed her the bottle of whiskey. "I don't feel much like killing anybody today."

With a huff, Sarah thrust the bottle back into his hands and followed it with the fabric and Maggie's bundle. "Then I'll stop them myself."

"It's going to be a shame when you lose some of those pretty teeth."

Taking time only to glare at him, Sarah bent down and scooped up the spittoon Maggie kept beside her doorway. Her skirts in one hand, weapon in the other, she marched toward the middle of the melee.

"That's some woman," Maggie said with a grin. Jake merely grunted. "Got grit."

"Go water down your stew."

Maggie just laughed. "She's got you, too. Hope I'm around when she figures it out."

A little breathless, Sarah dodged the rolling bodies. The

men were groaning and hissing as they struggled to land punches. The smell of stale whiskey and sweat rose from both of them. She had to scramble a bit for aim before she brought the brass down with a thunk on one head and then the other. A roar of laughter, then a few cheers, poured out the doorway of the saloon. Ignoring the sound, Sarah looked down at the two men, who were frowning at her and rubbing their heads.

"You should be ashamed of yourselves," she told them, in a tone that would have made Mother Superior proud. "Fighting in the street like a couple of schoolboys. You've done nothing but bloody your faces and make a spectacle of yourselves. Now stand up." Both men reached for their hats and struggled to their feet. "I'm sure whatever disagreement you have can be better solved by talking it out." Satisfied, Sarah nodded politely, then glided back across the street to where Jake and Maggie stood.

"There." She handed Maggie the spittoon. Her self-satisfied smirk was for Jake alone. "It was only a matter of getting their attention, then applying reason."

He glanced over her head to where the two men were wrestling in the dirt again. "Yes, ma'am." Taking her arm, he started up the street before she could get it in her head to do something else. "Did you learn to swing like that in your fancy school?"

"I had occasion to observe the nuns' techniques for handling disagreements."

"Ever get knocked on the head with a spittoon?"

She tilted her head, her eyes laughing under the cover of her lashes. "No, but I know what a wooden ruler feels like." Sarah glanced in the dry goods as she stopped by her wagon. Inside, she could see Liza flirting with a thin, gangly man with straw-colored hair and shiny brown boots.

"Is that Will Metcalf?"

Jake stowed the rest of her things in the back of the wagon. "Yeah."

"I think Liza's quite taken with him." She bit back a sigh. Romance was as far away from her right now as the beautiful house her father had built for her in his mind. Turning, she bumped into Jake's chest. His hands came up to steady her and stayed on her arms. Not so far away, she thought again. It wasn't far away at all when it could reach out and touch you.

"You got to watch where you're going."

"I usually do. I used to." He was going to kiss her again, right there in the center of town. She could feel it. She could almost taste it.

He wanted to. He wanted five minutes alone with her, though he knew there was no use, it was no good. "Sarah—"

"Good morning, Jake." Twirling her parasol, Carlotta sauntered up to the wagon. Smiling slightly she ignored the warning look he sent her and turned her attention to Sarah. She'd already decided to hate her, for what she was, for what she had. Her smile still in place, she skimmed her gaze up and down Sarah. Pure and proper and dull, she decided. Jake would be tired of her in a week. But in the meantime it would give her pleasure to make the little priss uncomfortable.

"Aren't you going to introduce me to your friend?"

Jake ignored her and kept a hand on Sarah's arm to steer her to the front of the wagon.

Sarah didn't recognize the basic female urge, the primal urge, to face the enemy down. She only knew she wouldn't have the woman smirking at her back. "I'm Sarah Conway." She didn't offer her hand, she simply nodded. It was as much of an insult as Carlotta's sneering scrutiny.

"I know who you are." Carlotta smiled, fully, even as

her eyes turned to blue ice. "I knew your pa. I knew him real well."

The blow hit home. Carlotta was delighted to see it. But when her eyes skimmed up to meet Jake's, most of the pleasure she felt died. She'd seen him look at men that way when they'd pushed him too far. With a toss of her head, she turned away. He'd come around, she told herself. Men always did.

His mouth grim, Jake reached for Sarah's arm again to help her into the wagon. The moment his fingers brushed her, she jerked away.

"Don't touch me." She had to turn, to grip the edge of the wagon, until she caught the breath Carlotta had knocked out of her. All of her illusions were shattered now. The idea of her father, her own father, with a woman like that was more than she could take.

He'd have preferred to walk away. Just turn and keep going. Infuriated, he dug his hands into his pockets. "Let me help you into the damn wagon, Sarah."

"I don't want your help." She whirled back to face him. "I don't want anything from you. Do you understand?"

"No, but then I don't figure I'm supposed to."

"Do you kiss her the same way you kissed me? Did you think of me the same way you think of her and women like her?"

His hand shot out to stop her before she could scramble into the wagon. "I wasn't thinking at all when I kissed you, and that was my mistake."

"Miss Conway." Samuel Carlson stopped his horse at the head of the wagon. His eyes stayed on Jake's as he dismounted. "Is there a problem?"

"No." Instinctively she stepped between the men. Carlson's gun had a handle of polished ivory, and it looked deadly and beautiful below his silver brocade vest. It no longer shocked her to realize that even a man as obviously cultured and educated as he wouldn't hesitate to use a weapon. "Mr. Redman's been an invaluable help to me since I arrived."

"I heard you'd had some trouble."

Sarah discovered she was digging her nails into her palms. Slowly, stiffly, she uncurled her fingers, but she could do nothing about the tension that was pounding at the base of her throat. It sprang, she knew, from the men, who stood on either side of her, watching each other, ready, almost eager.

"Yes. Fortunately, the damage wasn't extensive."

"I'm glad to hear that." At last Carlson shifted his gaze to Sarah. She heard her own sigh of relief. "Did you ride into town alone, Miss Conway?"

"Yes, I did. As a matter of fact, I'd better be on my way."

"I'd be obliged if you'd allow me to drive you back. It's a long ride for a woman alone."

"That's kind of you, Mr. Carlson. I couldn't impose."

"No imposition at all." Taking her arm, he helped her into the seat. "I've been meaning to ride out, pay my respects. I'd consider it a favor if you'd allow me to drive you."

She was about to refuse again when she looked at Jake. There was ice in his eyes. She imagined there would be a different look in them altogether when he looked at Carlotta.

"I'd love the company," she heard herself say, and she waited while Carlson tied his horse to the rear of the wagon. "Good day, Mr. Redman." Folding her hands in her lap, she let Carlson guide her team out of town.

They talked of nothing important for most of the drive. The weather, music, the theater. It was a pleasure, Sarah told herself, to spend an hour or two in the company of a man who understood art and appreciated beauty.

"I hope you won't take offense if I offer some advice, Miss Conway."

"Advice is always welcome." She smiled at him. "Even if it's not taken."

"I hope you'll take mine. Jake Redman is a dangerous man, the kind who brings trouble to everyone around him. Stay away from him, Miss Conway, for your own good."

She said nothing for a moment, surprised by the strength of the anger that rose up in her. Carlson had said nothing but the truth, and nothing she hadn't already told herself. "I appreciate your concern."

His voice was calm and quiet and laced with regret. "But you won't take my advice."

"I don't think it will be necessary. It's unlikely I'll be seeing Mr. Redman now that I've settled in."

Carlson shook his head and smiled. "I have offended you."

"Not at all. I understand your feelings for Jake—" She corrected herself carefully. "Mr. Redman. I'm sure the trouble between him and your brother was very distressing for you."

Carlson's mouth thinned. "It pains me to say that Jim brought that incident on himself. He's young and a bit wild yet. Redman's a different matter. He lives by his gun and his reputation with it."

"That sounds like no life at all."

"Now I've stirred your sympathies. That certainly wasn't my intention." He touched a hand lightly to hers. "You're a beautiful, sensitive woman. I wouldn't want to see you hurt."

She hadn't been called beautiful in what felt like a very long time. Since a waltz, she remembered, at a ball at Lucilla's big house. "Thank you, but I assure you I'm learning very quickly to take care of myself."

As they drove into the yard, the puppy bounded up, racing around the wagon and barking. "He's grown some," Carlson commented as Lafitte snapped at his ankles.

"Hush, now." Lafitte snarled when Carlson lifted Sarah from the wagon. "He has the makings of an excellent guard dog, I think. And, thank heaven, he gets along well with Lucius. May I offer you some coffee?"

"I'd like that." Once inside, Carlson took a long look. "I've had some difficulty picturing you here. A drawing room with flowered wallpaper and blue draperies would suit you."

She laughed a little as she put the coffee on. "I think it will be some time yet before I put up wallpaper and draperies. I'd like a real floor first. Please sit down."

From the tin on the shelf she took a few of the sugar cookies she'd baked earlier in the week. It pleased her to be able to offer him a napkin she'd sewed out of scrap material.

"It must be a lonely life for you."

"I haven't had time to be lonely, though I admit it's not what I'd hoped for."

"It's a pity your father never made the mine pay."

"It gave him hope." She thought of the journal she was reading. "He was a man who needed hope more than food."

"You're right about that." Carlson sipped at the coffee she served him. "You know, I offered to buy this place from him some time back."

"You did?" Sarah took the seat across from him. "Whatever for?"

"Sentiment." Carlson sent her an embarrassed smile. "Foolish, really. My grandfather once owned this land. He lost it in a poker game when I was a boy. It always infuriated him." He smiled again and sampled a cookie. "Of course, he had the ranch. Twelve hundred acres, with the best water that can be had in these parts. But he grumbled about losing that old mine until the day he died."

"There must be something about it that holds a man. It certainly held my father."

"Matt bought it from the gambler and dived right in. He always believed he'd find the mother lode, though I don't think there is one. After the old man died and I took over, I thought it might be fitting somehow for me to bring it back into the family. A tribute. But Matt, he wouldn't part with it."

"He had a dream," Sarah murmured. "It killed him, eventually."

"I'm sorry. I've upset you. I didn't mean to."

"It's nothing. I still miss him. I suppose I always will."

"It might not be healthy for you to stay here, so close to where he died."

"It's all I have."

Carlson reached over to pat her hand. "As I said, you're a sensitive woman. I was willing to buy this place from Matt. I'd be willing to buy it from you if you feel you'd like to sell."

"Sell?" Surprised, she looked over. The sun was streaming through the yellow curtains at the window. It made a stream of gold on the floor. Before long, the strength of it would fade the material. "That's very generous of you, Mr. Carlson."

"I'd be flattered if you'd call me Samuel."

"It's very generous, and very kind, Samuel." Rising, she walked to the window. Yes, the sun would bleach it out, the same way it bleached the land. She touched a hand to the wall. The adobe stayed cool. It was a kind of miracle, she thought. Like the endurance that kept men in this place. "I don't think I'm ready to give up here."

"You don't have to decide what you want now." He rose, as well, and moved over to lay a gentle hand on her shoulder. She smiled at the gesture. It was comforting to have friends who cared.

"It's been difficult, adjusting here. Yet I feel as though I can't leave, that in leaving I'd be deserting my father."

"I know what it is to lose family. It takes time to think straight again." He turned her to face him. "I can say that I feel I knew Matt enough to be sure he'd want the best for you. If you decide you want to let it go, all you have to do is tell me. We'll leave it an open offer."

"Thank you." She turned and found herself flustered when he lifted both her hands to his lips.

"I want to help you, Sarah. I hope you'll let me."

"Miss Conway."

She jolted, then sighed when she saw Lucius in the doorway. "Yes?"

He eyed Carlson, then turned his head to spit. "You want me to put this team away?"

"Please."

Lucius stayed where he was. "How about the extra horse?"

"I'll be riding out. Thank you for the company, Sarah."

"It was a pleasure."

As they stepped outside, Carlson replaced his hat. "I hope you'll let me call again."

"Of course." Sarah was forced to snatch up the dog when he came toward her guest, snarling and snapping. "Goodbye, Samuel."

She waited until he'd started out before she put the puppy down and walked over to Lucius.

"Lucius." She leaned over to speak to him as he unhitched the horses. "You were quite rude just now."

"If you say so, miss."

"Well, I do." Frustrated, she ducked under the horses to

join him. "Mr. Carlson was considerate enough to drive me back from town. You looked at him as though you wanted to shoot him in the head."

"Maybe."

"For heaven's sake. Why?"

"Some snakes don't rattle."

Casting her eyes to the sky, she gave up. Instead, she snatched the bottle of whiskey from the wagon and watched his eyes light up. "If you want this, take off your shirt."

His mouth dropped as if she'd hit him with a board. "Beg pardon, ma'am?"

"The pants, too. I want you to strip right down to the skin."

He groped at his neckcloth. "Mind if I ask why you'd be wanting me to do that, Miss Conway?"

"I'm going to wash your clothes. I've tolerated the smell of them—and you—quite long enough. While I'm washing them, you can take that extra cake of soap I bought and do the same with yourself."

"Now, miss, I—"

"If, and only if, you're clean, I'll give you this bottle. You get a pail of water and the soap and go into that shed. Toss your clothes out."

Not sure he cared for the arrangement, Lucius shifted his feet. "And if I don't?"

"Then I'll pour every drop of this into the dirt."

Lucius laid a hand on his heart as she stamped off. He was mortally afraid she'd do it.

Chapter 7

Sarah rolled up the sleeves of her oldest shirtwaist, hitched up her serviceable black skirt and went to work.

They'd be better off burned, she thought as she dunked Lucius's stiff denim pants into the stream. The water turned a mud brown instantly. With a sound of disgust, she dunked them again. It would take some doing to make them even marginally acceptable, but she was determined.

Cleanliness was next to godliness.

That had been one of the proverbs cross-stitched on Mother Superior's office wall. Well, she was going to get Lucius as close to God as was humanly possible. Whether he liked it or not.

Leaving the pants to soak, she picked up his faded blue shirt by the tips of her fingers. Deplorable, she decided as she dampened and scrubbed and soaked. Absolutely deplorable. She doubted the clothes had seen clean water in a year. Which meant Lucius's skin had been just as much in need of washing. She'd soon fix that.

She began to smile as she worked. The expression on his face when she'd threatened to empty out the whiskey had been something to see. Poor Lucius. He might look tough and crusty, but underneath he was just a sweet, misguided man who needed a woman to show him the way.

Most men did. At least that was what Lucilla had always said. As she beat Lucius's weathered shirt against the rocks, Sarah wondered what her friend would think of Jake

Redman. There was certainly nothing sweet about him, no matter how deep down a woman might dig. Though he could be kind. It baffled her that time and time again he had shown her that streak of good-heartedness. Always briefly, she added, her lips thinning. Always right before he did something inexcusable.

Like kissing the breath out of her. Kissing her until her blood was hot and her mind was empty and she wanted something she didn't even understand. He'd had no right to do it, and still less to walk away afterward, leaving her trembling and confused.

She should have slapped him. With that thought in mind, Sarah slapped the shirt on the water and gave a satisfied nod at the sound. She should have knocked the arrogance right out of him, and then it should have been she who walked away.

The next time... There would be no next time, she assured herself. If Jake Redman ever touched her again, she'd...she'd...melt like butter, she admitted. Oh, she hated him for making her wish he would touch her again.

When he looked at her, something happened, something frantic, something she'd never experienced before. Her heart beat just a little too fast, and dampness sprang out on the palms of her hands. A look was all that was necessary. His eyes were so dark, so penetrating. When he looked at her it was as if he could see everything she was, or could be, or wanted to be.

It was absurd. He was a man who lived by the gun, who took what he wanted without regret or compunction. All her life she'd been taught that the line between right and wrong was clear and wide and wasn't to be crossed.

To kill was the greatest sin, the most unforgivable. Yet he had killed, and would surely kill again. Knowing it, she couldn't care for him. But care she did. And want she did. And need.

Her hands were wrist-deep in water when she brought herself back. She had no business even thinking this way. Thinking about him. If she had to think of a man, she'd do better to think of Samuel Carlson. He was well-mannered, polished. He would know the proper way to treat a lady. There would be no wild, groping kisses from a man like him. A woman would be safe, cherished, cared for.

But she wished Jake had offered to drive her home.

This was nonsense. Sarah wrung out the shirt and rubbed her nose with the back of her damp hand. She'd had enough nonsense for the time being. She would wash thoughts of Jake away just as she washed the grime and grit and the good Lord knew what from Lucius's shirt.

She wanted her life to be tidy. Perhaps it wouldn't be as grand as she'd once imagined, but it would be tidy. Even here. Sitting back on her heels, she looked around. The sun was heading toward the buttes in the west. Slowly, like a big golden ball in a sky the color of Indian paintbrush. The rocks towered, their odd, somewhat mystical shapes rising up and up, some slender as needles, others rough and thick.

There was a light smell of juniper here, and the occasional rustle that didn't alarm her as it once would have. She watched an eagle soar, its wings spread wide. King of the sky. Below, the stream gurgled, making its lazy way over the rocks.

Why, it was beautiful. She lifted a hand to her throat, surprised to discover that it was aching. She hadn't seen it before, or hadn't wanted to. There was a wild, desolate, marvelous beauty here that man hadn't been able to touch. Or hadn't dared. If the land was lawless, perhaps it deserved to be.

For the first time since she had arrived, she felt a sense

of kinship, of belonging. Of peace. She'd been right to stay, because this was home. Hers. At long last, hers.

When she rose to spread the shirt over a rock, she was smiling. Then she saw the shadow, and she looked up quickly.

There were five of them. Their black hair was loose past their bare shoulders. All but one sat on a horse. It was he who stepped toward her, silent in knee-length moccasins. There was a scar, white and puckered, that ran from his temple, catching the corner of his eye, then curving like a sickle down his cheek. She saw that, and the blade of the knife he carried. Then she began to scream.

Lucius heard the rider coming and strapped his gunbelt on over his long underwear. With soap still lathered all over his face, he stepped out of the shed. Jake pulled up his mount and took a long, lazy look.

"Don't tell me it's spring already."

"Damn women." Lucius spit expertly.

"Ain't that the truth?" After easing off his horse, Jake tossed the reins over the rail. Lafitte immediately leaped up to rest his paws on his thigh. In the way dogs have, he grinned and his tongue lolled. "Going to a dance or something?"

"No, I ain't going anywhere." Lucius cast a vicious look toward the house. "She threatened me. Yes, sir, there's no two ways about it, it was a threat. Said less'n I took myself a bath and let her wash my clothes she'd pour out every last drop of whiskey in the bottle she brought."

With a grin of his own, Jake leaned against the rail and rolled a cigarette. "Maybe she's not as stupid as she looks."

"She looks okay," Lucius muttered. "Got a streak of stubborn in her, though." He wiped a soapy hand on the thigh of his long underwear. "What are you doing out here?"

"Came out to talk to you."

"Like hell. I got eyes. She ain't in there," he said when Jake continued to stare at the house.

"I said I came to talk to you." Annoyed, Jake flicked a match and lit his cigarette. "Have you done any checking in the mine?"

"I've taken a look. She don't give a body much free time." He picked up a rock and tossed it so that the puppy would have something to chase. "Always wanting something built or fixed up. Cooks right good, though." He patted his belly. "Can't complain about that."

"See anything?"

"I saw where Matt was working some, right enough. And the cave-in." He spit again. "Can't say I felt real good about digging my way past it. Now, maybe if you told me what it was I was supposed to be looking for."

"You'll know if you find it." He looked back at the house. She'd put curtains on the windows. "Does she ever go up there?"

"Goes up, not in. Sits by his grave sometimes. Breaks your heart."

"Sounds like you're going soft on her, old man." He reached down to give Lafitte a scratch on the head.

"Wouldn't talk if I was you." He only laughed when Jake looked at him. There weren't many men who would have dared. "Don't go icing up on me, boy. I've known you too long. Might interest you to know that Samuel Carlson paid a call."

Jake blew out smoke with a shrug. "I know." He waited, took another drag, then swore under his breath. "Did he stay long?"

"Long enough to make up to her. Kissing her hands, he was. Both of them."

"Is that so?" The fury burned low in his gut and spread

rapidly. Eyes narrowed, he flicked the cigarette away, half finished, and watched it smolder. "Where is she?"

"Down to the stream, I imagine."

Lucius smothered a laugh and bent down to pick up Lafitte before the puppy could scramble after Jake. "I wouldn't, if'n I was you, young fella. There's going to be fireworks fit for Independence Day."

Jake wasn't sure what he was going to do, but he didn't think Sarah was going to like it. He hoped she didn't. She needed a short rein, he decided. And he was going to see to it himself. Letting Carlson paw all over her. Just the thought of it made small, jagged claws of jealousy slice through him.

When he heard her scream, both guns were out of their holsters and in his hands in a heartbeat. He took the last quarter of a mile at a run, her screams and the sound of running horses echoing in his head.

When he reached the stream he saw the dust the ponies had kicked up. Even at a distance he recognized Little Bear's profile. There was a different kind of fire in him now. It burned ice-cold as he holstered his weapons. Lafitte came tearing down the path, snarling.

"You're too late again," Jake told the dog as he sniffed the ground and whined. He turned as Lucius came running in nothing more than his gunbelt and long johns.

"What happened?" Jake said nothing. Hunkering down, Lucius studied the marks left by the struggle. "'Paches." He saw his shirt, freshly washed and drying in the sun. "Damn it all to hell." Still swearing, he raced down the path toward Jake. "Let me get on my spare shirt and my boots. They don't have much of a lead."

"I'm going alone."

"There was four of them, maybe more."

"Five." Jake strode back into the clearing. "I ride alone."

"Listen, boy, even if it was Little Bear, that don't give you no guarantees. You weren't no more than kids last time, and you chose different ways."

"It was Little Bear, and I'm not looking for guarantees." He swung into the saddle. "I'm going to get her back."

Lucius put a hand on the saddle horn. "See that you do."

"If I'm not back tomorrow sundown, go get Barker. I'll leave a trail even he can follow." He kicked his horse into a gallop and headed north.

She hadn't fainted, but she wasn't so sure that was a blessing. She'd been tossed roughly onto the back of a horse, and she was forced to grip its mane to keep from tumbling off. The Indian with the scar rode behind her, calling out to his companions occasionally and gesturing with a new government-issue Winchester. He'd dragged her by her hair to get her astride the horse, and he still seemed fascinated by it. When she felt him push his nose into it, she closed her eyes, shuddered and prayed.

They rode fast, their ponies apparently tireless and obviously surefooted, as they left the flats for the rocks and the hills. The sun was merciless here. She felt it beating down on her head as she struggled not to weep. She didn't want to die weeping. They would undoubtedly kill her. But what frightened her more than whatever death was in store for her was what they would do to her first.

She'd heard stories, horrible, barbaric stories, about what was done to captive white women. Once she'd thought them all foolishness, like the stories of bogeymen conjured up to frighten small children. Now she feared that the stories were pale reflections of reality.

They climbed higher, to where the air cooled and the mountains burst to life with pine and fast-running streams. When the horses slowed, she slumped forward, her thighs screaming from the effort of the ride. They talked among themselves in words that meant nothing to her. Time had lost all meaning, as well. It had been hours. She was only sure of that because the sun was low and just beginning to turn the western sky red. Blood red.

They stopped, and for one wild moment she thought about kicking the horse and trying to ride free. Then she was being dragged to the ground. With the breath knocked from her, she tried to get her bearings.

Three of the men were filling water skins at the stream. One seemed hardly more than a boy, but she doubted age mattered. They watered their mounts and paid no attention to her.

Pushing herself up on her elbows, she saw the scarfaced Indian arguing with one she now took to be the leader. He had a starkly beautiful face, lean and chiseled and cold. There was an eagle feather in his hair, and around his neck was a string of what looked like small bleached bones. He studied her dispassionately, then signaled to the other man.

She began to pray again, silently, desperately, as the scarfaced brave advanced on her. He dragged her to her feet and began to toy with her hair. The leader barked out an order that the brave just snarled at. He reached for her throat. Sarah held her breath as he ripped the cameo from her shirtwaist. Apparently satisfied for the moment, he pushed her toward the stream and let her drink.

She did, greedily. Perhaps death wasn't as close as she'd feared. Perhaps somehow, somehow, she could evade it. She wouldn't despair, she told herself as she soothed her burning skin with the icy water. Someone would come after her. Someone.

Jake.

She nearly cried out his name when she was dragged to her feet again. Her captor had fastened her brooch to his buckskin vest. Like a trophy, she thought. Her mother's cameo wouldn't be a trophy for a savage. Furious, she reached for it, and was slapped to the ground. She felt the shirtwaist rip away from her shoulder as she was pulled up by it. Instinctively she began to fight, using teeth and nails. She heard a cry of pain, then rolling masculine laughter. As she kicked and squirmed, her hands were bound together with a leather strap. She was sobbing now, but with rage. Tossed astride the pony again, she felt her ankles bound tight under its belly.

There was the taste of blood in her mouth, and tears in her eyes. They continued to climb.

She dozed somehow. When the pain in her arms and legs grew unbearable, it seemed the best escape. The height was dizzying. They rode along the edge of a narrow canyon that seemed to drop forever. Into hell, she thought as her eyes drooped again. Straight into hell.

Wherever they were taking her, it was a different world, one of forests and rivers and sheer cliffs. It didn't matter. She would die or she would escape. There was nothing else.

Survival. That's all there is.

She hadn't understood what Jake had meant when he'd said that to her. Now she did. There were times when there was nothing but life or death. If she could escape, and had to kill to do so, then she would kill. If she could not escape, and they were planning what she feared they were, she would find a way to kill herself.

They climbed. Endlessly, it seemed to Sarah, they rode up a winding trail and into the twilight. Around her she could hear the call of night birds, high and musical, accented by the hollow hooting of an owl. The trees glowed gold and red, and as the wind rose it sounded through them. The air chilled, working through the torn shirtwaist. Only her pride remained as she shivered in silence.

Exhaustion had her dreaming. She was riding through the forest with Lucilla, chatting about the new bonnet they had seen that morning. They were laughing and talking about the men they would fall in love with and marry. They would be tall and strong and devastatingly handsome.

She dreamed of Jake—of a dream kiss, and a real one. She dreamed of him riding to her, sweeping her up on his big gray mount and taking her away. Holding her, warming her, keeping her safe.

Then the horses stopped.

Her heart was too weary even for prayer as her ankle bonds were cut. She was pulled unresisting from the horse, then sprawled on the ground when her legs buckled under her. There was no energy left in her for weeping, so she lay still, counting each breath. She must have slept, because when she came to again she heard the crackling of a fire and the quiet murmuring of men at a meal.

Biting back a moan, she tried to push herself up. Before she could, a hand was on her shoulder, rolling her onto her back.

Her captor leaned over her, his dark eyes gleaming in the firelight. He spoke, but the words meant nothing to her. She would fight him, she promised herself. Even knowing she would lose, she would fight. He touched her hair, running his fingers through it, lifting it and letting it fall. It must have pleased him, for he grinned at her before he took out his knife.

She thought, almost hoped, that he would slit her throat and be done with it. Instead, he began to cut her skirt away. She kicked, as viciously as she could, but he only parried the blows, then locked her legs with his own. Hearing her skirt rip, she struck out blindly with her bound hands. As he raised his own to strike her, there was a call from the campfire. Her kidnappers rose, bows and rifles at the ready.

She saw the rider come out of the gloom and into the flickering light. Another dream, she thought with a little sob. Then he looked at her. Strength poured back into her body, and she scrambled to her feet.

"Jake!"

She would have run to him, but she was yanked ruthlessly back. He gave no sign, barely glanced her way as he walked his horse toward the group of Apaches. He spoke, but the words were strange, incomprehensible to her.

"Much time has passed, Little Bear."

"I felt breath on my back today." Little Bear lowered his rifle and waited. "I thought never to see you again, Gray Eyes."

Slowly, ignoring the rage bubbling inside him, Jake dismounted. "Our paths have run apart. Now they come together again." He looked steadily into eyes he knew as well as he knew his own. There was between them a love few men would have understood. "I remember a promise made between boys. We swore in blood that one would never lift a hand against the other."

"The promise sworn in blood has not been forgotten." Little Bear held out his hand. They gripped firm, hand to elbow. "Will you eat?"

With a nod, Jake sat by the fire to share the venison. Out of the corner of his eye, he saw Sarah huddled on the ground, watching. Her face was pale with fear and exhaustion. He could see bruises of fatigue under eyes that were glazed with it. Her clothes were torn, and he knew, as he ate and drank, that she must be cold. But if he wanted her alive, there were traditions to be observed.

"Where is the rest of our tribe?"

"Dead. Lost. Running." Little Bear stared broodingly into the fire. "The long swords have cut us down like deer.

Those who are left are few and hide in the mountains. Still they come."

"Crooked Arm? Straw Basket?"

"They live. North, where the winters are long and the game is scarce." He turned his head again, and Jake saw a cold, depthless anger—one he understood. "The children do not laugh, Gray Eyes, nor do the women sing."

They talked, as the fire blazed, of shared memories, of people both had loved. Their bond was as strong as it had been when Jake had lived and learned and felt like an Apache. But they both knew that time had passed.

When the meal was over, Jake rose from the fire. "You have taken my woman, Little Bear. I have come to take her back."

Little Bear held up a hand before the scarred man beside him could speak. "She is not my prisoner, but Black Hawk's. It is not for me to return her to you."

"Then the promise can be kept between us." He turned to Black Hawk. "You have taken my woman."

"I have not finished with her." He put a hand on the hilt of his knife. "I will keep her."

He could have bargained with him. A rifle was worth more than a woman. But bargaining would have cost him face. He had claimed Sarah as his, and there was only one way to take her back.

"The one who lives will keep her." He unstrapped his guns, handing them to Little Bear. There were few men he would have trusted with his weapons. "I will speak with her." He moved to Sarah as Black Hawk began to chant in preparation for the fight.

"I hope you enjoyed your meal," she said, sniffing. "I actually thought you might have come to rescue me."

"I'm working on it."

"Yes, I could see that. Sitting by the fire, eating, telling stories. My hero."

His grin flashed as he hauled her against him for a long, hard kiss. "You're a hell of a woman, Sarah. Just sit tight and let me see what I can do."

"Take me home." Pride abandoned, she gripped the front of his shirt. "Please, just take me home."

"I will." He squeezed her hands as he removed them from his shirt. Then he rose, and he, too, began to chant. If there was magic, he wanted his share.

They stood side by side in the glow of the fire as the youngest warrior bound their left wrists together. The glitter of knives had Sarah pushing herself to her feet. Little Bear closed a hand over her arm.

"You cannot stop it," he said in calm, precise English.

"No!" She struggled as she watched the blades rise. "Oh, God, no!" They came down, whistling.

"I will spill your white blood, Gray Eyes," Black Hawk murmured as their blades scraped, edge to edge.

Locked wrist to wrist, they hacked, dodged, advanced. Jake fought in grim silence. If he lost, even as his blood poured out, Black Hawk would celebrate his victory by raping Sarah. The thought of it, the fury of it, broke his concentration, and Black Hawk pushed past his guard and sliced down his shoulder. Blood ran warm down his arm. Concentrating on the scent of it, he blocked Sarah from his mind and fought to survive.

In the frigid night air, their faces gleamed with sweat. The birds had flown away at the sound of blades and the smell of blood. The only sound now was the harsh breathing of the two men locked in combat, intent on the kill. The other men formed a loose circle around them, watching, the inevitability of death accepted.

Sarah stood with her bound hands at her mouth, holding back the need to scream and scream until she had no air left. At the first sight of Jake's blood she had closed her eyes tight. But fear had had them wide again in an instant.

Little Bear still held her arm, his grip light but inescapable. She already understood that she was to be a kind of prize for the survivor. As Jake narrowly deflected Black Hawk's blade, she turned to the man beside her.

"Please, if you stop it, let him live, I'll go with you willingly. I won't fight or try to escape."

For a moment, Little Bear took his eyes away from the combat. Gray Eyes had chosen his woman well. "Only death stops it now."

As she watched, both men tumbled to the ground. She saw Black Hawk's knife plunge into the dirt an inch from Jake's face. Even as he drew it out, Jake's knife was ripping into his flesh. They rolled toward the fire.

Jake didn't feel the heat, only an ice-cold rage. The fire seared the skin on his arm before he yanked free. The hilt of his knife was slick with his own sweat but the blade dripped red with his opponent's blood.

The horses whinnied and shied when the men rolled too close. Then they were in the shadows. Sarah could see only a dark blur and the sporadic gleam of a knife. But she could hear desperate grunts and the scrape of metal. Then she heard nothing but the sound of a man breathing hard. One man. With her heart in her throat, she waited to see who would come back into the light.

Bruised, bloodied, Jake walked to her. Saying nothing, he cut through her bonds with the blade of the stained knife. Still silent, he pushed it into his boot and took his guns back from Little Bear.

"He was a brave warrior," Little Bear said.

With pain and triumph singing through him, Jake

strapped on his gunbelt. "He died a warrior's death." He offered his hand again. "May the spirits ride with you, brother."

"And with you, Gray Eyes."

Jake held out a hand for Sarah. When he saw that she was swaying on her feet, he picked her up and carried her to his horse. "Hold on," he told her, swinging up into the saddle behind her. He rode out of camp without looking back, knowing he would never see Little Bear again.

She didn't want to cry, but she couldn't stop. Her only comfort was that her tears were silent and he couldn't hear them. Or so she thought. They'd ridden no more than ten minutes at a slow walk when he turned her around in the saddle to cradle her against him.

"You've had a bad time, Duchess. Go on and cry for a while."

So she wept shamelessly, her cheeks pressed against his chest, the movement of the horse lulling her. "I was so afraid." Her voice hitching, she clung to him. "He was going to—"

"I know. You don't want to think about it." He didn't. If he did, he'd lose the already-slippery grip he had on his control. "It's all over now."

"Will they come after us?"

"No."

"How can you be sure?" As the tears passed, the fear doubled back.

"It wouldn't be honorable."

"Honorable?" She lifted her head to look at him. In the moonlight his face looked hard as rock. "But they're Indians."

"That's right. They'll stand by their honor a lot longer than any white man."

"But—" She had forgotten for a moment the Apache in him. "You seemed to know them."

"I lived with them five years. Little Bear, the one with the eagle feather, is my cousin." He stopped and dismounted. "You're cold. I'll build a fire and you can rest awhile." He pulled a blanket out of his saddlebag and tossed it over her shoulders. Too tired to argue, Sarah wrapped it tight around herself and sat on the ground.

He had a fire burning quickly and started making coffee. Without hesitation, Sarah bit into the jerky he gave her and warmed her hands over the flames.

"The one you...fought with. Did you know him?"

"Yeah."

He'd killed for her, she thought, and had to struggle not to weep again. Perhaps it had been a member of his own family, an old friend. "I'm sorry," she managed.

"For what?" He poured coffee into a cup, then pushed it into her trembling hands.

"For all of it. They were just there, all at once. There was nothing I could do." She drank, needing the warmth badly. "When I was in school, we would read the papers, hear stories. I never really believed it. I was certain that the army had everything under control."

"You read about massacres," he said with a dull fury in his voice that had her looking up again. "About settlers slaughtered and wagon trains attacked. You read about savages scalping children. It's true enough. But did you read any about soldiers riding into camps and butchering, raping women, putting bullets in babies long after treaties were signed and promises made? Did you hear stories about poisoned food and contaminated blankets sent to the reservations?"

"But that can't be."

"The white man wants the land, and the land isn't his—or wasn't." He took out his knife and cleaned it in the dirt. "He'll take it, one way or the other."

She didn't want to believe it, but she could see the truth in his eyes. "I never knew."

"It won't go on much longer. Little Bear and men like him are nearly done."

"How did you choose? Between one life and the other?"

He moved his shoulders. "There wasn't much choice. There's not enough Apache in me to have been accepted as a warrior. And I was raised white, mostly. Red man. That's what they called my father when he was coming up outside an army post down around Tucson. He kept it. Maybe it was pride, maybe it wasn't."

He stopped, annoyed with himself. He'd never told anyone so much.

"You up to riding?"

She wanted him to go on, to tell her everything there was to tell about himself. Instinct held her back. If she pushed, she might never learn. "I can try." Smiling, she reached out to touch his arm. "I want to— Oh, you're bleeding."

He glanced down. "Here and there."

"Let me see. I should have tended these already." She was up on her knees, pulling away the rent material of his sleeve.

"Nothing a man likes better than to have his clothes ripped off by a pretty woman."

"I'll thank you to behave yourself," she told him, but she couldn't muffle a chuckle.

It was good to hear her laugh, even if only a little. Most of the horror had faded from her eyes. But he wanted it gone, all of it. "Heard you made Lucius strip down to the skin. He claimed you threatened him."

This time her laughter was warmer. "The man needed to be threatened. I wish you'd seen his face when I told him to take off his pants."

"I don't suppose you'd like me to do the same."

"Just the shirt should do. This arm certainly needs to be bandaged." She rose and, modesty prevailing, turned her back before she lifted the hem of her skirt to rip her petticoat.

"I'm obliged." He eased painfully out of his shirt. "I've been wondering, Duchess, just how many of those petticoats do you wear?"

"That's certainly not a subject for discussion. But it's fortunate that I…" She turned back to him, and the words slipped quietly down her throat. She'd never seen a man's chest before, had certainly never thought a man could be so beautiful. But he was firm and lean, with the dark skin taut over his rib cage and gleaming in the firelight. She felt the heat flash inside her, pressing and throbbing in her center and then spreading through her like a drug.

An owl hooted behind her and made her jolt. "I'll need some water." She was forced to clear her throat. "Those wounds should be cleaned."

With his eyes still on hers, he lifted the canteen. Saying nothing, she knelt beside him again to tend the cut that ran from his shoulder to his elbow.

"This is deep. You'll want a doctor to look at it."

"Yes, ma'am."

Her eyes flicked up to his, then quickly away. "It's likely to scar."

"I've got others."

Yes, she could see that. His was the body of a hero, scarred, disciplined and magnificent. "I've caused you a great deal of trouble."

"More than I figured on," he murmured as her fingers glided gently over his skin.

She tied the first bandage, then gave her attention to the slice in his side. "This one doesn't look as serious, but it must be painful."

Her voice had thickened. He could feel the flutter of her
breath on his skin. He winced as she cleaned the wound,
but it was the firelight on her hair that was making him
ache. He held his breath when she reached around him to
secure the bandage.

"There are some nicks," she murmured. Fascinated, she
touched her palm to his chest. "You'll need some salve."

He knew what he needed. His hand closed over her wrist.
Her pulse jumped, but she only stared, as if she were mes-
merized by the contrast of his skin against hers. Dazed,
she watched her own fingers spread and smooth over the
hard line of his chest.

The fire had warmed it, warmed her. Slowly she lifted
her head and looked at him. His eyes were dark, darker
than she'd ever seen them. Storm clouds, she thought. Or
gunsmoke. She thought she could hear her heart pounding in her head. Then there was no sound. No sound at all.

He reached for her face, just to rub his palm over her
cheek. Nothing in his life had ever seemed so soft or looked
so beautiful. The fire was in her eyes, glowing, heating.
There was passion there. He knew enough of women to
recognize it. Her cheeks, drained of color by fatigue, were
as delicate as glass.

He leaned toward her, his eyes open, ready for her to
shy away.

She leaned toward him, her pulse pounding, waiting
for him to take.

An inch apart, they hesitated, his breath merging with
hers. Softly, more softly than either of them would have
thought he could, he brushed his lips over hers. And heard
her sigh. Gently, with hands more used to molding the
grips of guns, he drew her to him. And felt her give. Her
lips parted, as they would only for him.

Boldly, as she had never known she could, she ran her

hands up his chest. Was he trembling? She murmured to him, lost in the wonder of it. His body was rigid with tension, even as he took the kiss deeper, gloriously deeper. She tasted the hot flavor of desire on his lips as they moved, restless and hungry, over hers.

Eager for more, she pressed against him, letting her arms link tight behind him, and her mouth tell him everything.

He felt the need burst through him like wildfire, searing his mind and loins and heart. Her name tore out of him as he twisted her in his arms and plundered her mouth. The flames beside them leaped, caught by the wind, and sent sparks shooting into the air. He felt her body strain against his, seeking more. Desperate, he tugged at the torn neck of her blouse.

She could only gasp when he covered her breast with his hand. His palm was rough with calluses, and the sensation made her arch and ache. Then his mouth was on her, hot and wet and greedy as it trailed down. Helpless, she dragged her hands through his hair.

She had faced death. This was life. This was love.

His lips raced over her until she was a mass of nerves and need. Recklessly she dragged his mouth back to hers and drove them both toward delirium. His hands were everywhere, pressing, bruising, exciting. With her breath hammering in and out of her lungs, she began to tremble.

His mouth was buried at her throat. The taste of her had seeped into him, and now it was all he knew, all he wanted to know. She was shuddering. Over and over, beneath his own, her body shook. Jake dug his fingers into the dirt as he fought to drag himself back. He'd forgotten what he was. What she was. Hadn't he proven that by nearly taking her on the ground? He heard her soft, breathless moan as he rolled away from her.

She was dizzy, dazed, desperate. With her eyes half

closed, she reached out. The moment she touched him, he was moving away, standing.

"Jake."

He felt as though he'd been shot, low in the gut, and would bleed for the rest of his life. In silence, he smothered the fire and began to break camp.

Sarah suddenly felt the cold, and she wrapped her arms around herself. "What's wrong?"

"We've got to ride."

"But..." Her skin still tingled where his hands had scraped over it. "I thought...that is, it seemed as though..."

"Damn it, woman, I said we've got to ride." He yanked a duster out of his saddlebag and tossed it to her. "Put that on."

She held it against her as she watched him secure his saddlebags again. She wouldn't cry. Biting her lip hard to make sure, she vowed she would never cry over him. He didn't want her. It had just been a whim. He preferred another kind of woman. After dragging the duster around her shoulders, she walked to the horse.

"I can mount," she said coldly when he took her arm.

With a nod, he stepped back, then vaulted into the saddle behind her.

Chapter 8

The crack of the rifle echoed over the rock and sent a lone hawk wheeling. Sarah gritted her teeth, cocked the lever and squeezed again. The empty whiskey bottle exploded. She was improving, she decided as she mopped her brow and reloaded. And she was determined to get better still.

Lucius wandered over, Lafitte dancing at his heels. "You got a good eye there, Miss Sarah."

"Thank you." She lowered the rifle to give the pup a scratch. Jake was right. He was going to be a big one. "I believe I do."

No one was going to have to rescue her again, not from a rattlesnake, not from Apache marauders, not from the wrath of God himself. In the two weeks since Jake had dropped her, without a word and apparently without a thought, on her doorstep, she'd increased her daily rifle practice. Her aim had sharpened a great deal since she'd taken to imagining that the empty bottles and cans were Jake's grinning face.

"I told you, Lucius, there's no need for you to watch my every move. What happened before wasn't your fault."

"I can't help feeling it was. You hired me on to keep a lookout around here. Then the first time my pants're down—so to speak, Miss Sarah—you're in trouble."

"I'm back now, and unharmed."

"And I'm mighty grateful for it. If Jake hadn't just ridden up… I'd have tried to get you back, Miss Sarah, but he was the man for it."

She bit back the unkind remark that sprang to mind. He had saved her, had risked his life to do so. Whatever had happened afterward couldn't diminish that.

"I'm very grateful to Mr. Redman, Lucius."

"Jake just done what he had to."

She remembered the knife fight with a shudder. "I sincerely hope he won't be required to do anything like it again."

"That's why I'm going to keep a better eye on you. I tell you the God's truth now, Miss Sarah, worrying after a woman's a troublesome thing. I ain't had to bother since my wife died."

"Why, Lucius, I never knew you'd been married."

"Some years back. Quiet Water was her name. She was mighty dear to me."

"You had an Indian wife?" Wanting to hear more, Sarah sat down on a rock, spreading her skirts.

He didn't talk about it often, at least not when he was sober. But he found he was making himself comfortable and telling his tale. "Yes, ma'am. She was Apache, one of Little Bear's tribe. Fact is, she'd've been some kind of aunt to him. I met her when I'd come out here to do some soldiering. Fought Cheyenne, mostly. That would have been back in '62. Didn't mind the fighting, but I sure got tired of the marching. I headed south some to do a little prospecting. Anyways, I met up with John Redman. That was Jake's pa."

"You knew Jake's father?"

"Knew him right well. Partnered up for a while. He and his missus had hit some hard times. Lot of people didn't care much for the idea of him being half-Apache." With a little laugh, he shrugged. "He told me once that some of his tribe didn't care much for the idea of him being half-white. So there you go."

"What kind of man was he?"

"Hardheaded, but real quiet. Didn't say much less'n you said something first. Could be funny. Sometimes it wouldn't occur to you for a minute or two that he'd made a joke. He was good for a laugh. Guess he was the best friend I ever had." He took out his bottle and was relieved when Sarah said nothing. "John had in mind to do some ranching, so I lent a hand here and there. That's how I came to meet Quiet Water."

Casually Sarah pleated her skirt. "I suppose you knew Jake as a boy."

"I'll say I did." Lucius let go a whistling laugh. "Tough little cuss. Could look a hole right through you. Ain't changed much. He was spending some time with his grandma's people. Would've thought he was one of them then, 'cept for the eyes. Course, he wasn't. They knew it and he knew it. Like John said, it's hard not being one or the other. I used to wonder what would've happened if Quiet Water and me had had kids."

"What happened to her, Lucius?"

"I had gone off looking for gold." His eyes narrowed as he stared off into the sun. "Seems a regiment rode through early one morning. Some settler claimed his stock was stolen, and that the Apaches had done it. So the soldiers came in, looking for trouble, hating Indians. Killed most everybody but those who made it up into the rocks."

"Oh, Lucius. Lucius, I'm so sorry." Unable to find words, she took both his hands in hers.

"When I come back, it was done. I was half-crazy, I guess. Rode around for days, not going anywhere. I guess I was hoping somebody'd come along and shoot me. Then I headed to the Redman place. They'd been burned out."

"Oh, dear God."

"Nothing left but charred wood and ashes."

"How horrible." She tightened her grip on his hands. "Oh, Lucius, it wasn't the soldiers?"

"No. Leastwise they weren't wearing uniforms. Seemed like some men from town got liquored up and decided they didn't want no breed that close by. John and his missus had had trouble before, like I said, but this went past hard words and threats. They started out to burn the barn, raise hell. One of them started shooting. Maybe they'd meant to all along, there's no saying. When it was over, they'd burned them out and left the family for dead."

Horror made her eyes dark and huge. "Jake. He would have been just a boy."

"Thirteen, fourteen, I reckon. But he was past being a boy. I found him where he'd buried his folks. He was just sitting there, between the two fresh graves. Had his pa's hunting knife in his hands. Still carries it."

She knew the knife. She'd seen it stained with blood, for her. But now all she could think of was the boy. "Oh, the poor child. He must have been so frightened."

"No, ma'am. I don't believe frightened's the word. He was chanting, like in a trance the Indians sometimes use. War chant, it was. He figured on going into town and finding the men who killed his folks."

"But you said he was only thirteen."

"I said he was past being a boy. Best I could do was talk him out of it for a time, till he learned to handle a gun better. He learned mighty fast. I ain't never seen a man do with a gun what Jake can do."

Though it was hot out, she rubbed the chill from her arms. "Did he...go back for them?"

"I don't rightly know. I never asked. I thought it best we move on until he had some years on him, so we headed south. Didn't know what to do for him. Bought him a horse, and we rode together awhile. I always figured he'd hook up with the wrong kind, but Jake was never much for hooking up with anybody. He'd've been about sixteen when we parted ways. Heard about him off and on. Then he rode into Lone Bluff a few months back."

"To lose everything that way." A tear ran down her cheek. "It's a wonder he's not filled with hate."

"He's got it in him, but it's cold. Me, I use the bottle, wash it away now and then. Jake uses something in here." He tapped his temple. "That boy holds more inside than anybody should have to. He ever lets it out, people better stand back."

She understood what he meant. Hadn't she seen it, that flat, dangerous look that came into his eyes? That expressionless stare that was more passionate than fury, more deadly than rage.

"You care for him."

"He's all I got that you might call family. Yeah, I got an affection for the boy." Lucius squinted over at her. "I figure you do, too."

"I don't know what I feel for him." That was a lie. She knew very well what she felt, how she felt. She was even coming to understand why she felt. He wasn't the man she had once imagined she would love, but he was the only man she ever would. "It doesn't matter what I feel," she said, "if he doesn't feel it back."

"Maybe he does. It might be hard for him to say it right out, but I always figure a woman's got a sense about those things."

"Not always." With a little sigh, she rose. "There's work to be done, Lucius."

"Yes'm."

"There is one question. What have you been doing in the mine?"

"The mine, Miss Sarah?"

"You said yourself I have a good eye. I know you've been going in there. I'd like to know why."

"Well, now." Fabricating wasn't Lucius's strong suit. He coughed and shifted his feet and peered off at nothing. "Just having a look around."

"For gold?"

"Could be."

"Do you think you'll find any?"

"Matt always figured there was a rich vein in that rock, and when Jake—" He broke off.

"When Jake what? Asked you to look?"

"Maybe he might have suggested it sometime."

"I see." Sarah looked up to the top of the ridge. She had always wondered what Jake wanted, she thought, her heart shattering. Perhaps she knew now. Gold seemed to pull at the men she loved. "I have no objection to you working the mine, Lucius. In fact, I think it's an excellent idea. You must let me know if you require any tools." When she looked back at him, her eyes were as cool and hard as any man's. "The next time you ride into town, you might mention to Jake that Sarah's Pride is mine."

"Yes, ma'am, if you'd like."

"I insist." She looked toward the road. "There's a buggy coming."

Lucius spit and hoped it wasn't Carlson. As far as he was concerned, the man had been too free with his visits to Sarah in the past few weeks.

It wasn't Carlson. As the buggy drew closer, Sarah saw it was a woman holding the reins. Not Liza, she realized with a pang of disappointment. The woman was dark and delicate and a stranger to her.

"Good morning." Sarah set the rifle against the wall of the house.

"Good morning, ma'am." The young woman sat in the buggy and sent Sarah a nervous smile. "You sure live a ways out."

"Yes." Since her visitor didn't seem in a hurry to alight, Sarah walked to the buggy. "I'm Sarah Conway."

"Yes, ma'am, I know. I'm Alice. Alice Johnson." She gave the puppy a bright, cheerful smile, then looked at Sarah again. "Pleased to meet you."

"It's nice to meet you, too, Miss Johnson. Would you like to come in for some tea?"

"Oh, no, ma'am, I couldn't."

Baffled by Alice's horrified expression, Sarah tried again. "Perhaps you're lost?"

"No, I've come to talk with you, but I couldn't come in. It wouldn't be fitting."

"Oh? Why?"

"Well, you see, Miss Conway, I'm one of Carlotta's girls."

Carlotta? Wide-eyed, Sarah looked her visitor over again. She was hardly more than a girl, a year or more younger than Sarah herself. Her face was scrubbed clean, and her dress was certainly modest. As Sarah stared, thick lashes lowered over her dark eyes and a blush rushed into her cheeks.

"Do you mean you work at the Silver Star?"

"Yes, ma'am, for nearly three months now."

"But—" Sarah swallowed the words when she saw Alice bite her lip. "Miss Johnson, if you've come to see me, I suggest we talk inside. It's much too hot to stand in the sun."

"I couldn't. Really, it wouldn't be fitting, Miss Conway."

"Fitting or not, I don't wish sunstroke on either of us.

Please, come in." Leaving the decision in the hands of her visitor, Sarah walked inside.

Alice hesitated. It didn't feel right, not when Miss Conway was a real lady. But if she went back and couldn't tell Carlotta that she'd done what she'd been sent for, she'd get slapped around for sure. Carlotta always knew when you lied. And you always paid for it.

Sarah heard the timid footsteps as she put water on to boil. Before she could turn and offer Alice a seat, the girl was bubbling.

"Oh, my, isn't this pretty? You've got a real nice place here, Miss Conway. Curtains and all."

"Thank you." Her smile was full and genuine. It was the first time she'd had company who had thought so. "I'm more and more at home here. Please, sit down, Miss Johnson. I'm making tea."

"It's real kind of you, but I don't feel right, you giving me tea. It ain't proper."

"This is my house, and you're my guest. Of course it's proper. I hope you'll enjoy these cookies. I made them only yesterday."

With her fingers plucking nervously at her skirt, Alice sat. "Thank you, ma'am. And don't worry. I won't tell a soul I came in and sat at your table."

Intrigued, Sarah poured the tea. "Why don't you tell me what brought you out to see me?"

"Carlotta. She's been looking at all the dresses you've been making for the ladies in town. They're real pretty, Miss Conway."

"Thank you."

"Just the other day, after Jake left—"

"Jake?"

"Yes'm." Hoping she was holding the cup properly, Alice drank. "He comes into the Silver Star pretty regular. Carlotta's real fond of him. She don't work much herself, you know. Unless it's somebody like Jake."

"Yes, I see." She waited for what was left of her heart to break. Instead, it swelled with fury. "I suppose she might find a man like him appealing."

"She surely does. All the girls got a fondness for Jake."

"I'm sure," she murmured.

"Well, like I was saying, Carlotta got it into her head one day after he left that we should have us some new clothes. Something classy, like ladies would wear. She told me Jake said you could sew some up for us."

"Did he?"

"Yes, ma'am. She said she thought Jake had a real fine idea there, and she sent me on out to see about it. I got me all the measurements."

"I'm sorry, Miss Johnson, I really couldn't. Be sure to tell Carlotta that I appreciate the offer."

"There's eight of us girls, miss, and Carlotta said she'd pay you in advance. I got the money."

"That's generous, but I can't do it. Would you like more tea?"

"I don't—" Confused, Alice looked at her cup. She didn't know anyone who'd ever said no to Carlotta. "If it's not too much trouble." She wanted to stretch out her visit, though she knew that, and the message she'd be taking back, would make Carlotta box her ears.

"Miss Johnson—"

"You can call me Alice, Miss Conway. Everybody does."

"Alice, then. Would you mind telling me how it was you came to work for Carlotta? You're very young to be… on your own."

"My daddy sold me off."

"*Sold* you?"

"There was ten of us at home, and another on the way.

Every time he got drunk he whipped one of us or made another. He got drunk a lot. Few months back, a man passed through and Daddy sold me for twenty dollars. I ran off as soon as I could. When I got to Lone Bluff I went to work for Carlotta. I know it ain't right and proper, but it's better than what I had. I get my meals and a bed to myself when I'm finished work." She gave a quick, uncomfortable shrug. "Most of the men are all right."

"Your father had no right to sell you, Alice."

"Sometimes there's right and there's what's done."

"If you wanted to leave Carlotta, I'm sure there would be other work for you in town. Proper work."

"Begging your pardon, Miss Conway, but that ain't true. None of the town ladies would hire me for anything. And they shouldn't. Why, how would they know if I'd been with one of their husbands?"

It was sound thinking, but Sarah shook her head. "If you decide to leave, I'll find work for you."

Alice stared at her, wide-eyed. "That's kind of you. I knew you were a real lady, Miss Conway, and I'm obliged. I'd better be heading back."

"If you'd like to visit again, I'd be happy to see you," Sarah told her as she walked her out.

"No, ma'am, that wouldn't be proper. Thank you for the tea, Miss Conway."

Sarah thought a great deal about Alice's visit. That night, as she read her father's journal by lamplight, she tried to imagine what it had been like. To be sold, she thought with an inward shudder. By her own father, like a horse or a steer. It was true that she, too, had spent years of her life without a real family, but she had always known her father loved her. What he had done, he had done with her best interests at heart.

Once she would have condemned Alice's choice out of hand. But now she thought she understood. It was all the girl knew. The cycle had begun with her father's callousness, and the girl was caught in it, helplessly moving in the same circle, selling herself time after time because she knew nothing else.

Had it been the same for Jake? Had the cruelty he'd lived through as a child forced him into a life of restlessness and violence? The scars he carried must run deep. And the hate. Sarah looked into the soft glow of the lamp. As Lucius had said, the hate ran cold.

She should have hated him. She wanted to, she wished the strong, destructive emotion would come, filling all the cracks in her feelings, blocking out everything else. With hate, a coolheaded, sharply honed hate, she would have felt in control again. She needed badly to feel in control again. But she didn't hate him. She couldn't.

Even though she knew he had spent the night with another woman, kissing another woman's lips, touching another woman's skin, she couldn't hate him. But she could grieve for her loss, for the death of a beauty that had never had a chance to bloom fully.

She had come to understand what they might have had together. She had almost come to accept that they belonged together, whatever their differences, whatever the risks. He would always live by his gun and by his own set of rules, but with her, briefly, perhaps reluctantly, he had shown such kindness, such tenderness.

There was a place for her in his heart. Sarah knew it. Beneath the rough-hewn exterior was a man who believed in justice, who was capable of small, endearing kindnesses. He'd allowed her to see that part of him, a part she knew he'd shared with few others.

Then why, the moment she had begun to soften toward

him, to accept him for what and who he was, had he turned
to another woman? A woman whose love could be bought
with a handful of coins?

What did it matter? With a sigh, she closed her father's
journal and prepared for bed. She had only fooled herself
into believing he could care for her. Whatever kindness
Jake had shown her would always war with his lawless nature and his restless heart. She wanted a home, a man by
her side and children at her feet. As long as she loved Jake,
she would go on wanting and never having.

Somehow, no matter how hard it was, no matter how
painful, she would stop loving him.

Jake hated himself for doing it, but he rode toward Sarah's place, a dozen excuses forming in his head. He wanted
to talk to Lucius and check on the progress in the mine. He
wanted to make sure she hadn't been bitten by a snake. He'd
wanted a ride, and her place was as good as any.

They were all lies.

He just wanted to see her. He just wanted to look at her,
hear her talk, smell her hair. He'd stayed away from her for
two weeks, hadn't he? He had a right… He had no rights,
he told himself as he rode into the yard. He had no rights,
and no business thinking about her the way he was thinking about her, wanting her the way he wanted her.

She deserved a man who could make her promises and
keep them, who could give her the kind of life she'd been
born to live.

He wasn't going to touch her again. That was a promise
he'd made himself when he'd ridden away from her the last
time. If he touched her, he wouldn't pull back. That would
only cause them both more misery.

He'd hurt her. He had seen that plain enough when he'd

left her. But that was nothing compared to what he would have done if he'd stayed.

It was quiet. Jake pulled up his mount and took a long, cautious look around, his hand hovering over the butt of his gun. The dog wasn't yapping, nor was there any smoke rising from the chimney. The saddle creaked as he dismounted.

He didn't knock, but pushed open the door and listened. There wasn't a sound from inside. He could see, as his eyes scanned from one corner to the next, that the cabin was empty and as tidy as a church. The curtains she'd sewed had already begun to fade, but they moved prettily in the hot wind. His shoulders relaxed.

She'd done something here. That was something else he had to admire about her. She'd taken less than nothing and made it a home. There were pictures on the walls. One was a watercolor of wildflowers in soft, dreamy hues. It looked like her, he thought as he took a closer study. All dewy and fresh and delicate. Flowers like that would wither fast if they weren't tended.

He moved to the next, his brows drawing together as he scanned it. It was a pencil drawing—a sketch, he figured she'd call it. He recognized the scene, the high, arrogant buttes, the sun-bleached rock. If you looked west from the stream you'd see it. It wasn't an empty place. The Apache knew the spirits that lived there. But oddly, as he studied the lines and shadows, he thought Sarah might know them, too. He would never have imagined her taking the time to draw something so stark and strong, much less hang it on the wall so that she would see it every time she turned around.

Somehow—he couldn't quite figure out the why of it—it suited her every bit as much as the wildflowers.

Annoyed with himself, he turned away. She knew something about magic, he figured. Didn't the cabin smell of her, so that his stomach kept tying itself in knots? He'd be better off out in the air—fifty miles away.

A book caught his eye as he started out. Without giving a thought to her privacy, he opened it. Apparently she'd started a diary. Unable to resist, he scanned the first page.

She'd described her arrival in Lone Bluff. He had to grin as he read over her recounting of the Apache raid and his timely arrival. She'd made him sound pretty impressive, even if she'd noted what she called his "infuriating and unchristian behavior."

There was a long passage about her father, and her feelings about him. He passed it by. Grief was to be respected, unless it needed to be shared. He chuckled out loud as she described her first night, the cold can of beans and the sounds that had kept her awake and trembling until morning. There were bits and pieces he found entertaining enough about the townspeople and her impressions of life in the West. Then he caught his name again.

"Jake Redman is an enigma." He puzzled over the word, sure he'd never heard it before. It sounded a little too fancy to be applied to him.

I don't know if one might call him a diamond in the rough, though rough he certainly is. Honesty forces me to admit that he has been of some help to me and shown glimmers of kindness. I can't resolve my true feelings about him, and I wonder why I find it necessary to try. He is a law unto himself and a man wholly lacking in manners and courtesy. His reputation is distressing, to say the least. He is what is referred to as a gunslinger, and he wears his weapons as smoothly as a gentleman wears a watch fob. Yet I believe if one dug deeply enough one might discover a great deal of goodness there. Fortunately, I have neither the time nor the inclination to do the digging.

Despite his manner and his style of living there is a certain, even a strong, attractiveness about him. He has fine eyes of clear gray, a mouth that some women might call poetic, particularly when he smiles, and truly beautiful hands.

He stopped there to frown down at his hands. They'd been called a lot of things, but beautiful wasn't one of them. He wasn't sure he cared for it. Still, she sure did have a way with words.

He turned the page and would have read on, but the slightest of sounds at his back had him whirling, his guns gripped firmly in his hands.

Lucius swore long and skillfully as he lowered his own pistol. "I ain't lived this long to have you blow holes in me."

Jake slipped his guns home. "You'd better be careful how you come up on a man. Didn't you see my horse?"

"Yeah, I saw it. Just making sure. Didn't expect to find you poking around in here." He glanced down at the book. Without a word, Jake shut it.

"I didn't expect to find the place deserted."

"I've been up to the mine." Lucius pulled a small bottle of whiskey from his pocket.

"And?"

"It's interesting." He took a long pull, then wiped his mouth with the back of his hand. "I can't figure how Matt got himself caught in that cave-in. He was pretty sharp, and I recollect them beams being secure enough. Looks to me like someone worked pretty hard to bring them down."

With a nod, Jake glanced at the watercolor on the wall. "Have you said anything to her yet?"

"Nope." He didn't think it was the best time to tell Jake

that Sarah had found him out. "There's something else I haven't mentioned." His face split into a grin as Jake looked at him. "There's gold in there, boy. Just like Matt always claimed. He'd found the mother lode." Lucius took a swig from the bottle, then corked it. "You figured on that?"

"Just a hunch."

"Want me to keep it under my hat?"

"For the time being."

"I don't care much for playing tricks on Miss Sarah, but I reckon you've got your reasons."

"I've got them."

"I won't ask you what they are. I won't ask you neither what reasons you got for not coming around lately. Miss Sarah, she's been looking a mite peaked since you brought her back from the hills."

"She's sick?" he asked, too quickly.

Lucius rubbed a hand over his mouth to hide a grin. "I figure she's got a fever, all right. Heart fever."

"She'll get over it," Jake muttered as he walked outside.

"You're looking peaked yourself." When Jake didn't answer, he tried again. "Sure is some woman. Looks soft, but that streak of stubborn keeps her going. See there?" He pointed to the vegetable patch. "She's got something growing there. Never thought I'd see a speck of green, but there you go. She waters that thing every day. Stubborn. A stubborn woman's just bound to make things happen."

"Where is she?"

Lucius had been hoping he'd ask. "Gone off driving with Carlson. He's been coming around here near every day. Drinks tea." He spit. "Kisses her fingers and calls her right out by her first name." It warmed his heart to see Jake's eyes harden. "Said something about taking her to see his ranch. Been gone better than an hour now."

* * *

"I don't know when I've spent a more pleasant day." Sarah rose from the glossy mahogany table in Carlson's dining room. "Or had a more delightful meal."

"The pleasure has been mine." Carlson took her hand. "All mine."

Sarah smiled and gently took her hand away. "You have such a beautiful home. I never expected to see anything like it out here."

"My grandfather loved beautiful things." He took her elbow. "I inherited that love from him. Most of the furniture was shipped in from Europe. We had to make some concessions to the land." He patted a thick adobe wall. "But there's no reason to sacrifice all our comforts. This painting—" He guided her to a portrait of a pale, elegant woman in blue silk. "My mother. She was my grandfather's pride and joy. His wife died before this house was completed. Everything he did from that day was for his daughter."

"She's lovely."

"She was. Even my grandfather's love and devotion couldn't keep her alive. The women in my family have always been delicate. This land is hard, too hard for the fragile. It baked the life out of her. I suppose that's why I worry about you."

"I'm not as delicate as you might think." She thought of the ride into the mountains with her hands and feet bound.

"You're strong-willed. I find that very attractive."

He took her hand again. Before she could decide how to respond, a man strode into the house. He was shorter and leaner than Carlson, but there was enough of a resemblance around the mouth and eyes for her to recognize him. His hat was pushed back so that it hung around his neck by its strap. Yellow dust coated his clothes. He hooked his thumbs in the pockets of his pants and looked at her in a way that made her blood chill.

"Well, now, what have we got here?"

"Miss Conway." There was a warning, mild but definite, in Carlson's voice. "My brother Jim. You'll have to excuse him. He's been working the cattle."

"Sam handles the money, I handle the rest. You didn't tell me we were having company." He swaggered closer. He carried the scents of leather and tobacco, but she found nothing appealing about it. "Such nice-looking company."

"I invited Miss Conway to lunch."

"And it was lovely, but I really should be getting back." And away, she thought, from Jim Carlson.

"You don't want to rush off the minute I get in." Grinning, Jim laid a dirty hand on the polished surface of a small table. "We don't get enough company here, at least not your kind. You're just as pretty as a picture." He glanced at his brother with a laugh Sarah didn't understand. "Just as pretty as a picture."

"You'd better wash up." Though his voice was mild, Carlson sent him a hard look. "We have some business to discuss when I get back."

"It's all business with Sam." Jim winked at Sarah. "Now, me, I got time for other things."

Sarah swallowed a sigh of relief when Carlson took her elbow again. "Good day, Mr. Carlson."

Jim watched her retreating back. "Yeah, good day to you. A real good day."

"You'll have to excuse him." Carlson helped Sarah into the waiting buggy. "Jim's a bit rough around the edges. I hope he didn't upset you."

"No, not at all," she said, struggling to keep a polite smile. With her hands folded in her lap, she began to chat about whatever came to mind.

"You seem to be adjusting well to your new life," Carlson commented.

"Actually, I'm enjoying it."

"For selfish reasons, I'm glad to hear it. I was afraid you'd lose heart and leave." He let the horses prance as he turned to smile at her. "I'm very glad you're staying." He pulled up so that they could have a last look at the ranch from the rise. The house spread out, rising two stories, glowing pink in the sunlight, its small glass windows glimmering. Neat paddocks and outbuildings dotted the land, which was cut through by a blue stream and ringed by hills.

"It's lovely, Samuel. You must be very proud of it."

"Pride isn't always enough. A place like this needs to be shared. I've regretted not having a family of my own to fill it. Until now I'd nearly given up hoping I'd find a woman to share it with me." He took her hand and brought it to his lips. "Sarah, nothing would make me happier than if that woman were you."

She wasn't sure she could speak, though she could hardly claim to be surprised. He'd made no secret about the fact that he was courting her. She studied his face in silence. He was everything she had dreamed of. Handsome, dashing, dependable, successful. Now he was offering her everything she had dreamed of. A home, a family, a full and happy life.

She wanted to say yes, to lift a hand to his cheek and smile. But she couldn't. She looked away, struggling to find the right words.

She saw him then. He was hardly more than a silhouette on the horizon. An anonymous man on horseback. But she knew without seeing his face, without hearing his voice, that it was Jake. That knowledge alone made her pulse beat fast and her body yearn.

Deliberately she turned away. "Samuel, I can't begin to tell you how flattered I am by your offer."

He sensed refusal, and though anger tightened within him, he only smiled. "Please, don't give me an answer now. I'd like you to think about it. Believe me, Sarah, I realize we've known each other only a short time and your feelings might not be as strong as mine. Give me a chance to change that."

"Thank you." She didn't object when he kissed her hand again. "I will think about it." That she promised herself. "I'm very grateful you're patient. There's so much on my mind right now. I've nearly got my life under control again, and now that I'm going to open the mine—"

"The mine?" His hand tightened on hers. "You're going to open the mine?"

"Yes." She gave him a puzzled look. "Is something wrong?"

"No, no, it's only that it's dangerous." It was a measure of his ambition that he was able to bring himself under control so quickly. "And I'm afraid doing so might distress you more than you realize. After all, the mine killed your father."

"I know. But it also gave him life. I feel strongly that he would have wanted me to continue there."

"Will you do something for me?"

"I'll try."

"Think about it carefully. You're too important to me. I would hate to have you waste yourself on an empty dream." With another smile, he clucked to the horses. "And if you marry me, I'll see that the mine is worked without causing you any heartache."

"I will think about it." But her mind was crowded with other thoughts as she looked over her shoulder at the lone rider on the hill.

Chapter 9

Sarah had never been more excited about a dance in her life. Nor had she ever worked harder. The moment the plans had been announced for a town dance to celebrate Independence Day, the orders for dresses began to pour in. She left all the chores to Lucius and sewed night and day.

Her fingers were cramped and her eyes burned, but she had earned enough to put through an order for the wood floor she wanted so badly.

After the floor, Sarah thought, she would order glass for the windows and a proper set of dishes. Then, when time and money allowed, she was going to have Lucius build her a real bedroom. With a little laugh, she closed her eyes and imagined it. If the mine came through, she would have that house with four bedrooms and a parlor, but for now she'd settle for a real floor beneath her feet.

Soon, she thought. But before floors and windows came the dance.

She might have made every frock as pretty and as fashionable as her skill allowed, but she wasn't about to be outdone. On the afternoon of the dance she took out her best silk dress. It was a pale lavender blue, the color of moonbeams in a forest. White lace flirted at the square-cut bodice that accented the line of her throat and a hint of shoulder. There were pert bows of a deeper lavender at the edge of each poufed sleeve.

She laced her stays so tightly that her ribs hurt, telling herself it would be worth it. With her hand mirror, she struggled to see different parts of herself and put them together in her mind for a complete image. The flounced skirt with the bows was flattering, she decided, and the matching velvet ribbon at her throat was a nice touch. She would have pinned her cameo to it, but that, like so much else, had been lost.

She wouldn't think about that tonight, she told herself as she patted her hair. She'd swept it up, and its weight had caused her to use every hairpin she could find. But, she thought with a nod, it looked effortless, curling ever so slightly at her ears and temples.

It was important that she look her best. Very important, she added, pulling on her long white gloves. If Jake was there, she wanted him to see just what he'd tossed aside. She swept on her white lace shawl, checked the contents of her reticule, then stepped outside.

"Glory be." Lucius stood by the wagon with his hat in his hand. He'd cleaned up without her having to remind him, and had even taken a razor to his chin. When she smiled at him, he decided that if he'd been ten years younger he'd have given Jake a run for his money.

"Lucius, how handsome you look."

"Hell, Miss Sarah. I mean—" He cleared his throat. "You sure look a sight."

Recognizing that as a compliment, Sarah smiled and held out a hand. With as much style as he could muster, Lucius helped her into the wagon.

"You're going to set them on their ears."

"I hope so." At least she hoped she set one person on his ear. "You're going to save a dance for me, aren't you, Lucius?"

"I'd be pleased to. If I do say so, I dance right well, drunk or sober."

"Perhaps you'll try it sober tonight."

* * *

Jake saw them ride into town. He was sitting at his window, smoking and watching some of the cowboys racing in the streets, waving their hats, shooting off guns and howling.

Independence Day, he thought, blowing smoke at the sky. Most of them figured they had a right to freedom and the land they'd claimed. He'd come to accept that they, and others like them, would take the Arizona Territory and the rest of the West. Black Hawk, and others like him, would never stop the rush.

And he was neither invader nor invaded.

Maybe that was why he had never tried to put his mark on the land. Not since he'd lost what his father had tried to build. It was better to keep whatever you owned light, light enough that it fit on your horse.

The town was full of noise and people. Most of the cowhands were going to get three-quarters drunk, and they were liable to end up shooting themselves instead of the targets Cody had set up for the marksmanship contest. He didn't much care. He just sat at the window and watched.

Then he saw her. It hurt. Unconsciously he rubbed a hand over his heart, where the ache centered. She laughed. He could hear the sound float right up to him and shimmer like water over his skin. The wanting, the pure strength of it, made him drag his eyes away. For survival.

But he looked back, unable to stop himself. She stepped out of the wagon and laughed again as Liza Cody ran out of her father's store. She twirled in a circle for Liza, and he saw all of her, the white skin of her throat, the hint of high, round breasts, the tiny waist, the glow in her eyes. The cigarette burned down to his fingers, and he cursed. But he didn't stop looking.

"You going to sit in the window all day or take me down like you promised?" Maggie came farther into the room, her hands on her hips. The boy hadn't heard a word. She tugged on his shoulder, ignored the name he called her and repeated herself.

"I never promised to do anything."

"You promised, all right, the night I poured you into that bed when you came in so drunk you couldn't stand."

He remembered the night clearly enough. It had been a week after he'd brought Sarah back from the mountains. A week since he'd been going to the Silver Star, trying to work up enough interest to take Carlotta or any other woman to bed. Drinking had been simpler, but getting blind drunk was something he'd never done before and didn't intend to do again.

"I could have gotten myself into bed well enough."

"You couldn't even crawl up the stairs. If there's one thing I know, it's a man who's too drunk to think. Now, are you going to take me down or are you going to back down?"

He grumbled but pushed himself away from the window. "Nothing worse than a nagging woman."

She only grinned and handed him his hat.

They had no more than stepped outside when John Cody came racing up. "Mr. Redman. Mr. Redman. I've been waiting for you."

"Yeah?" He pulled the boy's hat over his face. "Why's that?"

Delighted with the attention, Johnny grinned. "The contest. My pa's having a contest. Best shooting gets a brand-new saddle blanket. A red one. You're going to win, ain't you?"

"I wasn't figuring on it."

"How come? Nobody shoots better'n you. It's a real nice blanket, too."

"Go on, Jake." Maggie gave him a slap on the arm. "The boy's counting on you."

"I don't shoot for sport." He meant to walk on, but he saw Johnny's face fall. "A red blanket?"

The boy's eyes lit instantly. "Yessiree, about the prettiest one I ever seen."

"I guess we could look." Before the sentence was complete, Johnny had him by the hand and was pulling him across the street.

At the back of the store Cody had set up empty bottles and cans of varying sizes. Each contestant stood behind a line drawn in the dirt and took his best six shots. Broken glass littered the ground already.

"It costs two bits to enter," Johnny told him. "I got a short bit if you need it."

Jake looked at the dime the boy offered. The gesture touched him in a way that only those who had been offered very little through life would have understood. "Thanks, but I think I got two bits."

"You can shoot better than Jim Carlson. He's winning now." Johnny glanced over to where Jim was showing off a fancy railman's spin with his shiny new Smith & Wesson .44. "Can you do that?"

"Why? It doesn't help you shoot any better." He flipped a quarter to Johnny. "Why don't you go put my name down?"

"Yessir. Yessiree." He took time out to have a friendly shoving match with another boy, then raced away.

"Going to shoot for the blanket?" Lucius asked from behind him.

"Thinking about it." But he was watching Jim Carlson. He remembered that Jim rode a big white gelding. Jake had seen the gleam of a white horse riding away the night Sarah's shed had burned.

Lucius tipped his hat to Maggie. "Ma'am."

"That you, Lucius? I don't believe I've ever seen you with that beard shaved."

He colored up and stepped away. "I guess a man can shave now and then without a body gawking at him."

"I forgot you had a face under there," Jake commented as he watched Will Metcalf hit four out of six bottles. "You looking for a new red blanket, too?"

"Nope. Just thought I'd come around and tell you Burt Donley rode into town."

Only his eyes changed. "Is that so? I thought he was in Laramie."

"Not anymore. He came this way while you were in New Mexico. Started working for Carlson."

In an easy move, Jake turned and scanned the area behind him. "Donley doesn't punch cattle."

"Hasn't been known to. Could be Carlson hired him to do something else."

"Could be," Jake murmured, watching Donley walk toward the crowd.

He was a big man, burly at the shoulders, thick at the waist. He wore his graying hair long, so long it merged with his beard. And he was fast. Jake had good reason to know just how fast. If the law hadn't stepped in two years before, one of them would be dead now.

"Heard you had some trouble a while back."

"Some." Through the crowd, Jake's eyes met Donley's. They didn't need words. There was unfinished business between them.

As she stood beside Liza, Sarah watched Jake. And shivered. Something had come into his eyes. Something cold and deadly and inevitable. Then the crowd roared when the next contestant shattered all six bottles.

"Oh, look." Liza gave Sarah a quick shake. "Jake's going to shoot. I know it's wrong, but I've always wanted to see how he does it. You hear such stories. There was one—" Her mouth fell open when he drew his right hand and fired.

"I didn't even see him take it out," she whispered. "It was just in his hand, quick as a blink."

"He hit them all." Sarah wrapped her shawl tighter around her. He had hardly moved. His gun was still smoking when he slid it back in place.

Donley strode over, flipped a quarter and waited until more targets were set. Sarah watched his big hand curl over the butt of his gun. Then he drew and fired.

"Goodness. He hit all of them, too. That leaves Dave Jeffrey, Jim Carlson, Jake and Burt Donley."

"Who is he?" she asked, wondering why Jake looked like he wanted to kill him. "The big man in the leather vest."

"Donley? He works for Samuel Carlson. I've heard talk about him, too. The same kind of talk as you hear about Jake. Only…"

"Only?"

"Well, you know how I told you Johnny's been tagging after Jake, pestering him and talking his ear off? I can't say it worries me any. But if he got within ten feet of Burt Donley I'd skin him alive."

The crowd shifted as Cody brought the line back five feet. When the first man aimed and fired, missing two bottles, Sarah saw Johnny tug on Jake's arm and whisper something. To her surprise, Jake grinned and ruffled the boy's hair. There it was again, she thought. That goodness. That basic kindness. Yet she remembered the look that had come into his eyes only moments before.

Who are you? she wanted to ask.

As if he'd heard her, Jake turned his head. Their eyes met and held. She felt a flood of emotions rise up uncontrollably and again wished she could hate him for that alone.

"You keep looking at her like that," Maggie murmured at his side, "you're going to have to marry her or ride fast in the other direction."

"Shut up, Maggie."

She smiled as sweetly as if he'd kissed her cheek. "Just thought you'd like to know that Sam Carlson ain't too pleased by the way you two are carrying on."

Jake's gaze shifted and met Carlson's. He had come up to stand behind Sarah and lay a proprietary hand on her shoulder. Jake considered allowing himself the pleasure of shooting him for that alone. "He's got no claim."

"Not for lack of trying. Better move fast, boyo."

The onlookers cheered again as Jim Carlson nipped five out of six targets.

Taking his time, Jake reloaded his pistol, then moved to the line. The six shots sounded almost like one. When he lowered his Colt, six bottles had been shattered.

Donley took his place. Six shots, six hits.

The line was moved farther back.

"They can't do it from here," Liza whispered to Sarah. "No one could."

Sarah just shook her head. It wasn't a game anymore. There was something between the two men, something much deeper, much darker, than a simple contest of skill. Others sensed it, too. She could hear the murmur of the crowd and see the uneasy looks.

Jake moved behind the line. He scanned the targets, judging the distance, taking mental aim. Then he did what he did best. He drew and fired on instinct. Bottles exploded, one by one. There was nothing left but a single jagged base. Without pausing, he drew his other gun and shattered even that.

There was silence as Donley stepped forward. He drew, and the gun kicked in his hand with each shot. When he was done, a single bottle remained unbroken.

"Congratulations, Redman." Cody brought the blanket over, hoping to dispel some of the tension. Relief made him let out his breath audibly when Sheriff Barker strolled over.

"That was some shooting, boys." He gave each man a

casual nod. Will Metcalf stood at his shoulder as directed. "Good to get it out of your system with a few bottles. Either one of you catches a bullet tonight, there's sure no way I can doubt who put it there."

The warning was given with a smile that was friendly enough. Behind Sarah, Carlson gave a quick shake of his head. Without speaking, Donley made his way through the crowd, which parted for him.

"I ain't never seen nobody shoot like that." Johnny looked up at Jake with awe and wonder in his eyes.

Jake tossed the blanket to him. "There you go."

His eyes widened even farther. "I can have it?"

"You got a horse, don't you?"

"Yes, sir, I got me a bay pony."

"Red ought to look real nice on a bay. Why don't you go see?"

With a whoop, Johnny raced off, only to be caught by his mother. After a minor scuffle, he turned back, grinning. "Thanks, Mr. Redman. Thanks a lot."

"You sure did please that boy pink," Barker commented.

"I don't need a blanket."

Barker only shook his head. "You're a puzzle, Jake. I can't help but have a liking for you."

"That's a puzzle to me, Sheriff. Most lawmen got other feelings."

"Maybe so. Either way, I'd be obliged if you'd keep those guns holstered tonight. You wouldn't want to tell me what there is between you and Donley?"

Jake sent him an even look. "No."

"Didn't figure you would." He spit out tobacco juice. "Well, I'm going to have me some chicken and dance with my wife."

There were a dozen tables lined up along one side of the big canvas tent. Even before the music started, more than half of the food was gone. Women, young and old, were flirting, pleased to be shown off in their best dresses. When the fiddle started, couples swarmed onto the floor. Liza, in her pink muslin, grabbed Will's hand and pulled him with her. Carlson, dashing in his light brown suit and string tie, bowed to Sarah.

"I'd be honored if you'd step out with me, Sarah."

With a little laugh, she gave him a formal curtsy. "I'd be delighted."

The music was fast and cheerful. Despite the heat, the dancing followed suit. At the front of the tent the musicians fiddled and plucked and strummed tirelessly, and the caller wet his whistle with free beer. Couples swung and sashayed and kicked up their heels in a reel. It was different from the dances Sarah had attended in Philadelphia. Wonderfully different, she thought as she twirled in Lucius's arms. Hoots and hollers accompanied the music, as well as hand-clapping, foot-stamping and whistles.

"You were right, Lucius." Laughing, she laid a hand on her speeding heart when the music stopped.

"I was?"

"Yes, indeed. You're a fine dancer. And this is the best party I've ever been to." She leaned over impulsively and kissed his cheek.

"Well, now." His face turned beet red with embarrassed pleasure. "Why don't I fetch you a cup of that punch?"

"That would be lovely."

"Sarah!" Liza's face was nearly as pink as Lucius's when she rushed over and grabbed Sarah's arm.

"My goodness, what's wrong?"

"Nothing. Nothing in the world is wrong." Impatient, Liza dragged Sarah to a corner of the tent. "I just got to tell somebody or bust."

"Then tell me. I'd hate to see you rip the seams of that dress."

"I was just outside, taking a little air." She looked quickly right, then left. "Will came out after me. He kissed me."

"He did?"

"Twice. I guess my heart just about stopped."

One brow lifted, Sarah struggled with a smile. "I suppose that means you've decided to let him be your beau."

"We're getting married," Liza blurted out.

"Oh, Liza, really? That's wonderful." Delighted, Sarah threw her arms around her friend. "I'm so happy for you. When?"

"Well, he's got to talk to Pa first." Liza chewed her lip as she glanced toward her father. "But I know it's going to be all right. Pa likes Will."

"Of course he does. Liza, I can't tell you how happy I am for you."

"I know." When her eyes filled, Liza blinked and sniffled. "Oh, Lordy, I don't want to cry now."

"No, don't, or I'll start."

Laughing, Liza hugged her again. "I can't wait. I just can't wait. It'll be your turn before long. The way Samuel Carlson can't take his eyes off you. I have to admit, I used to have a crush on him." She gave a quick, wicked smile. "Mostly, I thought about using him to make Will jealous."

"I'm not going to marry Samuel. I don't think I'm ever going to get married."

"Oh, nonsense. If not Samuel, there's bound to be a man around here who'll catch your eye."

The musicians began to play again. A waltz. Half smiling, Sarah listened. "The trouble is," she heard herself saying, "one has, but he isn't the kind who thinks about marriage."

"But who—" Liza broke off when she saw Sarah's eyes

go dark. "Oh, my," she said under her breath as she watched Jake come into the tent and cross the room.

There might have been no one else there. No one at all. The moment he'd walked in everything had faded but the music, and him. She didn't see Carlson start toward her to claim the waltz. Nor did she see his jaw clench when he noted where her attention was focused. She only saw Jake coming toward her.

He didn't speak. He just stopped in front of her and held out a hand. Sarah flowed like water into his arms.

She thought it must be a dream. He was holding her, spinning her around and around the room while the music swelled in her head. His eyes never left hers. Without thinking, she lifted her hand from his shoulder to touch his face. And watched his eyes darken like storm clouds.

Flustered by her own behavior, she dropped her hand again. "I didn't imagine you would dance."

"My mother liked to."

"You haven't—" She broke off. It was shameless. The devil with it. "You haven't been by to see me."

"No."

He was never any help, Sarah thought. "Why?"

"You know why." He was crazy to be doing even this. Holding her, torturing himself. She had lowered her eyes at his words, but she raised them again now. The look was clear and challenging.

"Are you afraid to see me?"

"No." That was a lie, and he didn't lie often. "But you should be."

"You don't frighten me, Jake."

"You haven't got the sense to be scared, Sarah." When the music stopped, he held her a moment longer. "If you did, you'd run like hell any time I got close."

"You're the one doing the running." She drew out of his arms and walked away.

It was difficult to hold on to her composure, difficult not to fume and stamp and scream as she would have liked. With her teeth gritted, she stood up for the next dance with the first man who asked her. When she looked again, Jake was gone.

"Sarah." Carlson appeared at her side with a cup of lemonade.

"Thank you." Her small silk fan was hardly adequate for the July heat. "It's a lovely party, isn't it?"

"Yes. More so for me because you're here."

She sipped, using the drink as an excuse not to respond.

"I don't want to spoil your evening, Sarah, but I feel I must speak my mind."

"Of course. What is it?"

"You're stepping on very dangerous ground with Jake Redman."

"Oh." Her dander rose, and she fought it down again. "How is that, Samuel?"

"You must know him for what he is, my dear. A killer, a hired gun. A man like that will treat you with no more respect than he would a woman who was…less of a lady."

"Whatever you think of him, Samuel, Mr. Redman has come to my aid a number of times. If nothing else, I consider him a friend."

"He's no one's friend. Stay away from him, Sarah, for your own sake."

Her spine shot ramrod-straight. "That doesn't sound like advice any longer, but like a demand."

Recognizing the anger in her eyes, he shifted ground. "Consider it a request." He took her hand. "I like to think we have an understanding, Sarah."

"I'm sorry." Gently she took her hand from his. "We don't. I haven't agreed to marry you, Samuel. Until I do I feel no obligation to honor a request. Now, if you'll excuse me, I'd like some air. Alone."

Knowing she had been unnecessarily short with him, she hurried out of the tent.

The moon was up now, and nearly full. Taking the deep, long breaths Sister Madeleine had always claimed would calm an unhealthy temper, she studied it. Surely the moon had been just as big and white in the East. But it had never seemed so. Just as the sky had never seemed so vast or so crowded with stars. Or the men as impossible.

The breathing wasn't going to work, she discovered. She'd walk off her anger instead. She'd taken no more than five steps when the shadow of a man brought her up short. She watched Jake flick away a cigarette.

"It's a hot night for walking."

"Thank you for pointing that out," she said stiffly, and continued on her way.

"There's a lot of drinking going on tonight. A lot of men in town who don't get much chance to see pretty women, much less hold on to one. Walking alone's not smart."

"Your advice is noted." She stormed away, only to have her arm gripped.

"Do you have to be so ornery?"

"Yes." She yanked her arm free. "Now, if that's all you have to say, I'd like to be alone."

"I got more to say." He bit off the words, then dug into his pocket. "This belongs to you."

"Oh." She took the cameo, closing her fingers around it. "I thought it was gone. The Apache with the scar. He'd taken it. He was wearing it when—" When you killed him, she thought.

"I took it back. I've been meaning to give it to you, but it slipped my mind." That was another lie. He'd kept it because he'd wanted to have something of her, even for a little while.

"Thank you." She opened her bag and slipped the cameo inside. "It means a great deal to me." The sound of high, wild feminine laughter tightened her lips. Apparently there was a party at the Silver Star tonight, as well. She wouldn't soften toward him, not now, not ever again. "I'm surprised you're still here. I'd think a dance would be a bit tame for your tastes. Don't let me keep you."

"Damn it, I said I don't want you walking around alone."

Sarah looked down at the hand that had returned to her arm. "I don't believe I'm obliged to take orders from you. Now let go of me."

"Go back inside."

"I'll go where I want, when I want." She jerked free a second time. "And with whom I want."

"If you're talking about Carlson, I'm going to tell you now to stay away from him."

"Are you?" The temper that had bubbled inside her when one man had warned her boiled over at the nerve of this one. "You can tell me whatever you choose, but *I* don't choose to listen. I'll see Samuel when it pleases me to see him."

"So he can kiss your hand?" The anger he was keeping on a short rein strained for freedom. "So you can have the town talking about you spending the day at his place?"

"You have quite a nerve," she whispered. "You, who spends your time with—that woman. Paying her for attention. How dare you insinuate that there's anything improper in my behavior?" She stepped closer to stab a finger at his chest. "If I allow Samuel to kiss my hand, that's my affair. He's asked me to marry him."

The last thing she expected was to be hauled off her feet so that her slippers dangled several inches from the ground. "What did you say?"

"I said he asked me to marry him. Put me down."

He gave her a shake that sent hairpins flying. "I warn you, Duchess, you think long and hard about marrying him, because the same day you're his wife, you're his widow. That's a promise."

She had to swallow her heart, which was lodged in her throat. "Is a gun your answer for everything?"

Slowly, his eyes on hers, he set her down. "Stay here."

"I don't—"

He shook her again. "By God, you'll stay here. Right here, or I'll tie you to a rail like a bad-tempered horse."

Scowling after him, she rubbed the circulation back into her arms. Of all the rude, high-handed— Then her eyes grew wide. Oh, dear Lord, she thought. He's going to kill someone. Flinging a hand to her throat, she started to run. He caught her on his way back, when she was still two feet from the tent.

"Don't you ever listen?"

"I thought—I was afraid—"

"That I was going to put a bullet in Carlson's heart?" His mouth thinned. So she cared that much, to come running to save him. "There's time for that yet." Taking a firmer grip on her arm, he pulled her with him.

"What are you doing?"

"Taking you home."

"You are not." She tried and failed to dig in her heels. "I'm not going with you, and I'm not ready to go home."

"Too bad." Impatient with her struggles, he swooped her up.

"Stop this at once and put me down. I'll scream."

"Go right ahead." He dumped her on the wagon seat. She scrambled for the reins, but he was faster.

"Lucius will take me home when I choose to go home."

"Lucius is staying in town." Jake cracked the reins. "Now why don't you sit back and enjoy the ride? And keep quiet," he added when she opened her mouth. "Or I swear I'll gag you."

Chapter 10

Dignity. Despite the circumstances… No, Sarah thought, correcting herself, *because* of the circumstances, she would maintain her dignity. It might be difficult at the speed Jake was driving, and given the state of her own temper, but she would never, never forget she was a lady.

She wished she were a man so she could knock him flat.

Control. Jake kept his eyes focused over the horses' heads as they galloped steadily and wished it was as easy to control himself. It wasn't easy, but he'd used his control as effectively as he had his Colts for most of his life. He wasn't about to lose it now and do something he'd regret.

He thought it was a shame that a man couldn't slug a woman.

In stony silence, they drove under the fat, full moon. Some might consider it a night for romance, Sarah thought with a sniff. Not her. She was certain she'd never see another full moon without becoming furious. Dragging her off in the middle of a party, she fumed, trying to give her orders on her personal affairs. Threatening to tie her up like—like a horse, she remembered. Of all the high-handed, arrogant, ill-mannered— Taking a long, cautious breath, she blocked her thoughts.

She'd lose more than her dignity if she allowed herself to dwell on Jake Redman.

The dog sent up a fast, frantic barking as they drove into the yard. He scented Sarah and the tall man who always scratched him between the ears. Tongue lolling, he jumped at the side of the wagon, clearly pleased to have his mistress home. One look had him subsiding and slinking off again. She'd worn that same look when he'd tried to sharpen his teeth on one of her kid slippers.

The moment Jake had pulled the horses up in front of the house, Sarah gathered her skirts to step down. Haste and temper made her careless, and she caught the hem. Before she could remind herself about her dignity, she was tugging it free. She heard the silk rip.

"Now see what you've done."

Just as angry, but without the encumbrances, Jake climbed down from the opposite side. "If you'd have held on a minute, I'd have given you a hand."

"Oh, really?" With her chin lifted, she marched around the front of the wagon. "You've never done a gentlemanly thing in your life. You eat with your hat on, swear and ride in and out of here without so much as a good day or a goodbye."

He decided she looked much more likely to bite than her scrawny dog. "Those are powerful faults."

"Faults?" She lifted a brow and stepped closer. "I haven't begun to touch on your faults. If I began, I'd be a year older before I could finish. How dare you toss me in the wagon like a sack of meal and bring me back here against my wishes?"

She was stunning in the moonlight, her cheeks flushed with anger, her eyes glowing with it. "I got my reasons."

"Do you? I'd be fascinated to hear them."

So would he. He wasn't sure what had come over him, unless it was blind jealousy. That wasn't a thought he wanted to entertain. "Go to bed, Duchess."

"I have no intention of going anywhere." She grabbed his arm before he could lead the horses away. "And neither will you until you explain yourself. You accosted me, manhandled me and threatened to kill Samuel Carlson."

"It wasn't a threat." He took her hand by the wrist and dragged it away from his arm. "The next time he touches you, I'll kill him."

He meant it, Sarah realized. She stood rooted to the spot. The ways of the West might still be new to her, but she recognized murder when she saw it in a man's eyes. With her shawl flying behind her, she raced after him.

"Are you mad?"

"Maybe."

"What concern is my relationship with Samuel Carlson to you? I assure you that if I didn't wish Samuel, or any man, to touch me, I would not be touched."

"So you like it?" The horses shied nervously when he spun around to her. "You like having him hold you, put his hands over you, kiss you."

She would have suffered the tortures of hell rather than admit that Carlson had done no more than kiss her fingers. And that the only man who had done more was standing before her now. She stepped forward until she was toe-to-toe with him.

"I'll risk repeating myself and say that it's none of your business."

The way she lifted that chin, he thought, she was just asking to have it punched. "I figure it is." He dragged the horses inside the shed to unharness them.

"You figure incorrectly." Sarah followed him inside. Dignified or not, she was going to have her say. "What I do is my business, and mine alone. I've done nothing I'm ashamed of, and certainly nothing I feel requires justification to you. If I allow Samuel to court me, you have no say in the matter whatsoever."

"Is that what you call it?" He dragged the first horse into its stall. "Courting?"

She went icily still. "Have you another name for it?"

"Maybe I've been wrong about you." He took the second horse by the bridle as he studied Sarah. "I thought you were a bit choosier. Then again, you didn't pull back when I put my hands on you." He grabbed her wrist before she could have the satisfaction of slapping his face.

"How dare you?" Her breath heaved through her lips. "How dare you speak to me that way?" When she jerked free, her shawl fell to the ground unnoticed. "No, I didn't object when you touched me. By God, I wish I had. You make me feel—" The words backed up in her throat. Sarah dug her fingers into her palms until she could choke them free. "You made me feel things I still don't understand. You made me trust you, and those feelings, when it was all a lie. You made me want you when you didn't want me back. After you'd done that, you turned away as though it had meant nothing."

Pain clawed through his gut. What she was saying was true. The hurt shining from her eyes was real. "You're better off," he said quietly as he led the horse into a stall.

"I couldn't agree more." She wanted to weep. "But if you think that gives you any right to interfere in my life, you're wrong. Very wrong."

"You jumped mighty fast from my arms to his." Bitterness hardened the words even as he cursed himself for saying them.

"I?" It was too much—much more than she could bear. Driven by fury, she grabbed his shirt with both hands. "It wasn't I who jumped, it was you. You left me here without a word, then rode straight to the Silver Star. You kissed me, then rubbed my taste from your mouth so that you could kiss her."

"Who?" He caught her by the shoulder before she could rush back outside. "Who?"

"I have nothing more to say to you."

"You started it. Now finish it. Whose bed do you have me jumping in, Sarah?"

"Carlotta's." She threw the name at him with all the hurt and fury that was bottled up inside of her. "You left me to go to her. If that wasn't enough hurt and humiliation, you told her to hire me."

"Hire you?" Shock had his fingers tightening, bruising her flesh. "What the hell are you talking about?"

"You know very well you told her she should hire me to sew dresses for her and her—the others."

"Sew?" He didn't know if he should laugh or curse. Slowly he released his grip and let his hands fall to his sides. "Whatever else you think about me, you should know I'm not stupid."

"I don't know what I think about you." She was fighting back tears now, and it infuriated her.

It was the gleam of those tears that had him explaining when he would have preferred to keep silent. "I never told Carlotta to hire you, for anything. And I haven't been with—" He broke off, swearing. Before he could stride out, she snatched his arm again. She'd conquered her tears, but she couldn't stop her heart from pounding.

"Are you telling me that you haven't been to the Silver Star?"

"No. I'm not telling you that."

"I see." With a bitter little laugh, she rubbed her temple. "So you've simply found, and bought, another woman who suits you. Poor Carlotta. She must be devastated."

"It would take a hell of a lot more than that. And I haven't bought anything in the Silver Star but whiskey since you— since I got back to town."

"Why?" She had to force even a whisper through her lips.

"That's my business." Cursing himself, he started out again, only to have her rush to stop him.

"I asked you a question."

"I gave you my answer." He scooped up her shawl and pushed it into her hands. "Now go to bed."

She tossed the filmy lace on the ground again. "I'm not going anywhere, and neither are you until you tell me why you haven't been with her, or anyone."

"Because I can't stop thinking about you." Enraged, he shoved her back against the wall with a force that had pins scattering and her hair tumbling wild and free to her waist. He wanted to frighten her, frighten her half as much as she frightened him. "You're not safe with me, Duchess." He leaned close to her, dragging a hand roughly through her hair. "Remember that."

She pressed her damp hands against the wall. It wasn't fear she felt. The emotion was strong and driving, but it wasn't fear. "You don't want me."

"Wanting you's eating holes in me." His free hand slid up to circle her neck. "I'd rather be shot than feel the way you make me feel."

"How do I make you feel?" she murmured.

"Reckless." It was true, but it wasn't everything. "And that's not smart, not for either of us. I'll hurt you." He squeezed lightly, trying to prove it to them both. "And I won't give a damn. So you better run while I still have a mind to let you."

"I'm not running." Even if she had wanted to, it would have been impossible. Her legs were weak and trembling. She was already out of breath. "But you are." Knowing exactly what she was doing, what she was risking, she raised her chin. "Threats come easily to you. If you were the kind of man you say you are, and you wanted me, you'd take me. Right here, right now."

His eyes darkened. They were almost black as they bored into hers. She didn't wince as his fingers tightened painfully in her hair. Instead, she kept her chin up and dared him.

"Damn you." He brought his mouth down hard on hers. To scare her, he told himself as he pressed her back against the wall and took his fill. To make her see once and for all what he was. Ruthless, knowing she would bruise, he dragged his hands over her. He touched her the way he would have touched a girl at the Silver Star. Boldly, carelessly. He wanted to bring her to tears, to make her sob and tremble and beg him to leave her alone.

Maybe then he would be able to.

He heard her muffled cry against his mouth and tried to pull back. Her arms circled him, drawing him in.

She gave herself totally, unrestrainedly, to the embrace. He was trying to hurt her, she knew. But he couldn't. She would make him see that being in his arms would never cause her pain. She gasped, forced to grip him tighter to keep her balance, when his mouth roamed down her throat, spreading luxuriant heat. The scraping of his teeth against her skin had her moaning. Too aroused to be shocked by her own actions, she tugged at his shirt. She wanted to touch his skin again, wanted to feel the warmth of it.

He was losing himself in her. No, he was already lost. Her scent, the fragility of it, had his senses spinning. Her mouth, the hunger of it, clawed at his control. Then she said his name—it was a sigh, a prayer—and broke the last bonds.

He pulled her down into the hay, desperate for her. The silk of her dress rustled against his hands as he dragged it from her shoulders. A wildness was on him, peeling away right and wrong as he tore the silk away to find her.

Terror rose up to grab her by the throat. But it wasn't

terror of him. It was terror of the need that had taken possession of her. It ruled her, drove her beyond what could and could not be. As ruthless as he, she ripped at his shirt.

He was yanking at her laces, cursing them, cursing himself. Impatient with encumbrances, he shrugged out of his shirt, then sucked in his breath when her fingers dug into his flesh to pull him closer.

Hot, quick kisses raced over her face. She couldn't catch her breath, not even when he tore her laces loose. They rolled over on the hay as they fought to free themselves, and each other, of the civilized barrier of clothing. She arched when he filled his hands with her breasts, too steeped in pleasure to be ashamed of her nakedness. Her pulse hammered at dozens of points, making her thoughts spin and whirl and center only on him.

She was willow-slim, soft as the silk he'd torn, delicate as glass. For all her fragility, he couldn't fight her power over him. He could smell the hay, the horses, the night. He could see her eyes, her hair, her skin, as the moonlight pushed through the chinks in the shed to shimmer over them. Once more, just once more, he tried to bring himself to sanity. For her sake. For his own.

Then she lifted her arms to him and took him back.

He was lean and firm and strong. Sarah tossed her common sense aside and gave herself to the need, to the love. His eyes were dark, dangerously dark. His skin gleamed like copper in the shadowed light. She saw the scar that ran down his arm. As his mouth came bruisingly back to hers, she ran a gentle finger over it.

There was no turning back for either of them. The horses scraped the ground restlessly in their stalls. In the hills, a coyote sent up a wailing, lonesome song. They didn't hear. She heard her name as he whispered it. But that was all.

The hay scratched her bare skin as he covered her body

with his own. She only sighed. He felt the yielding, gloried in it. He tasted the heat and the honey as he drew her breast into his mouth. A breathless moan escaped her at this new intimacy. Then his tongue began to stroke, to tease.

The pleasure built, painful, beautiful, tugging at her center as his teeth tugged at her nipples. It was unbearable. It was glorious. She wanted to tell him, wanted to explain somehow, but she could only say his name over and over.

He felt her thigh tremble when he stroked a hand along it. Then he heard her gasp of surprise, her moan of desire, when he touched what no man had ever dared to touch.

His. He took her as gently as his grinding need would allow toward her first peak. She was his. She cried out, her body curving like a bow as she crested. The breath burned in his lungs as he crushed his mouth to hers and took her flying again.

She held on, rocked, dazed and desperate. So this was love. This was what a man and woman brought to each other in the privacy of the night. It was more, so much more, than she had ever dreamed. Tears streamed from her eyes to mix with the sweat that slicked her body and his.

"Please," she murmured against his mouth, unsure of what she was asking. "Please."

He didn't want to hurt her. With that part of his mind that still functioned he prayed he could take her painlessly. His breathing harsh and ragged, he entered her slowly, trying to soothe her with his mouth and his hands.

Lights exploded behind her eyes, brilliant white lights that flashed into every color she'd ever seen or imagined. The heat built and built until she was gasping from it, unaware that her nails had scraped down his back and dug in.

Then she was running, racing, speeding, toward something unknown, something urgently desired. Like life. Like breath. Like love. Instinct had her hips moving. Joy had her arms embracing.

She lost her innocence in a wild burst of pleasure that echoed endlessly.

The moonlight slanted across her face as she slept. He watched her. Though his body craved sleep, his mind couldn't rest. She looked almost too beautiful to be real, curled into the hay, her hair spread out, her skin glowing, covered by nothing more than the thin velvet ribbon around her neck.

He'd recognized the passion in her from the beginning. He had suppressed his own for too long not to recognize it when it was suppressed in another. She'd come to him openly, honestly, innocently. And of all the sins he'd ever committed, the greatest had been taking that innocence from her.

He'd had no right. He pressed his fingers against his eyes. He'd had no choice. The kind of need he'd felt for her—still felt, he realized—left no choice.

He was in love with her. He nearly laughed out loud. That kind of thinking was dangerous. Dangerous to Sarah. The things he loved always seemed to end up dead, destroyed. His gaze shifted. Her dress was bundled in a heap near her feet. On the pale silk lay his gunbelt.

That said it all, Jake decided. He and Sarah didn't belong together any more than his Colts and her silk dress did. He didn't belong with anyone.

He shifted, started to rise, but Sarah stirred and reached for his hand. "Jake."

"Yeah." Just the way she said his name made desire quicken in him.

Slowly, a smile curving her lips, she opened her eyes. She hadn't been dreaming, she thought. He was here, with her. She could smell the hay, feel it. She could see the glint of his eyes in the shadowed light. Her smile faded.

"What's wrong?"

"Nothing's wrong." Turning away, he reached for his pants.

"Why are you angry?"

"I'm not angry." He yanked his pants over his hips as he rose. "Why the hell should I be angry?"

"I don't know." She was determined to be calm. Nothing as beautiful as what had happened between them was going to be spoiled by harsh words. She found her chemise, noted that one shoulder strap was torn and slipped it on. "Are you going somewhere?"

He picked up his gunbelt because it troubled him to see it with her things. "I don't think I'd care to walk back to town, and Lucius has my horse."

"I see. Is that the only reason you're staying?"

He turned, ready to swear at her. She was standing very straight, her hair drifting like clouds around her face and shoulders. Her chemise skimmed her thighs and dipped erotically low at one breast. Because his mouth had gone dry, he could only shake his head.

She smiled then, and held out a hand. "Come to the house with me. Stay with me."

It seemed he still had no choice. He closed his hand over hers.

Sarah awoke with Lafitte licking her face. "Go away," she muttered, and turned over.

"You asked me to stay." Jake hooked an arm around her waist. He watched her eyes fly open, saw the shock, the remembering and the pleasure.

"I was talking to the dog." She snuggled closer. Surely there was no more wonderful way to wake up than in the arms of the man you loved. "He figured out how to climb up, but he hasn't figured out how to get down."

Jake leaned over to pat Lafitte's head. "Jump," he said, then rolled Sarah on top of him.

"Is it morning?"

"Nope." He slid a hand up to cup her breast as he kissed her.

"But the sun's up— Oh…" It dimmed as his hands moved over her.

Day. Night. Summer. Winter. What did time matter? He was here, with her, taking her back to all those wonderful places he had shown her. She went willingly at dawn, as she had on the blanket of hay and then again and again on the narrow cot as the moon had set.

He taught her everything a woman could know about the pleasures of love, about needs stirred and needs met. He showed her what it was like to love like lightning and thunder. And he showed her what it was to love like soft rain. She learned that desire could be a pain, burning hot through the blood. She learned it could be a joy, rushing sweet under the skin.

But, though she was still unaware of it, she taught him much more, taught him that there could be beauty, and comfort, and hope.

They came together with the sun rising higher and the heat of the day chasing behind it.

Later, when she was alone in the cabin, Sarah cooled and bathed her skin. This was how it could be, she thought dreamily. Early every morning she would heat the coffee while he fed the stock and fetched fresh water from the stream. She would cook for him and tend the house. Together they would make something out of the land, out of their lives. Something good and fine.

They would start a family. She pressed a hand lightly

against her stomach and wondered if one had already begun. What a beautiful way to make a child, she thought, running her fingers over her damp skin. What a perfect way.

She caught herself blushing and patted her skin dry. It wasn't right to think that way, not when they weren't married. Not when he hadn't even asked her. Would he? Sarah slipped on her shirtwaist and buttoned it quickly. Hadn't she herself said he wasn't the kind of man who thought of marriage?

And yet... Could he love her the way he had loved her and not want to spend his life with her?

What had Mrs. O'Rourke said? Sarah thought back as she finished dressing. It had been something about a smart woman bringing a man around to marriage and making him think it had been his idea all along. With a light laugh, she turned toward the stove. She considered herself a very smart woman.

"Something funny?"

She glanced around as Jake walked in. "No, not really. I guess I'm just happy."

He set a basket of eggs on the table. "I haven't gathered eggs since my mother—for a long time."

As casually as she could, she took the eggs and started preparations for breakfast. "Did your mother have chickens when you were a boy?"

"Yeah. Is that coffee hot?"

"Sit down. I'll pour you some."

He didn't want to talk about his past, she decided. Perhaps the time wasn't right. Yet.

"I was able to get a slab of bacon from Mr. Cobb." She sliced it competently while the pan heated. "I've thought about getting a few pigs. Lucius is going to grumble when I ask him to build a sty, but I don't think he'd complain about eating ham. I don't suppose you know anything about raising pigs?"

Would you listen to her? Jake thought as he tilted back in her chair. The duchess from Philadelphia talking about raising pigs. "You deserve better," he heard himself say.

The bacon sizzled as she poured the coffee. "Better than what?"

"Than this place. Why don't you go back east, Sarah, and live like you were meant to?"

She brought the cup to him. "Is that what you want, Jake? You want me to go?"

"It's not a matter of what I want."

She stood beside him, looking down. "I'd like to hear what you want."

Their eyes held. He'd had some time to think, and think clearly. But nothing seemed clear enough when he looked at her. "Coffee," he said, taking the cup.

"Your wants are admirably simple. Take your hat off at my table." She snatched it off his head and set it aside.

He just grinned, running a hand through his hair. "Yes, ma'am. Good coffee, Duchess."

"It's nice to know I do something that pleases you." She let out a yelp when he grabbed her from behind and spun her around.

"You do a lot that pleases me." He kissed her, hard and long. "A whole lot."

"Really?" She tried to keep her tone aloof, but her arms had already wound around his neck. "A pity I can't say the same."

"I guess that was some other woman who had her hands all over me last night." Her laugh was muffled against his lips. "I brought your things over from the shed. Dress is a little worse for wear. Four petticoats." He nipped her earlobe. "I hope you don't pile that many on every day around here."

"I don't intend to discuss—"

"And that contraption you lace yourself into. Lucky you don't pass out. Can't figure you need it. Your waist's no bigger around than my two hands. I ought to know." He proved it by spanning her. "Why do you want to strap yourself into that thing?"

"I have no intention of discussing my undergarments with you."

"I took them off you. Seems I should be able to talk about them."

Blushing to the roots of her hair, she struggled away. "The bacon's burning."

He took his seat again and picked up his coffee. "How many of those petticoats do you have on now?"

After rescuing the bacon, she sent him a quick, flirtatious look over her shoulder. "You'll just have to find out for yourself." Pleased at the way his brows shot up, she went back to her cooking.

He was no longer certain how to handle her. With breakfast on the table, the scents wafting cozily in the air, and Sarah sitting across from him, Jake searched his mind for something to say.

"I saw your pictures on the wall. You draw real nice."

"Thank you. I've always enjoyed it. If I'd known that my father was living here—that is, if I'd known how a few sketches would brighten the house up—I would have sent him some. I did send a small watercolor." She frowned a little. "It was a self-portrait from last Christmas. I thought he might like to know what I looked like since I'd grown up. It's strange. He had all the letters I'd written to him in that little tin box in the loft, but the sketch is nowhere to be found. I've been meaning to ask the sheriff if he might have forgotten to give it to me."

"If Barker had it, he'd have seen you got it back." He didn't care for the direction his thoughts were taking. "You sure it got this far? Mail gets lost."

"Oh, yes. He wrote me after he received it. Liza also mentioned that my father had been rather taken with it and had brought it into the store to show around."

"Might turn up."

"I suppose." She shrugged. "I've given this place a thorough cleaning, but I might not have come across it. I'll look again when Lucius puts in the floor."

"What floor?"

"The wooden floor. I've ordered boards." She broke off a bite of biscuit. "Actually, I ordered extra. I have my heart set on a real bedroom. Out the west wall, I think. My sewing money's coming in very handy."

"Sarah, last night you said something about Carlotta telling you I'd given her some idea about having you sew for her." He watched her stiffen up immediately. "When did you talk to her?"

"I didn't. I have no intention of talking to that woman."

He rolled his tongue into his cheek. He doubted Sarah would be pleased to know that her tone amused him. "Where did you hear that from?"

"Alice Johnson. She works in…that place. Apparently Carlotta had her drive out here to negotiate for my services."

"Alice?" He cast his mind back, juggling faces with names. "She's the little one—dark hair, big eyes?"

Sarah drew in a quiet, indignant breath. "That's an accurate description. You seem to know the staff of the Silver Star very well."

"I don't know as I'd call them staff, but yeah, I know one from the other."

Rising, she snatched up his empty plate. "And I'm sure they know you quite well." When he just grinned, she had to fight back the urge to knock the look off his face with the cast-iron skillet. "I'll thank you to stop smirking at me."

"Yes, ma'am." But he went right on. "You sure are pretty when you get fired up."

"If that's a compliment," she said, wishing it didn't make her want to smile, "you're wasting your breath."

"I ain't much on compliments. But you're pretty, and that's a fact. I guess you're about the prettiest thing I've ever seen. Especially when you're riled."

"Is that why you continue to go out of your way to annoy me?"

"I expect. Come here."

She smoothed down her skirt. "I will not."

He rose slowly. "You're ornery, too. Can't figure why it appeals to me." He dragged her to him. After a moment's feigned struggle, she laughed up at him.

"I'll have to remember to stay ornery and annoyed, then."

He said nothing. The way she'd looked up at him had knocked the breath out of his body. He pulled her closer, holding on, wishing. Content, Sarah nuzzled his shoulder. Before he could draw her back, she framed his face with her hands and brushed her lips over his.

"You're still tying me up in knots," he muttered.

"That's good. I don't intend to stop."

He stepped back, then gripped her hands with his. "Which one did he kiss?"

"I don't know what you mean."

"Carlson." She gave a surprised gasp when his fingers tightened on hers. "Which hand did he kiss?"

Sarah kept her eyes on his. "Both."

She watched the fury come then, and was amazed at how quickly, how completely, he masked it. But it was still there. She could feel it rippling through him. "Jake—"

He shook his head. Then, in a gesture that left her limp, he brought her hands to his lips. Then he dropped them, obviously uncomfortable, and dug his own hands into his pockets.

"I don't want you to let him do it again."

"I won't."

Her response should have relaxed him, but his tension doubled. "Just like that?"

"Yes, just like that."

He turned away and began to pace. Her brow lifted. She realized she'd never before seen him make an unnecessary movement. If he took a step, it was to go toward or away.

"I've got no right." There was fury in his voice. The same kind she heard outside the tent the night before. In contrast, hers was soft and soothing.

"You have every right. The only right. I'm in love with you."

Now he didn't move at all. He froze as a man might when he heard a trigger cocked at the back of his head. She simply waited, her hands folded at her waist, her eyes calm and clear.

"You don't know what you're saying," he managed at last.

"Of course I do, and so do you." With her eyes on his, she walked to him. "Do you think I could have been with you as I was last night, this morning, if I didn't love you?"

He stepped back before she could touch him. It had been so long since he'd been loved that he'd forgotten what it could feel like. It filled him like a river, and its currents were strong.

"I've got nothing for you, Sarah. Nothing."

"Yourself." She reached a hand to his cheek. "I'm not asking for anything."

"You're mixing up what happened last night with—"

"With what?" she challenged. "Do you think because you were the first man that I don't know the difference between love and…lust? Can you tell me it's been like that for you before, with anyone? Can you?"

No, he couldn't. And he couldn't tell her it would never be that way with anyone but her. "Lucius will be back soon," he said instead. "I'll go down and get the water you wanted before I leave."

And that was all? she thought. Damn him for turning his back on her again. He didn't believe her, she thought. He thought she was just being foolish and romantic… But no, no, that wasn't right, she realized. That wasn't it at all.

It came to her abruptly and with crystalline clarity. He did believe her, and that was why he had turned away. He was as frightened and confused by her love as she had been by the land. It was just as foreign to him. Just as difficult to understand and accept.

She could change that. Taking a long, cleansing breath, she turned to her dishes. She could change that in the same way she had changed herself. She embraced the land now, called it her own. One day he would do the same with her.

She heard the door open again, and she turned, smiling. "Jake—"

But it was Burt Donley who filled the doorway.

Chapter 11

"Where's Redman?"

Panic came first, and it showed in her wide, wild eyes. She was still holding the skillet, and she had one mad thought of heaving it at his head. But his hand was curled over the butt of his gun. She saw in his eyes what she had never seen in Jake's, what she realized she'd never seen in any man's, not even in those of the Apache who had kidnapped her. A desire, even an eagerness, to kill.

He stepped inside, and through the thickness of his beard she saw that he was smiling. "I asked you, where's Redman?"

"He's not here." It surprised her how calm a voice could sound even when a heart was pounding. She had a man to protect. The man she loved. "I don't believe I asked you in."

His smile widened into a grin. "You ain't going to tell me he brought you all the way out here last night and then left a pretty thing like you all alone?"

She was terrified Jake would come back. And terrified he wouldn't. She had no choice but to hold her ground. "I'm not telling you anything. But as you can see, I'm alone."

"I can see that, real plain. Funny, 'cause his horse is in town and he ain't." He picked up a biscuit from the bowl on the table with his wide, blunt-edged fingers, studied it, then bit in. "Word is he spends time out here."

"Mr. Redman occasionally visits. I'll be sure to tell him you were looking for him, if and when I see him."

"You do that. You be sure and do that." He took another bite, chewing slowly, watching her.

"Good day, then."

But he didn't leave. He only walked closer. "You're prettier than I recollect."

She moistened her lips, knowing they were trembling. "I don't believe we've met."

"No, but I've seen you." She strained backward when he put a hand to her hair. "You don't favor your pa none."

"You'll have to excuse me." She tried to step to the side, but he blocked her.

"He sure did set some store by you. A man can see why." He pushed the rest of the biscuit into his mouth, chewing as he reached down to toy with the small bow at her collar. "Too bad he got himself killed over that mine and left you orphaned. Smart man would've kept himself alive. Smart man would've seen the sense in that."

She shifted again, and was again blocked. "He could hardly be blamed for an accident."

"Maybe we'll talk about that later." Enjoying her trembling, he tugged the little bow loose. "You look smarter than your pa was."

Lafitte burst in, snarling. Donley had his hand on the butt of his gun when Sarah grabbed his arm. "No, please. He's hardly more than a puppy." Moving quickly, she gathered the growling dog up. "There's no need for you to hurt him. He's harmless."

"Donley likes killing harmless things." Jake spoke from the doorway. The men stood ten feet apart, Jake backed by sun, Donley by shadow. "There was a man in Laramie— more of a boy, really. Daniel Little Deer was harmless, wasn't he, Donley?"

"He was a breed." Donley's teeth gleamed through his

beard. "I don't think no more of killing a breed than a sick horse."

"And it's easier when it's back-shooting."

"I ain't shooting at your back, Redman."

"Move aside, Sarah."

"Jake, please—"

"Move aside." He was over the sick fear he'd felt when he'd seen Donley's horse outside the house. He was cold, killing-cold. His guns hung low on his hips, and his hands were limber and ready.

Donley shifted, settling his weight evenly. "I've waited a long time for this."

"Some of us get lucky," Jake murmured, "and wait a long time to die."

"When I've killed you, I'm going to have the woman, and the gold." His hand slapped the butt of his gun. The .44 was aimed heart-high. He was fast.

The sound of a gunshot exploded, ripping through the still morning air. Sarah watched in horror as Donley stumbled, forward, then back. A red stain spread across his shirt and his leather vest before he fell by the stone hearth and lay still.

Jake stood in the doorway, his face expressionless, his mind calm and cold. He'd never once felt the rush some men spoke of that came from killing. To him it was neither power nor curse. It was survival.

"Oh, God." Pressed back against the wall, Sarah stared. Lafitte leaped out of her limp arms to crouch, growling, by Donley's gun hand. Her vision grayed, wavered, then snapped back when Jake gripped her arms.

"Did he hurt you?"

"No, I—"

"Get outside."

Hysteria bubbled up in her throat. A man was dead,

lying dead on her floor, and the one holding her looked like a stranger. "Jake—"

"Get outside," he repeated, doing his best to shield her from the man he'd killed. "Go on into the shed or down to the stream." When she only continued to stare, he pulled her to the door and shoved her out. "Do what I tell you."

"What—what are you going to do?"

"I'm going to take him into town."

Giving in to weakness, she leaned on the rail, dragging in gulps of the hot, dusty air as though it were water. "What will they do to you? You killed him."

"Barker'll take me at my word. Or he'll hang me."

"No, but—" Nausea was churning now, coating her skin with a thin, clammy sweat. "He wanted to kill you. He came looking for you."

"That's right." He took both her arms again because he wanted her to look at him, really look. "And tomorrow, next week, next month, there'll be someone else who comes looking for me. I got fast hands, Sarah, and somebody's always going to want to prove they got faster. One day they'll be right."

"You can change. It can change. It has to." She struggled out of his hold, only to throw her arms around him. "You can't want to live this way."

"What I want and what is have always been two different things." He pushed her away. "I care about you." It was easy to mean it, hard to say it. "That's why I'm telling you to walk away."

He'd just killed a man in front of her eyes. And killed him coldly. Even through her horror she'd seen that. But it hadn't left him untouched. What she saw now was the frustration and anger of a man caught in a trap. He needed someone to offer him a way out, or at least the hope of one. If she could do nothing else, she could give him hope.

"No." She stepped forward to frame his face with her hands. "I can't. I won't."

Her hands were trembling. Cold and trembling, he thought as he reached for them. "You're a damn fool."

"Yes. I'm quite sure you're right. But I love you."

He couldn't have begun to tell her what it did to him inside when she said that. When he looked into her eyes and saw that she meant it. He pulled her against him for a rough, hungry kiss. "Go away from the house. I don't want you here when I bring him out."

She nodded, took a long breath and stepped back. The sickness had passed, though the raw feeling inside remained. "Once I was sure there was only right and wrong, and that to kill another person was the greatest wrong. But there isn't only right and wrong, Jake. What you did, what you had to do, kept you alive. There's nothing more important to me than that." She paused and touched his hand. "Come back."

He watched her, as he had watched her once before, start up the rise to her father's grave. When she was gone, he went back inside.

Two days passed, and Sarah tried to follow her daily routine and not to wonder why Jake hadn't ridden back to her. It seemed everyone else had paid her a visit, but not Jake. Barker had come out and, in his usual take-your-time way, questioned her about Burt Donley. It seemed no more than a token investigation to Sarah. Barker, either because he was lazy or because he was a shrewd judge of character, had taken Jake at his word.

The story had spread quickly. Soon after Barker, Liza and Johnny had driven up to hear the details and eat oatmeal cookies. Before she had left, Liza had chased Johnny outside to pester Lucius so that she could spend an hour talking about Will and her upcoming wedding. She was to have a new dress, and she had already ordered the pink silk and the pattern from Santa Fe.

The following morning, the sound of a rider approaching had Sarah rushing out of the chicken coop, eggs banging dangerously against each other in the basket she carried. She struggled to mask her disappointment when she saw Samuel Carlson.

"Sarah." He dismounted quickly, and would have taken her hand, but she used both to grip the handle of the basket. "I've been worried about you."

"There's no need." She smiled as he tied his horse at the rail.

"I was shocked to learn that Donley and Redman had drawn guns right here in your house. It's a miracle you weren't injured."

"I'm sure I would have been if Jake hadn't come back when he did. Donley was...very threatening."

"I feel responsible."

"You?" She stopped in front of the house. "Why?"

"Donley worked for me. I knew what kind of man he was." There was a grimness around his eyes and mouth as he spoke. "I can't say I had any trouble with him until Redman came back to town."

"It was Donley who sought Jake out, Samuel." Her voice sharpened with the need to defend him. "It was he who deliberately provoked a fight. I was there."

"Of course." He laid a soothing hand on her arm. Manners prevented him from stepping inside the house without an invitation. He was shrewd enough to see that something had changed, and that he wouldn't get one. "I detest the fact that you were forced to witness a killing, and in your own home. It must distress you to stay here now."

"No." She glanced over her shoulder. It had been difficult, the first time she had gone inside afterward. There were still traces of dried blood in the dirt, the sight of which had given Johnny ghoulish pleasure. But it was her home. "I'm not as frail as that."

"You're a strong woman, Sarah, but a sensitive one. I'm concerned about you."

"It's kind of you to be. Your friendship is a great comfort to me."

"Sarah." He touched a gentle hand to her cheek. "You must realize that I want to be much more than your friend."

"I know." Regret was in her eyes, in her voice. "It's not possible, Samuel. I'm sorry."

She saw the anger mar his face, and was surprised by the depth of it before he brought it under control again. "It's Redman, isn't it?"

She felt it would be dishonorable, and insulting, to lie to him. "Yes."

"I thought you were more sensible, Sarah. You're an intelligent, gently bred woman. You must understand that Redman is a dangerous man, a man without scruples. He lives by violence. It's part of him."

She smiled a little. "He describes himself the same way. I believe you're both wrong."

"He'll only hurt you."

"Perhaps, but I can't change my feelings. Nor do I wish to." Regret had her reaching out to touch his arm. "I'm sorry, Samuel."

"I have faith that in time you'll get over this infatuation. I can be patient."

"Samuel, I don't—"

"Don't distress yourself." He patted her hand. "Along with patience, I have confidence. You were meant to belong to me, Sarah." He stepped back to untie his horse. Inside, he was boiling with rage. He wanted this woman, and what belonged to her—and he intended to have them, one way or the other.

When he turned to stand beside his mount with his reins in his hands, his face was touched only with affection and concern. "This doesn't change the fact that I worry about you, living out here all alone."

"I'm not alone. I have Lucius."

Carlson cast a slow, meaningful look around the yard.

"He's up in the mine," Sarah explained. "If there was trouble, he'd come down quickly enough."

"The mine." Carlson cast his eyes up at the rock. "At least promise me that you won't go inside. It's a dangerous place."

"Gold doesn't lure me." She smiled again, relieved that they would remain friends.

He swung gracefully into the saddle. "Gold lures everyone."

She watched him ride off. Perhaps he was right, she mused. Gold had a lure. Even though in her heart she didn't believe she'd ever see the mine pay, it was exciting knowing there was always a chance. It kept Lucius in the dark and the dust for hours on end. Her father had died for it.

Even Jake, she thought, wasn't immune. It was he who had asked Lucius to pick up where her father had left off. She had yet to discover why. With death on his mind, Donley's last words had been… A glimmer of suspicion broke into her mind.

I'm going to have the woman, and the gold.

Why should a man like Donley speak of gold before he drew his gun? Why would a worthless mine be on his mind at such a time? Or was it worthless?

Her promise to Samuel forgotten, she started toward the rise.

A movement caught her eye and, turning around again,

she scanned the road. Someone was coming, on foot. Even as she watched, the figure stumbled and fell. Sarah had her skirts in her hand and was running before the figure struggled to stand again.

"Alice!" Sarah quickened her pace. The girl was obviously hurt, but until Sarah reached her, catching her before she fell again, she couldn't see how badly.

"Oh, dear Lord." Gripping the sobbing girl around the waist, she helped her toward the house. "What happened? Who did this to you?"

"Miss Conway..." Alice could hardly speak through her bruised and bloodied lips. Her left eye was blackened and swollen nearly shut. There were ugly scratches, like the rake of fingernails, down her cheek, and every breath she took came out with a hitch of pain.

"All right, don't worry, just lean on me. We're nearly there."

"Didn't know where else to go," Alice managed. "Shouldn't be here."

"Don't try to talk yet. Let me get you inside. Oh, Lucius." Half stumbling herself, Sarah looked up with relief as he came hurrying down the rocks. "Help me get her inside, up to bed. She's badly hurt."

"What in the holy hell—?" Wheezing a bit from the exertion, he picked Alice up in his scrawny arms. "You know who this girl is, Miss Sarah?"

"Yes. Take her up to my bed, Lucius. I'll get some water."

Alice swooned as he struggled to carry her up the ladder to the loft. "She's done passed out."

"That may be a blessing for the moment." Moving quickly, Sarah gathered fresh water and clean cloths. "She must be in dreadful pain. I can't see how she managed to get all the way out here on foot."

"She's taken a mighty beating."

He stepped out of the way as best he could when Sarah climbed the stairs to sit on the edge of the bed. Gently she began to bathe Alice's face. When she loosened the girl's bodice, he cleared his throat and turned his back.

"Oh, my God." With trembling hands, Sarah unfastened the rest of the buttons. "Help me get this dress off of her, Lucius. It looks as though she's been whipped."

His sense of propriety was overcome by the sight of the welts on Alice's back and shoulders. "Yeah, she's been whipped." The cotton of her dress stuck to the raw, open sores. "Whipped worse'n a dog. I'd like to get my hands on the bastard who done this."

Sarah found her own hands were clenched with fury. "There's some salve on the shelf over the stove, Lucius. Fetch it for me." She did her best to bathe and cool the wounds. As Alice's eyes fluttered open and she moaned, Sarah soothed her in a low, calming voice. "Try not to move, Alice. We're going to take care of you. You're safe now. I promise you you're safe."

"Hurts."

"I know. Oh, I know." There were tears stinging her eyes as she took the salve from Lucius and began to stroke it over the puffy welts.

It was a slow, painful process. Though Sarah's fingers were light and gentle, Alice whimpered each time she touched her. Her back was striped to the waist with angry red lines, some of which had broken open and were bleeding. With sweat trickling down her face, Sarah tended and bandaged, talking, always talking.

"Would you like another sip of water?"

"Please." With Sarah's hand cradling her head, Alice drank from the cup. "I'm sorry, Miss Conway." She lay back weakly as Sarah held a cool cloth to her swollen eye.

"I know I shouldn't have come here. It ain't right, but I wasn't thinking straight."

"You did quite right by coming."

"You was—were—so nice to me before. And I was afraid if I didn't get away…"

"You aren't to worry." Sarah applied salve to her facial scratches. "In a few days you'll be feeling much better. Then we can think about what's to be done. For now, you'll stay right here."

"I can't—"

"You can and you will." Setting the salve aside, Sarah took her hand. "Do you feel strong enough to tell us what happened? Did a man—one of your customers—do this to you?"

"No, ma'am." Alice moistened her swollen lips. "It was Carlotta."

"Carlotta?" Sarah's eyes narrowed to slits. "Are you saying that Carlotta beat you like this?"

"I ain't never seen her so mad. Sometimes she gets mean if something don't go her way, or if she's been drinking too much you get a slap or two. She went crazy. I think she might've killed me if the other girls hadn't broke in the door and started screaming."

"Why? Why would she hurt you like this?"

"I can't say for sure. I done something wrong." Her voice slurred, and her eyes dropped shut. "She was mad, powerful mad, after Jake came by. They had words. Nancy, she's one of the other girls, listened outside of Carlotta's office. He said something to set her off, I expect. Nancy said she was yelling. Said something about you, Miss Conway, I don't rightly know what. When he left she went crazy. Started smashing things. I went on up to my room. She came after me, beat me worse'n Pa ever did. Eli, he brought me out."

"Eli's the big black Carlotta has working for her," Lucius explained.

"He drove me out as far as he could. She finds out, she'll make him sorry. Took a belt to me," she murmured as sleep took her under. "Kept hitting me and hitting me, saying it was my fault Jake don't come around no more."

"Bitch," Lucius said viciously. Then he wiped his mouth. "'Scuse me, Miss Sarah."

"No excuse necessary. I couldn't agree more." There was a rage running through her, hotter and huger than anything she'd ever experienced. She stared at the girl asleep in her bed, her small, pretty face bruised and swollen. She remembered each welt she'd tended. "Hitch up the wagon, Lucius."

"Yes'm. You want me to go somewheres?"

"No, I'm going. I want you to stay with Alice."

"I'll hitch it up, Miss Sarah, but if you're thinking about talking to the sheriff, it won't do much good. Alice here ain't going to talk to him like she done with you. She'd be too scared."

"I'm not going to the sheriff, Lucius. Just hitch up the wagon."

She pushed the horses hard, pleased that the fury didn't subside as she approached town. She wanted the fury. Since she'd come west she'd learned to accept many things—the grief, the violence, the labor. Perhaps the land was lawless, but there were times and reasons, even here, for justice.

Johnny raced out of the dry goods as Sarah rode by, then raced back in again to complain to Liza that Sarah hadn't waved at him. She hadn't even seen him. There was only one face in her mind now. She drew up in front of the Silver Star.

Three women lounged in what might have been called a parlor. The late-morning heat had them half dozing in their petticoats and their feathered wraps. The room itself was dim and almost airless. Vivid red drapes hung limp at the windows. Gold leaf glowed dull and dusty on the frames of the mirrors.

As Sarah entered, a heavy-eyed redhead popped up from her sprawled position on a settee. She plopped back again with a howling laugh. "Well, look here, girls, we got ourselves some company. Get out the teacups."

The others looked over. One of them hitched her wrap up around her shoulders. Her hands folded, Sarah stood in the doorway and took it all in.

So this was a bordello. She couldn't say she saw anything remotely exciting. It looked more like a badly furnished parlor in need of a good dusting. There was a heavy floral scent of mixed perfumes that merged, none too appealingly, with plain sweat. Carefully, finger by finger, Sarah drew off her driving gloves.

"I'd like to speak with Carlotta, please. Will someone tell her I'm here?"

No one moved. The women merely exchanged looks. The redhead went back to examining her nails. After a long breath, Sarah tried another tactic.

"I'm here to speak with her about Alice." That caught their attention. Every one of the women looked over at her. "She'll be staying with me until she's well."

Now the redhead rose. Her flowered wrap slid down her shoulders with the movement. "You took Alice in?"

"Yes. She needs care, Miss—"

"I'm Nancy." She took a quick look behind her. "How come somebody like you's going to see to Alice?"

"Because she needs it. I'd be grateful to you if you would tell Carlotta I'd like to speak with her."

"I reckon I could do that." The redhead pulled her wrap up. "You tell Alice we was asking about her."

"I'll be glad to."

While Nancy disappeared up the stairs, Sarah tried to ignore the other women's stares. She had changed to one of her best day dresses. Sarah thought the dove gray very distinguished, particularly with its black trim. Her matching hat had been purchased just before her trip west and was the latest Paris fashion. Apparently it wasn't proper attire for a bordello, she thought as she watched Carlotta descend the stairs.

The owner of the Silver Star was resplendent in her trademark red. The silk slithered down her tall, curvaceous body, clinging, shifting, swaying. Her high white breasts rose like offerings from the scalloped bodice, which was threaded with silver threads. In her hand she carried a matching fan. As she flicked it in front of her face, the heavy scent of roses filled the room.

Despite her feelings, Sarah couldn't deny that the woman was stunning. In another place, another time, she could have been a queen.

"My, my, this is a rare honor, Miss Conway."

She'd been drinking. Sarah caught the scent of whiskey under the perfume. "This is hardly a social call."

"Now you disappoint me." Her painted mouth curved. "I can always use a new girl around here. Isn't that right… ladies?"

The other women shifted uncomfortably and remained tactfully silent.

"I thought maybe you'd come in looking for work." Still waving the fan, she strolled around Sarah, sizing her up. "Little scrawny," she said. "But some men like that. Could use some fixing up, right, girls? Little more here." She patted Sarah's unrouged cheek. "Little less there." She flicked a hand at the neckline of Sarah dress. "You might make a tolerable living."

"I don't believe I'd care to...work for you, Carlotta."

"That so?" Her eyes, already hardened by the whiskey, iced over. "Too much of a lady to take pay for it, but not too much of a lady to give it away."

Sarah curled her fingers into a fist, then forced them to relax again. She would not resort to violence, or be driven to it. "No. I wouldn't care to work for anyone who beats their employees. Alice is with me now, Carlotta, and she'll stay with me. If you ever put your hands on her again, I'll see to it that you're thrown in jail."

"Oh, will you?" An angry flush darkened cheeks already bright with rouge. "I'll put my hands on who I please." She stabbed the fan into Sarah's chest. "No prim-faced bitch from back east is going to come into my place and tell me different."

With surprising ease, Sarah reached out and snapped the fan in two. "I just have." She had only an instant to brace herself for the slap. It knocked her backward. To balance herself she grabbed a table and sent a statuette crashing to the floor.

"Your kind makes me sick." Carlotta's voice was high and brittle as she leaned toward Sarah. Whiskey and anger had taken hold of her and twisted her striking face. "Looking as though they wouldn't let a man touch them. But you'll spread your legs as easy as any. You think because you went to school and lived in a big house that makes you special? You're nothing out here, nothing." She scooped up a fat plaster cherub and sent it crashing into the wall.

"The fact that I went to school and lived in a house isn't all that separates us." Sarah's voice was a sharp contrast to Carlotta's in its calmness. "You don't make me sick, Carlotta. You only make me sorry."

"I don't need pity from you. I made this place. I got something, and nobody handed it to me. Nobody ever gave

me money for fine dresses and fancy hats. I earned it."
Breasts heaving, she stepped closer. "You think you got
Jake dangling on a string, honey, you're wrong. Soon as
he's had his fill of you, he'll be back. What he's doing to
you on these hot, sweaty nights, he'll be doing to me."

"No." Amazingly, Sarah's voice was still calm. "Even
if he comes back and puts your price in your hands, you'll
never have what I have with him. You know it," Sarah said
quietly. "And that's why you hate me." With her eyes on
Carlotta, she began to pull on her gloves again. Her hands
would tremble any moment. She knew it, and she wanted to
be on her way first. "But the issue here is Alice, not Jake.
She is no longer in your employ."

"I'll tell that slut when she's through here."

It happened so quickly, Sarah was hardly aware of it. She
had managed to hold her temper during Carlotta's insulting
tirade against her own person. But to hear Alice called by
that vile name while the girl was lying helpless and hurt
was too much. Her ungloved hand shot out and connected
hard with the side of Carlotta's face.

The three women, and the one who had come creeping
down the stairs to look in on the commotion, let out gasps
of surprise in unison. Sarah barely had time to feel the satisfaction of her action when Carlotta had her by the hair.
They tumbled to the floor in a flurry of skirts.

Sarah shrieked as Carlotta tried to pull her hair out by
the roots. She had handfuls of it, tugging and ripping while
she cursed wildly. Fighting the pain, Sarah swung out and
connected with soft flesh. She heard Carlotta grunt, and
they rolled across the rug. Crockery smashed as they col-
lided with a table, each trying to land a blow or defend
against one. Sarah took a fist in the stomach with a gasp,
but managed to evade a lethal swipe of Carlotta's red-tipped
nails.

There was hate in Carlotta's eyes, a wild, almost mad hate. Sarah grabbed her wrist and twisted, knowing that if the other woman got her hands on her throat she'd squeeze until all her breath was gone.

She had no intention of being strangled, or pummeled. Her own rage had her rolling on top of her opponent and grabbing a handful of dyed hair. When she felt teeth sink into her arm, she cried out and yanked with all her strength, jerking Carlotta's head back and bringing out a howl of rage and pain. Other screams rose up, but Sarah was lost in the battle. She yanked and clawed and tore as viciously as Carlotta. They were equals now, with no barriers of class or background. A lamp shattered in a shower of glass as the two writhing bodies careened into another table.

"What in the hell is going on here?" Barker burst into the parlor. He took one look at the scene on the floor and shut his eyes. He'd rather have faced five armed, drunken cowboys than a pair of scratching women. "Break it up," he ordered as the two of them tumbled across the floor. "Somebody's going to get hurt here." He shook his head and sighed. "Most likely me."

He stepped into the melee just as Jake strode through the parlor doors.

"Let's pull them apart," Barker said heavily. "Take your pick." But Jake was already hauling Sarah up off the floor. She kicked out, her breath hissing as she tried to struggle away.

"Pull in your claws, Duchess." He clamped an arm around her waist as Barker restrained Carlotta.

"Get her out of here." Carlotta shoved away from Barker and stood, her dress ripped at both shoulders, her hair in wild tufts. "I want that bitch out of here and in jail. She came in here and started breaking up my place."

"Now, that don't seem quite logical," Barker mused.

"Miss Sarah, you want to tell me what you're doing in a place like this?"

"Business." She tossed her hair out of her eyes. "Personal business."

"Well, looks to me like you've finished with your business here. Why don't you go on along home now?"

Sarah drew on her dignity like a cape over her torn dress. "Thank you, Sheriff." She cast one last look at Carlotta. "I am quite finished here." She glided toward the door to the secret admiration of Carlotta's girls.

"Just one damn minute." Jake took her arm the second she stepped outside. She had time now for embarrassment when she noted the size of the crowd she'd drawn.

"If you'll excuse me," she said stiffly, "I must get home." She reached up to tidy her tousled hair. "My hat."

"I think I saw what was left of it back in there." Jake ran his tongue over his teeth as he looked at her. She had a bruise beginning under her eye. It would make up to be a pretty good shiner by the end of the day. Her fashionable gray dress was ripped down one arm, and her hair looked as though she'd been through a windstorm. Thoughtfully, he tucked his hands in his pockets. Carlotta had looked a hell of a lot worse.

"Duchess, a man wouldn't know it to look at you, but you're a real firebrand."

Grimly she brushed at her rumpled skirts. "I can see that amuses you."

"I have to say it does." He smiled, and her teeth snapped together. "I guess I'm flattered, but you didn't have to get yourself in a catfight over me."

Her mouth dropped open. The man looked positively delighted. She was scratched and bruised and aching and humiliated, and he looked as though his grin might just split his face. Over him? she thought, and made herself return the smile.

"So you think I fought with Carlotta over you, because I was jealous?"

"Can't think of another reason."

"Oh, I'll give you a reason." She brought her fist up and caught him neatly on the jaw. He was holding a hand to his face and staring after her when Barker strolled out.

"She's got what you might call a mean right hook." In the street, people howled and snickered as Sarah climbed into the wagon and drove off. "Son," Barker said with a hand on Jake's shoulder, "you're the fastest hand I ever saw with those Colts of yours. You play a fine game of poker, and you hold your whiskey like a man. But you got a hell of a lot to learn about women."

"Apparently," Jake murmured. He walked across to O'Riley's and untied his horse.

Sarah seethed as she raced the wagon toward home. She'd made a spectacle of herself. She'd engaged in a crude, despicable sparring match with a woman with no morals. She'd brought half the town out into the street to stare and snicker at her. And then, to top it all off, she'd had to endure Jake Redman's grinning face.

She'd shown him. Sarah tossed her head up and spurred the horses on. Her hand might possibly be broken, but she'd shown him. The colossal conceit of the man, to believe that she would stoop to such a level out of petty jealousy.

She wished she'd torn Carlotta's brass-colored hair out by its black roots.

Not over him, she reminded herself. At least not very much over him.

She heard the rider coming up fast and looked over her shoulder. With a quick gasp of alarm, she cracked the reins. She would not speak to him now. Jake Redman could go to the devil, as far as she was concerned. And he could take his grin with him.

But her sturdy workhorses were no match for his mustang. Nor was her driving skill a match for his riding. Even as she cursed him, he came up beside her. She had a flash, clear as a bell, of how he'd looked when he'd raced beside the stagecoach, firing over his shoulder. He looked just as untamed and dangerous now.

"Stop that damn thing."

Chin up, she cracked the reins again.

One of these days somebody was going to teach her to listen, Jake thought. It might just be today. He judged the timing and rhythm, then leaped from his horse into the wagon. Surefooted, he stepped over onto the seat, and though she fought him furiously he pulled the horses in.

"What the hell's got into you, woman?" He scrambled for a hold as she shoved him aside and tried to jump out.

"Take your hands off me. I won't be handled this way."

"Handling you is a sight more work than I care for." He snatched his hand out of range before she could bite him. "Haven't you had enough scratching for one day? Sit down before you hurt yourself."

"You want the blasted wagon, take it. I won't ride with you."

"You'll ride with me, all right." Out of patience, he twisted her into his lap and silenced her. She squirmed and pushed and held herself as rigid as iron. Then she melted. He felt the give, slow, easy, inevitable. In her. In himself. As her lips parted for his, he forgot about keeping her quiet and just took what he kept trying to tell himself he couldn't have.

"You pack a punch, Duchess." He drew her away to rub a hand over his chin. "In a lot of ways. You want to tell me what that was for?"

She pulled away, furious that she'd gone soft with just one kiss. "For assuming that I was jealous and would fight over any worthless man."

"So now I'm worthless. Well, that may be, but you seem to like having me around."

She did her best to straighten what was left of her dress. "Perhaps I do."

He needed to know it more than he'd imagined. Jake took her chin in his hand and turned her to face him. "You change your mind?"

Again she softened, this time because she saw the doubt in his eyes. "No, I haven't changed my mind." She drew a long breath. "Even though you didn't come back and you've been to the Silver Star to see Carlotta."

"You sure do hear things. Can't imagine what you'd know if you lived closer to town. Stay in the wagon." He recognized the look in her eye by now. "Stay in the wagon, Sarah, until I get my horse tied on. I'll just catch you again if you run."

"I won't run." She brought her chin up again and stared straight ahead. When he'd joined her again, she continued her silence. Jake clucked to the horses and started off.

"I like to know why a woman's mad at me. Why don't you tell me how you know I've been to Carlotta's?"

"Alice told me."

"Alice Johnson?"

"That's right. Your friend Carlotta nearly beat her to death."

He brought the horses up short. "What?"

Her fury bounded back and poured over him. "You heard what I said. She beat that poor girl as cruelly as anyone can be beaten. Eli helped Alice get out of town. Then she walked the rest of the way to my place."

"Is she going to be all right?"

"With time and care."

"And you're going to give it to her?"

"Yes." Her eyes dared him. "Do you have any objections?"

"No." He touched her face, gently, in a way that was new to him. Abruptly he snatched his hand back and snapped the reins again. "You went into the Silver Star to have it out with Carlotta over Alice."

"I've never been so furious." Sarah lifted a hand to where Jake had touched her. "Alice is hardly more than a child. No matter what she did, she didn't deserve that kind of treatment."

"Did she tell you why Carlotta did it?"

"She didn't seem to know, only that she must have made some kind of mistake. Alice did say that Carlotta was in a temper after you had been there."

He said nothing for a moment as he put the pieces together. "And she took it out on Alice."

"Why did you go? Why did you go to Carlotta? If there's something you…" She hadn't any idea how to phrase it properly. "If I don't know enough about your needs… I realize I don't have any experience in these matters, but I—"

She found her mouth crushed again in a kiss that was half hungry, half angry. "There's never been anyone else who's known so much about what I need." He watched her face clear into a smile. "I went to see Carlotta to tell her I don't care much for having my name used as a reference."

"So she took it out on Alice, because Alice was the one who'd come to talk to me." Sarah shook her head and tried not to let her temper take over again. "Alice only told me what Carlotta wanted her to tell me. It didn't work the way she'd planned, and Alice paid for it."

"That's about the size of it."

Sarah linked her fingers again and set them in her lap. "Is that the only reason you went to Carlotta?"

"No." He waited for the look. The look of passionate fury. "I went for that, and to tell her to stay away from you. Of course, I didn't know at the time that you were going to go and bloody her lip."

"Did I?" She tried and failed to bank down the pleasure she felt at the news. "Did I really?"

"And her nose. Guess you were a little too involved to notice."

"I've never struck anyone before in my life." She tried to keep her voice prim, then gave up. "I liked it."

With a laugh, Jake pulled her to his side. "You're a real wildcat, Duchess."

Chapter 12

Jake learned something new when he watched Sarah with Alice. He had always assumed that a woman who had been raised in the sheltered, privileged world would ignore, even condemn, one who lived as Alice lived. There were many decent women, as they called themselves, who would have turned Alice away as if she were a rabid dog.

Not Sarah.

And it was more than what he supposed she would have called Christian charity. He'd run into his share of people who liked to consider themselves good Christians. They had charity, all right, unless they came across somebody who looked different, thought different. There had been plenty of Christian women who had swept their skirts aside from his own mother because she'd married a man of mixed blood.

They went into church on Sundays and quoted the Scriptures and professed to love their neighbor. But when their neighbor didn't fit their image of what was right, love turned to hate quickly enough.

With Sarah it wasn't just words. It was compassion, caring, and an understanding he hadn't expected from her. He could hear, as he sat at the table, the simple kindness in her voice as she talked to the girl and tended her wounds.

As for Alice, it was obvious the girl adored Sarah. He'd yet to see her, as Sarah claimed her patient wasn't up to visitors. But he could hear the shyness and the respect in her voice when she answered Sarah's questions.

She'd fought for Alice. He couldn't quite get over that. Most people wouldn't fight for anything unless it was their own, or something they wanted to own. It had taken pride, and maybe what people called valor, for her to walk into a place like the Silver Star and face Carlotta down. And she'd done it. He glanced up toward the loft. She'd more than done it. She'd held her own.

Rising, he walked outside to where Lucius was doing his best to teach an uncooperative Lafitte to shake hands.

"Damn it, boy, did I say jump all over me? No, you flea-brained mongrel, I said shake." Lucius pushed the dog's rump down and grabbed a paw. "Shake. Get it?" Lafitte leaped up again and licked Lucius's face.

"Doesn't appear so," Jake commented.

"Fool dog." But Lucius rubbed the pup's belly when he rolled over. "Grows on you, though." He squinted up at Jake. "Something around here seems to be growing on you, too."

"Somebody had to bring her back."

"Reckon so." He waited until Jake crouched to scratch the puppy's head. "You want to tell me how Miss Sarah came to look like she'd been in a fistfight?"

"She looked like she was in a fistfight because she was in a fistfight."

Lucius snorted and spit. "Like hell."

"With Carlotta."

Lucius's cloudy eyes widened, and then he let out a bark of laughter that had Lafitte racing in circles. "Ain't that a hoot? Are you telling me that our Miss Sarah went in and gave Carlotta what for?"

"She gave her a bloody nose." Jake looked over with a grin. "And pulled out more than a little of her hair."

"Sweet Jesus, I'd've given two pints of whiskey to've seen that. Did you?"

Chuckling, Jake pulled on Lafitte's ears. "The tail end of it. When I walked in, the two of them were rolling over the floor, spitting like cats. I figure Carlotta outweighs Sarah by ten pounds or more, but Sarah was sitting on her, skirts hiked up and blood in her eye. It was one hell of a sight."

"She's got spunk." Lucius pulled out his whiskey and toasted Sarah with a healthy gulp. "I knew she had something in her head when she tore out of here." Feeling generous, he handed the bottle to Jake. "Never would have thought she'd set her mind on poking a fist into Carlotta. But nobody ever deserved it more. You seen Alice?"

"No." Jake let the whiskey spread fire through him. "Sarah's got the idea that it's not fitting for me to talk to the girl until she's covered up or something."

"I carried her in myself, and I don't mind saying I ain't seen no woman's face ever smashed up so bad. Took a belt to her, too, from the looks of it. Her back and shoulders all come up in welts. Jake, you wouldn't whup a dog the way that girl was whupped. That Carlotta must be crazy."

"Mean and crazy's two different things." He handed Lucius the bottle. "Carlotta's just mean."

"Reckon you'd know her pretty well."

Jake watched Lucius take another long sip. "I paid for her a few times, sometime back. Doesn't mean I know her."

"Soon plop my ass next to a rattler's." Lucius handed the bottle back to Jake again, then fell into a fit of coughing. "Miss Sarah, I didn't hear you come out."

"So I surmised," she said with a coolness that had Lucius coughing again. "Perhaps you gentlemen have finished drinking whiskey and exchanging crude comments and would like to wash for supper. If not, you're welcome to eat out here in the dirt." With that she turned on her heel, making certain she banged the door shut behind her.

"Ooo-whee." Lucius snatched back the bottle and took another drink. "She's got a mighty sharp tongue for such a sweet face. I tell you, boy, you'll have to mind your step if'n you hitch up with her."

Jake was still staring at the door, thinking how beautiful she'd looked, black eye and all, standing there like a queen addressing her subjects. "I ain't planning on hitching up with anyone."

"Maybe you are and maybe you ain't." Lucius rose and brushed off his pants. A little dirt and she'd have them off him again and in the stream. "But she's got plans, all right. And a woman like that's hard to say no to."

Sarah spoke politely at supper, as if she were entertaining at a formal party. Her hair was swept up and tidied, and she'd changed her dress. She was wearing the green one that set off her hair and eyes. The stew was served in ironstone bowls, but the way she did it, it could have been a restaurant meal on fancy china.

It made him think, as he hadn't in years, of his mother and how she had liked to fuss over Sunday supper.

She said nothing about the encounter in town, and it was clear that she didn't care to have the subject brought up. It was hard to believe she was the same woman he'd dragged off the floor in the Silver Star. But he noticed that she winced now and then. He bit into a hunk of fresh bread and held back a grin. She was hurting, all right, and more than her pride, from the look of it. As he ate he entertained thoughts of how he would ease those hurts when the sun went down.

"Would you like some more stew, Lucius?"

"No, ma'am." He patted his belly. "Full as a tick. If it's all the same to you, I'll just go take a walk before I feed the stock and such. Going to be a pretty night." He sent them both what he thought was a bland look. "I'll sleep like a log after a meal like this. Yessir. I don't believe I'll stir till morning." He scraped back his chair and reached for his hat. "Mighty fine meal, Miss Sarah."

"Thank you, Lucius."

Jake tipped back his chair. "I wouldn't mind a walk myself."

Sarah had to smile at the way Lucius began to whistle after he'd closed the door. "You go ahead."

He took her hand as she rose. "I'd like it better if you went with me."

She smiled. He'd never asked her to do something as ordinary, and as romantic, as going for a walk. Thank goodness she hadn't forgotten how to flirt. "Why, that's nice of you, but I have to see to the dishes. And Alice may be waking soon. I think she could eat a bit now."

"I imagine I could occupy myself for an hour or two. We'll take a walk when you're done."

She sent him a look from under lowered lashes. "Maybe." Then she laughed as he sent her spinning into his lap. "Why, Mr. Redman. You are quite a brute."

He ran a finger lightly over the bruise under her eye. "Then you'd best be careful. Kiss me, Sarah."

She smiled when her lips were an inch from his. "And if I don't?"

"But you will." He traced her bottom lip with his tongue. "You will."

She did, sinking into it, into him. Her arms wound around him, slender and eager. Her mouth opened like a flower in sunlight. They softened against him even as they heated. They yielded even as they demanded.

"Don't be long," he murmured. He kissed her again,

passion simmering, then set her on her feet. She let out a long, shaky breath when he closed the door behind him.

With Alice settled for the night and the day's work behind her, Sarah stepped out into the quieting light of early evening. It was still too warm to bother with a shawl, but she pushed her sleeves down past her elbows and buttoned the cuffs. There were bruises on her arms that she didn't care to dwell on.

From where she stood she could hear Lucius in the shed, talking to Lafitte. He'd become more his dog than hers, Sarah thought with a laugh. Or perhaps they'd both become something of hers.

As the land had.

She closed her eyes and let the light breeze flutter over her face. She could, if she concentrated hard enough, catch the faintest whiff of sage. And she could, if she used enough imagination, picture what it would be like to sit on the porch she envisioned having, watching the sun go down every evening while Jake rolled a cigarette and listened with her to the music of the night.

Bringing herself back, she looked around. Where was he? She stepped farther out into the yard when she heard the sound of hammer against wood. She saw him, a few yards from the chicken coop, beating an old post into the ground. He'd taken his shirt off, and she could see the light sheen of sweat over his lean torso and the rippling and bunching of his muscles as he swung the heavy hammer down.

Her thoughts flew back to the way his arms had swung her into heat, into passion. The hands that gripped the thick, worn handle of the hammer now had roamed over her, touching, taking whatever they chose.

And she had touched, wantonly, even greedily, that long, limber body, taking it, accepting it as her own.

Her breath shuddered out as she watched him bend and

lift and pound. Was it wrong to have such thoughts, such wonderful, exciting visions? How could it be, when she loved so completely? She wanted his heart, but oh, she wanted his body, as well, and she could find no shame in it.

His head came up quickly, as she imagined an animal's might when it caught a scent. And he had. Though she was several yards away, he had sensed her, the trace of lilac, the subtlety of woman. He straightened, and just as she had looked her fill of him, he looked his of her.

She might have stepped from a cool terrace to walk in a garden. The wind played with her skirts and her hair, but gently. The backdrop of the setting sun was like glory behind her. Her eyes, as she walked toward him, were wide and dark and aware.

"You've got a way of moving, Duchess, that makes my mouth water."

"I don't think that's what the good sisters intended when they taught me posture. But I'm glad." She moved naturally to his arms, to his lips. "Very glad."

For the first time in his life he felt awkward with a woman, and he drew her away. "I'm sweaty."

"I know." She pulled a handkerchief from her pocket and dabbed at his face. "What are you doing?"

She made him feel like a boy fumbling over his first dance. "You said you wanted pigs. You need a pen." He picked up his shirt and shrugged it on. "What are you doing?"

"Watching you." She put a hand to his chest, where the shirt lay open. "Remembering. Wondering if you want me as much as you did."

He took her hand before she could tear what was inside of him loose. "No, I don't. I want you more." He picked up his gunbelt, but instead of strapping it on he draped it over his shoulder. "Why don't we go for that walk?"

Content, she slipped her hand into his. "When I first came here I wondered what it was that had kept my father, rooted him here. At first I thought it was only for me, because he wanted so badly to provide what he thought I'd need. That grieved me. I can't tell you how much." She glanced up as they passed the rise that led to his grave. "Later I began to see that even though that was part of it, perhaps the most important part to him, he was also happy here. It eases the loss to know he was happy."

They started down the path to the stream she had come to know so well.

"I didn't figure you'd stick." Her hand felt right, easy and right, tucked in his. "When I brought you out here the first time, you looked as if someone had dropped you on your head."

"It felt as though someone had. Losing him... Well, the truth is, I'd lost him years and years ago. To me, he's exactly the same as he was the day he left. Maybe there's something good about that. I never told you he had spun me a tale." At the stream she settled down on her favorite rock and listened to the water's melody. "He told me of the fine house he'd built after he'd struck the rich vein of gold in Sarah's Pride. He painted me a picture of it with his words. Four bedrooms, a parlor with the windows facing west, a wide porch with big round columns." She smiled a little and watched the sun glow over the buttes. "Maybe he thought I needed that, and maybe I did, to see myself as mistress of a fine, big house with curving stairs and high, cool walls."

He could see it, and her. "It was what you were made for."

"It's you I was made for." Rising, she held out her hands.

"I want you, Sarah. I can't offer you much more than a blanket to spread on the ground."

She glanced over at the small pile of supplies he'd already brought down to the stream. She moved to it and lifted the blanket.

It was twilight when they lowered to it. The air had softened. The wind was only a rustle in the thin brush. Overhead the sky arched, a deep, ever-darkening blue. Under the wool of the blanket the ground was hard and unforgiving. She lifted her arms to him and they left the rest behind.

It was as it had been the first time, and yet different. The hunger was there, and the impatient pull of desire. With it was a knowledge of the wonder, the magic, they could make between them. A little slower now, a little surer, they moved together.

There was urgency in his kiss. She could feel it. But beneath it was a tenderness she had dreamed of, hoped for. Seduced by that alone, she murmured his name. Beneath her palm, his cheek was rough. Under her fingers, his skin was smooth. His body, like his mind, like his heart, was a contrast that drew her, compelled her to learn more.

A deep, drugging languor filled her as he began to undress her. There was no frantic rush, as there had been before. His fingers were slow and sure as they moved down the small covered buttons. She felt the air whisper against her skin as he parted the material. Then it was his mouth, warmer, sweeter, moving over her. Her sigh was like music.

He wanted to give her something he'd never given another woman. The kind of care she deserved. Tenderness was new to him, but it came easily now as he peeled off layer after layer to find her. He sucked in his breath as her fingers fumbled with the buttons at his waist. Her touch wasn't hesitant, but it was still innocent. It would always be. And her innocence aroused him as skill never could have.

She removed the layers he'd covered himself with. Not layers of cotton or leather, but layers of cynicism and aloofness, the armor he'd used to survive, just as he'd used his

pistols. With her he was helpless, more vulnerable than he
had been since childhood. With her he felt more of a man
than he had ever hoped to be.

She felt the change, an explosion of feelings and needs
and desires, as he dragged her up into his arms to crush his
mouth against hers. What moved through him poured into
her, leaving her breathless, shaken and impossibly strong.
Without understanding, without needing to, she answered
him with everything in her heart.

Then came the storm, wild, windy, wailing. Rocked by
it, she cried out as he drove her up, up, into an airless, rushing cloud of passion. Sensations raced through her—the
sound of her own desperate moans, the scrape of his face
against her skin as he journeyed down her trembling body,
the taste of him that lingered on her lips, on her tongue,
as he did mad, unspeakably wonderful things to her. Lost,
driven beyond reason, she pressed his head closer to her.

She was like something wild that had just been un-
chained. He could feel the shocked delight ripple through
her when he touched her moist heat with his tongue. He
thought her response was like a miracle, though he'd long
ago stopped believing in them. There was little he could
give her besides the pleasures of her own body. But at least
that, he would do.

Sliding upward, he covered her mouth with his. And
filled her.

Long after her hands had slipped limply from his back,
long after their breathing had calmed and leveled, he lay
over her, his face buried in her hair. She'd brought him
peace, and though he knew it wouldn't last, for now she'd
brought him peace of mind, of body, of heart.

He hadn't wanted to love, hadn't dared to risk it. Even

now, when it was no longer possible to hide it from himself, he couldn't tell her.

"Lucius was right," she murmured against his ear.

"Mmm?"

"It's a pretty night." She ran her hands up his back. "A very pretty night."

"Am I hurting you?"

"No." She gripped her own wrists so that she could hold him closer. "Don't move yet."

"I'm heavy, and you've got some colorful bruises."

If she'd had the energy, she might have laughed. "I'd forgotten about them."

"I put some on you myself last night." He lifted his head to look down at her. "I don't know much about going easy."

"I'm not complaining."

"You should." Fascinated, he stroked a finger down her cheek. "You're so beautiful. Like something I made up."

She turned her lips into his palm as her eyes filled. "You've never told me you thought I was beautiful."

"Sure I did." He shifted then, frustrated by his own lack of words. "I should have."

She curled comfortably against his side. "I feel beautiful right now."

They lay in contented silence, looking up at the sky.

"What's an enigma?" he asked her.

"Hmm? Oh, it's a puzzle. Something difficult to understand. Why?"

"I guess I heard it somewhere." He thought of her diary, and her description of him, but couldn't see how it applied. He'd always seen himself as being exactly what he appeared to be. "You're getting cold."

"A little."

Sitting up, he pushed through her discarded undergarments for her chemise. She smiled, lifting her arms over her head. Her lips curved when she saw his gaze slide over her skin. When he pulled the cotton over her, she linked her hands behind his neck.

"I was hoping to stay warm a different way."

With a laugh, he slid a hand down over her hip. "I remember telling you once before you were a quick study." Experimentally he pushed the strap of her chemise off her shoulder. "You want to do something for me?"

"Yes." She nuzzled his lips. "Very much."

"Go on over and stand in that stream."

Confused, she drew back. "I beg your pardon?"

"Nobody says that better than you, Duchess. I'll swear to that." He kissed her again, in a light, friendly manner that pleased and puzzled her.

"You want to go wading?"

"Not exactly." He toyed with the strap. Women wore the damnedest things. Then they covered them all up anyhow. "I thought you'd go stand in the stream wearing just this little thing. Like you did that first night."

"What first night?" Her puzzled smile faded as he traced his fingertip along the edge of her bodice. "That first— You! You were watching me while I—"

"I was just making sure you didn't get yourself into any trouble."

"That's disgraceful." She tried to pull away, but he held her still.

"I started thinking then and there how much I'd like to get my hands on you. Had some trouble sleeping that night." He lowered his lips to the curve of her throat and began to nibble. "Fact is, I haven't had a good night's sleep since I set eyes on you."

"Stop it." She turned her head, but it only made it easier for him to find her mouth.

"Are you going to go stand in the stream?"

"I am not." She smothered a laugh when he rolled her onto the blanket again. "I'm going to get dressed and go back to the house to check on Alice."

"No need. Lucius is keeping an eye on her."

"Oh, I see. You've already decided that for me."

"I guess you could put it like that. You're not going anywhere but this blanket. And maybe the stream, once I talk you into it."

"You won't talk me into it. I have no intention of sleeping outside."

"I don't figure on sleeping much at all." He stretched out on his back again and gathered her close. "Haven't you ever slept outside before, looked at the sky? Counted stars?"

"No." But, of course, tonight she would. She wanted nothing more. She turned her head to study his profile. "Have you ever counted stars, Jake?"

"When I was a kid." He stroked a hand lazily up and down her arm. "My mother used to say there were pictures. She'd point them out to me sometimes, but I could never find them again."

"I'll show you one." Sarah took his hand and began to draw in the air. "It's a horse. A winged horse. Pegasus," she added. Then she caught her breath. "Look, a shooting star." She watched, his hand held in hers, as it arced across the sky. She closed her eyes quickly, then made a wish. "Will you tell me about your mother?"

For a long moment he said nothing, but continued to stare up at the sky. The arc of light was gone, without a trace. "She was a teacher." Sarah's gaze flicked up quickly to his face. "She'd come out here from St. Louis."

"And met your father?"

"I don't know much about that. He wanted to learn to read and write, and she taught him. She set a lot of store by reading."

"And while she was teaching him, they fell in love."

He smiled a little. It sounded nice the way she said it. "I guess they did. She married him. It wouldn't have been easy, with him being half Apache. They wanted to build something. I remember the way my father used to talk about taking the land and making it work for him. Leaving something behind."

She understood that, because it was what she wanted for herself. "Were they happy?"

"They laughed a lot. My mother used to sing. He always talked about buying her a piano one day, so she could play again like she did in St. Louis. She'd just laugh and say she wanted lace curtains first. I'd forgotten that," he murmured. "She wanted lace curtains."

She turned her face into his shoulder because she felt his pain as her own. "Lucius told me what happened to them. To you. I'm so sorry."

He hadn't known he needed to talk about it, needed to tell her. "They came in from town…eight, ten of them, I've never been sure." His voice was quiet now, his eyes on the sky. He could still see them, as he hadn't allowed himself to see them for years. "They lit the barn first. Maybe if my father had stayed in the house, let them shoot and shout and trample, they'd have left the rest. But they'd have come back. He knew it. He took his rifle and went out to protect what was his. They shot him right outside the door."

Sarah held him tighter, seeing it with him.

"We ran out. They tasted blood now, like wolves, wild-eyed, teeth bared. She was crying, holding on to my father and crying. Inside the barn, the horses were screaming. The sky was lit up so I could see their faces while they torched the rest."

And he could smell the smoke as he lay there, could

hear the crackle of greedy flames and his mother's pitiful weeping.

"I picked up the rifle. That's the first time I ever wanted to kill. It's like a fever in the blood. Like a hand has ahold of you, squeezing. She started to scream. I saw one of the riders take aim at me. I had the rifle in my hands, but I was slow. Better with a bow or a knife back then. She threw herself up and in front of me so when he pulled the trigger the bullet went in her."

Sarah tightened her arms around him as tears ran fast and silent down her cheeks.

"One of them hit me with a rifle butt as he rode by. It was morning before I came to. They'd burned everything. The house was still smoking—even when it cooled there was nothing in it worth keeping. The ground was hard there, and I got dizzy a few times, so it took me all day to bury them. I slept there that night, between the two graves. I told myself that if I lived until morning I'd find the men who'd done it and kill them. I was still alive in the morning."

She said nothing, could say nothing. It wasn't necessary to ask what he'd done. He'd learned to use a gun, and use it well. And he had found the men, or some of them.

"When Lucius came, I told him what happened. That was the last time I told anyone."

"Don't." She turned to lay her body across his. "Don't think about it anymore."

He could feel her tears on his chest, the warmth of them. As far as he knew, no one had ever cried for him before. Taking her hand, he kissed it. "Show me that picture in the sky, Sarah."

Turning, keeping her hand in his, she began to trace the stars. The time for tears, for regrets—and, she hoped, for revenge—was done. "The stars aren't as big in the East, or as bright." They lay quietly for a while, wrapped close, listening to the night sounds. "I used to jump every time I heard a coyote. Now I like listening for them. Every night, when I read my father's journal—"

"Matt kept a journal?" He sat up as he asked, dragging her with him.

"Why, yes." There was an intensity in his eyes that made her heart skip erratically. "What is it?"

"Have you read it?"

"Not all of it. I've been reading a few pages each night."

He suddenly realized that he was digging his fingers into her arms. He relaxed them. "Will you let me read it?"

Her heart was steady again, but something cold was inching its way over her skin. "Yes. If you tell me why you want to."

He turned away to reach casually in his saddlebag for his tobacco pouch and papers. "I just want to read it."

She waited while he rolled a cigarette. "All right. I trust you. When are you going to trust me, Jake?"

He struck a match on a rock. The flame illuminated his face. "What do you mean?"

"Why did you ask Lucius to work in the mine?"

He flicked the match out, then tossed it aside. The scent of tobacco stung the air. "Maybe I thought Matt would have liked it."

Determined, she put a hand to his face and turned it toward hers. "Why?"

"A feeling I had, that's all." Shifting away, he blew out a stream of smoke. "People usually have a reason for setting fires, Sarah. There was only one I could figure when it came to you. Somebody didn't want you there."

"That's ridiculous. I hardly knew anyone at that point. The sheriff said it was drifters." She curled her hands in her lap as she studied his face. "You don't think it was."

"No. Maybe Barker does, and maybe he doesn't. There's

only one thing on this land that anyone could want. That's gold."

Impatient, Sarah sat back on her heels. "But there isn't any gold."

"Yes, there is." Jake drew deep on his cigarette and watched the range of expressions cross her face.

"What are you talking about?"

"Lucius found the mother lode, just the way Matt did." He glanced at the glowing tip of his cigarette. "You're going to be a rich woman, Duchess."

"Wait." She pressed a hand to her temple. It was beginning to throb. "Are you telling me that the mine is really worth something?"

"More than something, according to Lucius."

"I can't believe it." With a quick, confused laugh, she shook her head. "I never thought it was anything but a dream. Just this morning, I'd begun to wonder, but— How long have you known?"

"A while."

"A while?" she repeated, looking back at him. "And you didn't think it important enough to mention to me?"

"I figured it was important enough not to." He took a last drag before crushing the cigarette out. "I've never known a woman who could keep her mouth shut."

"Is that so?"

"Yes, ma'am."

"I'm perfectly capable of keeping my mouth shut, as you so eloquently put it. But why should I?"

There was no way to tell her but straight out. "Matt found the gold, and then he was dead."

"There was an accident…" she began. Suddenly cold, she hugged her elbows. He didn't have to speak for her to see what was in his mind. "You're trying to tell me that my father was murdered. That can't be." She started to scramble up, but he took her arms and held her still.

"Ten years he worked the mine and scratched a few handfuls of gold from it. Then he hits, hits big. The minute he does, there's a cave-in, and he's dead."

"I don't want to think about it."

"You're going to think about it." He gave her a quick shake. "The mine's yours now, and the gold in it. I'm not going to let what happened to Matt happen to you." His hands gentled and slid up to frame her face. "Not to you."

She closed her eyes. She couldn't take it in, not all at once. Fear, hysteria and fresh grief tangled within her. She lifted her hands to his wrists and held on until she felt herself calming. He was right. She had to think about it. Then she would act. When she opened her eyes, they were clear and steady.

"Tell me what you want me to do."

"Trust me." He touched his lips to hers, then laid her back gently on the blanket. She'd given him peace early in the night. Now, as the night deepened, he would try to do the same for her.

Chapter 13

"I'm feeling lots better, Miss Conway." Alice took the tin cup and sipped gingerly.

She didn't want to complain about her back, or about the pain that still galloped along it despite the cooling salve. The morning light showed her facial bruises in heart-wrenching detail and caused the girl to look even younger and smaller and more vulnerable. Though the scratches on her cheeks were no longer red and angry, Sarah judged it would be several days before they faded.

"You look better." It wasn't strictly true, and Sarah vowed to keep her patient away from a mirror a bit longer. Though the swelling had eased considerably, she was still worried about Alice's eye and had already decided to drive into town later and talk with the doctor.

"Try a little of this soft-boiled egg. You need your strength."

"Yes, ma'am." Privately Alice thought the glossy wet yolk looked more like a slimy eye than food. But if Sarah had told her to eat a fried scorpion she'd have opened her mouth and swallowed. "Miss Conway?"

"Yes, Alice?" Sarah spooned up more egg.

"I'm beholden to you for taking me in like you did, and I can't— Miss Conway, you gave me your own bed last night. It ain't fitting."

Smiling a little, Sarah set the plate aside. "Alice, I assure you, I was quite comfortable last night."

"But, Miss Conway—"

"Alice, if you keep this up I'm going to think you're ungrateful."

"Oh!" Something close to horror flashed in Alice's eyes. "No, ma'am."

"Well, then." Because the response was exactly what she'd expected, Sarah rose. She remembered that the nuns had nursed with compassion tempered with brisk practicality. "You can show your gratitude by being a good patient and getting some more rest. If you're feeling up to it later, I'll have Lucius bring you down and we can sit and talk awhile."

"I'd like that. Miss Conway, if it hadn't been for you and Eli, I think I'd've died. I was hoping... Well, I got some money saved. It ain't much, but I'd like you to have it for all your trouble."

"I don't want your money, Alice."

The girl flushed and looked away. "I know you're probably thinking about where it comes from, but—"

"No." She took Alice's hand firmly in hers. "That has nothing to do with it." Pride, Sarah thought. She had plenty of her own. Alice was entitled to hers. "Alice, did Eli want money for driving you out of town?"

"No, but...he's a friend."

"I'd like to be your friend, if you'd let me. You rest now, and we'll talk about all this later." She gave Alice's hand a reassuring squeeze before she picked up the empty dishes and started down the ladder. She barely muffled a squeal when hands closed around her waist.

"Told you you didn't need that corset."

Sarah sent Jake what she hoped was an indignant look over her shoulder. "Is that why I couldn't find it when I dressed this morning?"

"Just doing you a favor." Before she could decide whether

to laugh or lecture, he was whirling her around and kissing her.

"Jake, Alice is—"

"Not likely to faint if she figures out what I'm doing." But he set her aside, because he liked the way the sunlight streamed through the curtains and onto her hair. "You're mighty nice to look at, Duchess."

It was foolish to blush, but her color rose. "Why don't you sit down, and you can look at me some more while I fix you breakfast?"

"I'd like to, but I've got some things to see to." He touched her again, just a fingertip to the single wispy curl that had escaped from the neat bun on top of her head. "Sarah, will you let me have Matt's journal?"

Both the grief and the dread showed clearly in her eyes before she lowered them. During the night, after love and before sleep, she had thought of little else but what Jake had told her. Part of her wondered if she would be better off not knowing, not being sure. But another part, the same part that had kept her from turning back and going east again, had already accepted what needed to be done.

"Yes." She walked to the hearth to work the rock loose. "I found this the first night. His journal, what must have been his savings, and the deed to Sarah's Pride."

When she held the book out to him, Jake resisted the urge to open it there and then. If he found what he thought he would find, he would have business to take care of before he said anything else to her. "I'll take it along with me, if it's all the same to you."

She opened her mouth to object, wanting the matter settled once and for all. But he'd asked for her trust. Perhaps this was the way to show him he had it. "All right."

"And the deed? Will you let me hold on to it until we have some answers?"

In answer, she offered it to him, without hesitation, without question. For a moment they held the deed, and the dream, between them. "Just like that?" he murmured.

"Yes." She smiled and released her hold. "Just like that."

That her trust was so easily given, so total in her eyes, left him groping for words. "Sarah, I want..." What? he wondered as he stared down at her. To guard and protect, to love and possess? She was like something cool and sweet that had poured into him and washed away years of bitter thirst. But he didn't have the words, he thought. And he didn't have the right.

"I'll take care of this."

She lifted a brow. There had been something else, something in his eyes. She wanted it back, so that she could see it, understand it. "I thought *we* were going to take care of it."

"No." He cupped her chin in his hand. "You're going to leave this to me. I don't want anything to happen to you."

Her brow was still lifted as her lips curved. "Why?"

"Because I don't. I want you to—" Whatever he might have said was postponed. He moved to the window quickly. "You've got company coming." As he spotted the buggy, his shoulders relaxed. "Looks like Mrs. Cody and her girl."

"Oh." Sarah's hands shot up automatically to straighten her hair. "I must look— Oh, how would I know? I haven't had a chance to so much as glance in the mirror."

"Wouldn't matter much." Without glancing back, he pulled open the door. "Too bad you're so homely."

Muttering, she pulled off her apron and followed him outside. Then memory came flooding back and had her biting her lip. "I imagine they would have heard all about the, ah, incident yesterday."

"I expect." Jake secured the deed and the journal in the saddlebags that he'd tossed over the rail.

"You needn't look so amused." She fiddled nervously

with the cameo at her throat, then put on her brightest smile. "Good morning, Mrs. Cody. Liza."

"Good morning, Sarah." Anne Cody brought the horses to a stop. "I hope you don't mind an early call."

"Not at all." But her fingers were busy pleating her skirt. She was afraid there was a lecture coming. The good sisters had given Sarah more than what she considered her share over the past twelve years. "I'm always delighted to see you," she added. "Both of you."

Anne glanced over at the dog, who'd run out to bark at the horses. "My, he's grown some, hasn't he?" She held out a hand. "Mr. Redman?"

Jake stepped over to help her, then Liza, down, remaining silent until he'd slung his saddlebags over his shoulder. "I'd best be on my way." He touched a hand to his hat. "Ladies."

"Mr. Redman." Anne held up a hand in the gesture she used to stop her children from rushing out before their chores were finished. "Might I have a word with you?"

He shifted his bags until their weight fell evenly. "Yes, ma'am."

"My son John has been dogging your heels these last weeks. I'm surprised you put up with it."

Jake didn't imagine it pleased her, either, to have the boy spending time with him. "He hasn't made a pest of himself."

Curious, Anne studied his face. "That's a kind thing to say, Mr. Redman, when I'm sure he's done just that."

"Johnny was born a pest," Liza put in, earning a slow, measured look from her mother.

"It appears my children have that in common." With Liza effectively silenced, Anne turned back to Jake. "He's been going through what most boys his age go through, I expect. Fascinated with guns, gunfights. Gunfighters. I don't mind saying it's given me some worry."

"I'll keep my distance," Jake said, and turned to leave.

"Mr. Redman." Anne hadn't raised two willful children without knowing how to add the right tone of authority to her voice. "I'll have my say."

"Ma." Both Liza's cheeks and voice paled when she saw the look in Jake's eyes. Cold, she thought, and moistened her lips. She'd never seen eyes so cold. "Maybe we should let Mr. Redman be on his way."

"Your mother's got something to say," Jake said quietly. "I reckon she ought to say it."

"Thank you." Pleased, Anne drew off her riding gloves. "Johnny was real excited about what happened here between you and Burt Donley."

"Mrs. Cody," Sarah began, only to be silenced by a look from both her and Jake.

"As I was saying," Anne continued, "Johnny hardly talked about anything else for days. He figured having a shoot-out made a man a man and gave him something to strut about. Even started pestering his pa for a Peacemaker." She glanced down at the guns on Jake's hips. "Wooden grip, he said. Nothing fancy, like some of the glory boys wear. Just a good solid Colt. Mr. Cody and I had just about run clean out of patience with the boy. Then, just yesterday, he came home and told me something." She paused, measuring her words. "He said that killing somebody in a gunfight or any other way doesn't make a man grown-up or important. He said that a smart man doesn't look for trouble. He walks away from it when he can, and faces it when he can't."

For the first time, Anne smiled. "I guess I'd been telling him pretty near the same, but it didn't get through coming from me or his pa. Made me wonder who got him thinking that way." She offered her hand again. "I wanted to tell you I'm obliged."

Jake stared at the hand before taking it. It was the kind of gesture, one of gratitude, even friendship, that had rarely been made to him. "He's a smart boy, Mrs. Cody. He'd have come around to it."

"Sooner or later." Anne stepped toward the door of the house and then she turned back. "Maggie O'Rourke thinks a lot of you. I guess I found out why. I won't keep you any longer, Mr. Redman."

Not quite sure how to respond, he touched his hat before he started toward the paddock to saddle his horse.

"That's quite a man, Sarah," Anne commented. "If I were you, I'd want to go say a proper goodbye."

"Yes, I…" She looked at Anne, then back toward Jake, torn between manners and longings.

"You won't mind if I fix tea, will you?" Anne asked as she disappeared inside.

"No, please, make yourself at home." Sarah looked toward Jake again. "I'll only be a minute." Gathering her skirts, she ran. "Jake!" He turned, the saddle held in both hands, and enjoyed the flash of legs and petticoats. "Wait. I—" She stopped, a hand on her heart, when she realized she was not only out of breath but hadn't any idea what she wanted to say to him. "Are you… When will you be back?"

The mustang shifted and nickered softly as Jake settled the saddle in place. "Haven't left yet."

She hated feeling foolish, and hated even more the idea that he could swing onto his horse and ride out of her life for days at a time. Perhaps patience would do the job.

"I was hoping you'd come back for supper."

He tossed up a stirrup to tighten the cinch. "You asking me to supper?"

"Unless you've something else you'd rather be doing."

His hand snaked out, fast and smooth, to snag her arm before she could flounce away. "It's not often I get invitations to supper from pretty ladies." His grip firm, he glanced back toward the house. Things were changing, he decided, and changing fast, when he looked at the adobe cabin and thought of home. He still didn't know what the hell to do about it.

"If I'd known you'd need so long to think about it," Sarah said between her teeth, "I wouldn't have bothered. You can just—" But before she could tell him he swept her off her feet.

"You sure do get fired up easy." He brought his mouth down hard on hers to taste the heat and the honey. "That's one of the things I like about you."

"Put me down." But her arms encircled his neck. "Mrs. Cody might see." Then she laughed and kissed him again as he swung her down. "Well, will you come to supper or not?"

He vaulted into the saddle in one fluid, economical motion. His eyes were shadowed by the brim of his hat when he looked down at her. "Yeah, I'll come to supper."

"It'll be ready at seven," she called after him as he spurred his horse into a gallop. She watched until dust and distance obscured him. Gathering her skirts again, she ran back to the house. The laughter that was bubbling in her throat dried up when she heard Alice's weeping.

Liza stood by the stove, the kettle steaming in her hand. "Sarah, Ma's..." But Sarah was already rushing up the ladder, ready to defend the girl.

Anne Cody held the weeping Alice in her arms, rocking her gently. One wide, capable hand was stroking the girl's dark hair.

"There now, honey, you cry it all out," she murmured. "Then it'll be behind you." Wanting quiet, she sent Sarah a warning glance. Her own eyes were damp. Slowly Sarah descended the ladder.

"Alice called for you," Liza explained, still holding the kettle. "Ma went up to see what she needed." Liza set the sputtering kettle aside. Tea was the last thing on her mind. "Sarah, what's going on?"

"I'm not sure I know."

Liza cast another look toward the loft and said in a low voice. "Was she…that girl…really beaten?"

"Yes." The memory of it had Sarah touching a fingertip to the bruise under her own eye. "Horribly. Liza, I've never known one person was capable of hurting another so viciously." She needed to be busy, Sarah decided. There was too much to think about. Her father, the mine, Jake, Alice. After running a distracted hand over her hair, she began to slice honey cake.

"Did she really work for Carlotta?"

"Yes. Liza, she's just a girl, younger than you and I."

"Really?" Torn between sympathy and fascination, Liza edged closer to Sarah. "But she… Well, I mean, at the Silver Star she must have…"

"She didn't know anything else." Sarah looked down at her hands. Honey cake and tea. There had been a time when she had thought life was as ordered and simple as that. "Her father sold her. Sold her to a man for twenty dollars."

"But that's—" The curiosity in Liza's eyes heated to fury. "Why, he's the one who should be beat. Her own pa. Somebody ought to—"

"Hush, Liza." Anne slipped quietly down the ladder. "No one deserves to be beat."

"Ma. Sarah says that girl's pa sold her. Sold her off for money, like a horse."

Anne paused in the act of brushing down her skirts. "Is that true, Sarah?"

"Yes. She ran away and ended up at the Silver Star."

Anne's lips tightened as she fought back words that even

her husband had never heard her utter. "I'd dearly love that tea now."

"Oh, yes." Sarah hurried back to the stove. "I'm sorry. Please sit down." She set out the napkins she'd made out of blue checked gingham. "I hope you'll enjoy this honey cake. It's a recipe from the cook of a very dear friend of mine in Philadelphia." As she offered the plate, Philadelphia and everyone in it seemed years away.

"Thank you, dear." Anne waited for Sarah to sit down, then said, "Alice is sleeping now. I wasn't sure you'd done the right thing by taking her in here. Truth is, I drove out this morning because I was concerned."

"I had to take her in."

"No, you didn't." When Sarah bristled, Anne laid a hand on hers. "But you did what was right, and I'm proud of you. That girl needs help." With a sigh, she sat back and looked at her own daughter. Pretty Liza, she thought, always so bright and curious. And safe, she reflected, adding a quick prayer of thanksgiving. Her children had always had a full plate and a solid roof over their heads—and a father who loved them. She made up her mind to thank her husband very soon.

"Alice Johnson has had nothing but hard times." Anne took a sip of tea. Her mind was made up. She had only to convince her husband. At that thought her lips curved a little. It was never hard to convince a man whose heart was soft and open. The other ladies in town would be a bit more difficult, but she'd bring them around. The challenge of it made her smile widen and the light of battle glint in her eyes.

"What that girl needs is some proper work and a real home. When she's on her feet again, I think she should come work at the store."

"Oh, Mrs. Cody."

Anne brushed Sarah's stunned gratitude aside. "Once Liza's married to Will I'm going to need new help. She can take Liza's room in the house, as well…as part of her wage."

Sarah fumbled for words, then gave up and simply leaned over to wrap her arms around Anne. "It's kind of you," she managed. "So kind. I've spoken with Alice about just that, but she pointed out that the women in town wouldn't accept her after she'd worked at the Silver Star."

"You don't know Ma." Pride shimmered in Liza's voice. "She'll bring the ladies around, every one. Won't you, Ma?"

Anne patted her hair. "You can put money on it." Satisfied, she broke off a corner of the honey cake. "Sarah, now that we've got that settled, I feel I have to talk to you about the…visit you paid to the Silver Star yesterday."

"Visit?" Though she knew it was hopeless, Sarah covered the bruise under her eyes with her fingers.

"You know, when you tangled with Carlotta," Liza put in. "Everyone in town's talking about how you wrestled with her and even punched Jake Redman. I wish I'd seen it." She caught her mother's eye and grimaced. "Well, I do."

"Oh, Lord." This time Sarah covered her entire face. "Everyone?"

"Mrs. Miller was standing just outside when the sheriff went in." Liza took a healthy bite of cake. "You know how she loves to carry tales."

When Sarah just groaned, Anne shook her head at Liza. "Honey, you eat some more of that cake and keep your mouth busy. Now, Sarah." Anne pried Sarah's hands away from her face. "I have to say I was a mite surprised to hear that you'd gone in that place and had a hair-pulling match with that woman. Truth is, a nice young girl like you shouldn't even know about places and people like that."

"Can't live in Lone Bluff two days and not know

about Carlotta," Liza said past a mouthful of cake. "Even Johnny—"

"Liza." Anne held up a single finger. "Chew. Seeing as you're without kin of your own, Sarah, I figured I'd come on out and speak to you about it." She took another sip of tea while Sarah waited to be lectured. "Well, blast it, now that I've seen that girl up there, I wished I'd taken a good yank at Carlotta, myself."

"Ma!" Delighted, Liza slapped both hands to her mouth. "You wouldn't."

"No." Anne flushed a little and shifted in her chair. "But I'd like to. Now, I'm not saying I want to hear about you going back there, Sarah."

"No." Sarah managed a rueful smile. "I think I've finished any business I might have at the Silver Star."

"Popped you a good one, did she?" Anne commented studying Sarah's eye.

"Yes." Sarah grinned irrepressibly. "But I gave her a bloody nose. It's quite possible that I broke it."

"Really. Oh, I do wish I'd seen that." Ready to be impressed, Liza leaned forward, only to straighten again at a look from Anne. "Well, it's not as if I'd go inside myself."

"Not if you want to keep the hide on your bottom," Anne said calmly. She smoothed her hair, took another sip of tea, then gave up. "Well, darn it, are you going to tell us what it looks like in there or not?"

With a laugh, Sarah propped her elbows on the table and told them.

Scheming came naturally to Carlotta. As she lay in the wide feather bed, she ran through all the wrongs that had been done to her and her plans for making them right. The light was dim, with only two thin cracks appearing past the sides of the drawn shades. It was a large room by the

Silver Star's standards. She'd had the walls between two smaller rooms removed to fashion her own private quarters, sacrificing the money one extra girl would have made her for comfort.

For Carlotta, money and comfort were one and the same. She wanted plenty of both.

Though it was barely nine, she poured a glass of whiskey from the bottle that was always at her bedside. The hot, powerful taste filled the craving she awoke with every morning. Sipping and thinking, she cast her eyes around the room.

The walls were papered in a somewhat virulent red-and-silver stripe she found rich and elegant. Thick red drapes, too heavy for the blistering Arizona summers, hung at the windows. They made her think, smugly, of queens and palaces. The carpet echoed the color and was badly in need of cleaning. She rarely noticed the dirt.

On the mirrored vanity, which was decorated with painted cherubs, was a silver brush set with an elaborate *C* worked into the design. It was the only monogram she used. Carlotta had no last name, at least none she cared to remember.

Her mother had always had a man in her bed. Carlotta had gone to sleep most nights on a straw pallet in the corner, her lullaby the grunts and groans of sex. It had made her sick, the way men had pounded themselves into her mother. But that had been nothing compared to the disgust she had felt for her mother's weeping when the men were gone.

Crying and sniveling and begging God's forgiveness, Carlotta thought. Her mother had been the whore of that frigid little town in the Carolina mountains, but she hadn't had the guts to make it work for her.

Always claimed she was doing it to feed her little girl, Carlotta remembered with a sneer. She poured more whiskey into the glass. If that had been so, why had her little girl gone hungry so many nights? In the dim light, Carlotta studied the deep amber liquid. Because Ma was just as fond of whiskey as I am, she decided. She drank, and savored the taste.

The difference between you and me, Ma, she thought to herself, is that I ain't ashamed—not of the whiskey, not of the men. And I made something of myself.

Did you cry when I left? Carlotta laughed as she thought back to the night she'd left the smelly, windowless shack for the last time. She'd been fifteen and she'd saved nearly thirty dollars she'd made selling herself to trappers. Men paid more for youth. Carlotta had learned quickly. Her mother had never known her daughter was her stiffest competition.

She despised them all. Every man who'd pushed himself into her. She took their money, arched her hips and loathed them. Hate made a potent catalyst for passion. Her customers went away satisfied, and she saved every coin.

One night she'd packed her meager belongings, stolen another twenty dollars from the can her mother kept hidden in the rafters and headed west.

She'd worked saloons in the early years, enjoying the fancy clothes and bottles of paint. Her affair with whiskey had blossomed and helped her smile and seduce hungry-eyed cowboys and rough-handed drifters. She'd saved, keeping her mouth firmly shut about the bonuses she wheedled from men.

When she'd turned eighteen she had had enough to open her own place. A far cry from the Silver Star, Carlotta remembered. Her first brothel had been hardly more than a shack in a stinking cattle town in east Texas. But she'd made certain her girls were as young and pretty as she could get.

She'd had a brief affair with a gambler who'd sported brocade vests and string ties. He'd filled her head with talk of crystal chandeliers and red carpets. When she'd moved on, she'd taken his pearl stickpin, two hundred in cash and her own profits.

Then she'd opened the Silver Star.

One day she'd move on again, on to California. But she intended to do it in style. She'd have those crystal chandeliers, she vowed. And a white porcelain tub with gold handles. Gold.

Carlotta felt a pleasure flow through her, a pleasure as fluid as the whiskey. It was gold she needed to bring her dream to full life. And gold she intended to have.

The man beside her was the tool she would use to gain it.

Jim Carlson. Carlotta looked down at his face. It was rough with several days' growth of beard and slack from sleep, sex and whiskey. She knew him for a fool, hot-tempered, small-minded and easily manipulated. Still, he was better-looking than many she had taken into her bed. His body was tough and lean, but she preferred young, limber bodies. Like Jake's.

Scowling, Carlotta took another drink. She'd broken her most important rule with Jake Redman. She'd let herself want him, really want him, in a way she'd never desired another man. Her body had responded to his so that for the first time in her life she hadn't feigned the ecstasy men wanted from a whore. She'd felt it. Now she craved it, as she craved whiskey, and gold, and power.

With Jake, desire was a hot, tight fist in her gut. Not just because he had a style in bed most men who came to her didn't feel obliged to employ. Because Jake Redman held something of himself back, something she sensed was powerful and exciting. Something she wanted for herself.

And had been on her way to getting, she thought, before that pasty-faced bitch had come to town.

She had a lot to pay Miss Sarah Conway back for. Thoughtful, Carlotta touched a hand to her bruised cheek. A whole lot. Pay her back she would, and in doing so she would take Jake and the gold.

Jim Carlson, though he was unaware of it, was going to help her on all counts.

Setting the empty glass aside, Carlotta picked up a hand mirror. The bruises annoyed her, but they would fade. The faint lines fanning out from her eyes and bracketing her mouth would not. They would only deepen. She cursed and pushed the mirror aside. With a pleased smile, she ran both hands down her body. It was long, smooth-skinned and curvaceous.

It was her body men wanted and her body she had used, and would continue to use, to get what life had cheated her of.

She shifted, took Jim in her hand and brought him breathlessly awake.

"God Almighty, Carlotta." Groaning, he tried to roll over and into her.

"In a hurry, Jim?" She evaded him expertly, all the while using her skill to keep him aroused.

"Thought you'd burned the life out of me last night." He shuddered. "Glad to find out it ain't so."

"I want to talk to you, Jim."

"Talk." He filled his hands with her breasts. "Honey, I got better ways to spend my money than talk."

She let him suck and nuzzle, calculating how far she could let him go and keep him in line. Rooting about like a puppy, she thought in disgust while she stroked his hair.

"Your money ran out at dawn, sweetheart."

"I got more." He bit her, hard. Because she knew he expected it, she gave a soft moan of pleasure.

"House rules, Jim. Money first."

He swore at her and considered taking his pleasure as he chose. But if he forced her and managed to avoid getting tossed out by Eli, the doors of the Silver Star would be barred to him. He had money, he thought. And a need that was rock-hard.

When he started to shift, Carlotta trailed a finger down his arm. "Talk, Jim, and I'll…" With a long sigh, she arched back so that he could look his fill. "I'll give you the rest for free."

Sweat beaded on his upper lip as he studied her. "You don't do nothing for free."

Deliberately she ran a hand over her breast and down her rib cage and stroked the soft swell of her belly. "Talk. We're going to talk first." Her lips curved as she watched him swallow. "About gold." When he stiffened, her smile only widened. "Don't worry, Jim. I haven't told anyone, have I? I've never said a word about how you and Donley killed old Matt Conway."

"I was drunk when I told you about that." He wiped a hand over the back of his mouth as fear and desire twined inside him. "A man says all kinds of things when he's drunk."

That made her laugh. She pillowed her head on her folded arms. "Nobody knows that better than a whore or a wife, Jim, honey. Relax. Who was the one who told you old Matt had finally hit? Who was the one who told you his daughter was coming and you had to move fast? Don't try dealing from the bottom with me, sweetheart. It's business, remember. Yours and mine."

After pushing himself up in bed, he reached bad-temperedly for the whiskey bottle. "I told you once Sam got things worked out you'd get your share."

"And what does Sam have to work out?" She let him take a swallow, two. It never hurt to loosen a man's tongue, but there were some who went from relaxed to mean with whiskey. With Jim the line was all too easily crossed. She took the bottle back.

"We've already been through this," he muttered. He no longer felt like having sex, and he sure as hell didn't want to talk.

"If Sam had some idea about getting that Conway bitch to the altar to get his hands on the deed, he's had time enough. Everybody in town knows she doesn't have her eye on your brother, but on Jake Redman."

"How about you?" He tapped a finger, none too gently, against her bruised cheekbone. "Who do you have those blue eyes on?"

"The main chance, sweetheart. Always the main chance." She ran her tongue over her lips, grimly pleased with the way Jim's eyes followed the movement. The surest way to lead a man, she knew, was from a point just below his gunbelt. She rose, knowing the shuttered light would be flattering to her skin. Slowly she ran her hands up her body, letting them linger on her breasts.

"You know, Jim," she began, slipping into a thin red negligee that was as transparent as glass, "I've always been drawn to men who take risks, who know what they want and take it." She left the negligee open as she walked back toward the bed. "That night you came in and told me how you and Donley had dragged Matt up to the mine and how you'd killed him because he wouldn't hand over the deed. You told me just how you'd killed him, how you'd hurt him first. Remember that night, Jim? You and me sure had ourselves a good time after we came upstairs."

He wet his lips. Her nipples were dark and just out of reach. "I remember."

"It was exciting. Knowing you'd just come from killing a man. Killing him to get what you wanted. I knew I was with a real man." The negligee fell carelessly off one shoulder. "Trouble is, nothing's happened since. I keep waiting."

"I told you. Sam's going—"

"The hell with Sam." She battled back her temper to smile at him. "He's too slow, too careful. A real man takes action. If he wants the Conway girl, why doesn't he just take her? Or you could take her for him." She moved closer, letting the idea take root. "She's all that's in the way, Jim. You deal with her—and I ain't talking about firing one of her sheds." The quick wariness in his eyes pleased her. "Hurt her, Jim. She'll hand over the deed quick enough. Then kill her." She murmured the words like a love song. "When she's dead, you come to me. We can do anything you want." She stood beside the bed, glorious and gleaming. "Anything. And it won't cost you a cent."

She didn't cry out when his hand clamped over her wrist. Their faces were close, each of them aroused in different ways, for different reasons.

"You'll take care of her?"

"Yes, damn you. Come here."

Carlotta smiled bitterly at the ceiling while Jim collapsed on top of her.

From her window an hour later, Carlotta watched as Jake rode into town. Her hands clenched into fists—from anger, yes, but also from a stab of desire. Soon, she thought, very soon, he'd come back to her.

She turned as Jim pulled up his pants. She was smiling.

"I think it's a real good time for you to pay Sarah Conway a visit."

Chapter 14

When Jake walked into Maggie's, she set her fisted hands on her hips and looked him up and down with a sniff.

"Fine time to be strolling in, boyo." What she wanted was gossip, and she hoped to annoy it out of him. "Can't figure why a man would be paying good money for a bed and never sleep in it."

"I pay for your chicken and dumplings, too, but I ain't stupid enough to eat them." He started resignedly up the stairs, knowing she would follow.

"You don't seem to be suffering any from lack of food." With the audacity she'd been born with, she poked a finger in his ribs. "Must be getting meals someplace."

"Must be."

"Sarah a good cook, is she?"

Saying nothing, he pushed open the door to his room.

"Don't go pokering up on me, Jake, my boy." Maggie swiped a dustcloth here and there. "It's too late. Every blessed soul in town saw the way you looked at her at the dance. Then there was the way you rode out of town after her when she socked you in the jaw." The dark, furious glint in his eyes had Maggie cackling. "That's more like it. Always said you could drop a man dead with a look as quick as with those guns of yours. No need to draw on me, though. I figure Sarah Conway's just what you need."

"Do you?" Jake tossed his saddlebags on the bed. He considered starting to strip to get rid of her. But he'd tried that before, and it hadn't budged her an inch. "I reckon you want to tell me why before you leave me the hell alone."

"Like to see the back of me, would you?" She just laughed again and patted his cheek. "More than one man's considered it my best side."

He barely managed to control a grin. He was damned if he knew why the nosy old woman appealed to him. "Why don't you get yourself another husband, Maggie? Then you could nag him."

"You'd miss me."

"I reckon some dogs miss the fleas once they manage to scratch them off." Then he sat by the window, propping his back against one side and his boot against the other.

"Somebody's got to bite at you. Might as well be me. I got something to say about you and Sarah Conway."

Staring out the window, he frowned. "It won't be anything I haven't said to myself. Go away, Maggie."

"Now listen to me, boy," she said in an abruptly serious tone. "There's some who're born to the pretty. They slide out of their mothers and straight into silk and satin. Then there's others who have to fight and claw and scratch for every good thing. We know something about that, you and me."

Still frowning, he looked back at her. With a nod, she continued. "Some go hungry, and some have their bellies full. The sweet Lord himself knows why he set things up that way, and no one else. But he didn't make the one man better than the other. It's men themselves who decide if they're going to be strong or weak—and that's the same as good or bad. Sometimes there's a woman who shoves them one way or the other. You take ahold of Sarah Conway, Jake. She'll shove you right enough."

"Could work the other way around," he murmured. "A woman's easier to shove than a man."

Maggie's brows rose in two amused peaks. "Jake, my boy, you've got a lot to learn about women."

It was the second time in so many days he'd been told that, Jake mused when Maggie clicked the door shut behind her. But it wasn't a woman he had to think about now.

It was gold. And it was murder.

He took Matt Conway's journal and started to read.

Unlike Sarah, Jake didn't bother with the early pages. He scanned a few at the middle, where Matt had written of working the mine and of his hopes for a big strike. There were mentions of Sarah here and there, of Matt's regrets at leaving her behind, of his pride in the letters she wrote him. And always he wrote of his longing to send for her.

He had wanted to build her a home first, a real home, like the one he'd described to her. The mine would do it, or so he had thought. Throughout the pages, his confidence never wavered.

Each time I enter, I feel it. Not just hope, but certainty. Today. Each time I'm sure it will be today. There is gold here, enough to give my Sarah the life of a princess—the life I had wanted so badly to give her mother. How alike they are. The miniature Sarah sent me for Christmas might be my own lost, lovely Ellen. Looking at it each night before I sleep makes me grieve for the little girl I left behind and ache for the young woman my daughter has become.

So there had been a painting, Jake mused. Questions might be answered once it was found. He skipped on, toward the end.

In my years of prospecting, I've learned that success is as elusive as any dream. A man may have a map and tools, he may have skill and persistence. But there is one factor that cannot be bought, cannot be learned. Luck. Without it a man can dig and hammer for years with the vein he seeks always inches out of reach. As I have been. Sweet God, as I have been.

Was it the hand of chance that caused my own to slip, that had me sprawled in the dirt nursing my bruised and bloody fingers and cursing God as I learned to curse him so eloquently? And when I stumbled, half-blind with tears of frustration and pain, was it his hand that led me deeper into the tunnel, swinging my pick like a madman?

There it was, under my still-bleeding fingers. Glinting dull against the dark rock. It ran like a river, back, back into the dark mouth of the mine, narrow, then widening. I know it cannot be, yet to me it seemed to shimmer and pulse like a living thing. Gold. At long last.

I am not ashamed that I sat on the dusty floor of the mine, my lamp between my knees, and wept.

He'd found it, Jake thought as he frowned over the words. It was no longer just a hunch, a feeling, but fact. Matt Conway had found his gold, and he'd died. Perhaps there would be an answer to why and how in the remaining pages.

Do men grow more foolish with age? Perhaps. Perhaps. But then, whiskey makes fools of young and old. There need be no excuses. A man finds his heart's desire after years of sweat. To what does he turn? A woman, and a bottle. I found both at the Silver Star.

It had been my intention to keep my discovery to myself for a little longer. Sarah's letter changed that. She's coming. My own little girl is already on her way to join me. There is no way to prepare her for what she will find. Thank God I will soon be able to give her all that I promised.

It wasn't my intent to tell Carlotta of the gold, or of Sarah's arrival. Whiskey and weakness. Undoubtedly I paid for my lack of discretion with a vicious head the next morning. And the visit from Samuel Carlson.

Could it be coincidence that now, after all these years, he wants the mine? His offer was generous. Too generous for me to believe the purchase was to be made from sentiment on his part. Perhaps my suspicions are unfounded. He took my refusal in good temper, leaving the offer open. Yet there was something, something in the way he held his brother and his man Donley to silence—like holding wild dogs on a leash. Tomorrow I will ride into town and tell Barker about my discovery. It may be wise to hire a few men to help me work the mine. The sooner it is begun, the sooner I can build my Sarah the house she believes is already waiting for her.

It was the last entry. Closing the book, Jake rose. He had his answers.

"Miss Sarah, seeing as you're going into town and all…"

Sarah sighed as she adjusted her straw bonnet. "Again, Lucius?"

He scratched his grizzled beard. "A man gets powerful thirsty doing all this work."

"Very well." She'd managed to cure him of his abhorrence of water. Easing him away from his passion for whiskey would take a bit more time.

"I'm obliged, Miss Sarah." He grinned at her. In the weeks he'd been working for her he'd discovered she had a soft heart—and a tough mind. "You check on that wood you ordered. I'll be right pleased to put that floor in for you when it gets here."

Easily said, she mused, when the wood was still hundreds of miles away. "You might finish building the pen Jake started. I intend to inquire about buying some piglets while I'm in town."

"Yes'm." He spit. He'd build the cursed pen, but he'd be damned if he'd tend pigs. "Miss Sarah, I'm getting a mite low on tobacco."

Whiskey and tobacco, Sarah thought, rolling her eyes heavenward. What would Mother Superior have said? "I'll see to it. You look in on Alice regularly, Lucius. See that she has a bit of that broth and rests."

She heard him grumble about being a nursemaid and snagged her lip to keep it from curving. "I'll be back by three. I'm going to fix a very special meal tonight." She gave him a final glance. "You'll want to change your shirt." She cracked the reins and headed out before she allowed herself to laugh.

Life was glorious. Life was, she thought as she let the horses prance, magnificent. Perhaps she was rich, as Jake had said, but the gold no longer mattered. So many things that had seemed so important only a short time before really meant nothing at all.

She was in love, beautifully, wildly, in love, and all the gold in the world couldn't buy what she was feeling.

She would make him happy. It would take some time, some care and more than a little patience, but she would make Jake Redman see that together they could have everything two people could want. A home, children, roots, a lifetime.

What they had brought to each other had changed them both. She was not the same woman who had boarded the train in Philadelphia. How far she'd come, Sarah reflected as she scanned the distant buttes. Not just in miles. It was much more than miles. Only weeks before she'd been certain her happiness depended on having a new bonnet. She laughed as the hot wind tugged at the brim of the one she wore now. She had come to Lone Bluff with dreams of fine parties and china dishes. She hadn't found them. But she had found more, much more.

And she had changed him. She could see it in the way he looked at her, in the way he reached for her as he slept, just to hold her, to keep her close. Perhaps the words were difficult for him to say. She could wait.

Now that she had found him, nothing and no one would keep her from being with him.

She saw the rider coming, and for an instant her smile bloomed. But it wasn't Jake. Sarah watched Jim Carlson slow his horse to a trot as he crossed the road in front of her. She intended to ride by with a brief nod of greeting, but he blocked her way.

"Morning, ma'am." He shifted in his saddle to lean toward her. The stink of whiskey colored his words. "All alone?"

"Good morning, Mr. Carlson. I'm on my way to town, and I'm afraid I'm a bit pressed for time."

"That so?" It was going to be easier than he'd thought. He wouldn't have to go through Lucius to get to her. "Now that's a shame, since I was just riding out to see you."

"Oh?" She didn't care for the look in his eyes, and the smell of whiskey on his breath didn't seem harmless, as it did with Lucius. "Is there something I can do for you, Mr. Carlson?"

"There sure is." Slowly, his eyes on hers, he drew his gun. "Step on out of the wagon."

"You must be mad." She'd frozen at the first sight of

the barrel, but now, instinctively, her fingers inched toward her rifle.

"I wouldn't touch that rifle, ma'am. It'd be a shame for me to put a hole in that pretty white hand of yours. Now, I said get out of the wagon."

"Jake will kill you if you touch me."

He'd already thought that one through. That was the reason he was altering Carlotta's plan to suit himself. He wasn't going to kill Sarah here and now, unless she did something stupid. "Oh, I got plans for Redman, honey, don't you worry. You just step out of that wagon before I have to put a bullet in your horses."

She didn't doubt he would, or that he would shoot her in the back should she try to run. Trapped, she stepped down and stood stiffly beside the wagon.

"God Almighty, you got looks, Sarah. That's why Sam took to you." With his gun still in his hand, Jim slid out of the saddle. "You got those fine lady looks like our mama did. You saw her picture at the house. Sam, he's mighty fond of pictures." He grinned again. When he reached out to touch Sarah's face, she hissed and jerked it aside. "But you, you got some fire. Mama was just crazy. Plumb crazy." He stepped forward so that his body pushed hers against the side of the wagon. "Sam told you she was delicate, didn't he? That's the word he uses. Crazy was what she was, so that the old man would lock her up sometimes for days. One day when he opened up the door he found her hanging dead with a pretty pink silk scarf around her neck."

Horror leaped into her eyes and warred with fear. "Let me go. If Samuel finds out what you've done, he'll—"

"You think I run scared of Sam?" Laughing, Jim forced Sarah's face back to his. "Maybe you figure he's smoother than me, got more brains. But we're blood." His fingers bit into her skin. "Don't forget it. You ever let him get this

close, let him do what he wanted? Or did you save yourself for that breed?"

She slapped him with all the force of her fear and rage.
Then she was clawing at him, blindly, with some mad hope
of getting to his horse. She felt the barrel of the gun press
into the soft underside of her jaw and heard the click of
the hammer.

"Try that again and I'll leave what's left of you here for
the buzzards, gold or no gold. Your pa tried to get away,
too." The stunned look in her eyes pleased him, gave him
the edge he wanted. "You think on what happened to him
and take care." He was breathing quickly, his finger trembling on the trigger. He'd lied when he'd said he wasn't
scared of his brother. If it hadn't been for the rage Sam
would heap on him, Jim would have sent a bullet into her.
"Now you're going to do just like I say, and you'll stay alive
a while longer."

"Interesting reading." Barker squinted down at Matt's
journal while he fanned the hot, still air around his face
with his hat. "Matt had a fine way of putting words on
paper."

"Fine or not, it's plain enough." Jake fidgeted at the
window, annoyed with himself for coming to the law with
something he could, and should, have handled himself.
Sarah's doing, he thought. He hadn't even felt the shove.

"It's plain that Matt thought he'd found gold."

"He'd found it. Lucius dug through to where Matt was
working. It's there, just the way Matt wrote."

Thoughtful, Barker closed the book and leaned back in
his chair. "Poor old Matt. Finally makes the big strike, then
gets caught in a cave-in."

"He was dead before those beams gave way."

Taking his time, Barker pushed a cozy plug of tobacco in

his cheek. "Well, now, maybe you think so, and maybe I'm doing some pondering on it, but this here journal isn't proof. It's not going to be easy to ride out to the Carlson ranch and talk to Sam about murder with no more than a book in my hand. Now hold on," he added when Jake snatched the book from the desk. "I didn't say I wasn't going out, I just said it wasn't going to be easy." Still fanning himself with his hat, he sat back in his chair. He wanted to think it through, and think it through carefully. The Carlson family had a long reach. He was more concerned about that than about the quick temper and gun of young Jim.

"Got a question for you, Jake. Why'd you bring me that journal instead of riding on out and putting a hole in the Carlson brothers?"

Jake skimmed his eyes over Barker's comfortable paunch. "My deep and abiding respect for the law."

After a bark of laughter, the sheriff spit a stream of tobacco juice into the spittoon. "I once knew a woman—before Mrs. Barker—who lied as smooth as that. Couldn't help but admire her." With a sigh, he perched his hat on his head. "Whatever your reason, you brought it, so I'm duty-bound to do something about it. Got to tell you, nothing's more tiring than duty." He reached unenthusiastically for his gunbelt as the door burst open.

"Sheriff." Nancy stood, darting glances over her shoulder and tugging restlessly at the shoulder of her hastily donned dress. "I got to talk to you."

"You'll just have to hold on to it till I get back. One of them cowboys got a little too enthusiastic over at the Silver Star, I ain't getting worked up about it."

"You'd better listen." Nancy stood firm in front of the door. "I'm only doing this 'cause of Alice." She glanced at Jake then. "Carlotta'd strip my skin if she found out I come, but I figured Miss Conway done right by Alice, I ought to do right by her."

"Quit babbling. If you're hell-bent on talking, say it."

"It's Carlotta." Nancy kept her voice low, as if it might carry back to the Silver Star. "She's been feeling real mean since yesterday."

"Carlotta was born feeling mean," Barker muttered. Then he waved to Nancy to continue. "All right, finish it out."

"Last night she took Jim Carlson up. She don't usually let men stay overnight in her room, but he was still there this morning. My room's next to hers, and I heard them talking."

Jake took her arm to draw her farther into the room. "Why don't you tell me what you heard?"

"She was talking about how Jim and Donley killed Matt Conway, and how he was supposed to take care of Matt's girl." She yelped when Jake's fingers bit into her arm. "I didn't have no part in it. I'm telling you what I heard 'cause she took Alice in after Carlotta near killed her."

"Looks like I'd better have a talk with Carlotta," Barker mused, straightening his hat.

"No, you can't." Fear for her own skin had her yanking free of Jake. "She'll kill me. That's the God's truth. Anyways, it's too late for that."

"Why?" Jake caught her again before she could dash out the door.

She'd gone this far, Nancy thought, dragging the back of her hand over her mouth. She might as well finish. "Carlotta said Jim was to scare Miss Conway good, hurt her. Then, when he had the deed to the mine, he was to kill her. He rode out an hour ago, and I couldn't get away till now."

Jake was already through the door and halfway to his horse when Barker caught up with him. "Will and me'll be right behind you."

There had been times when killing had come easily to Jake, so easily that after it was done he'd felt nothing. This time would be different. He knew it, felt it, as he sped down the road toward Sarah's house. If Jim Carlson was ahead of him and he got within range, he would kill him without question. It would be easy. And it would be a pleasure.

He heard the horses behind him, but he didn't look back.

His own mount seemed to sense the urgency and lengthened his strides until his powerful legs were a blur and the dust was a yellow wall behind them.

When Jake saw the wagon, the cold rage dropped into his gut and turned into a hot, bubbling fear. He vaulted from the saddle beside the two horses, which stood slack-hipped and drowsy.

Surprisingly agile, Barker slipped down beside him. "Take it easy." He began to place a hand on Jake's shoulder, but then he thought better of it. "If he took her off somewhere, we'll track him." He held up a hand before any of the men with him could speak. Along with Will were three men from town, including John Cody, who still wore his store apron. "We take care of our own here, Jake. We'll get her back."

In silence, Jake bent down to pick up the cameo lying facedown in the road. Its slender pin was snapped. There were a few pale blue threads clinging to the broken point. The signs told him she'd struggled, and the picture of her frightened and fighting clawed at him. The signs also told him where she was being taken. With the broach in his pocket, he jumped into the saddle and rode hard for the Carlson ranch.

Her hands were bound together and tied to the saddle horn. If it had been possible, she would have jumped to the ground. Though there was nowhere to run, at least she would have had the satisfaction of making him sweat.

Everything Jake had said was true—about the gold, about her father's death. Sarah had no doubt that the man responsible for it all was sitting behind her.

At first she thought he was taking her into the hills, or to the desert, where he could kill her and leave her body hidden. But she saw, with some confusion, the graceful lines of the Carlson ranch house in the shallow valley below.

It was a peaceful scene, lovely despite the waves of radiant heat rising up from the ground. She heard a dog bark. As they approached, Samuel burst out of the house, hatless and pale, to stare at his brother.

"What in God's name have you done?"

Jim loosened the rope around the saddle horn, then lifted Sarah to the ground. "Brought you a present."

"Sarah, my dear." His mouth grim, Carlson tugged at her bonds. "I'm speechless. There's no way I could ever…" He let his words trail off and began to massage the raw skin of her wrists. "He must be drunk. Stable that horse, damn you," he shouted at Jim. "Then come inside. You've a great deal to answer for."

It stunned her, left her limp, when Jim merely shrugged and led his horse away. It must be a joke, a bizarre joke, she thought, bringing her trembling hands to her lips. But it wasn't. She knew it was much too deadly to be a joke.

"Samuel—"

"My dear, I don't know what to say." He slipped a supporting arm around her waist. "I can't begin to apologize for my brother's outrageous behavior. Are you hurt? Dear Lord, your dress is torn." He had her by the shoulders then, and the look in his eyes froze her blood. "Did he touch you, molest you?"

She managed to shake her head, once, then twice. Then

the words came. "Samuel, he killed my father. It was for the gold. There's gold in the mine. He must have found out and he—he murdered my father."

She was breathless now, her hands clinging to his trim black vest. He only stared at her, stared until she wanted to scream. "Samuel, you must believe me."

"You're overwrought," he said stiffly. "And no wonder. Come in out of the heat."

"But he—"

"You needn't worry about Jim." He led her inside the thick adobe walls. "He won't bother you again. You have my word. I want you to wait in my office." His voice was quiet, soothing, as he led her past his mother's portrait and into a room. "Try to relax. I'll take care of everything."

"Samuel, please be careful. He might—he could hurt you."

"No." He patted her hand as he eased her into a chair. "He'll do exactly what I tell him."

When the door shut, she covered her face with her hands. For a moment she let the hysteria she'd fought off take control. He'd intended to kill her. She was certain of it, from the way he'd looked at her, the way he'd smiled at her. Why in God's name had he brought her here, where she would be protected by Samuel?

Protected. After letting out a shaky breath, she waited until her heartbeat leveled and the need to scream passed. She was safe now. But it wasn't over. She closed her eyes briefly. It was far from over.

It was madness. Jim Carlson was as mad as his poor mother had been, but instead of killing himself he had killed her father. She wanted to weep, to let the new, aching grief come. But she couldn't. She couldn't weep, and she couldn't sit.

Rising, she began to pace. The room was small but beautifully furnished. There were delicate porcelain figurines and a painting in fragile pastels. It reflected Samuel's elegant taste and eye for beauty. How unalike the brothers were, she thought.

Cain and Abel.

With a hand on her heart, she rushed to the door. She could never have borne the guilt if one brother killed another over her.

But the door was locked. For a moment she thought it was only her nerves making her fumble. After a deep breath she tried the knob again. It resisted.

Whirling around, she stared at the room. Locked in? But why? For her own protection? Samuel must have thought she would be safer behind a locked door until he came back for her.

And if it was Jim who came back with the key? Her heart thudding in her throat, she began a frantic search for a weapon.

She pulled out desk drawers, pushing ruthlessly through papers. If not a pistol, she thought, then a knife, even a letter opener. She would not be defenseless. Not again. She tugged open the middle drawer, and the brass pulls knocked against the glossy mahogany. Her hand froze when she saw the miniature. Her miniature.

Like a sleepwalker, she reached for it, staring blindly.

It was the self-portrait that she had painted the year before, the one she had shipped to her father for Christmas. The one, Sarah realized as her fingers closed over it, that he had shown with pride to his friends in town. The one that had been missing from his possessions. Missing because it had been taken by his murderer.

When the key turned in the lock, she didn't bother to close the drawer or to hide what she held in her hand. Instead, she rose and faced him.

"It was you," she murmured as Samuel Carlson closed and locked the door behind him. "You killed my father."

Chapter 15

Carlson crossed the room until only the desk was between them. "Sarah." His voice was almost a sigh, a sigh touched with patience. In his hand he carried a delicate cup filled with fragrant tea. But she noted that he had strapped on his gun. "I realize how upset you must be after Jim's inexcusable behavior. Now, why don't you sit down, compose yourself?"

"You killed my father," she repeated. It was rage she felt now, waves of it.

"That's ridiculous." The words were said gently. "I haven't killed anyone. Here, my dear. I've brought you some tea. It should help calm you."

The quiet sincerity in his eyes caused her to falter. He must have sensed it, because he smiled and stepped forward. Instantly she backed away. "Why was this in your desk?"

Carlson looked at the miniature in her hand. "A woman should never intrude on a man's personal belongings." His voice became indulgent as he set the cup on the desk. "But since you have, I'll confess. I can be faulted for being overly romantic, I suppose. The moment I saw it, I fell in love with you. The moment I saw your face, I wanted you." He held out a hand, palm up, as if he were asking for a dance. "Come, Sarah, you can't condemn me for that."

Confused, she shook her head. "Tell me how this came to be in your drawer when it belonged to my father."

Impatience clouded his face, and he dropped his hand to his side. "Isn't baring my soul enough for you? You knew, right from the beginning, you knew the way I felt about you. You deceived me." There was more than impatience in his face now. Something else was building in him. Something that had the bright, hot taste of fear clogging her throat.

"I don't know what you're talking about, Samuel." She spaced her words carefully and kept her eyes on his. "But you're right. I'm upset, and I'm not myself. I'd prefer to go home now and discuss all of this later." With the miniature still clutched in her hand, she stepped around the desk and toward the door. The violence with which he grabbed her and shoved her back against the wall had her head reeling.

"It's too late. Jim's interference has changed everything. His interference, and your prying. I was patient with you, Sarah. Now it's too late."

His face was close to hers—close enough for her to see clearly what was in his eyes. She wondered, as the blood drained slowly from her face, how it was that she'd never seen it before. The madness was bright and deadly. She tried to speak and found she had to swallow first.

"Samuel, you're hurting me."

"I would have made you a queen." He took one hand and brought it up to stroke her face. She cringed, but his eyes warned her not to move. "I would have given you everything a woman could want. Silk." He traced a finger over her cheekbone. "Diamonds." Then he ran it lightly down her throat. "Gold." His hand tightened abruptly around her windpipe. Before she could begin to struggle, it was loosened again. "Gold, Sarah. It belonged to me, truly to me. My grandfather had no right to lose that part of my heritage. And your father...he had no right to deny me what was already mine."

"He did it for me." Perhaps she could calm him, if only

she could remain calm herself, before it was too late. "He only wanted to see that I was taken care of."

"Of course." He nodded, as if he were pleased that she understood. "Of course he did. As I do. It would have been yours as much as mine. I would never have let you suffer because I had taken it back. As my wife, you would have had every luxury. We would have gone back east together. That was always my plan. I was going to follow you back east and court you. But you stayed. You should never have stayed, Sarah. This isn't the place for you. I knew it the moment I saw your picture. It was there, in that miserable little cabin, beside the cot. I found it while I was looking for the deed to the mine."

His face changed again. He looked petulant now, like a boy who had been denied an extra piece of pie. "I was very annoyed that my brother and Donley killed Matt. Clumsy. They were only to…convince him to turn over the deed. Then, of course, it was up to me to think of causing the cave-in to cover up what they'd done. I never found the deed. But I found your picture."

She didn't think he was aware of how viciously his fingers were digging into her arms. She was almost certain he was no longer aware of how much he was telling her. She remained silent and still, knowing her only hope now was time.

"Delicate," he murmured. "Such a delicate face. The innocence shining in the eyes, the soft curve of the mouth. It was a lie, wasn't it, Sarah?" The violence sprang back into his face, and she could only shake her head and wait. "There was no delicacy, no innocence. You toyed with me, offering me smiles, only smiles, while you gave yourself to Redman like a whore. He should be dead for touching what belonged to me. You should both be dead."

She prepared to scream. She prepared to fight for what she knew was her life.

"Sam!" The banging on the door brought with it a mixture of fear and relief.

Swearing, Carlson dragged Sarah to the door to unlock it. "Goddamn it, I told you to go back and get rid of the wagon and team."

"Riders coming in." The sweat on Jim's face attested to the fact that he had already ridden, and ridden hard. "It's Redman and the sheriff, with some men from town." He glanced at Sarah. "They'll be looking for her."

When Sarah tried to break away, Samuel locked an arm around her throat. "You've ruined everything, bringing her here."

"I only did it 'cause you wanted her. I could've taken care of her back on the road. Hell, I could've taken care of her the night we torched her shed, but you said you didn't want her hurt none."

Carlson tightened his grip as Sarah clawed at his arm. Her vision grayed from lack of air. As if from a distance, she heard the voices, one mixing into the other.

"How long?"

"Ten minutes, no more... Kill her now."

"Not here, you idiot... Hold them off... In the hills."

Sarah's last thought before she lost consciousness was that Jake was coming, but too late.

"You listen to me." Barker stopped the men on the rise above the Carlson ranch. But it was Jake he was looking at. "I know you'd like to ride in there hell-bent, but you take a minute to think. If they've got her, we've got to go slow."

"They've got her." In his mind, the Carlson brothers were already dead.

"Then let's make sure we get her back in one piece. Will,

I want you to break off, ease on over to the barn. John, I'd be obliged if you'd circle around the back. I don't want any shooting until it's necessary." With a nod, he spurred his horse.

Jim watched them coming and wiped the sweat off his brow. His men were all out on the range. Not that they'd have been any good, he thought. The only one who'd have backed them against the sheriff was Donley. And he was dead. Wetting his lips, he levered the rifle in the window.

He had to wait until they got close. That was what Sam had told him. Wait until they got close. Then he was to kill as many as he could. Starting with Redman.

Sweat dripped down into his eyes. His fingers twitched.

Sam had sent Donley to kill Redman, Jim remembered. But it was Donley who'd been buried. Now he was going to do it. He wet his lips when he caught Jake in the sight. He was going to do it right. But nerves had his finger jerking on the trigger.

Jake felt the bullet whiz past his cheek. Like lightning, he kicked one foot free of the stirrup to slide halfway down the side of his horse. Gun drawn, he rode toward the house while Barker shouted orders. He could hear the men scrambling for cover and returning fire, but his mind was on one thing and one thing alone.

Getting inside to Sarah.

Outside the doors, he leaped off. When he kicked them open, his second gun was drawn. The hall and the foyer were empty. He could hear the shouts of men and peppering gunfire. With a quick glance for any sign of her, he started up the stairs.

Jim Carlson's back was to him when he broke open the door.

"Where is she?" Jake didn't flinch when a bullet from outside plowed into the wall beside him.

From his crouched position, Jim turned slowly. "Sam's

got her." With a grin, he swung his rifle up. For months he'd wanted another chance to kill Jake Redman. Now he took it.

He was still grinning as he fell forward. Jake slid his smoking guns back in their holsters. Moving quickly, he began to search the house.

Barker met him on the steps. "She ain't here. I found this on the floor." In his hand he held Sarah's miniature.

Jake's eyes flicked up to Barker's. They held there only seconds, but Barker knew he would never forget the look in them. Later he would tell his wife it was the look of a man whose soul had gotten loose.

Turning on his heel, Jake headed outside, with Barker close behind.

"Oh, God." For the first time since Jake had known him, Barker moved with speed. Pushing past Jake, he raced to where two of his men were carrying Will Metcalf.

"He isn't dead." John Cody laid Will down and held his head. "But we have to get him back to town, to the doc."

Barker crouched down as Will's eyes fluttered open. "You're going to be all right, son."

"Took me by surprise," Will managed, struggling not to gasp at the pain as Cody pressed a pad to the hole in his shoulder. "Was Sam Carlson, Sheriff. He had her—I saw he had her on the horse. Think they headed west."

"Good job, Will." Barker used his own bandanna to wipe the sweat off his deputy's brow. "One of you men hitch up a wagon, get some blankets. You get this boy to the doctor, John. Redman and I'll go after Carlson."

But when he stood, all he saw of Jake was the dust his mustang kicked up as he galloped west.

Sarah came to slowly, nausea rising in her throat. Moaning, she choked it back and tried to lift a hand to her spinning head. Both wrists were bound tight to the saddle horn.

For a moment she thought she was still with Jim. Then she remembered.

The horse was climbing, picking its way up through dusty, dung-colored rock. She watched loose dirt and stones dislodged by the horse's hooves fall down a dizzying ravine. The man behind her was breathing hard. Fighting for calm, she tried to mark the trail they were taking and remember it. When she escaped—and she would—she didn't intend to wander helplessly through the rocks.

He stopped the horse near the edge of a canyon. She could see the thin silver line of a river far below. An eagle called as he swooped into the wide opening, then returned to a nest built in the high rock wall.

"Samuel, please—" She cried out when he pulled the rope from around her wrists and dragged her roughly to the ground. One look warned her that the calm, sane words she had meant to use would never reach him.

There was a bright, glazed light in his eyes. His face was pale and drenched with sweat. His hair was dark with it. She watched his eyes dart here and there, as if he expected something to leap out from behind a huddle of rock.

The man who had swept off his hat and kissed her fingers wasn't here with her now. If he had ever been part of Samuel Carlson, he had vanished. The man who stood over her was mad, and as savage as any beast that lived in the hills.

"What are you going to do?"

"He's coming." Still breathing rapidly, Carlson swiped a hand over his mouth. "I saw him behind us. When he comes for you, I'll be ready." He reached down to drag her to her feet. "I'm going to kill him, Sarah. Kill him like a dog." He pulled out his gun and rubbed the barrel against her cheek, gently, like a caress. "You're going to watch. I want you to watch me kill him. Then you'll understand. It's important that you understand. A man like that deserves to die by a gun. He's nothing, less than nothing. A crude gunslinger with Indian blood. He put his hands on you." A whimper escaped her as he dragged a hand through her hair. "I'm going to kill him for you, Sarah. Then we're going away, you and I."

"No." She wrenched free. The canyon was at her back when she faced him. If she had stumbled another step she would have fallen back into nothing. There was fear. The taste of it was bitter in her throat. But it wasn't for herself. Jake would come, she knew, and someone would die. "I won't go anywhere with you. It's over, Samuel. You must see that. They know what you've done, and they'll hunt you down."

"A potbellied sheriff?" He laughed and, before she could evade him, closed his hand over her arm. "Not likely. This is a big country, Sarah. They won't find us."

"I won't go with you." The pain when he squeezed her arm nearly buckled her knees. "I'll get away."

"If I must, I'll keep you locked up, the way my mother was locked up. For your own good."

She heard the horse even as he did and screamed out a warning. "No, Jake, he'll kill you!" Then she screamed again, this time in pain, as Carlson bent her arm behind her back. Calmly he put the gun to her temple.

"It's her I'll kill, Redman. Come out slow and keep your hands where I can see them, or the first bullet goes in her brain." He twisted her arm ruthlessly because he wanted Jake to hear her cry out again. He wanted Jake to hear the pain. "Now, Redman, or I'll kill her and toss her body over the edge."

"No. Oh, no." Tears blurred her vision as she watched Jake step out into the open. "Please don't. It won't gain you anything to kill him. I'll go with you." She tried to turn her head to look into Carlson's eyes. "I'll go anywhere you want."

"Not gain anything?" Carlson laughed again, and it echoed off the rocks and air. "Satisfaction, my dear. I'll gain satisfaction."

"Are you hurt?" Jake asked quietly.

"No." She shook her head, praying she could will him back behind the rock, back to safety. "No, he hasn't hurt me. He won't if you go back."

"But you're wrong, my dear, quite wrong." Carlson bent his head close to hers, amused by the quick fury in Jake's eyes when he brushed his lips over Sarah's hair. "I'll have to, you see, because you won't understand. Unless I kill him for you, you won't understand. Your gunbelt, Redman." Carlson drew back the hammer for emphasis and kept the gun tight against Sarah's temple. "Take it off, slowly, very slowly, and kick it aside."

"No!" She began to struggle, only to have him drag her arm farther up her back. "I'll kill you myself." She wept in rage and fear. "I swear it."

"When I'm done here, my dear, you'll do exactly what I say, when I say. In time you'll understand this was for the best. Drop the belt, Redman." Carlson smiled at him and jerked his head to indicate that he wanted the guns kicked away. "That's fine." He took the gun away from Sarah's temple to point it at Jake's heart. "You know, I've never killed a man before. It always seemed more civilized to hire someone—someone like yourself." His smile widened. "But I believe I'm going to enjoy it a great deal."

"You might." Jake watched his eyes. He could only hope Sarah had the sense to run when it was over. Barker couldn't be far behind. "Maybe you'll enjoy it more when I tell you I killed your brother."

The muscles in Carlson's cheek twitched. "You bastard."

Sarah screamed and threw her weight against his gun hand. She felt the explosion, as if the bullet had driven into her. Then she was on her knees. Life poured out of her when she saw Jake sprawled on the ground, blood seeping from his side.

"No. Oh, God, no."

Carlson threw back his head and laughed at the sky. "I was right. I enjoyed it. But he's not dead yet. Not quite yet." His lips stretched back from his teeth as he lifted the gun again.

She didn't think. There was no room for thought in a mind swamped with grief. She reached out and felt the smooth grip of Jake's gun in her hand. Kneeling in the dirt, she balanced it and aimed. "Samuel," she murmured, and waited for him to turn his head.

The gun jumped in her hand when she fired. The sound of the shot echoed on and on and on. He just stared at her. Afraid she'd missed, Sarah drew back the hammer and calmly prepared to fire again.

Then he stumbled. He stared at her as his hand reached up to press against the blood that blossomed on his shirt-front. Without a sound, he fell back. He groped once in the air, then tumbled off the edge and into the canyon.

Her hand went limp on the gun. Then the shudders began, racking shudders, as she crawled to Jake. He'd pushed himself up on one elbow, and he held his knife in his hand. She was weeping as she tore at her petticoats to pad the wound in his side.

"I thought he'd killed you. You looked—" There was so much blood, she thought frantically as she tore more cloth. "You need a doctor. I'll get you on the horse as soon as—" She broke off again as her voice began to hitch. "It was crazy, absolutely crazy, for you to come out in the open like that. I thought you had more sense."

"So did I." The pain was searing, centering in his side and flowing out in waves of heat. He wanted to touch her, just once more, before he died. "Sarah…"

"Don't talk." Tears clogged her throat. His blood seeped through the pad and onto her hands. "Just lie still. I'm going to take care of you. Damn you, I won't let you die."

He couldn't see her face. Tired of the effort, he closed his eyes. He thought, but couldn't be sure, that he heard horses coming. "You're a hell of a woman," he murmured, and passed out.

When he awoke, it was dark. There was a bitter taste in his mouth and a hollow throbbing at the base of his skull. The pain in his side was still there, but dull now, and constant. He lay still and wondered how long he'd been in hell.

He closed his eyes again, thinking it didn't matter how long he'd been there, since he wouldn't be leaving. Then he smelled her, smelled the soft scent that was Sarah. Though it cost him dearly, he opened his eyes again and tried to sit up.

"No, don't." She was there, murmuring to him, pressing him gently back on a pillow, then laying a cool cloth against his hot face.

"How long—" He could only manage two whispered words before the strength leaked out of him.

"Don't worry." Cradling his head with her arm, she brought a cup to his lips. "Drink a little. Then you'll sleep again. I'm right here with you," she continued when he coughed and tried to turn his head away.

"Can't—" He tried to focus on her face, but saw only a silhouette. It was Sarah, though. "Can't be in hell," he murmured, then sank back into the darkness.

When he awoke again, it was daylight. And she was there, leaning over him, smiling, murmuring something he couldn't quite understand. But there were tears drying on her cheeks, cheeks that were too pale. She sat beside him, took his hand and held it against her lips. Even as he struggled to speak, he lost consciousness again.

She thought it would drive her mad, the way he drifted in and out of consciousness that first week, with the fever burning through him and the doctor giving her no hope. Hour after hour, day after day, she sat beside him, bathing his hot skin, soothing when the chills racked him, praying when he fell back into that deep, silent sleep.

What had he said that day when he'd awakened? Pacing to the window, the one Maggie had told her Jake had sometimes sat in, she drew the curtain aside to look down at the empty street. He'd said it couldn't be hell. But he'd been wrong, Sarah thought. It was hell, and she was mired in it, terrified each day that he would leave her.

So much blood. He'd lost so much blood. By the time Barker had ridden up she'd nearly managed to stop it, but the ride back to town had cost him more. She had stanched still more while the doctor had cut and probed into his side to remove the bullet. She hadn't known that watching the bullet come out of him would be as bad as watching it go in.

Then the fever had raced through him, vicious and merciless. In a week he'd been awake only a handful of minutes, often delirious, sometimes speaking in what Lucius had told her was Apache. If it didn't break soon, she knew, no matter how hard she prayed, no matter how hard she fought, it would take him.

Sarah moved back to the bed to sit beside him and watch over him in the pale light of dawn.

Time drifted, for her even as it did for him. She lost track of minutes, then hours, then days. When morning came she held his hand in hers and thought over the time they'd had together. His hands had been strong, she thought. Biting back a sob, she laid her forehead on his shoulder. And gentle, too, she remembered. When he'd touched her. When he'd taught her.

With him she'd found something lovely, something powerful. A sunrise. A fast river. A storm. She knew now that love, desire, passion and affection could be one emotion for one man. From that first frantic discovery in the hay to the soft, sweet loving by the stream, he'd given her more than most women had in a lifetime.

"But I'm greedy," she murmured to him. "I want more. Jake, don't leave me. Don't cheat me out of what we could have." She blinked back tears when she heard the door open behind her.

"How is he?"

"The same." Sarah rose and waited while Maggie set a tray on the bureau. She'd long ago stopped arguing about eating. It had taken her only a few days to realize that if she wanted the strength to stay with Jake she needed food.

"Don't worry none about this breakfast, because Anne Cody made it up for you."

Sarah dashed away the hated, weakening tears. "That was kind of her."

"She asked about our boy here, and wanted you to know that Alice is doing just fine."

"I'm glad." Without interest, she folded back the cloth so that steam rose fragrantly from the biscuits.

"Looks like Carlotta skipped town."

"It doesn't matter." With no more interest than she had in the biscuits, she looked at her own face in the mirror. Behind her reflection, she could see Jake lying motionless in the bed. "The damage is done."

"Child, you need sleep, and not what you get sitting up in that chair all night. You go on and use my room. I'll stay with him."

"I can't." Sarah ignored the biscuits and took the coffee. "Sometimes he calls for me, and I'm afraid if I'm not here he might...slip away. That's foolish, I suppose, but I just can't leave him, Maggie."

"I know." Because she did, Maggie set a comforting hand on Sarah's shoulder. The noise at the door had her turning back. "What are you doing sneaking around here, young John Cody?"

Johnny slipped into the doorway and stood with his hat crushed in his hands. "Just wanted to see him, is all."

"A sickroom ain't no place for nasty little boys."

"It's all right." Sarah waved him in and summoned up a smile. "I'm sure Jake would be pleased that you'd taken the time to visit him."

"He ain't going to die, is he, Sarah?"

"No." She found the confidence she'd lost during the night. "No, he isn't going to die, Johnny."

"Ma says you're taking real good care of him." He reached out a hand, then balled it at his side again.

"It's all right, boy," Maggie said, softening. "You can pet him as long as he don't know it. I do it myself."

Gingerly Johnny stroked a hand along Jake's forehead. "He's pretty hot."

"Yes, but the fever's going to break soon." Sarah laid a hand on Johnny's shoulder. "Very soon."

"Will's better," he said, giving Sarah a hopeful smile. "He's got his arm in a sling and all, but he's getting around just fine and dandy. Won't even let Liza fuss no more."

"Before long Jake won't let me fuss, either."

Hours later she dozed, lulled by the afternoon sun. She slept lightly, her head nestled against the wing of the chair and her hands in her lap on top of her journal. She'd written everything she felt, hoped, despaired of on those pages. Someone called her name, and she lifted a hand as if to brush the voice away. She only wanted to sleep.

"Sarah."

Now her eyes flew open, and she bolted out of the chair.
Jake was half sitting up in bed, his brows drawn together
in annoyance or confusion. And his eyes, she noted, were
focused, alert and direct on hers.

"What the hell's going on?" he asked her. Then he
watched, astonished, as she collapsed on the side of the
bed and wept.

It was three weeks before he had the strength to do more
than stand on his own feet. He had time to think—perhaps
too much time—but when he tried to do anything he found
himself weak as a baby.

It infuriated him, disgusted him. When he swore at Maggie twice in one morning, she told Sarah their patient was
well on the road to recovery.

"He's a tough one, Jake is," Maggie went on as they
climbed the steps to his room together. "Said he was damn
sick and tired of having females poking him, pouring things
into him and trying to give him baths."

"So much for gratitude," Sarah said with a laugh. Then
she swayed and clutched the banister for support.

Maggie grabbed her arm. "Honey, are you all right?"

"Yes. Silly." Shrugging it off, Sarah waited for the diz-
ziness to pass. "I'm just tired yet, I think." One look at
Maggie's shrewd face had her giving up and sitting carefully on the riser.

"How far along are you?"

It surprised Sarah that the direct question didn't make her
blush. Instead, she smiled. "About a month." She knew the
exact moment when she had conceived Jake's child, on the
riverbank under the moon. "I had the obvious sign, of course.
Then, for the last few days, I haven't been able to keep anything down in the morning."

"I know." Pleased as a partridge, Maggie cackled. "Honey,
I knew you were breeding three days ago, when you turned

green at the sight of Anne Cody's flapjacks. Ain't Jake just going to fall on his face?"

"I haven't told him," Sarah said quickly. "I don't want him to know until he's...until we've..." She propped her chin in her hands. "Not yet, Maggie."

"That's for you to decide."

"Yes, and you won't say anything...to anyone?"

"Not a peep."

Satisfied, Sarah rose and started up the stairs again. "The doctor said he'd be up and around in a couple of days. We haven't been able to talk about anything important since he's been healing." She knocked on the door to his room before pushing it open.

The bed was empty.

"What— Maggie!"

"He was there an hour ago. I don't know where—" But she was talking to air, as Sarah was flying down the stairs again.

"Sarah! Sarah!" His hand wrapped around a licorice whip, Johnny raced toward her. "I just saw Jake riding out of town. He sure looked a lot better."

"Which way?" She grabbed the surprised boy by the shoulders. "Which way did he go?"

"That way." He pointed. "I called after him, but I guess he didn't hear me."

"Damned hardheaded man," Maggie muttered from the doorway.

"So he thinks he can just ride off," Sarah said between her teeth. "Well, Jake Redman is in for a surprise. I need a horse, Maggie. And a rifle."

He'd thought it through. He'd had nothing but time to think over the last weeks. She'd be mad, he figured. He almost smiled. Mad enough to spit, he imagined, but she'd get over it. In time she'd find someone who was right for her. Who was good for her.

Talking to her wouldn't have helped. He'd never known a more stubborn woman. So he'd saddled up and ridden out of Lone Bluff the way he'd ridden out of countless towns before. Only this time it hurt. Not just the pain from his still-healing wound, but an ache deeper, sharper, than anything that could be caused by a bullet.

He'd get over it, too, he told himself. He'd just been fooling himself, letting himself pretend that she could belong to him.

He'd never forget how she'd looked, kneeling in the dirt with his gun in her hand. His gun. And there had been horror in her eyes. He'd taught her to kill, and he wasn't sure he could live with that.

The way he figured it, she'd saved his life. The best he could do for her was return the favor and get out of hers.

She was rich now. Jake remembered how excited Lucius had been when he'd come to visit, talking on and on about the mine and how the gold was all but ready to fall into a man's hands. She could go back east, or she could stay and build that big house with the parlor she'd told him about.

And he would…he would go on drifting.

When he heard the rider coming, instinct had him wheeling his horse around and reaching for his gun. He swore, rubbing his hand on his thigh, as Sarah closed the distance between them.

"You bastard."

He acknowledged her with a nod. There was only one way to handle her now, one way to make certain she turned around and left. Before just looking at her made him want to crawl.

"Didn't know you could ride, Duchess. You come out all this way to tell me goodbye?"

"I have more than that to say." Her hands balled on the reins while she fought with her temper. "Not a word, Jake, to me, to anyone? Just saddle up and ride out?"

"That's right. When it's time to move on, you move."

"So you're telling me you have no reason to stay?"

"That's right." He knew the truth sometimes hurt, but he hadn't known a lie could. "You're a mighty pretty woman, Duchess. You'll be hard to top."

He saw the hurt glow in her eyes before her chin came up. "That's a compliment? Well, you're quite right, Jake. I'll be very hard to top. You'll never love another woman the way you love me. Or want one," she said, more quietly. "Or need one."

"Go on back, Sarah." He started to turn his horse but stopped short when she drew the rifle out of its holster and aimed it heart-high. "You want to point that someplace else?"

For an answer, she lowered it a few strategic inches, smiling when his brow lifted. "Ever hear the one about hell's fury, Jake?"

"I get the idea." He shifted slightly. "Duchess, if it's all the same to you, I'd rather you pointed it back at my chest."

"Get off your horse."

"Damn it, Sarah."

"I said off." She cocked the lever in two sharp movements. "Now."

He leaned forward in the saddle. "How do I know that's even loaded?"

"How do you know it's loaded?" She smiled, brought it up to her eye and fired. His hat flew off his head.

"Are you crazy?" Stunned, he dragged a hand through his hair. He could almost feel the heat. "You damn near killed me."

"I hit what I aim at. Isn't that what you said I should learn to do?" She cocked the rifle again. "Now get off that horse before I shoot something more vital off you."

Swearing, he slid down. "What the hell are you trying to prove with all this?"

"Just hold it right there." She dropped to the ground. Giddiness washed over her, and she had to lean one hand against her mount.

"Sarah—"

"I said hold it right there." She shook her head to clear it.

"Are you sick?"

"No." Steady again, she smiled. "I've never felt better in my life."

"Just crazy, then." He relaxed a little, but her pallor worried him. "Well, if you've a mind to kill me after spending the better part of a month keeping me alive, go ahead."

"You're damn right I kept you alive, and I didn't do it so you could leave me the minute you could stand up. I did it because I love you, because you're everything I want and everything I intend to have. Now you tell me, you stand there and tell me why you left."

"I already told you. It was time."

"You're a liar. Worse, you're a coward."

Her words had the effect she'd hoped for. The cool, almost bored look in his eyes sizzled into heat. "Don't push me, Sarah."

"I haven't begun to push you. I'll start by telling you why you got on that horse and rode away. You left because you were afraid. Of me. No, not even of me, of yourself and what you feel for me." Her chin was up, a challenge in her eyes as she dared him to say it was untrue. "You loved me enough to stand unarmed in front of a madman, but not enough to face your own heart."

"You don't know what I feel."

"Don't I? If you believe that, you're a fool, as well as

a liar." The fresh flash of fury in his eyes delighted her. "Don't you think I knew every time you touched me, every time you kissed me?" He was silent, and she drew a long breath. "Well, you can get on that horse and you can ride, you can run into the hills, to the next town. You can keep running until you're hundreds of miles away. Maybe you'll be fast enough, just fast enough to get away from me. But before you do you're going to tell me."

"Tell you what?"

"I want you to tell me you love me."

He studied her. Her eyes glowed with determination, and her cheeks were flushed with anger. Her hair, caught by the wind, was blowing back. He should have known then and there that he'd never had anywhere to run.

"A man'll say most anything when a woman's pointing a rifle at his belly."

"Then say it."

He bent to pick up his hat, slapping it against his thighs twice to loosen the dust. Idly he poked his finger through the hole in the crown.

"I love you, Sarah." He settled the hat on his head. "Now do you want to put that thing away?"

The temper went out of her eyes, and with it the glint of hope. Without a word, she turned to secure the rifle in the holder. "Well, I had to threaten it out of you, but at least I heard you say it once. Go ahead and ride off. I won't stop you. No one's holding a gun on you now."

She wouldn't cry. No, she swore to herself she wouldn't hold him with tears. Fighting them back, she tried to struggle back into the saddle. He touched her arm, lightly, not holding, when he wanted more than anything he'd ever wanted in his life to hold her.

"I love you, Sarah," he said again. "More than I should. A hell of a lot more than I can stand."

She closed her eyes, praying that what she did now would be right for both of them. Slowly she turned toward him, but she kept her hands at her sides. "If you ride away now, I'll come after you. No matter where you go, I'll be there. I'll make your life hell, I swear it."

He couldn't stop the smile any more than he could stop his hand from reaching up to touch her face. "And if I don't ride away?"

"I'll only make your life hell some of the time."

"I guess that's a better bargain." He lowered his head to kiss her gently. Then, with a groan, he crushed her hard against him. "I don't think I'd've gotten very far, even if you hadn't shot at me."

"No use taking chances. Lucky for you I was trying to shoot over your head."

He only sighed and drew her away. "You owe me a hat, Duchess." Still amazed, he drew it off to poke at the hole. "I guess I'd have to marry any woman who could handle a gun like that."

"Is that a proposal?"

He shrugged and stuck his hat back on his head. "Sounded like it."

She lifted a brow. "And it's the best you can do?"

"I haven't got any five-dollar words." Disgusted, he started back to his horse. Then he stopped and turned back. She was waiting, her arms folded, a half smile on her face. So he swore at her. "There's a preacher comes into town once every few weeks. He can marry us proper enough, with whatever kind of fuss you figure would satisfy you. I'll build you a house, between the mine and the town, with a parlor if that's what you want, and a wood floor, and a real bedroom."

To her it was the most eloquent of proposals. She held out her hands. "We'll need two."

"Two what?"

"Two bedrooms," she said when his hands closed over hers again.

"Listen, Duchess, I've heard they've got some odd ways of doing things back east, but I'm damned if my wife is going to sleep in another room."

"Oh, no." Her smile lit up her face. "I'm going to sleep in the same room, the same bed as you, every night for the rest of my life. But we'll need two bedrooms. At least we will by spring."

"I don't see why—" Then he did, so abruptly, so stunningly, that he could only stare at her. If she had taken the rifle back out and driven it butt first into his gut he would have been less shaken. His fingers went slack on hers, then dropped away. "Are you sure?"

"Yes." She held her breath. "There's going to be a child. Our child."

He wasn't sure he could move, and was less sure he could speak. Slowly, carefully, he framed her face with his hands and kissed her. Then, when emotions swamped him, he simply rested his forehead against hers. "Two bedrooms," he murmured. "To start."

Content, she wrapped her arms around his waist. "Yes. To start."

* * * * *